BLACK APPLE

A NOVEL

JOAN CRATE

PHYLLIS BRUCE EDITIONS

SIMON & SCHUSTER CANADA

New York   London   Toronto   Sydney   New Delhi

Simon & Schuster Canada
A Division of Simon & Schuster, Inc.
166 King Street East, Suite 300
Toronto, Ontario   M5A 1J3

Phyllis Bruce Editions, published by Simon & Schuster Canada

This Simon & Schuster Canada edition March 2016

SIMON & SCHUSTER CANADA and colophon are registered trademarks of Simon & Schuster, Inc.

For information about special discounts for bulk purchases, please contact Simon & Schuster Special Sales at 1-800-268-3216 or CustomerService@simonandschuster.ca.

Library and Archives Canada Cataloguing in Publication

Crate, Joan, 1953–, author
Black apple : a novel / Joan Crate.

Issued in print and electronic formats.
ISBN 978-1-4767-9516-4 (bound).—ISBN 978-1-4767-9518-8 (ebook)

I. Title.

PS8555.R338B53   2016   C813'.54   C2015-905966-6
C2015-905967-4

Manufactured in the United States of America

1   3   5   7   9   10   8   6   4   2

ISBN 978-1-4767-9516-4
ISBN 978-1-4767-9518-8 (ebook)

For Augie, Peggy, and too many others

PART ONE

1

Baby Bird

PAPA OPENED THE DOOR slowly. "What do you want?" he said in English.

"I'm Father Alphonses," a white man's voice said. Then came a stream of sound. Rose, cross-legged on the floor while Mama braided her hair, made out just a few of the words. "School," "must," "law" louder than the rest.

Mama stopped braiding. "Lie down with Kiaa-yo," she hissed, pushing Rose towards the nest of hides. Mama stood, pressing herself against the wall where the men couldn't see. Catching Rose's eye, she signalled her to pull the hide over her head.

Under the fur, Rose couldn't make out the words anymore. Kiaa-yo threw out his arms and legs, making crying sounds, so Rose pushed up the soft cover with one hand and put a finger in his mouth, letting him suck.

"You'd better leave," Papa said.

"We'll bring in the RCMP," one of them yelled back.

She peeked out, and that's when it happened. Oh, Papa with his *what can I do?* look stepped backward into the house, no longer fierce, his colours breaking apart like the reflection of the moon in runoff water.

The men barged in, but Mama stepped forward and stood in front of them.

"Mrs. Whitewater, I'm here to escort your daughter to St. Mark's Residential School for Girls," said the man with the white stripe at his throat. "This is Mr. Higgins, the Indian agent. Now if you'll just get—ah, there she is." He pulled the hide back on Rose and Kiaa-yo.

Mama started coughing. The lard man pushed her aside. Oh, now Mama was changing just like Papa, her colour draining.

She ran to Mama, let her mother hold her against her soft body, rocking gently.

"Rose," Mama whispered, "my little Sinopaki."

"No packing necessary. All her clothing will be provided," the man with the white stripe said, but Mama wouldn't let her go, and Rose wouldn't let go of Mama. The man grasped Rose's arm with cold fingers, but she pulled away. Kiaa-yo screamed.

Run!

She flew to the door, where Papa slumped against the wall. He was mad and scared and just like sand spilling out of an old cloth bag. But suddenly he stood up straight and stepped in front of her. He stopped her from reaching the door.

"Papa?"

He opened his lips, but the words caught in his mouth. Nothing came out but spit. He didn't say it, but *Why did I stop you?* splattered over his face.

"Hurry up, Rose," the lard man behind her yelled.

Walking between these strangers, these bad men, she gulped and burned. They had come to her house, and now they were taking her away. She wanted to run, but her feet were wobbly and all wrong.

Mama and Papa had told her that men might be coming, but they hadn't said she would have to go all alone, that they would stay behind. These *a-ita-pi-ooy* were stealing her. People eaters. She cried into her hands, snot-slimy. Ahead, the stripe man was a black smear against the old carriage road.

A machine sat on the side of the road. *Car*. She had seen cars before, had even been in a big one called a "truck" with her mama, Mama's sister Aunt Angelique, and her new husband, Forest Fox Crown. The truck growled and chewed the ground. It charged way too fast, making trees uproot and fly by the windows. No, she wouldn't get in this car.

The lard man came up behind her, opened the front door, and wedged himself behind the wheel. The stripe man pulled the back door open and pushed his cold hand against her shoulder. "Get in, Rose."

Oh, and she had to. She scooted along the seat as far away from him as she could get. The car smelled bad. Not tree, water, moss, meat, blood, or berry. Like the stink that blew in from that mining town to the west, that Black Apple.

He climbed in the front next to the lard man and turned to her. "By the way, I'm Father Alphonses. This is Mr. Higgins," his voice way too loud.

Mr. Higgins said nothing. He acted like he couldn't see her anymore. The car snorted and they jerked down the road, trees and bushes whooshing by.

"Papa," she cried.

"Quiet, Rose," Father Alphonses said.

"Jesus Bloody Christ!" Mr. Higgins shouted as the car bounced and they all shot to the roof. "Excuse me, Father, but these shit roads are wrecking the undercarriage. Excuse me for saying so."

The backseat squeaked under her bum. Rose threw all her weight onto her feet, half standing. The car turned suddenly and she tumbled back. The squeaking under her was terrible, the sound of a baby bird crying out for its mother and flapping its bony wings in her throat. The car rumbled onto that great grey road.

They drove faster, and the bird cried even louder, underneath and inside her. Its mama didn't hear, couldn't answer, wouldn't come. She kept swallowing so she wouldn't throw up.

"Clean sheets," Father Alphonses said, pretend-friendly. "You'll like that. And there will be other children your age. You'll learn manners and discipline, but most important of all, Rose, the holy sisters will teach you the Word of God. You will be saved. Do you know what *saved* means?"

Bird bones in her throat. She could hardly breathe, so she put her head down on the floor and pushed her feet up over the seat. Closing her eyes, she tried to fly away, but her head throbbed and throw-up pushed from her belly down to her throat. She swallowed it back, one foot against the door handle.

"Stop that." Father Alphonses' voice was full of thistles. "Sit up properly."

No, she wouldn't. Not even if her head burst open on the car floor, a big fat puffball. Behind her eyes, she jumped in Napi's river and paddled around, water shooting up her nose until she choked and sputtered, and Mr. Higgins said, "What's she doing back there?" Rose put her face back underwater trying to swim away from those men, but when she came up for air, she was still in the car—they were all still in the car.

"Sit up, Rose."

The baby bird started calling out again and it sounded like *Mama, Papa, Mama, Papa* over and over, and Father Alphonses said, "Stop that," so she shut her mouth and held her breath, diving deep to get away from the bird and the men and the thistles.

The car rumbled to a stop.

Sitting up, she peered out the window. Aunt Angelique's Reserve! Oh, they had driven east and she knew where they were. There was the band office, and there, the church, with kids, mamas, papas, grandmas, and grandpas everywhere. She spotted Aunt Angelique's round red-checked skirt. The youngest two of her six new stepchildren clung to Angelique's hands.

"*Na-a,*" she cried, pressing against the glass. Aunt Angelique didn't hear, so she pounded her fist and screamed, "*Na-a!*"

"Quiet!" Father Alphonses said, reaching over and cuffing her across the head.

She didn't care what he did, that stupid mean stripe man with cold hands!

"*Na-a!*" she screamed.

Mr. Higgins pulled up a button on his car door. "I'm going to check with the bus driver, Father. Get her to shut up and stop—"

She pulled up the button on her door, pushed out, and ran. "Aunt Angelique!"

Auntie turned. She opened her arms, and Rose tumbled into the aroma of wood smoke and delicious *imis-tsi-kitan*, her face pressed to Auntie's soft belly.

When she opened her eyes and looked around, she saw kids being bustled towards two yellow buses. Boys bunched outside the doors of one bus, girls outside the other. A piece of ice shivered down her back.

"There you are," said Father Alphonses.

"No!" She grabbed the soft flesh at Aunt Angelique's hips and clung.

"Ow!" cried Auntie. Rose's little stepcousins backed up and stared. "Sinopaki, let go." Angelique pried Rose's fingers off and placed her broad hand on the nape of Rose's neck. "*Kaakoo!*" she ordered, steering her towards the bus. "You have to go to school."

Father Alphonses made a throat sound. He was right behind her. She had nowhere to run.

"Bye-bye, Sinopaki." Bending, Aunt Angelique rubbed a thick cheek against her nose. Then she stepped away and grabbed the hands of her own children, her new children who were Forest Fox Crown's and not really hers at all!

Eyes on the dirty black-licorice steps, she climbed into the bus. Kids were squeezed in everywhere. That awful Father Alphonses plunked himself down on the front seat, so she pushed to the very back and squished beside a bony girl with big teeth.

So many kids! She had seen some of them before on visits to the Reserve, had played with a few of them when they had waving arms and flying feet. But today these girls were scrubbed shiny, their hair pulled into tight braids. She touched her own hair. Mama hadn't been able to finish braiding it. The bad men had come, and now it was unravelling.

All around her the girls were quiet, each pair of eyes stuck to the green seat directly in front. Small girls huddled close to bigger ones. Rose spotted Aunt Angelique's two oldest stepdaughters sitting in the front row across from Father Alphonses. They turned to look at her, but they didn't nod or smile. "Your auntie isn't our real mother," they had told her at the wedding. "You're not our cousin." She wiped her nose on the back of her hand and swallowed down the baby bird still flapping in her throat.

The bus shuddered and moved away from mamas, papas, grandpas, grandmas, and Aunt Angelique, some of them waving kerchiefs, flying patches of colour that grew smaller and smaller until they disappeared, like fireflies going out. Soon there was just a plume of dust billowing into the too-blue sky.

She turned to the front. Hills rose and fell, and Rose's tummy rose and fell too. Cottonwoods and wolf willows thinned until ahead in the distance was nothing but a line of yellow grasses drawn between the road and a big empty sky. Nothing but space. The bus was taking them to nowhere.

2

Mother Grace

PULLING ON BLOOMERS under her white cotton nightdress, Mother Grace winced as splinters of pain jabbed her right shoulder. Automatically she swallowed the curse in her mouth. Cursing was a matter of tone and intent, she had always contended, and though she used the names of the Holy Family frequently, she never took them in vain. *Non*, she uttered the names of God, Jesus Christ, and the Holy Virgin Mother as a supplication, a sort of abbreviated prayer for divine blessing, and, when need be, an intervention.

But pain forced the blasphemies—the ones her father and older brothers had so many years before spit at stillborn calves and broken fences—to form in her voice box and rub it raw. These days it seemed to take all her willpower to maintain a dignified silence and not throw those curses, like small black stones, at her layers of clothing, the splintery wooden ironing board, heavy books, and pestering sisters.

She had risen early, as she did every year on the first day of school, well before sunrise, when all the sisters were still snoring in their narrow beds. Dressing as quickly as she could manage, she tried to think about what lay ahead. But it was no use. Her mind couldn't get past the ache seeping through her. *Mal à la tête. Rhumatisme.* And with everything she had to do.

Down the stairs and to chapel. She hoped a feeling of piety would overtake her as it sometimes did. But not today. As she entered, she crossed herself with holy water, then climbed the red-carpeted steps to the altar.

She recalled how grand the carpet had looked twenty-two years before when she first arrived at St. Mark's, how it made her think of the blood of Jesus Himself. Now it was threadbare, worn under the feet and knees of three generations of students. And no money would be sent in the foreseeable future to replace it. Everything these days went to the war effort, the Second World War, and there was simply no more trimming to be done from the meagre St. Mark's budget. It was wartime, this terrible war having started just two decades after the first, which, if she remembered correctly, was the war that was supposed to end them all. *Dieu, ayez pitié*, the government of Canada had forgotten the residential schools.

She forced herself to kneel. *Most holy and adored Trinity, one God in three Persons, I praise you and give you thanks.* She went straight to a request to God for guidance, as she did on the first day of every new school year, but halfway through, her insincerity dismayed her and she couldn't finish. Rising from her knees was difficult, and all she could think about were the aspirins upstairs in the bathroom cabinet and how foolish she had been not to take two before coming down. Now she'd have to go all the way back up, being extra quiet so as not to wake the young, nervous Sister Cilla, always a light sleeper. Or Sister Joan, who in the last few years had taken it upon herself to keep a critical eye on the daily routine of the convent and all its incumbents, particularly her, Mother Grace. She lit a candle to the Virgin, Mother of Divine Providence, and one to glorious St. Mark, who, through the grace of God our Father, became a great evangelist preaching the Good News of Christ. Her prayers were stiff as a hymnbook cover, her spirit dark as the sky glowering through the chapel windows.

In the kitchen, she made herself a cup of instant coffee. The floors creaked horribly, and she hoped none of the sisters would hear her and come running downstairs: *Mother Grace, what are you doing up so early? Why, you mustn't tire yourself, Mother Grace.* Well meaning, but bothersome! Most of the sisters were well meaning. Down the hall to the main entrance she shuffled, inhaling the satisfying smells of disinfectant and floor polish. In a few hours, children would pile through the front door and into the foyer, where framed photographs of past and present sisters, priests, the bishop, and the cardinal of Canada hung. *Les sauvages,* she had once called the children.

She rubbed her left hand down her right shoulder and let her fingers bite into the painful flesh. No pleasant shivers of excitement this year. No nostalgia either. Draining the last of her instant coffee, she found herself wondering how long it had been since she'd had a really good cup. Decades, it seemed, prairie water being so alkaline. She set the cup and saucer down.

Surely it wasn't dread she was feeling. Weariness perhaps. *Ennui.* She pulled off her glasses and polished the lenses with a handkerchief from her sleeve. Instinctively, her half-blind eyes fluttered towards the first light of morning creeping through the window above the front door. The shape of a large, dark bird loomed overhead. She gasped.

Foolish old woman. Just the crucifix, that accursed piece of whittled wood with Jesus' crude head drooping over his childlike body at an alarming angle, his mouth and eyes gouges of agony. She'd never liked it, but it had been brought by the Benedictine Bishop von Tettenborn all the way from Germany when the school first opened thirty-one years ago, and since Father David often referred to it in his sermons, there was no discreet way to have it replaced by a more pleasing effigy.

Mother Grace was reaching for her cup and saucer to take back to the kitchen when her eyes were drawn to the photographs that lined the wall. There they were, past and present: the religious community of St. Mark's. Father David was a good twenty years younger in his photo, with a healthy head of hair and an almost convincing smile. These days, he did little more than sleep, nibble, and complain, the old goat. Brother Abraham—who looked after the chickens and the elderly cow that had remained at St. Mark's after St. Gerard's Residential School for Boys, twenty miles to the south, was built eight years ago—had a more recent picture. "Dumb as a doorstop," she had heard Sister Joan remark about Abe more than once, and there was no denying it, though the man did come in handy, supplying them with fresh chicken and eggs and carrying heavy loads.

Hélas, Father Damien! His death three years ago had altered things at St. Mark's, that was certain. In fact, his position at the school had yet to be filled. Since his passing she had, for all intents and purposes, run St. Mark's without an interfering Oblate so much as looking over her shoulder. It was a state of affairs with which she was not unhappy.

Down three rows was a photo of the young sister who had died in the girls' dormitory not a week after Damien's body was found sprawled beneath the top hayloft of the old barn. Sister Mary of Bethany. Mother Grace pried the photo from its hook. Then she pulled Father Damien's photo from the wall. For a moment, she felt triumphant. She'd bury the two pictures under a pile of paperwork, and perhaps no one would notice they were missing. Surely it was her right to edit the unseemly from St. Mark's past. And from her own. Since the deaths of Damien and Mary of Bethany, she had felt a growing deficiency in her daily life; she was no longer satisfied by her role as Mother General of St. Mark's Residential School for Girls. Sometimes she felt as if she no longer knew her purpose. Or if, indeed, she had one.

Just that March, she had turned sixty years old. And with her birthday, passed at the school without mention, came regret, came questions, and, *oui*, desire for fulfilment—something worthy, a call to the future of sorts. As always, she used prayer and meditation to address her moments of uncertainty, yet this new longing remained. Reached in old age, it was very different from her obsession with the pure body and unblemished soul of her Saviour, Jesus Christ, that had filled her as a young woman. She closed her eyes, remembering the glow of her Beloved's skin touching hers as she had knelt in prayer, His breath and counsel warm in her ear, His eyes watching her as she slept. No, that sort of personal relationship with the Lord was long gone. Nor did she feel the same strong ambition for personal recognition that had begun once she took her final vows. *Oui.* She had once been sure of an important destiny. But over the years, nothing much had come of it. Surely this time God would provide. *Crois en Dieu*, she told herself wearily. *Aie foi en Jésus.* Trust in the Almighty.

She studied her own photograph on the wall. Not unflattering, she thought, surprised by the serenity of that framed smile. As she turned away, she felt her conscience pinch. Vanity, a venial sin.

She went to her office. She would hide the photos of Father Damien and Sister Mary of Bethany. She would forget all about them and the dismal lives they represented. Pulling open the bottom drawer of her file cabinet, she shoved the wretched pair to the back. Things needed to change at the school, and she would do everything she could to make sure that this time it was a change for the better.

Clang, clang, clang! Mother Grace almost jumped out of her skin. It was Sister Joan, of course, marching along the upstairs hall, ringing her hand bell as if this were Armageddon and she the seven angels in one righteous body awakening the dead. *Lord, give me patience*, Mother Grace prayed. *Give me strength.* She waited in her office until she heard the sisters climb downstairs and enter the chapel for Matins. Then she went to join them.

At breakfast, Mother Grace rose from her seat at the first table. "Father David, Brother Abe, Sisters: Our charges will soon be arriving. We will once again embark on our mission of saving the souls and educating the Indian children of this great land." She looked around at the faces. Sister Margaret didn't even attempt to hide her look of disdain, her mouth turning down at the corners where it collided with her many chins. Sitting beside her on the left—the goat to Margaret's sheep— Sister Joan stared at her with an expression that she no doubt thought to be one of world-weary wisdom. Only Sister Bernadette and young

Sister Cilla looked as if they were fully awake, focused and ready to meet the day.

"Sister Joan, please lead our prayer," she said in order to wipe the smug expression off the woman's face. As Joan droned on, Mother Grace tried to uncover the hope buried deep in her breast, bring it forth to serve God, and do her duty as the superior of the school. "Amen," she chimed in with the others.

It shouldn't be so terribly difficult, this duty. The Church was doing the Indian race a great favour in bringing them the Lord and an education. She herself had loved convent school, which for all intents and purposes was similar to residential school. Her school had provided her a wonderful opportunity, it had changed her young life, and she persisted in thinking of her arrival there as the result of a series of preordained events.

L'Académie l'Annonciation in Montpetit was the same school her mother had gone to, and Maman had spoken of it so often and so fondly to her that she found the surroundings familiar from her very first day. She was thirteen years and six months old when she first entered the school, but already work-weary, already *mûre*, ready to be plucked from the world and placed in the winepress of the Lord, as Sister Francis of Assisi had so aptly put it.

The serene atmosphere of l'Annonciation, its routine and the relatively small number of chores, were a welcome change from the noise and gruelling work she had been accustomed to on the farm. At the two-room schoolhouse in Tête Rouge, a half hour away by horseback, she had missed as many days as she had attended. Like her two older brothers, she was needed at home. L'Annonciation had freed her from a life of drudgery.

"Let me take your dish, Mother Grace." Sister Bernadette snatched her bowl from under her. "It's going to be a busy day."

Already the others were scuttling about, filling basins in the kitchen, some heading down the hall to set up chairs in the gymnasium. She'd better fetch the lists from her office to keep the proceedings orderly.

3

St. Mark's

ON THE BUS, Rose was half asleep, her head lolling on the sharp shoulder next to her, when the girl abruptly shook her off.

"St. Mark's," the girl breathed, her eyes widening, body tensing.

Rose squinted out the front window, trying to see, but suddenly girls were leaning forward, bobbing up and stretching on tiptoes, hands clutching their neighbours' fingers and arms.

"Stay seated!" Father Alphonses roared above the din.

As the girls sat down, Rose caught sight of a stout building rising above a yard of packed dirt. The peaked roof fell over the brick walls like a frown. The bus turned, and she glimpsed a smaller building behind what must be the school—a barn maybe—its red paint ragged. And beyond that, for just a split second, a field bathed in shadow, small crosses leaning from lumps of soil. And then the brick building blocked out everything else.

"You will disembark from the bus row by row," Father Alphonses instructed, "starting with the first row."

Rose let the bony, big-toothed girl shove in front of her, and she followed her sloppy leather shoes—boy's shoes, she realized, and way too big—off the bus.

The school was colourless inside, the walls and ceiling white, the staircase and doors dark.

"Snip, snap!" a white lady in a long black robe yelled, clapping her hands.

She trailed the line of girls down a hall and into a room bigger than even the Band Council chamber on the Reserve. It overflowed with kids, whole bunches of girls sitting on wooden chairs, more pouring through the doors. She followed the slapping heels of the toothy girl's shoes down an aisle of chairs, stopping when they stopped.

"Sit," another white lady in a black robe ordered. They all sat down on squeaky chairs. "Quiet!" The lady walked down the aisle, stopping by each of them. When she stood over Rose, she grabbed her hand and pressed a piece of paper in it. "Your number. Stand up when it's called." She moved on to the toothy girl.

Rose held on to the paper in that big hot room of kids shuffling and crying. The sounds pushed her into a corner of herself, and she closed her eyes. Sunshine. A few hornets buzzed around her, and she ran to her creek and jumped in, spraying her legs giggly cold. She hopped onto the bank and ran to the trap shack, where Papa sat on a stump, scraping rust from steel.

A steel trap clamped her shoulder. "That's you, Rose. Your number." Father Alphonses leaned over and snatched the scrap of paper from her palm. He pointed to a line of girls.

Numbly she followed. Someone pushed her head in a basin of water and scrubbed her scalp with sharp fingers, not soft like Mama's. Her face was scraped with a wet cloth. Another lady combed her wet hair, then chopped it with a pair of scissors. It thunked to the floor like something dead.

More fingers on her, unbuttoning the dress Mama had made, red with green, black, and white diamonds stitched on the front, her very favourite, and she said, "No," pushing the hand away, but it grabbed her hair and yanked the dress from her shoulders, pulling it down.

"Arms up."

The dark, heavy dress that was pushed over her head smelled of damp corners and dirty feet.

Rose crunched her eyes shut. There, behind her eyes, the sun had already set and the sky was dark.

4

The Naming

MOTHER GRACE COULDN'T stop the frown forming on her face. The school floors, scrubbed with ammonia over the summer, then waxed and buffed into penitence the previous week, were now covered in dusty footprints. The white school walls, washed by the two youngest sisters over a six-day period, were pocked by dirty handprints. And all around her—chatter, wailing, and the harsh sounds of an unchristian language. Hardly even the semblance of order! She turned as she heard what she hoped was the last bus of the day rumble into the schoolyard. Pulling open the front door, she kicked the door stop in place, her old knees scowling.

"This way, girls," she called, waving at the untidy cluster huddled outside the bus door.

Most of this group looked decent enough, but as they drew close, her nostrils twitched at the scent of bear grease wafting from a couple of heads. The majority wore brightly coloured dresses, some with trousers underneath, and several had shoes on their feet—a good sign with the current shortage at the school—though some girls were in moccasins. Two or three had nothing but streaks of dirt on their feet. A little girl crying her eyes out shuffled forward in a ratty pair of pink bedroom slippers, for heaven's sake.

"I'll take care of them, Mother Grace," a sister called, rushing up from behind her.

As Mother Grace started back to the dining hall to assume her role as supervisor, a classroom door opened and a flock of freshly cropped girls spilled out. Just ahead of her, senior girls in school uniforms dawdled.

"Move on," she ordered, clapping her hands.

Turning the corner to the staff dining room, she spotted the stork-like figure of young Sister Priscilla—now "Cilla," apparently because she thought it easier for the younger girls to pronounce—hovering over a group of distraught little girls, seemingly torn between whether to comfort or admonish them. Near the entrance to the kitchen, roosting on what appeared to be her own office chair, was Sister Margaret, a Bible in her hands and impatience scribbled over her doughy face.

Coming up beside Sister Margaret, Mother Grace said, "Let's begin," with a lightness she didn't feel. Already, it had been an arduous day, and she yearned to sit down on the very chair Margaret had obviously wheeled, without permission, from her office. But she would not succumb to anger or complaint. After all, Sister Margaret was elderly, beleaguered by lumbago, and as far as she could tell, a paucity of spirit. She, the Mother General, would rise above.

Sister Cilla herded her charges forward, then came up and stood by Mother Grace's side.

"Your name?" Mother Grace asked each girl. Sister Cilla recorded each response on a sheet of foolscap. At least where possible. Unfortunately, there were always those children whose parents had, for whatever reason, given them Blackfoot names, or "unpronounceable monikers" as she referred to them. Those she replaced with scriptural names.

"Sootaki," the little girl before her croaked.

"I beg your pardon?" Sister Cilla asked.

"Sootaki."

Cilla glanced up, and Mother Grace allowed herself a barely audible sigh before tilting her chin towards Sister Margaret. Placing her hands on Sootaki's shoulders, Cilla steered the girl to the seated nun.

"Anataki," whispered the very next child.

Sister Cilla looked askance, but Mother Grace gestured again with her chin, and that girl too was dispatched to Sister Margaret.

Mother Grace's naming system wasn't without its problems. Since female names were less prevalent than male names in the Bible, the same name was sometimes given to more than one girl at the school—though, to avoid confusion in the classroom, no two girls in the same year shared the same name. Hence the pen, paper, and lists, a bothersome but necessary business.

Sister Margaret leaned towards the two girls in front of her, making Mother Grace's office chair groan. "I'm going to give you proper names, you little beggars. Let's see what we have here." Slowly she flipped through the Bible.

Mother Grace suspected Sister Margaret was making as much of a production as possible out of the simple act of renaming. Sister Margaret had often voiced her objection to the scriptural naming policy, saying how she, the dormitory supervisor, would call out one name and have two or three girls of different ages come running. She advocated adding saints' names to the roster. "Nice ones," she'd said, "like Agatha, Bridget, Perpetua, or even Margaret." Perhaps if Sister Margaret hadn't brought up her suggestion so often, Mother Grace would have considered it.

"Anne," Sister Margaret finally announced to the first girl. "Ruth," she barked at the second. Sister Cilla wrote down the names, and the girls hurried to kitchen, where a sister was handing out nightclothes.

Thankfully, after the first two, the names of the new little girls this year were quite acceptable, though there seemed to be a proliferation of Marys. "Marie," Mother Grace said to the second one. "Maryanne," to the third.

*   *   *

Rose kept her eyes on the nun at the front of the line, the questioner with the glasses and lined face. That nun asked each girl her name, her words sounding different from the way the other nuns said them, turned up at the edges. The questioner wasn't tall like the young one next to her. Not fat like the one sitting in the chair. But she held her head up, like she was in charge. And her headdress, Rose could see, was different from the others'—black where theirs were white, white where theirs were black. She was chief, all right, the "Mother General" she had heard the other nuns talk about as they scrubbed, shoved, and snipped her.

Her turn now. "Your name?"

"Ro-ose," she stuttered. At least that wouldn't be changed like the Indian names of those two other girls. English names weren't changed, Mama had said. That's why her official name was Rose, though her real name was Sinopaki, which meant kit fox.

"Rose," the chief nun repeated, her eyes behind the glasses sky-bright. Or like a bluebottle fly. "That's certainly not a biblical name."

Rose bit her lip against the throb of tears.

The long-bone nun sprang forward. *"I am a rose of Sharon, a lily of the valleys,"* she blurted.

The Mother General glanced up at the tall sister. "Ah, yes. Song of Solomon." She closed her eyes and went inside herself.

Everyone watched, and Rose sucked her lip. The girls behind her started shuffling. The fat name changer moved, making her chair shiver.

Suddenly a new nun grew out of the space beside the shivering chair. Rose blinked, but there she was, young, as young as the tall one nearby, but this one's skirt was bunched around her waist, showing the bottom part of her legs, her narrow ankles and bare feet. The new nun leaned against the wall, watching them all with a fed-up look, her headdress crooked.

Then Mother General made a throat noise and opened her blue eyes, and when Rose looked back, the new nun was melting away. Gone!

Oh. She wasn't sure what had happened, and when she looked up at Mother Grace, she saw she wasn't sure either. Mother Grace blinked like she didn't even know how long she'd had her eyes closed.

"Rose Marie," she said, staring strong, right at her, with her sky-fly eyes. Then she raised her chin, glancing at the long-bone nun with her paper and pen, then over to the fat one in the chair. "Rose Marie," she repeated, louder.

As she stood in line for her nightclothes, Sinopaki, Rose, now Rose Marie, sucked blood from her bottom lip. Her eyes smarted and her head banged. First that nun appearing and disappearing right in front of her, and then her name being changed.

Name changes happened sometimes, she knew. It was normal. Her papa was first Bull Calf, *Matoom onista*, she remembered, named by his parents for his bawling cry. At school, the priests had renamed him "Michel" after a dead one. After that, he ran away from his school. Mama didn't like Papa saying that in front of her, but he did, he ran away, and after he got caught and was brought back to his school a few times, everyone on his Reserve called him "Piitaa," because, like an eagle, he was always flying. Still later, after he ran far, far away into Mama's country, he was given the name "Blessed Wolf" after the four-legged who had helped him find food and finally led Grandfather Whitewater to him. The spirit wolf had saved her papa, had given him power. Sure, names got changed. She knew that. But under her skin, she was still Sinopaki.

At supper, the ache in Rose Marie's chest grew big. Clank of dishes on the wooden table. Snatch of white hands and a chipped bowl full of greasy water with floating skin and mushy green.

"Chicken stew," a sister said.

She could hardly swallow it. The chicken skin was bumpy, there was hardly any meat, and stuff that shouldn't be cooked was boiled into slime. She wiped her nose on her sleeve and tried to eat, but someone beside her was crying, and the stew came back up to her mouth. She choked.

She tried to chew and not throw up. She tried not to cry.

Finally, Sister Cilla stood, her finger shaking at them. "Tomorrow you'll have to finish every scrap in your dish. Now back upstairs to the dormitory, first-year girls. It's time to get ready for bed."

Up the way-too-many steps they followed Sister Cilla and marched into the room that was almost as big as that gymnasium.

"Go find your bed in the back two rows," Sister Cilla ordered. "Remember, your number is on the bedpost."

A clump of squiggles was all *number* meant to Rose Marie, and she was pretty sure that's all it meant to the other first-year girls. She found her bed because she had bunched her nightdress in a ball at the bottom, the way she liked to put clothes, fur, and other soft things.

"Into your nightdresses," Sister Cilla called.

Rose Marie looked at the other girls pulling their uniforms over their heads, and she did the same.

Sister Cilla went around and helped the ones getting stuck. "Straighten your arms." She tugged hard.

When everyone was changed, Sister went to the centre aisle, pressed her hands together, and looked at them one by one. "Time for our prayer. Repeat after me: *Now I lay me down to sleep—*"

A few of the girls couldn't speak English well, and everyone talked at different speeds, some fast, some slow. Rose Marie couldn't get any sound out at all.

"In the name of the Father, the Son, and the Holy Ghost," Sister Cilla said, crossing herself.

This part Rose Marie knew. Mama had taken her to church a few times when they had visited Auntie Connie and Aunt Angelique on the Reserve. Seeing all the hands rising, falling, and crisscrossing, she had copied them. She had learned how to kneel and fold her hands too, and to lower her head at the right time. Now she closed her eyes like Sister Cilla, but she couldn't make the too-big room with high-up beds go away. She thought of Papa's traps, how when they were rusty, they made a hurt sound—and the animals in them too, when they weren't dead. The beds made the same sound. She opened her eyes and watched Sister Cilla, whose long black dress was a shadow that ate up her whole body. Her long-bone hands were just a little sun-browned, like they were only half there, and there was a gold ring on her finger, like that one Forest Fox Crown gave Aunt Angelique in the moon of sore eyes.

"Let's try that again, girls. *Now I lay me down to sleep.*"

Rose Marie looked over at the next bed, and the bed after that, and all around her at all the heads with just-chopped hair. Some of the mouths in some of the heads were saying the prayer and some were open holes with sad dribbling out.

Two beds away, one of the girls was shaking. She looked like she was choking, and she sounded like it too. The choking spread to Rose Marie, and she tried to close her mouth to stop the sounds, but they burst out anyway. She pressed her lips together and clamped her hand over them. She didn't want to cry in front of all these kids and that tall nun. Way at the front of the room, a light hung from a wire over the only door, just one way to escape. Oh, she wanted Mama and Papa, and while gurgles leaked from her mouth, she prayed, *Mama and Papa, come get me.*

"I didn't hear everyone," Sister Cilla said. "We're going to say the prayer over until everyone knows it. Then we will kneel by our beds and pray properly from start to finish."

Rose Marie's knees, elbows, and fingers felt itchy-tingly. She bent her legs, straightened them, bounced on her toes, and swung her head and not-enough hair from one side to the other. The room jarred back and forth like the Indian agent's mud-coloured car had jarred the sky and ground that morning. She felt dizzy-sick, and the small amount of slimy chicken stew she had swallowed was turning hard and hot in her tummy.

The door smacked open with a bang and Sister Margaret lumbered through, turning to the big girls behind her. "Halt." She dragged a chair over and lowered herself. "Come on," she ordered, waving the girls in with an arm packed like sausage in its black sleeve.

Sister Cilla waited for the too-many girls. Rose Marie knew what Papa thought about so many people stuck together, like in the towns, that one called Black Apple near them and the one named Hilltop near her aunties' Reserve. People packed in without enough space for their spirits to move. The air tightened in that big room that wasn't big enough. Like a snare around her chest. As she tried to breathe, her fingers came undone and started curling around nothing.

"Stand still," Sister Cilla yelled.

Run! Rose Marie's brain said. She had tried to run away when the men came to take her, but Papa had stood in her way. Now she darted towards the door that led to the hall that led to the stairs that led to the big front door that opened on the whole wide world.

"Stop!" Sister Cilla shouted. "Stop this instant, Rose Marie!"

A breeze blew cold on her neck where her hair used to fall. She would not stop!

Sister Cilla called, "Sister! Sister Margaret!"

"Great heavens!" Sister Margaret gasped, heaving herself up and lumbering towards Rose Marie.

The girl turned, racing down another row of beds, flying past the older girls fishing nightdresses from cupboards and then back towards the door. Oh, and there was Sister Cilla loping on her long-bone legs, skirt flapping like a crow.

Sister Cilla dove. Rose Marie pulled back. Sister crashed into the door, slamming it shut with a crunch-bone sound.

Back up the centre aisle she raced, Sister Cilla limping behind. All the girls were watching her, their faces blurring by. Sister Cilla's long arm shot out and grabbed air. Rose Marie dove under a bed. Sliding on her belly, she could smell lye soap on her skin. And fear.

Girls got down on all fours to watch. Some jumped on their beds and bounced, the springs screeching. Rose Marie was back on her feet, running. A big girl hooted. Wind blowing inside her head made her eyes dizzy.

"Go, go, go!" girls shrieked. They laughed and clapped their hands.

Grasping a bedpost, Rose Marie swung around a corner. Sister Cilla!

"Stop," Sister ordered.

She spun towards the door, but Sister Margaret had planted herself in front of it. Rose Marie scurried under another bed, crab-scrambling, goose-pimply cold and sweating hot.

"Stop," Sister Cilla repeated, her cheeks flushing.

The girls on the beds swallowed their giggles. Rose Marie skittered out the other side.

"Stop!" both sisters shouted together. The girls stopped bouncing. The room, except for the drumbeat of her bare feet, grew quiet.

"Rose Marie!" Sister Cilla yelled, so loud the high-up windows shook. That's when she saw how small those windows were, how impossible the banged-shut door was to get through with Sister Margaret parked right in front. She'd never reach the hall or the staircase leading down to the next one. She would never get to the big wooden door that led to the road and the Reserve and her home. Trapped.

Sister Cilla strode from the side aisle to join Sister Margaret. The two sisters stood between her and the door. Cold clawed its way up her legs, numbing inch by inch. *A-pis-tot-oki, na-tot-sich-pi*, she prayed.

Breasts heaving, Sister Margaret stomped towards her, raised one sausage arm, and smacked her face. Rose Marie flew to the floor.

Later, her nosebleed stanched, her face stinging nettles, she knelt by her bed and prayed with the other first-year girls:

> *Now I lay me down to sleep,*
> *I pray the Lord my soul to keep.*
> *If I should die before I wake,*
> *I pray the Lord my soul to please, please, please take!*

5

Stealing Anne

FROM HER VERY first night at St. Mark's, Rose Marie was bothered by the shadows in the dormitory. Dark pools ran into each other and clumped together, forming shapes. Oh, they were just shadows made by the only light left on at night, that one bulb dangling in the entrance; they had to be. "Please make them just shadows," she muttered while the other first-year girls recited their bedtime prayer. Stuck in this school, crowded by kids, nuns, pointers, desks, and rules, she was alone, so terribly lonely. "Parents," she whispered to herself in her bed, *"N'iiko-si,"* then *"Na Nik-sist,"* Mama, and *"Na Ki-na-nin,"* Papa, just to hear the names that bloomed familiar smells, touch and warmth, such safety. Growing less familiar every day, here in the school, where she didn't feel safe at all.

Sootaki, named Anne by big fat Sister Margaret and her big fat Bible, slept one row up. That first night, after Rose Marie had run through the dormitory, after Sister Margaret had smacked her across the face and Sister Cilla had shoved toilet paper up her nose to stop the bleeding—after all that, when she was back standing beside her metal bed, Sister Cilla ordered, "Girls, pay attention and stand up straight."

Lifting her chin, she felt blood trickle down her throat, but she managed to stop crying. As Sister Cilla moved towards her, she stiffened. But Sister wasn't coming for her. Instead she stopped at the row in front and looked at Sootaki, who was making signs to an older cousin up front.

"Anne," she said. "Stand up straight, arms at your sides."

Sootaki—now Anne—immediately did as she was told.

"You must pay attention, Anne. We're about to say our prayers."

Sootaki, Rose Marie could see, had already become "Anne."

The following morning, all the first-year girls were herded into Sister Joan's classroom and told to sit at hard wooden desks. That's when Sootaki's name was changed again.

Sister Joan, striding back and forth in front of the class, skirts chewing, showed the girls how to sit properly with their hands clasped in front of them. "Like this," she said, holding her arms out and fitting the fingers of one hand through the fingers of the other. Up and down the rows Sister Joan strode, making sure each set of hands was properly clasped. "Feet flat on the floor." She jabbed at crossed knees.

Rose Marie had to scrunch forward on her seat to get her feet to reach the floor. Her nose still hurt from Sister Margaret's slap, and it felt big as a puffball and all prickly.

"Very good. Now I will explain roll call," Sister Joan announced. "When I say your name, you will put up your hand like this." She raised her arm above her head. "Once I've spotted you, you will say dis-tinct-ly, 'Present, Sister Joan.' Is that clear, class?"

Everyone was quiet, and Sister Joan folded her lips, making them disappear. "When I ask the class a question, you will answer in unison, 'Yes, Sister Joan.' Is that clear?"

Some of the girls, Rose Marie included, began to answer, "Yes, Sister Joan," but others sat still as gophers at the side of a road, and the ones answering, not sure they should be, stopped, voices tripping backwards to silence.

Sister Joan made a huffing sound. "Answer me. Is that clear, class?"

Some girls stared at the shorn nape of the student in front; some looked down at their desks, their folded hands, their feet flat on the floor; some shuffled, but no one answered.

"Class," Sister Joan bellowed, "I told you, when I ask a question, you will answer—" Her lips disappeared again. "Fine, fine," she said, spit flying. "Let's concentrate on roll call, shall we? When I call your name, you will raise your hand and answer, 'Present, Sister Joan.' Then you will put your arm down and fold your hands once more on your desk." Sister Joan, eyes bulging, folded her hands in front of her again, for everyone to see. "Martha!" she barked.

No one answered.

"Martha!" Sister Joan's voice was louder, her face blotching red. "Is there a Martha in this room? Where is Martha?"

A girl third seat from the front raised a shaky arm.

"Martha?" Sister Joan demanded.

Martha nodded.

"You will raise your hand and say, 'Present, Sister Joan,'" she croaked, her face a stain.

"Present, Sister Joan," Martha whispered.

Things went better after that, and Rose Marie relaxed a little. While Sister Joan called out names, she let her bottom slide back on the seat a little so only her toes touched the floor.

"Anne," Sister Joan called.

Just as Sootaki, sitting right beside Rose Marie, raised her hand, another voice rang out, loud and clear. "Present, Sister Joan."

Rose Marie followed the direction of Sootaki's eyes and looked at Anataki in the far row, saw her lower her hand, fold it into her other hand, and stare at her desk.

Sootaki leaned forward and glared at Anataki, trying to catch her eye, but Anataki wouldn't look up.

Sister kept calling out names, her head lifting and falling.

"Ruth," Sister Joan called. "Ruth?"

There was still no answer, and Sister Joan glared. "For goodness' sake, is Ruth here?"

Beside Rose Marie, Sootaki slowly raised her hand. "I'm not—" she began, but Sister Joan cut in.

" 'Present, Sister Joan.' That's what you say! You raise your hand as soon as your name is called, and you answer smartly, 'Present, Sister Joan.' We don't have all day, Ruth."

That evening in the dormitory, when the first-, second-, and third-year girls were standing in line for the bathroom, the older girls returned to the dormitory from kitchen and laundry duties. Sootaki's older cousin Bertha marched up to Anataki and shoved her to the floor.

"Smarten up, *Ruth*!" she hissed, kicking her. "You're *Ruth*, not Anne."

Anataki got back up and looked around, her expression stupid as the chickens that pecked the ground in front of Brother Abraham's barn.

"What's going on here?" Sister Margaret called as she lumbered into the room. "You," she said to Anataki as Bertha slipped away. "Don't just stand there. What's your name?"

"Anne," Anataki answered softly.

"Well, move up, Anne. We don't have all night."

Sootaki, leaving the bathroom, frowned when she heard the name "Anne." She went straight to her cousins clumped at Bertha's bed, and the four girls turned to glare at Anataki. But Anataki didn't seem to notice.

Following right behind Anataki in line, Rose Marie was itchy-tingly. Anataki had picked the wrong girl, she thought. With her big cousins, oh, Sootaki was the wrong one to steal a name from.

* * *

The next day as students lined up for lunch in the cafeteria, Bertha cut in, pushing Anataki out of line. "Tell the sisters," she ordered, "you're Ruth, not Anne."

After lunch, when the first-year girls filed back to Sister Joan's class, Sootaki whispered to Anataki, "You tell Sister Joan you're Ruth or my big relatives and me gonna beat you up."

Rose Marie watched. No emotion showed on Anataki's face. Nothing at all.

That night as Anataki walked out of a toilet stall, Bertha, standing at the sink, threw down her toothbrush and punched her in the face.

Anataki staggered back, hitting a stall door, her expression switching from shock to anger. And then her face went blank as the bathroom wall. She turned and walked away. She didn't tell Sister Margaret or Sister Cilla about taking the wrong name. Nor about being punched either.

The fourth evening after four morning roll calls when Anataki had answered "Present, Sister Joan" so fast Sootaki hadn't had time to open her mouth, Sootaki slow-walked up to Sister Margaret, her three cousins waving her on.

"Sister Margaret," she stammered, pointing at Anataki, "that girl over there took my name."

"What?" Sister Margaret demanded. Looking over at Anataki, she couldn't suppress a yawn.

Bertha blustered up. "My cousin's the one you named Anne, Sister Margaret. That girl over there was named Ruth, but now she's pretending to be Anne." Bertha's two sisters, coming up moving beside her, nodded vigorously, and Sootaki said, "Really truly, Sister Margaret."

Sister Margaret came over to Anataki, who was sitting on her bed pulling off her stockings. "You. I hear you're not going by the name I gave you."

Anataki raised her eyes as far as Sister Margaret's breasts, lowered them, and murmured, "Name? Name Anne, Sister Margaret."

"Didn't I give you the name Ruth?" Sister's voice was loud enough to reach everyone, especially Sootaki and her three cousins giggling into their hands.

"Name?" Anataki repeated, her eyes reaching Sister Margaret's chins before falling to the floor. "Anne, Sister Margaret."

Sister Margaret glared. Anataki's jaw was swollen on one side, and Sister must have noticed this, must have wondered if maybe there had been a fight. A four-against-one fight.

Sister reached over and patted Anataki's head. "You're not from the Reserve, are you? You're from the country. No speak good English?" she asked loudly. "Never mind. I'll tell that other one." And she made her way over to Sootaki, standing with her cousins.

"You're Ruth," Sister Margaret told Sootaki firmly. "The other girl is Anne."

The four girls started clamouring, but Sister Margaret raised a thick hand. "That's all there is to it! Now get on with you, you little beggars."

She motioned to Sister Cilla, who was helping the little ones put on their nightdresses, and when Cilla hurried over, told her, "I need to straighten you out about this name business. That one there's Anne. The one with the cousins is Ruth."

Waving off Sister Cilla's "But I think you're mistaken—" Sister Margaret fixed her with a steely gaze. "I believe I'm the senior supervisor here," she said, then hollered over to Anataki, "No more trouble, *Anne*."

"—ataki," the little girl whispered.

Rose Marie, a few feet away, heard her finish her name, her old name, the Blackfoot name she had decided, secretly, to keep. She looked into Anataki's face and saw a coyote dart behind her eyes. A coyote chasing a chicken. Quick. Then the chicken look was on her face again, dull and stupid.

She thought maybe she liked that girl, that Anataki.

6

Girls, So Many of Them

N O POINT IN denying it, Mother Grace was having difficulties. Perhaps it was the ridiculous allowance with which she was expected to run the school. Since the Second World War had begun, going on five years now, the already inadequate residential school budget had been cut to the bone. *Oui*, and subsequently, a shortage of supplies and the necessary rationing of coal. Conditions conspired against her. Unusually brisk weather blew in from the Rockies. The cold aggravated her rheumatism, and the dwindling light affected her mood. Night fell sooner each evening, stayed later each morning, and darkness settled grain by grain like sand in her joints.

It was possible the children's behaviour really *was* worse this year, as some of the sisters complained, their smiles less frequent, their anger and melancholy more pervasive. Heavens, the despondency she saw in those little brown children whose skin never seemed quite clean. Not to mention the moodiness of the sisters themselves, their pinched faces and barbed quips.

Whatever caused it, by the third week just two days into the new school year, Mother Grace was more unsure of herself than ever, second-guessing every decision enacted in the past and hesitant about making new ones. Her self-doubt chewed holes in morning prayer, the celebration of Mass, the orders she gave, and, worst of all, her conviction. *Mon Dieu*, hiding the photos of Sister Mary of Bethany and Father Damien had not removed them from her thoughts. They haunted her still, their unexpected deaths, their futile lives.

She couldn't confide in any of the sisters. That was partly due to the alliance Sisters Joan and Margaret seemed to have forged against her. Sister Bernadette was generally loyal and good-natured, but she was also uncomplicated—unable, perhaps, to fully comprehend Mother Grace's concerns. Sister Lucy was getting a little hard of hearing, and Mother Grace was not inclined to raise her voice in this school of a thousand ears. Sister Cilla, a delightful young woman in many ways, was inexperienced. And, of course, in her position it was inappropriate to speak of personal matters to the sisters. She couldn't bring herself to approach any of them. Nor old Father David, growing more remote by the day.

Among the mortal, there was only Father Patrick, dear Patrick, her true confessor and closest friend. And, as always, he was a hundred miles away, in the Badlands. She snatched a few sheets of stationery and her favourite fountain pen from her desk drawer.

Dear Patrick,

I pray that God continues to hold you to His loving bosom. I my-self am troubled and wish for nothing more than your warm presence.

In this school of cold drafts, I too am cold, full of self-doubt. These days I question procedure. I question intent, and most of all, I question myself. I know that running the school with a disciplined routine is necessary to make it a place of order rather than chaos, God's house rather than the Devil's workshop. If you were here, you would tell me that the residential schools are hardly houses of God and that we should incorporate some of the Indians' (many would say both primitive and blasphemous) rituals at the schools as a way to engage them. You are a wise and kind man, dearest, but some-

times, I fear, too kind. I know you favour day schools rather than residential ones, but wouldn't they impede our mission of making the Indian race God-fearing citizens of the Dominion?

I wonder: What is my purpose? Comfort me, Pat. I can't seem to find solace anywhere else, though new students have come to us again this year, and I tell myself there is always promise in that.

I will admit that one child in particular has piqued my interest: a first-year girl whose name I altered. I suppose it was her expression I noticed: inquisitiveness with a touch of defiance. It reminded me of myself in childhood. If Sister Priscilla hadn't interrupted with a quotation from Song of Solomon, reminding me that roses too are God's work, I might have allowed Sister Margaret to replace "Rose" with any biblical name she pleased: "Agar" perhaps, "Gomer," even "Haggith." But the bereft gaze of another little girl whose name had been changed just minutes before deterred me and I allowed "Rose" to remain, simply adding a reference to our Holy Mother.

Sister Cilla's outburst took me aback. In this time, at this age, Song of Solomon seems to elicit in my heart not joy, but turmoil.

She put her pen down. Was it unseemly to say more? If she were able to talk to Patrick in person as she had as a novice, the subject would unfold quite naturally. There was nothing, it seemed, they were unable to discuss candidly. Yet writing was different. Putting her innermost thoughts on a page made them tangible. What if Patrick did not follow his usual practice of tossing her letter into his wood stove, and someone else read it? Dear, dear Patrick with his bright eyes and quick mind, his strong body. *Ça alors*, a strong body no more, she feared.

The truth is that Song of Solomon is full of the material extravagance that I have sacrificed in the service of God—the silver, gold, and precious stones, not to mention the physical sensuality—and so Sister Cilla's reference to the book has disturbed me.

She thought of the thighs compared to jewels, the belly, "a heap of wheat set about with lilies." *Oui*, she remembered the verses well, recalled the giggling they had instigated in her dormitory at convent school. Amid the violent history, petty jealousies, the miracles, prophecies and wisdom of the Bible, the Song of Solomon had seemed profane. Yet, as she grew older, she related her ardour for her Lord Jesus Christ to the Song of Solomon. *Hélas*, her passion for the sacrifice of His flesh, the gift of His holy love!

At the age of seventeen, she had decided to pledge herself to Him, to become His bride. Jesus alone would be her life's mate. She waited for graduation, then travelled east to Montreal to enter the Mother House of Les Sœurs d'Amour Fraternelle (translated in English— rather unfortunately, she had always thought—as the Sisters of Brotherly Love).

As a postulant, she had deeply felt her commitment to Jesus, talking to Him at the end of each day as one would a husband, imagining His hand on her hair, His arm brushing hers as He spoke, the delightful tingle of skin on holy skin.

"What a day I've had," she would tell Him. "Already I'm fed up with the routine of the Mother House: clean, cook, eat, pray, and, above all, follow orders. Is that serving You, *mon amour*? Should I be patient?" And she'd laugh, listening for the rumble of His loving voice in her ear. Sometimes she swore she could hear it.

What a fool she'd been! She recalled her confessor brusquely reminding her that Jesus was her husband only in the fact that she was dedicating herself to His service, the one man in her heart and life. An all-but-forgotten heat spread down her neck. She had been shameful. Perhaps. Yet devoted.

A year later, she and her companion walked into a university theology class, Portrayals of the Holy Spirit, given by Father Patrick McBain.

She touched her throat just above the high collar of her habit. An old throat, creped as her mother's ancient church dress. She had grown old here on the edge of the vast prairie, mountains looming in the west like bad omens. The possibility of another life outside the Church, one that included the sensuous, the fulfilment and praise of the body, gone. Forever and ever.

I miss you terribly, Patrick. Forgive me my ramblings.
  Yours in Christ,
    Grace

She folded the sheets, then impulsively pressed the letter to her lips before placing it in an envelope.

After typing the students' names in alphabetized class lists, Mother Grace opened her office door just as the bell rang, signalling the end of the school day. Girls foamed into the hallway.

"I just can't believe it," Esther Fox Crown gushed to her pal Susie Running Rabbit as they rushed past. "I said, 'Don't come over here and try to be my friend after what you said about me wearing lipstick. I only tried it on.' She just looked at me. Then I said, 'What are you going to do, tell Sister on me?'"

Behind them, Adele pushed down the hall calling to her older sister, "Esther, wait up!"

A few of the quiet girls strolled by. One of them, the painfully shy Abigail Bull, saw Mother Grace watching, dropped her eyes to the floor, and turned abruptly up the stairs.

"Watch where you're going, you little brats," Bertha Bright Eye shrieked, shoving a second-year girl out of her way. "Come on, let's sneak outside." She grabbed Anne-Marie Shot One Side's arm and steered her down the hall.

Sister Joan was heading her way, so Mother Grace closed her office door to a crack. She heard Leah Spotted Calf and Prissy Youngman running behind, calling, "Sister, Sister Joan, can we do anything to help?

"Yes, girls," Sister Joan answered curtly. "You can wipe down the blackboard for me. This way. Snip, snap."

Mother Grace sat down. Girls. So many of them. God help us.

7

Fire Worms

ROSE MARIE TRIED hard to fit in at school that whole windy month of September, but things weren't right. She felt hot and tingly-itchy sitting in the too-big desk in a colourless classroom, and sometimes she saw that new sister with the bunched-up skirt who always disappeared again. Maybe she was seeing backwards, at what people used to be. It made her want to run, but she wasn't allowed to run inside the school "under any circumstances," Sister Joan had said. Sitting in her desk, she squirmed, rocked, and scratched, but she could never get calm. She wanted out, needed out.

Whenever she could, she peered through the class and dining rooms' small windows and watched the land and sky. Sagebrush blew across the schoolyard towards the barn they weren't allowed to go near. Beyond the barn, she could glimpse a patch of that field they couldn't even talk about, the shade of a bruise, tender to the eyes. Going up from the nuns' floor to the dorm on the third floor, if she looked at just the right moment, she could catch a glimpse of that field with its crooked white crosses, and they made her want to run even more. She longed to be outside all the time, not just for a few minutes at recess, lunch, and after school. She wanted far away from the too-many kids and nuns. She wanted bushes, grass, and sky, with no one in sight but

Mama with Kiaa-yo in her arms, and Papa coming down the trail, his eyes and arms spraying midday sun. Maybe even a friend.

Somewhere to the east of the old chicken barn they had to stay away from, she figured there was a marsh, because ducks flew low going and coming, and there were a few grey geese too. Maybe muskrat lived there. Maybe frogs. She didn't know which animal-people were in this flat place, though she had seen gophers around the school, and, in the distance, a few prong-horned antelope, their noses sweeping the earth and poking the air, their scents calling *Come get me.* "Moon of making babies," Mama called this time.

The antelopes' constant grazing warned of a coyote moon and dark months. Oh, if she just walked away from this horrible, crowded place, she would find the land beyond the school with its long rolling yawns and the mountains turned to small blue sighs in the distance. But she wasn't allowed.

Until Aunt Angelique's marriage to Forest Fox Crown, she had been around other kids only when families visited or sick people came to Papa for healing. He was Blessed Wolf, the medicine man. She had no cousins except the two grown-big sons of Auntie Connie, and they had gone east to Coulee to work, disappearing into the coal mines at the time of first melt. Even after Aunt Angelique's marriage, Esther and Adele Fox Crown had told her, "Your aunt, she's not our mother, you know. Our mother died." The second day of school, Adele said, "Don't hang around us." She didn't even try.

But now there was that one girl. "Anataki," she started saying to her, whispering the last part of her name so that anyone close by heard only "Anne."

As soon as they began sitting together at meals and chasing each other at recess, Ruth and her cousins taunted them. "Midget," they jeered. "The Name-Stealer and the Midget. What a good pair!" Pretty soon other kids joined in. Rose Marie didn't know about Anataki, but she was getting pissed off.

* * *

One night, just before lights-out, she was the only one at the bathroom sink. She turned on the tap, which was like an all-at-once creek flowing fast, and splashed water on her face. As she turned the water off, she heard someone creeping behind her. She looked up. Ruth! Ruth's arm smashed her head down on the sink. Dizzy black blotches swam before her eyes. But she leapt. She hit and bit Ruth. Ruth screamed. She grabbed Ruth's throat and squeezed. Ruth gasped, her mouth opening and closing like a fish drowning in air.

A yank from behind. Oh! Her hair ripped from her scalp.

"Get off my relative!" Bertha screamed.

She wouldn't let go of Ruth. If she did, the two of them would kill her. She clung to Ruth's neck, watched her face darken and her eyes bulge. Bertha pulled Rose Marie's hair harder, ripping another patch from her head. Rose Marie tried to twist Ruth's head quick, the way Mama twisted the heads of birds she caught in snares, breaking their necks.

"Stop that!" thundered Sister Margaret.

Rose Marie could hear Sister wheezing behind. She let go. Ruth staggered and dropped to her knees.

Bertha punched her in the side of the head. Sister Margaret clamped one hand to the back of Bertha's neck, the other to hers. She half marched, half dragged them to the dormitory. All the girls stopped moving and stared.

"Get away from your bed, Susie," Sister Margaret ordered. "Sister Cilla, bring my stick!" Sister Margaret slammed both Rose Marie and Bertha against a bed. "Bend over."

Side by side, they hunched over, palms pressed to the mattress.

Sister Margaret snatched the stick from Sister Cilla and, without hesitating, swung it with a whoosh against Bertha's bum. Then Rose Marie's. Whack and whack and whack. Rose Marie's bones clattered and screamed. Sister Margaret kept hitting them, one, then the other. Rose Marie bit her lip bloody. She was not going to cry. Beside her, Bertha's face was tied in a knot. The stick kept whooshing and hammering. The room filled with splotchy black bruises. Bertha started sobbing.

"Bertha, you may go to your bed now. Kneel down and pray for forgiveness," Sister Margaret rasped.

Rose Marie turned her head and poured hate on Sister Margaret. Her bum and legs screamed, her eyes blurred, but she wouldn't cry.

"Stay where you are, you little beggar!" Sister Margaret shouted.

She turned back to the bed, and Sister swung her stick one, two, three times more.

"Sister Margaret . . ." Sister Cilla said.

Rose Marie fell into the bed, her body hammered full of rusty nails.

"Get up!" Sister Margaret hollered.

"Sister Margaret!" Sister Cilla repeated.

"This one's got to learn her lesson." Sister Margaret swung the stick again.

"Sister Margaret!" Sister Cilla yelled real loud.

The stick whistled. The blade of Mama's chopping knife slammed down on moose meat. Rose Marie screamed. She would whack Sister Margaret back. She would shove Mama's chopping knife in her guts.

"Enough!" Sister Cilla reached for the stick and Sister Margaret staggered back, letting her take it. "Go to your bed, Rose Marie."

Rose Marie felt like a live fish tossed in a hot pan. Shakily she made her way past the smudge of faces, head high. *No tears, see.*

Anataki gave her that coyote look, and Rose Marie forced herself to grin like it was nothing, like she couldn't care less, like those nuns could do anything at all to her and it wouldn't change her one bit. The sisters couldn't see her face, but some of the girls did.

After that, none of the first-years bugged her. A few big girls picked on her still. She was so small maybe they thought they could get away with it. Then, on the way to class or in the cafeteria line, she would poke them in the bum with her pencil, knock their food tray, or trip them up. She got back at them, all right.

When a big girl called her "Midget," she laughed. "Bird Beak," she jeered, and the other kids giggled. "Knuckle Bones," she called Leah Spotted Calf. "Duck Waddle," to that stupid Sarah Keeper. If they were mean, she was meaner. Then sometimes a girl got her back again, hit or pinched her. Tit-for-tat, like Sister Joan always said before she strapped them. So Rose Marie put stones in their shoes or hid their stockings. One morning when she was about to brush her teeth, she saw that someone had spit on her toothbrush. She wondered if this tit-for-tat would ever end.

Anataki knew how to get back at the mean ones too. She had learned from her brothers how to mimic. "Oh my," she said, flipping her hair like Adele Fox Crown had learned from Esther. "These old-way Indians, they're not as fabulous as I am."

Soon there was much less name-calling of Rose Marie and Anataki. The other girls—well, except sometimes for Bertha and her sisters— mostly stayed away.

Neither one of them, Rose Marie and Taki soon learned, could stomach the school food. In the morning when they lined up for breakfast, Sister Bernadette slapped something called "porridge" in their bowls. Some days it was a thin soup with small lumps that slid over their teeth and down their throats, so all they had to do was spoon and swallow. "Slimeballs," they called it. Other days the porridge was gooey as prairie gumbo and stuck in their throats until mouthfuls of water pushed it down into a hard wedge in their tummies. "Glue," Anne named it. Once or twice, Sister Bernadette managed to make it *just right*—"Baby Bear," Rose Marie said, remembering the story Sister Cilla had read them one noon hour when every one of the first-years was sick in bed. In the book, the bears were just like people but without any powers. And they wore stupid white people's clothes.

When "Baby Bear" was being served, Rose Marie managed to eat all her porridge and keep it down.

Anataki wasn't so lucky. She was almost a head taller and not at all sparrow-boned when school started, but by the middle of October, she was thin, her spine a staircase, her ribs tree branches. It was pancakes with Rogers Golden Syrup, served on the Sabbath, that made Taki's mouth water. She had a sweet tooth, and Rose Marie always let her have one of her two pancakes. Those breakfasts Anataki ate quickly, her eyes shining, syrup dripping from her bottom lip.

Lunch was usually a slice or two of doughy or stale bread, sometimes fried in the bacon grease collected from Father David and Brother Abraham's breakfasts, and occasionally served with leftovers from supper the night before. Once in a while there were baked beans.

Supper was mostly mashed potatoes served the same way as the breakfast porridge, in "slimeballs," "glue," and, occasionally, "Baby Bear style." Chicken stew was a watery broth in which one of Brother Abraham's scrawny, plucked, but still-clawed hens was boiled overnight with mushed vegetables, or sometimes a fried egg. Aside from the scraps of dry fish doled out on Fridays, there was little meat, and meat was what both girls longed for.

"Guess what I dreamed about last night?" Rose Marie whispered to Taki in the cafeteria line at breakfast one morning.

"You got to sleep, finally?"

"Yeah. And I dreamt up a big bowl of rabbit stew. Mmm."

"I love that. Deer stew too." Taki grinned. One of her teeth was loose, and it stuck out at an angle.

"Moose," Rose Marie said as Sister Bernadette ladled a glop of glue in her bowl.

"Dry meat, the chewy kind." Taki stared at the lump in her own bowl. "Rosie, I feel sick."

"You're as thin as a stick. You have to eat, even if it *is* glue."

Even when Taki did eat her porridge, it often came back up in the schoolyard at recess.

"If you don't eat it, you won't get used to it. Taki, you'll starve."

"No, I won't. It's just the porridge." Anataki slapped the back of her spoon against the lump in her bowl, watching it bounce. "I can eat potatoes if they're slimeballs, but not glue. Yesterday I ate my carrots, didn't I? And the bread."

"That's because the carrots weren't cooked, and there was jam for the bread."

Once a week, Sister Bernadette spooned out a dollop of jam, bright and quivering, beside a slice of bread. Usually it was strawberry jam, but sometimes it was raspberry, sometimes saskatoon—bright red or purple, dancing under the overhead lights.

Taki smacked her lips and laughed. "I love jam," she said, her nostrils quivering. "It smells like summer."

Once the jam was spooned onto her plate, she always picked up her glass of milk made from yucky powder and held it out, ready to fling at Ruth's big cousins if they reached over and stuck a finger in her meal. They were still mad about Ruth's name.

"Rude," Rose Marie jeered at Bertha. "Her name should be Rude, not Ruth, because she is—just like you."

By the end of October, both Rose Marie and Anataki were feeling not so sick, not so lonely anymore, though Taki was skinny as a bone, and Rose Marie still got hot and squirmy when she had to sit still in her desk for long. And she had trouble falling asleep at bedtime because she was afraid of seeing backwards all night long, and not just in bits. Kids, ones who weren't really there, thin and grey, sometimes crept through the dormitory. Sometimes that awful sister too. At least they left again.

Anataki's before life had been different from hers, so her stories were always fun to listen to. *Fas-cin-ating*—a new word she had learned from Sister Joan. "Girls, I think you'll find the saints' lives *fas-cin-ating*." Then she droned out the most boring story of some guy who did nothing but pray or a crazy lady who lived behind a brick wall on purpose.

In the moon of first flowers, Taki's family always moved to the United States of America, on the other side of the invisible line. "My papa and uncle tend a buffalo herd that Great-Grandfather rescued during the last days of the great *ii-nii*."

Rose Marie knew that word. *Buffalo.* Her papa had once drawn a picture of one of the big animals in the dirt but she had never seen a real live one.

"Great-Grandfather and his family drove the *ii-nii* to the south country with lots of water and that *soyo-toi-yis* grass the buffalo love to eat. That was long ago when the second big change began. My relations watch over the herd, taking the sick and old ones for food. Spring, summer, and fall, that's what we eat: buffalo meat, buffalo stew, soup made from buffalo bones. I used to get sick of all that buffalo." She widened her eyes. "I miss it now. Sooooo good!"

Some days Rose Marie even liked class. Some things Sister Joan taught were kind of interesting, like how to spell *Rose Marie* with big and little letters, other places in the Dominion of Canada that she hadn't known about, and even Moses up that mountain with the voice of God. As she listened, her body turned into a lake, the surface gently rippling, the centre calm. On those days, she could make herself sit still, her hands folded, toes touching the floor, and listen to Sister Joan. She could hold a pencil in her hand, print *A, B, C* in her notebook and *1, 2, 3* on the blackboard. Usually she was the first one to answer Sister Joan's questions, like *If I have four chickens and three run away, how many do I have left?* Sister would look at her with what might have been a smile if she hadn't made her lips disappear. "Good, good," she'd say, as if it wasn't really good at all.

Other days her tummy was all squirmy inside. Awful, horrible things had started to grow there. "Fire worms," she told Taki. "And they're getting worser."

One day she couldn't sit still any longer. When Sister Joan turned her back on the class to print the date on the board, Rose Marie got up from her desk and crept to the door. Sister Joan turned and rushed over, yanking the back of her school uniform.

"You will stand in the corner, Rose Marie," she said, dragging her to the back of the room.

Everyone turned to watch, so Rose Marie scrunched up her nose at them.

In the corner, she lowered her head and closed her eyes. *Summer sun, but not too hot. She ran to her creek and jumped from stone to stone, the water a fish dance of deep-down green and surface flash. The fire worms in her tummy slowed down. She splashed in the cold water, then hopped to the bank. The fire worms shrank. By the time she was skipping around the woodpile, her outside skin was perfectly cool, her tummy still.*

"Rose Marie, you will now stand on one leg," Sister Joan shouted from the front of the class.

The eyes of all the kids were on her again. As she raised her leg, fire worms wriggled inside. She slammed her foot down, *bang*, and tried to bang, bang, bang them out.

Sister Joan's footsteps. "All right, young lady." Her hand hooked Rose Marie's arm and pinched. "I've had just about enough of you." Sister marched her out of the classroom and down the hall. She took her big key ring from around her waist and unlocked a door. The broom closet. "Get in there and stay in there." Spit flew from Sister Joan's mouth and flecked Rose Marie's forehead. "You asked for this, missy!" She banged the door shut. *Click*. She locked it.

Rose Marie stared into the pitch-black until the outline of the door appeared. She picked up a musty string mop and whapped it against the door. She threw a tin of floor wax, the lid flying off. Wind howled and the stinking mop with its string worms whipped around her. She jumped up and down, banging her fists against the walls and crying out, "Papa, Mama, Papa, Mama, come get me!"

Her knees turned to jelly. She tumbled to the floor. *Ayaoo A Pis-totoki, Is Pommokit*, she murmured, a prayer she was not even allowed to say. "No Indian language," the sisters were always yelling. "English only."

She lay in the dark. So quiet. She wanted to drift like the specks of dust in the stream of light falling from the door crack. Then she remembered running through the schoolyard with Taki's hand in hers as they jumped in other girls' skipping ropes or rammed through game circles, making everyone yell. She laughed right out loud. Not everything was bad. Almost, but not everyone.

In the moon of first snow, Mama and Papa came to the school. Finally. Forest Fox Crown and Aunt Angelique had picked them up in Forest's truck and driven them to St. Mark's for visiting day.

Rose Marie glimpsed them at the back of the chapel during Mass, all four adults sitting together—and baby Kiaa-yo too. Her breath filled with tickles and she bit her hand so she wouldn't laugh out loud through the weird words that Sister Joan had tried to teach them. That Mother Grace was watching her, so she mumbled along with the big girls. *Deus tu conversus vivificabis nos.* She didn't know what the words meant, but she remembered them, and Mother Grace was watching, and if she didn't try those words, she would burst out laughing. *Et cum spiritu tuo.*

After Mass, she forgot that stupid rule about not running in the hall, and she ran to Papa and he scooped her up. She burrowed in his arms of light, and when he put her down, Mama pulled her to her soft bannock belly and held her tight. Turning to her baby brother, she rubbed her nose against his, making him sputter and laugh.

"My girl, my girl," Papa said, patting her head.

Mama whispered "Sinopaki," her secret name, and she felt good.

They sat in the downstairs visiting room, Rose Marie on Papa's knee, while Forest Fox Crown and Aunt Angelique went upstairs to the big girls' visiting room to see Adele and Esther. Kiaa-yo squirmed and she tickled his tummy. Mama unbuttoned her dress and fed him, which was a Bad Thing to Do, Rose Marie could tell from the gasp on Sister Lucy's face.

She slid off Papa's knee and jumped over his stretched-out legs. Sister Lucy opened her mouth, but she didn't say anything about no running, no jumping, no having fun, so she kept jumping until Mama was finished feeding Kiaa-yo.

"*Pohk Kiaayo,*" Mama crooned, and she handed the baby to Rose Marie. "*Pohk Sinopaki.*" They belonged to each other, all of them.

"*N'iiko-si,*" she whispered back.

"I don't know when we'll be back," Mama said when Forest Fox Crown and Aunt Angelique came downstairs way too soon. "Depends if we can get a ride." She looked at Forest, but he was staring down, fingers rubbing his shiny yellow keys.

"Be good," Mama said to her.

"*N'iiko-si,*" she whispered back. My parents.

That night the wind howled, and the school was shivery cold.

"That's because Mother Grace won't allow Brother Abe to keep the furnace burning at night," one of the older students had told them in the dormitory as the first-years were changing for bed. It was Leah, a big helper-girl who worked at even more jobs than she had to. She was folding pillowcases on her bed. "There's only so much money for coal," she added importantly. "The war's on, you know."

They nodded.

"My dad's at the war," said Martha Buffalo, her voice shivery.

"My uncle," said another girl.

"My big brother's in the mine," added another.

Sister Cilla strode down the centre aisle to the little girls in the back two rows. "Kneel," she ordered, and they smoothed their nightdresses over bony knees and knelt on the freezing floor.

"Now I lay me down to sleep," they recited through chattering teeth.

But Rose Marie had her own prayer.

"Let me sleep the whole night through."

"Let me dream all the cold and rules away."

Sister Cilla clapped her hands. "All right, up you get and into bed."

They climbed between icy sheets. The winter would be long and harsh, Rose Marie could tell. It might never end.

8

Beasts of the Field

THE FIRST TWO WEEKS of November were uncharacteristically grey. Sister Joan, Mother Grace noticed, was in a foul mood, displeased by the weather as well as her class of fourteen first-year girls.

She was complaining to Sister Margaret as they walked together down the stairs to Matins. "The more we try to acculturate them, the worse they get. 'You cannot learn unless you sit still and listen,' I tell them, but it's no use. Senseless, most of them."

Mother Grace coughed and Sister Joan looked down the stairs at her, eyes narrowed.

Rose Marie was discontented too. It was the fire worms or never being outdoors, or maybe the winter sun, all wrapped up in bandages of cloud. She scratched and fiddled in her desk, and finally, during counting, she slipped out of class and into the hall.

"Get back here!" Sister Joan yelled, her head popping from the door, arm waving.

Rose Marie started running for the big front door.

"Sister Cilla," Sister Joan yelled. "Get her!"

Oh dear, Sister Cilla with her long legs coming down the stairs.

Rose Marie sped up, but with a jump and two long lopes, Sister had her by the nape. She tried to shake Sister off, but she held her the way Mama did when she wanted her to "stay still a minute, eh?" The way Aunt Angelique had when she made her take the bus to this stupid old school. Sister Margaret and Sister Joan did it too. They all grabbed her tight by the neck and made her do what she didn't want to!

As Sister marched her back to class, Rose Marie looked up from the corner of her eye. Sister Cilla didn't even seem mad. Her cheeks were pink and she was almost-smiling. Maybe Sister *liked* chasing her. Maybe all Sister Cilla wanted was to run down the halls as fast as she could and never ever stop.

At the back of the classroom, Sister Joan made her turn her hands up just like she had with Martha the week before when she couldn't stop laughing. Sister whacked Rose Marie with the pointer, whacked until her palms were screeching *ow, ow, ow!* But, unlike Martha, she didn't cry.

The next day, the sun was just an old yellow scab stuck on the classroom window. Rose Marie wanted to peel it off and find the real sun underneath, bright and warm. She swayed in her desk, trying to calm the fire worms burning her tummy.

Sister Joan pulled a long skipping rope out of her desk drawer. "Fine!" She marched up the aisle, shoved Rose Marie against the back of her seat, and wrapped the skipping rope around her, tying her to the desk. "There. And if I hear a sound out of you, Rose Marie, I'll tape your mouth shut too!"

Fine, she thought to herself.

When Sister Joan was writing numbers on the board—*4, 5, 6*—she wiggled the rope loose. By *12, 13, 14*, she had slipped out of the coils. Taki gave her a *you're gonna get it* look, but she didn't care.

* * *

"Like greased lightning," Sister Joan hissed to Sister Margaret in the hallway as they headed for lunch. "She dashed out to the schoolyard. Without a coat, of course. What am I to do with the little heathen?"

Mother Grace, coming out of her office, heard the venom in Sister Joan's voice and wondered if she should intervene, possibly preventing a rash action on Joan's part. It wouldn't be the first time Sister Joan— nor Sister Margaret, for that matter—had overreacted to an unruly child. But both sisters could be difficult, Sister Margaret stubborn and Sister Joan so very defiant.

I'll speak to them when I have the energy, she thought as she made her way down the hall.

Later that day, she sat at her desk writing a funding request to the Oblates, who ran most of the Catholic residential schools, on behalf of Father David.

A child's voice pierced her office door, and she dropped her pen. The sound seemed to be coming from the dining room or the kitchen. A student in distress? Probably one of the girls on supper duty had cut a finger while slicing carrots or perhaps burnt herself while lighting the stove. Surely the situation was being taken care of by one of the sisters.

But the noise persisted. There was something primal in it, some sort of feral outrage that caused a shudder to pass through her entire body. Perhaps an animal had come into the school and been caught by Brother Abraham, a small animal trapped and possibly injured, dangerous even. She should get up. She should hurry down the hall and find out just what was taking place. The cries continued, terrible, rising and falling. She sat unmoving in her chair, chilled to the marrow of her bones.

She should get up, but she felt poorly. She had a great deal of paperwork to take care of. She simply didn't have the strength. Nor the motivation. The problem would very likely resolve itself.

* * *

Rose Marie lay on her bed, a lump of raw meat. A hammer pounded the left side of her skull just above her eye. Beds scraped across the floor, their springs crying out like small birds. From the high northwest windows, light pulsed, broke apart, and dropped on her, small punches blackening her eyes and jamming her down a dark hole. She fell.

Light blasted her awake. She heard the moan of an animal caught in Papa's trap.

O Sacred Heart of Jesus, filled with infinite love, broken by our ingratitude, and pierced by our sins, a nun prayed by her bed. She didn't recognize the voice. When she opened her eyes, she saw it was that new nun, the one who always disappeared again, the one she saw backwards.

She drifted in and out of sleep, and the nun faded and returned, her voice a thread carried by air currents. *Take every faculty of our souls and bodies.* The prayer wafted her to a nest of hides she sank into, at home, home at last and not hurting.

Mother Grace floated above. Her papery hand blurred as it reached and touched her forehead. The hammer came down again, slamming her eye shut. Mother Grace and Sister Cilla made her sit up and, oh, pulled off her school dress.

"No, it hurts!"

"Sinopaki," Mama whispered.

Then that trapped animal again, a little fox moaning until the sky pushed down and stubbed her out.

Taki's face was next to hers. *"Assa, assa!"*

"Get away from her, Anne," Sister Margaret ordered.

Other girls passed by her bed, staring with *oh my* eyes.

* * *

Her skull cracked under a weight, and water seeped in. Taki had placed something cold and wet over her eye.

"Rosie, please don't make that sound."

"Is she all right?" Sister Cilla asked, long fingers crossing her flat chest.

Taki pulled a scratchy blanket up to her chin.

"Don't. It hurts," she murmured.

"You talked, Rosie. Sister Cilla, she talked!"

Mother Grace came with a flashlight and stroked her aching hair. "How could she do this to you? Such a bright girl, she always says. Stubborn, but nevertheless—"

The dorm was dark, full of sleeping girls, but someone, something, was stirring. It pulled at her, wanting her to look up, to see.

Once, at home, when she was supposed to be asleep, she had felt the same need to open her eyes and peer out of her nest of skins. Mama was sewing in a circle of lamplight as she always did the nights Papa was away in the bush. A fire flickered from the mouth of the stove, lighting Mama and the rising-falling waves of her breasts and baby-belly, the glinting needle poking down and pulling up through the cloth—a warm sleepy song. She was about to settle back in her bed when she noticed something pouring through the air like thin milk, oh, just like the spirits she had seen flowing from birds caught in Mama's snares, or the spurt of four-leggeds escaping Papa's traps of steel and pain, leaving their bodies behind.

Heart drumming, she watched milk curdle into arms and legs. Not forming an animal or a bird but the shape of a lady. She looked over at Mama, who hadn't even noticed.

She wanted to call, *Mama, watch out,* but the lady-shape was filling with colour. A dress—red, blue, and yellow, gathered at the waist with a brass-studded belt that glittered crazily in the lamplight. A face. Like Mama's, but older, thinner, and there, painted with a white streak down the nose, yellow slashes across the cheeks and a red sun on the forehead. She watched the lady-shape glide across the room to Mama.

Mama raised her head. She gasped. "My mother!" Then a murmur: "How I miss you."

Goose pimples shivered up and down Rose's arms.

"Not yet," Mama whispered, her voice dropping so low that Rose could hardly hear. "I'm not ready. You must go alone." Mama straightened in her chair, her needle held upright. "Mother, go alone."

And *sta-ao,* the shadow spirit, faded away.

Here in the cold school, in her hard bed with rusty springs, in her pain, Rose Marie did not want to look up and see *sta-ao.* "No, no, no." She crawled under her blanket, her breath fast as sparrows flitting through trees, small black bruises shifting ache from one part of her body to another. But that pull, that *look up* call. Rose Marie raised herself on an elbow and peered towards the entrance.

There. She was right under the light, that sister who appeared and disappeared—young and kind of pretty, dressed in the same habit the other sisters wore. She had tied an apron around her waist just like Sister Bernadette, but she had pulled her habit over the apron, making it shorter so that the curvy part of her lower legs showed. The sister, Rose Marie could see, wasn't tall like Sister Cilla, but taller than Esther who wasn't really her cousin. Now the sister walked to the door, her skirt swaying from side to side just like Esther's always did. Oh, and she turned to nothing.

The following morning, right after Matins, Mother Grace made sure Rose Marie was doing as well as could be expected. She gave her an aspirin with a little water and then climbed down the two flights of stairs to her office. Something had to be done about the beating. But what exactly had taken place?

Sister Bernadette knew. Bernadette's eyes had burned bright at supper, worry creasing her forehead. She had stared at her food, unable to eat.

"Does anyone know the whereabouts of Sister Joan?" Mother Grace had asked.

All the sisters shook their heads, not one of them meeting her eyes.

She drew her shawl around her. Yes, something definitely had to be done. Bruises were already beginning to appear on the girl. She would be as spotted as a calf by the afternoon. The worst of it was the goose egg over her left eye, an eye that seemed to lose focus when she drew near and the child tried to look at her. If only she had been more decisive the previous morning, had responded as soon as she had heard the cries. *God, forgive me.*

A light tap on her office door. As Sister Bernadette stepped in, what flitted through Mother Grace's mind was *The mountain has come to Mohammed.* "Yes, Sister?"

"I guess Rose Marie was a nuisance yesterday," Sister Bernadette said, sitting on the edge of the chair across from her. "You know, Mother Grace, swinging her head, grinning at her friend Anne across the room a few rows over, fidgeting in her seat, the things she does. We all know how she can't sit still."

"Go on, Sister."

"Well, Sister Joan got it in her head that Rose Marie was mocking her."

"Mocking her?" Mother Grace leaned forward, wincing at the jabs of pain in her elbows.

"You see, Rose Marie's behaviour is dreadful, but she always knows the answers to Sister Joan's questions. Sister Joan got it in her head that the girl was making a joke of her"—Bernadette shifted in her seat—"her 'honest endeavours.' That's how she put it."

"You'd better tell me exactly what happened, Sister Bernadette."

The sister adjusted her skirt. "I was heading back to the kitchen from the, you know"—she pointed behind her towards the toilet—"Mother Grace, and up ahead I saw them. Sister Joan had the girl by the ear and was hauling her to the kitchen. By the time I got there, she had the electrical cord from the cupboard—the one from the frying pan—in her hand, Mother Grace, and she was swinging it at Rose Marie, hitting her again and again. 'Stand still!' she kept shouting, and the girl did. She didn't make a sound at first, so I thought it might not be hurting too much. Then she started making this noise, a terrible sound, and I said, 'I think that's enough, Sister Joan.' She's my senior, you know, but I did say, 'You should stop now, Sister Joan.' I did." Sister Bernadette started to snivel.

"Do you have a hankie, Sister?"

Bernadette tugged one from her pocket and gurgled into it. "'Get out of here,' Sister Joan said to me. 'This is none of your concern.' She kept swinging the cord, and it made a sound, like, like *thunk*. 'I'll give you something to cry about, Rose Marie,' she said. 'And you, Sister Bernadette, stop squawking like a goddamned chicken!'" Sister Bernadette blew her nose. "The girl stumbled against my cutting block. She collapsed on the floor, and Sister Joan . . . Sister Joan, she kicked her, Mother Grace."

"Kicked her?" Her office listed like a ship at sea.

"I stopped her, Mother Grace. I came to my senses, and I ran up and pushed Sister Joan away." She dabbed her nose. "'Spare the rod and spoil the child,' Sister Joan said. Just like Sister Margaret's always saying. Then she left."

"And the child?"

"I wrapped ice in a tea towel and put it on her eye. Then I took her up to bed. I should have put her in the infirmary, I know, but she could barely walk."

"Why did you not come to—"

"I know. I should have come to you, but she fell asleep immediately and I didn't want to move her. I didn't want to make trouble." Sister Bernadette gurgled into her hankie again.

"One doesn't let someone with any kind of head injury fall asleep, Sister."

"Oh dear, Mother Grace. But she looked so peaceful. I checked her, just to make sure—"

"The child was breathing?"

"Yes."

Spineless, Mother Grace thought. Then she wondered if she would have done anything differently. In fact, *she* had sat in her office and done nothing, absolutely nothing. "Tell Sister Joan I want to see her."

Sister Bernadette left her office, still snivelling.

Mother Grace was nervous about talking to Sister Joan; she couldn't deny it. She turned to the pile of bills on her desk, but when she tried to total the figures, she lost count. On the fourth attempt, she simply picked them up and threw them in her file cabinet. Her palms were damp. What was taking Sister Joan so long? She shuffled a pile of books over to the bookcase, checked the date and phases of the moon on her calendar, and returned to her desk. Her hands were so damp she had to keep drying them on her skirt. Her nails were a disgrace, she noticed. She sat down and was rummaging through her desk for a nail file when she heard Sister Joan clear her throat.

Glancing at her clock, she saw it had been an hour and seven minutes since she told Sister Bernadette to summon Joan. In just ten minutes, classes started.

"Come in, Sister," she said. "And shut the door."

As soon as Sister Joan was inside, she asked, "Sister, what is the meaning of this act of violence you perpetrated on Rose Marie White-water?" Her voice wavered only slightly.

Sister Joan lifted her chin. "The girl in question was undermining my authority in the classroom." Her voice was shrill. "Setting a bad example for the other students. I tried every other form of punishment

available to me. There was nothing else to do. I simply did what had
to be done. What no one else in this school has the courage to do."
Sister Joan pursed her lips in that superior way she had and looked
down at Mother Grace, challenge in her eyes.

"Why did you not come to me?"

Sister Joan snorted, just as Sister Margaret was always doing. Like
a bull. An insubordinate bull intent on whipping the earth under its
feet to a dust storm, its anger both righteous and demonic. A bull that
thought nothing could stop it.

As a child on the farm, Mother Grace had had dealings with bulls,
and she knew that a great deal of damage could be wreaked by beasts
of the field who thought they were wild animals. Her own uncle had
been killed by a plough horse, for heaven's sake. Trampled to death.
She felt heat course through her breast and rise to her head. She was
angry, she realized. *En colère.* And it felt good.

"It is true, Sister Joan, that as yet no guidelines for corporal punishment have been issued by our superiors, neither the Church nor the
government of Canada. *Except* that it must be given in the presence
of the school principal. Are you aware of that?"

Again Sister Joan snorted.

"In fact, until this very afternoon, I never believed guidelines were
needed. Let faith and common sense lead the sisters, I have always
maintained. Today, Sister Joan, you have proven me wrong." She rose,
startled by her sudden agility.

Sister Joan took a step back.

"*Blessed are the merciful, for they shall obtain mercy!*" she said, the
words sounding strange to her. They seemed to break from a room
in the core of her body, one that she had not been in for some time.
"*Suffer the little children to come unto me and forbid them not; for of such
is the kingdom of God.*" She stepped from behind her desk and moved
closer to Sister Joan, who took another step back.

"The words of Jesus, our Saviour. *Dieu soit loué.* I cannot begin to
tell you how very disappointed I am in you, Sister. How shameful your

brutality, and against a child, one of the youngest in the school and certainly the smallest!" She took another step forward, enjoying Joan's discomfort—her downcast eyes and purpling skin—as she backed her through the door. "You must pray to Him for guidance and forgiveness at all times of worship and an hour before sleep for two weeks. That is your penance! Do you understand?" Her voice was booming, loud enough, she realized with surprise, to be heard throughout the first floor.

Joan's head twitched up and down.

"Good. *Let the word of Christ dwell in you.*"

She watched Sister Joan jerk open the door and bolt down the hall.

"I will be watching!" she cried after her.

A victory! She sat down as a wave of elation washed over. Looking through her office window, she observed the distant snow-covered mountains peering through whiffs of cloud like clouds themselves, like a presence, uncertain and undefined—like God, she thought—and she let it fill her. As her gaze fell to the prairie, vast, stretching everywhere around her, cold and empty, her elation ebbed away. Perhaps a very small victory.

Later, she wished she hadn't made that last remark. Arrogance. Yet she could not stop feeling somewhat pleased with herself. As she hadn't been for over three years. She hoped it was possible to maintain the clarity her righteous anger had provided.

9

Visiting Hour

DAYS SHRANK AND nights stretched. A blizzard hit at the end of the hunting moon. Rose Marie remembered Papa telling her, "That's when the *mi-yiks-sop-oyi* swagger from the highest mountain peaks and swoop in." *Mi-yiks-sop-oyi*, then *aahki-tsimii*—snow blowing, biting, freezing fingers and toes. At home, they had always stayed inside, all together, Papa telling stories, Mama feeding wood into the stove and making spruce tea. But this school was way, way east of home, east of the Reserve, even, and the wind grew bigger and madder as it swept over the plain, slamming fists against the brick school and making threats through the chinks. *I'm coming for you. I'll get you.* No one was allowed outside. The cold, the cramped-up space, and the not-enough-to-eat could bring sickness, Rose Marie knew.

At night, the girls pretended to be asleep until Sister Cilla finished her last dormitory check. Then the big girls rose from their beds, tiptoed to the wardrobes, took off their nightdresses, pulled on uniforms and woollen stockings, tugged their nightdresses overtop, and helped the little ones do the same. Like all the others, Rose Marie tucked her head under her blanket and folded her shivery knees to her chest, but even in the extra clothes, she was cold and couldn't get to sleep. *I'll get you.*

Everyone had a cough, and some students had to go to the hospital room—the "infirmary," the sisters called it.

Rose Marie wasn't the only one who kept waking at night, tossing and turning, digging into her skinny blankets. Some of the older girls invited younger sisters or cousins into their beds and snuggled them to sleep. All by herself, Rose Marie shivered.

"Move over," Anataki grunted one night, then slid into Rose Marie's bed and wrapped her twig arms and legs around her.

For the first time since she had arrived at St. Mark's, Rose Marie slept peacefully the whole night through. She did not look up from her bed to see shadows clot together under the entrance light. Instead, she dreamt back to the shores of Mama's and Papa's bodies, and she, a small warm pond between them.

"I had the bestest dream," Taki whispered to her the next morning as they huddled under the blanket. It was early, just after Sister Joan had clanged the bell downstairs on the nuns' floor, and other than the shifting of sleeping girls, the dorm was still quiet. "We were across the invisible line at my relatives' summer camp in Montana. Mama was cooking supper over the fire, and it smelled so good, and me and my brothers were fighting over whose turn it was to ride and who had to get the water. Sik-apsii is so bossy just because he's the oldest and Awa-kaasii always thinks he can beat him up, but he can't, and they don't even want to let me have a turn on the horse, and the *ii-nii* started to move and all that dust turned red against the sun." She stuck her tongue in the space where her front tooth had been and grinned. "It even felt nice and warm."

Rose Marie could almost see it—the buffalo hurling into the red horizon. She could hear one brother slap the arm of the other, and Taki shout, "It's my turn to ride, *kiis-to-wawa*," as she ran for the horses.

A creak on the stairs. "Oh-oh," Taki said. In the morning, Sister Margaret always carried her stick, and she whacked it down on the legs of any girls she caught sleeping in the same bed.

"I'll wake Susanna and Martha. You get Josephine and Maria!" They leapt up and scampered along the rows of beds, hissing, "Wake up, Sister's coming!"

The first *isi-ksopo* blustered in, warm, from the west, and the snow turned slushy. In the schoolyard, girls stamped their heels to make a squishing sound until their feet were soaked from the wet seeping through holes in their boots to the darned lumps in their stockings.

But as the wind died, a cold front moved in from the north.

The second Sunday in December, just before Mass, Mother Grace sat in her office, reflecting. Her desk overflowed with correspondence—bills, notices, and catechism lessons—but it seemed to her that God was directing her thoughts elsewhere, summoning her to examine her actions and beliefs. She decided to pray that the seven gifts of the Holy Spirit be strengthened within her: wisdom, understanding, knowledge, counsel, fortitude, piety, and fear of the Lord. Those gifts would help her meet the challenges ahead.

Seven years before she had received a letter from the Mother House appointing her *la révérende mère provinciale* of Les Sœurs d'Amour Fraternelle. Eight weeks before the appointment, Sister Joan had sent the Mother Superior in Montreal a telegram informing her of the not-unexpected death of ninety-two-year-old Mother Paul Pius at the school.

Caught up in her own excitement, Sister Grace, so suddenly *Mother* Grace, wasn't aware that as weeks had turned to months without word from the Mother House, Sister Joan had grown increasingly optimistic that her role of "interim administrator," as she had proclaimed herself, would be elevated to that of "superior," in theory, a position under the leadership of Father David, but in practice, the unchallenged head of the school. It was a wish she had not failed to convey to her good friend and co-administrator, Sister Grace. It was Grace's knowledge of this ambition, she suspected, as much as her later promotion, that Sister Joan was never able to forgive.

Mother Grace had taken her appointment as superior at St. Mark's to be a sign from God; He had chosen her for this position, and she was eager finally to confront the weighty destiny she had believed to be hers since she took her vows. In fact, she now realized, she had been both blind and prideful.

Things had gone well at first. After just one month in her new position, she had not only prevailed upon Father Alphonses to bring volunteer workers from both Hilltop and the Reserve to the school, but she had elicited the promise of extra funding from the Oblates, having written a persuasive letter on Father David's behalf. From that point on, Father David—or Father Damien, should David be unavailable—had only to sign her letters and, at times, practise a modicum of conviviality when parishioners arrived with hammers and wood. Several repairs, long overdue, were made or scheduled at St. Mark's, and morale, with the exception of Sister Joan's, improved greatly. Mother Grace then turned her hand to systemizing the administration, drawing up and balancing a feasible budget, and taking over the ordering of supplies.

"Don't stir the pot if it's already boiling," she had overheard Father David mutter to Father Damien. "Let Gracie do all the work if she's so hell-bent on it." *Mais oui*, that had been just fine with her.

At the start of the next school year, she had been determined to institute a new, more liberal visiting practice. Every Sunday, the girls' parents would be allowed at St. Mark's for Mass. Afterwards, they could visit their children in one of two rooms, a small one off the school's entrance for the little girls and a classroom upstairs for the older ones. Parents with both first-year and older students would be allowed to take the younger ones with them to the room set aside for older girls.

Father David had complained that such a practice was in direct opposition to the government of Canada's policy of assimilation, but she had argued passionately. "How can we reach the children if we do not also encourage enlightenment in their parents?" She had been quite pleased with her oratory in those days. That was before it came back to bite her, as Sister Margaret would put it.

"Our job is not done when our students leave this school. We must continue to reach out to all the Indian race, to instruct and guide on an ongoing basis," she had argued.

And it had worked. Father David, with Father Damien following his lead, had grudgingly withdrawn his objections. Even dear Father Patrick had expressed his admiration for her "progressive" visiting policy, and a few other Catholic residential schools had followed her course of action, including, not a year later, the new St. Gerard's School for Boys, to the south. To this day, parents still complained about their sons and daughters having to attend different schools, but it was for the best, Mother Grace was convinced. St. Mark's had become overcrowded with the influx of students from Antelope Hills after that school burned down and, besides, boys distracted girls from their studies.

She had been optimistic. Mother Paul Pius and most of the sisters, including her, had thought that the opening of St. Gerard's would solve most of their problems. And it might have, if the staffing had been handled properly. Lifting her glasses, she pressed a finger and thumb against her aching eyes. No use crying over spilt milk, as Sister Bernadette was always saying.

Now, as for the past seven years, students were seated in the chapel, and then parents and younger siblings were led to rows of chairs at the back. After Mass, visiting hour would begin.

"Eyes straight ahead," Sister Joan ordered the first-year girls. "No looking at the back of chapel to see who might be there. You are in the presence of God."

"Crabby God," Taki whispered.

Rose Marie's parents hadn't visited since the moon of first snow. Even Forest Fox Crown came only once in a while and seldom with Aunt Angelique. He nodded at her, but never said anything, just tramped upstairs to visit stupid Adele and stupider Esther.

Taki's parents hardly ever visited either. They lived far, far away. Most Sundays, about half the girls were without visitors, so the sisters gave them three choices of how to spend visiting hour: help the sisters prepare lunch, take a Sunday school lesson with Sister Cilla, or play in the recreation room and clean it after. No one seemed to notice that Anataki and Rose Marie snuck up to the dormitory and played dolls under their beds. They had tied string around washcloths to make the dolls' heads, and when Rose Marie found some cotton pads by one of the wardrobes, they made those the bodies, attaching them to the heads with safety pins. At night, they tucked the dolls under their pillows.

This particular Sunday, Rose Marie was looking at the spikes stuck through Jesus' feet at the front of the chapel when she heard Kiaa-yo babble from the back. She spun around and waved frantically at Mama and Papa.

Taki drove a bony elbow into her ribs. "Sister Margaret!"

Father David, all in white, told them the Christ Child was coming. Mother Mary had been chosen by God. *That which is conceived in her is of the Holy Ghost.* It was the most important event in history, Sister Joan had told them that week in class. *The Word was made flesh.* Yet, with every phrase Father David spoke—*the sacrifice we offer*—came a scary feeling. Something big was happening, was about to happen. Rose Marie could feel the air tighten like a snare, like the string she had tied around her dolly's head.

The birth of Christ was a good, a happy thing; she knew that for sure. At least in the beginning. But then things turned bad for Jesus. And for his patient papa, especially his worried-sick mama. *Mother of Mercy. To you we cry, poor banished children of Eve; to you we send up our sighs, mourning, and weeping in this valley of tears.*

Sitting beside Taki in the pew, Rose Marie felt like she was about
to cry. After the angels, the star, and the three wise men came all kinds
of hurt, and finally, oh, the cross, the nails and blood.

After Mass, as she and Anataki walked out of chapel, she glimpsed
Mama. Oh, Mama! She dropped Taki's hand and was about to call out,
to run to her, but she stopped herself. Mama hadn't seen her. She was
gazing through the window, watching snow swirl in the wind. Light
rose from Mama's skin and shimmered like the halos around Mary and
Jesus' heads. She was quiet-calm, sadness and light at the same time.
Then Mama turned, grinned, and opened her arms.

Rose Marie could feel the bones under Mama's dress. They shuddered as Mama coughed, and then the sun dogs came, pulling at her
warmth, making it spill into the dry school air. She cried, and Mama
stroked her head as she always did, as she didn't do anymore because
she was so far, far away.

"Sinopaki."

"*Na-a.*"

Arm in arm, they walked into the visiting room. Papa was there with
Kiaa-yo on his knee. He laughed a flash of orange when he saw her.

"How come you never visit me?" she wanted to know, ducking
under Papa's arm. "How come Forest Fox Crown can't bring you?"

"The roads are bad," Mama said, coughing again. She kept coughing
until her eyes ran. Her hankie had a spot of red mixed in with yellow,
bright as the sometimes-jam Sister Bernadette gave them to eat, as the
winter nosebleeds that spread flowers over Rose Marie's white cotton
pillowcase. Way too red.

"Forest has to go west to our place, all the way back, and then farther east to the school," Papa answered. "Then, after the visit, he has
to go all the way to our place and all—"

"Why don't you get your own truck?"

"No money," Papa said. His bright energy sank back into his skin,
and he glanced down. She waited for him to say, "Don't worry, it'll

work out okay," like he usually did, but he didn't say it. He just kept looking at his moccasins.

The fire worms were crawling through her tummy, so she started to jump. "I'm going to huff and puff and blow your house in," she sang, blowing in Kiaa-yo's face. She blew too hard, and he started to cry.

"Mama has to go away," Papa said.

Mama unbuttoned her dress to feed Kiaa-yo.

"No, Mama," she said. "Sister Lucy—" But Mama didn't understand or couldn't hear. She pressed the baby's head to her breast.

"Red Rover, Red Rover, send Kiaa-yo over," she shouted.

Sister Lucy, she could see from the corner of her eye, was frowning.

"Joseph. Send Joseph over."

"Stay still," Papa said, his hand on her arm.

She would *not* stay still! She jumped over his feet, but Papa caught her arm.

"Assa," he whispered, trying to pull her close.

"No!" She went limp and fell to the floor. Papa had to drag her to him.

"Mama has been sick. She has to go to the sanitorium."

"Red Rover, Red Rover!" she yelled, climbing back up and struggling to free herself from Papa's grip.

Sister Lucy frowned and shook her head.

"I have to tell you something, Sinopaki," Papa said. "It's a healing place. *San-i-tor-i-um.* Until Mama's well again." His mouth was a crooked grey line and clouds blotted up his voice. "The old medicine isn't working. I'll be taking Kiaa-yo up north to my sister's until Mama is well again." He put his arms around her, his sinewy arms, and she sank into them. "You have to stay with the nuns over the Christmas holiday."

"No, Papa!" She yanked herself from him.

"Have to. Mama and I and Father Alphonses talked to your Mother Grace." Papa pushed his chin in the direction of her office. "I'll come back and see you as soon as I can."

"Sinopaki," Mama cooed, chucking her under the chin with one hand, covering her own mouth with the other. *"Kimmat-aki."* My poor girl. Mama tried to hug her, but, no, she wouldn't let her.

Jumping up and down, she screamed, *"Red Rover, Red Rover, send Joseph over!"*

Abruptly, Sister Lucy stood up. "Visiting hour is over!"

10

New Territory

MOTHER GRACE ORDERED Sister Cilla to move Rose Marie's things down to the second floor and into the spare bedroom. "She won't be returning home for the holidays, not with her mother so ill." She had decided to have the child stay in the bedroom left vacant by the death, three and a half years ago, of Sister Mary of Bethany. After all, Rose Marie was a bright girl, if somewhat unruly. This way Mother Grace could keep an eye on the child and determine what she needed and what she was capable of.

For the first two days, Rose Marie seemed subdued, her behaviour much better than when the other students were at the school, and the sisters were both surprised and relieved. Then the girl's aunt came for a visit on Sunday, and the following morning Sister Margaret reported that she had heard Rose Marie talking to herself during the night. "Once she yelled, 'Go alone' or some fool thing. Why, I marched right in and set the girl straight once and for all."

Mother Grace sighed. Sister Margaret was always doing something "once and for all."

That night, after Compline, as the sisters undressed in their rooms, they heard Rose Marie climb the stairs and race around the girls' dormitory overhead, her bare feet thrumming the floor. Sister Cilla, in only her underblouse and petticoat, climbed the stairs two at a time and flicked on the lights.

"Rose Marie," she ordered, "stop that. You should be in bed, sound asleep."

Rose Marie slowed but didn't stop, and, expecting a chase, Sister Cilla hurried towards her. But the girl let her take her hand and lead her to the door and down the stairs.

"She went to her room quiet as a lamb," she told Mother Grace as they brushed their teeth in the sisters' bathroom that night. "I said, 'Don't forget to say your prayers, Rose Marie,' but she didn't answer."

The next morning at breakfast, Mother Grace issued instructions to send Rose Marie out in the schoolyard to play each morning, providing the weather was suitable. "And she is to be given chores for the remainder of the day."

"She's just a first-year," Sister Cilla protested.

Sister Margaret harrumphed, and Mother Grace felt it necessary to recount how she'd been changing diapers, scrubbing floors, and cooking meals at Rose Marie's age. "Giving the child work to do will not only help her develop a sense of duty but also keep her energy in check."

"Unlikely," Sister Joan remarked sourly. "That girl is impossible . . ." Her voice trailed off when Mother Grace looked sharply at her.

After that, Rose Marie ended up doing most of her tearing about the schoolyard after breakfast, arriving back inside an hour or so later with a runny nose and her energy, thankfully, drained. Sister Bernadette had her clean the dining hall tables once she was out of her coat and boots. She would have liked to put the child to work washing dishes, a chore that, during the winter, left her own hands red and sore, but Rose Marie was too small to reach the sink.

The fourth day of Christmas break, the sky was clear, the sun bright, and the temperature "a mere four below with no wind," Brother Abe announced as he stamped his boots at the kitchen door.

"Brother Abraham, take them off. Don't go trailing snow all the way—" Mother Grace called after him, but he pretended not to hear. *Immortel!* The man was a child himself. She turned her attention to Sister Bernadette, scuttling to the toilet. "Tell Rose Marie to join us in the dining room for meals instead of eating alone in the kitchen."

Sure enough, when the child saw an egg, a slice of toast, and a spoonful of jam on her breakfast plate, her eyes lit up like the ragged Christmas tree in the corner that Father Alphonses had brought them from Hilltop.

"Goody goody!" She clapped her hands, and the sisters smiled indulgently.

An hour later, Mother Grace came out of her office with letters to mail. She'd get Brother Abe to drive her and Sister Cilla to Hilltop, where she'd buy stamps, post the letters, pick up powdered milk, and, if she had extra change, a few more lights for the tree. In a fit of generosity, she decided to take along Rose Marie to see the Nativity scene at the church.

She called down the hallway, but there was no answer. She popped into the kitchen to see if the child was helping Sister Bernadette, but she wasn't, so she sent Sister Cilla upstairs to check her bedroom. Perhaps she was playing with that rag she called a doll.

"No," Sister Cilla shouted down the stairs, "Rose Marie's not in her room, nor in the dormitory."

Moses. Marching into the kitchen, Mother Grace put a halt to lunch preparations. "The child's whereabouts is a more pressing problem, Sister Bernadette."

She and Sister Bernadette tracked down Sister Joan, sorting out lessons in her classroom.

"I haven't seen Rose Marie all morning," Sister Joan reported, not bothering to raise her head.

"Do you know where Sister Margaret is?" Mother Grace enquired, but Sister Joan merely shrugged.

Up the stairs Mother Grace and Sister Bernadette rushed, Grace's knees grumbling. They located Sister Margaret snoring in her bedroom. "Margaret, wake up," Mother Grace demanded. "Have you seen Rose Marie?"

"My, well, yes," Sister Margaret muttered, struggling into a sitting position. "She might have said something about going back outside, but that was, let's see, just before I came up to—meditate. I must have dozed off." She sniffed. "Not much more than an hour ago."

Mon Dieu! Back down the stairs on her aching legs Mother Grace went, the others close behind. She ordered Bernadette, Joan, and Priscilla to the schoolyard, while she and Sister Lucy peered through every window on the main floor, front and back. Nowhere could the child be seen.

She pulled on her overcoat and rushed as best she could in her slippery black oxfords through the snow to Brother Abe, at work in the barn, Sister Cilla close on her heels.

Chickens squawking all around him, Brother Abe looked up from raking straw, clearly annoyed. "Mother Grace, yer upsetting the chick—"

"We are looking for the child, Brother Abraham. Rose Marie."

"Hmm." He examined a filthy glove. "I seen that little girl head past the barn to the east this morning. I yelled after her, asking where she thought she was going. 'To the marsh,' she told me. I jes' figured you knew about it."

Mother Grace's heart dropped to her kidneys. She leaned against a barn post and tightened her thighs against the sudden urge to urinate. Did Brother Abe have a single brain cell in his head? she wondered. The child could be miles away by now, completely lost, with no one, nothing in sight but patches of yellow grass poking up through drifts of snow.

"I'll go to the marsh," Sister Cilla blurted, and before Mother Grace realized Cilla meant right now, the young woman was loping in her boots over the prairie snow towards the marsh, over a mile away, her black skirt waving like a flag and nothing around her but the blanket she had grabbed from a pile of dirty laundry as she ran out the back door.

"*Imbécile,*" Mother Grace shouted at Brother Abe. "Go after her!"

As soon as he left the barn, she searched out a dark corner. Gathering her skirt in her hands, she squatted. Watching her urine drive a hole in the straw jarred her back to her childhood. On the family farm, she had often lifted her skirt and pissed in the chicken-infested yard, despite her hatred of the creatures. Even as a small girl, she had been independent, doing as she liked, yet responsible to a fault. In control. What had happened to her these past three years?

She pulled up her bloomers and wandered through the barn, keeping as much distance from the birds as possible. Looking around, she realized she hadn't been near the building since Brother Abe found Father Damien's body outside, directly under the top hayloft door, and burst into her office, his face white as flour. She shuddered now, seeing the barnyard clearly in her mind's eye, Damien's body face down, his bloodied fingers hooking clumps of muck as if he had been trying to crawl away—for help, no doubt. Brother Abe had knelt, turned him over with a squelching sound, and the eyes—Father Damien's dead eyes—had stared up at her, rusty as a discarded plough blade flaking away. Perhaps that's what had first kindled her despair. Abandoned, he had looked, even by God.

She raised a hand to a splintery wall for support. St. Mark's fetid past was coming back to her with surprising clarity. This time she must face it.

Just five days after Father Damien's body was found in the barnyard, poor Sister Lucy discovered Sister Mary of Bethany lying lifeless on a bed in the girls' dormitory. *Mon Dieu,* it had all been too much to bear! It wasn't simply the tragedy of two lives destroyed so suddenly, seemingly without warning; it was also her own ignorance—though, at the time, she had defined it to herself as *innocence*.

She had believed she was running what Sister Joan called "a tight ship," but, in fact, it had been laden with stowaways and disease. For at least a year, since she couldn't avoid the girls' dormitory altogether, she had shunned the barn with its noise, stink, and unsettling memories, not even glimpsing it through a window. Yet it was part of St. Mark's, part of her responsibility. *Mon Dieu*, how she had neglected that duty since the tragedies. She had not only a right but a duty to be here, however unpleasant. She inhaled the odor of straw and chicken manure. Now it held her old and powerful smell too. She had marked her territory.

Brother Abe was the first to arrive back at the school. "I couldn't catch up to that sister," he reported to Mother Grace as she met him at the front door. "Runs like the wind. I never seen nothing like it in a nun before. I headed back to the barn to get these for supper." Gripped in his filthy glove were two headless chickens, their blood dripping onto the floor. He turned to take them to the kitchen.

"Brother Abraham," Mother Grace called after him, "surely you don't mean to tell me you left a small child and an unsuitably dressed sister on the frozen prairie in the midst of winter, do you?"

"It's okay," he answered, glancing back at her. "Sister Cilla had the little one in her sights, and a truck was coming down the road. I seen it stop and a farmer get out. He started out after them, so they'll be all right." He swung through the kitchen door, shouting, "Sister Bernadette, I got something for you. Them hens was pecking these two near to death, so I chopped off their heads and brung them."

It wasn't the first time Mother Grace had to bite her lip to stop from cursing Brother Abe, the *imbécile*.

As it turned out, she didn't have to worry for long. Just as she was heading to the front door to scan the horizon, Sister Cilla burst through, Rose Marie, red-faced and runny-nosed, tucked under her arm. Behind Cilla was a tall thin man in an open parka, overalls, and boots, a straw summer hat perched absurdly on his head.

Ignoring him, she snapped at Sister Cilla, "Next time you're going outside on a winter's day, dress for it!" Then she turned to the man. "Who are you?"

"Olaf Johanson at your service, ma'am," he announced, stepping forward.

Mother Grace took his accent to be Scandinavian. Heavens, she hoped he wasn't a Lutheran.

Sweeping the hat off his head, he bowed clumsily. "Father Alphonses said you be needing a pig or two at the school, yah?"

"What?" The cold had been detrimental to her knees, shoulders, and wrists, and now that both Rose Marie and Sister Cilla were safely back at the school, her mind was registering the extent of her discomfort. "Let me sit down," she muttered, hobbling over to a dining hall bench, Sister Cilla, Rose Marie, and Olaf Johanson trailing behind. She really had no time for any more foolishness.

"I brung you a pig," Olaf said. "Father Alphonses, he said you were pretty short of food at the school, yah? It's in my truck."

Fortunately, the pig was already butchered and wrapped neatly in brown paper packages. Brother Abraham helped Olaf unload the meat from the back of his truck, and Sister Bernadette happily inspected each bundle with its childish print in grease pen. "Pork chops," she cried, elated. "Shoulder roast. Spare ribs!"

"Enough, Sister Bernadette," Mother Grace reprimanded, and Bernadette's voice dropped to a squeak as she stuffed the first few packages in the small upstairs freezer.

The rest of the meat Sister Bernadette directed to the large freezer downstairs. While the men bustled in and out, bringing cold air with them, Sister Bernadette strutted around the kitchen and into the dining hall, chattering about how nice it would be to have pork and how pleased she was that Mr. Johanson had cut the chops and roasts in portions of just the right size. By the kitchen stove, Sister Cilla, uncharacteristically animated, rubbed Rose Marie's hands, called to the men, and joined Sister Bernadette with her own enthused utterances. *Mon Dieu*, it was like a country social!

Mother Grace folded her arms on one of the dining room tables and laid her head down, completely exhausted. She was slipping into sleep when voices rose in the kitchen. Brother Abe, Olaf, and the two sisters were laughing loudly, being far too familiar. Just then, Sister Bernadette called through the door, saying she was about to make tea.

"Can I bring you a cup, Mother Grace?"

"Yes, you may," she snapped. After all the commotion of the day, she wanted nothing more than a warm drink and a hot-water bottle. She lowered her head again and drifted off.

Stirring sometime later, she noticed her tea had not been delivered. Was Sister Bernadette so busy giggling like a schoolgirl that she had forgotten her? Hearing another wave of laughter from the kitchen, she cupped a hand over her ear and listened, feeling like the chaperone at a child's party.

"Do you know how to take a pig to the vet?" Olaf asked in his singsong accent. "In a ham-bulance, yah."

Giggles and guffaws.

"Why do the pig go to Las Vegas?"

"Why?" the sisters murmured.

"To play the slop machine!"

It was simply too much for a sane person to tolerate. She rose and made her way to the kitchen, where Rose Marie was timidly observing the spectacle of four foolish adults from behind the stove, clearly the only one with an ounce of sense. As Mother Grace glanced at her, Rose Marie gave her an odd expression: her eyes were cast in what appeared to be world-weary resignation, her mouth folded in an impish grin. It was as if the child could appreciate Mother Grace's frustration at the unseemly behaviour of the sisters while finding the whole scene humorous. It was, of course, and for an instant, she felt a smile form on her own lips. Then she remembered herself.

"Rose Marie, please set the tables for supper. It appears everyone else is far too busy."

As the adults turned to her, she approached the farmer. "Thank you so much for your generosity, Mr. Johanson. We at St. Mark's are indebted to you. Brother Abraham, will you see Mr. Johanson out?"

"I was going to bring you tea, Mother Grace, but you fell asleep," Sister Bernadette cried, but Mother Grace waved the woman silent and headed for the stairs and her bottle of aspirins.

Merde! she exclaimed to herself, more because she had a *reason* to be angry than because of anger itself. Surprisingly, her irritation was all but gone.

11

Voices

HER LITTLE BEDROOM on the nuns' floor spoke to Rose Marie. Prayers whispered from the walls: *God our Father, Jesus Christ, my Lord. I adore You profoundly. How I want to adore You.*

The sound seemed to be coming from the walls. "Hush," Rose Marie whispered, but it was no use.

Please help me to know You that I might live faithfully as a follower of Christ, came the voice.

She turned on the mattress, hands jammed to her ears.

Most Holy Trinity.

She shoved her head under the pillow.

I believe, I adore, I love You. By the infinite merits of His Most Sacred Heart.

Instead of blocking the words, the pillow drove them inside her skull, where they bounced and clattered, worser than even the fire worms . . . *poor sinners like me. I pray, Mother of God, that through your intercession, I will answer the call to religious life and be inspired.*

"Be quiet!" she screamed. Sobs swelled through her brain, and blurted through her ears. "Whoever you are, be quiet!" Springing up on her bed, she jumped on the mattress to knock out the sound.

Then she saw her. Oh, that nun! In a nightdress. Throwing herself on her knees, her face scrunched up like she was cut or burnt or beaten. Her nightcap plopped on the floor, revealing short, bristly hair. *I implore you, Jesus*, that nun cried. *Come to me now. Show yourself, Jesus!*

"Shut up!" Rose Marie yelled. "Go away!"

And she did. The nun melted into the wall.

"Mama," Rose Marie whispered as she climbed under the covers and pulled them over her head. "Help me. Even if you're in that san-i-tor-i-um." But Mama didn't come to her, couldn't help. Anataki was far away for the holidays and wouldn't be squeezing into bed beside her with whispers, giggles, and summer dreams. Even though the shadow nun had left, Rose Marie was scared. Night wrapped her up, squeezing everything out until she was as flat as the sheet under her on that shadow sister's bed.

The morning of January 3, Rose Marie moved her nightdress, school uniform, underwear, stockings, face cloth, and toothbrush back to the dormitory. She had a hard time sitting through lunch with the sisters, and she took only a few bites of the "perfectly good ham sandwich" Sister Bernadette had made her.

"It's yummy, Sister Bernadette. It's just—"

"No wonder you're skin and bones," Sister Margaret remarked, and Sister Joan tilted her head forward to get past Sister Margaret's big fat bosoms and give her a dirty look.

When Sister Margaret and Sister Joan started talking about "all the work, what with the students returning today," Sister Cilla patted Rose Marie's hand and whispered, "Eat what you can, dear. In another half hour, we'll be running around like crazy."

Once the sisters were finished with their meal, Rose Marie was on her feet, not even thinking of clearing their plates. She skipped out of the dining hall before Sister Bernadette could call her, threw on her coat, boots, and mitts, and ran outside. Squinting down the road, she couldn't see any of the school buses rumbling towards the school, so she took off down the trail to the barn, where she wasn't even sup-posed to be, ran back, then around the school one, two—five times until she was hot and panting.

Soon the yellow school buses arrived, one teetering over the white horizon, and then another. Three buses, all in a row, wheezed up to the school and stopped to let the girls scramble off.

"Anataki!" she cried, not caring if the sisters heard her use the not-allowed name. Throwing her arms around her friend, she breathed in the smell of snow and smoke. Clutching hands, the two of them jumped up and down, squealing.

"What's the point?" Sister Margaret, a few feet away, demanded of Sister Joan. "We send them home for two weeks, and once they get back, we have to start civilizing them all over again."

"*Acculturating* them," Sister Joan corrected her.

Rose Marie didn't care what they said. Taki was back! "You want to go upstairs and play dolls?" she whispered, and as soon as Sister Joan started the "orderly procedure" of lineups, they snuck up to the dormitory.

Once they were sitting on the floor under Rose Marie's bed, Taki reached into the waistband of her skirt. "I got something for you, Rosie." She pulled a packet wrapped in white hide.

"What is it?"

"Unwrap it and see."

Rose Marie did, and inside she found a blob of bread twice as big as her hand.

"*Imis-tsi-kitan*, Rosie."

Rose Marie brought it to her mouth, and that's when she smelled Mama's fingers wrapping dough around a willow stick and cooking it over a fire, the trees singing around them in sharp green notes, the creek gurgling, and, oh, she shoved half the piece in her mouth and closed her eyes, allowing the taste to fill her.

12

Forgiving Ruth

JANUARY WAS A dark, stunted month that stumbled headlong into February with its screaming winds, coughs, and scalding foreheads. By midmonth, a full third of the girls had fevers.

On St. Valentine's Day, which Sister Margaret proclaimed to a weepy Sister Cilla "the most stupid day in all Creation," both dormitory supervisors had to take shifts watching over those students confined to their beds. The very sickest girls were tucked in the six beds of the infirmary, a small room off the dormitory, and Sisters Margaret and Cilla kept an eye on them as well as the sick girls in the dorm, while the healthy senior girls were put to work doing the extra laundry.

Sister Bernadette trotted up to assist once she was through with meal preparation. "I wish I had a bit of sugar to make a cake to honour St. Valentine." She sighed as she pulled a clean sheet over a stained mattress.

Sister Margaret snorted. "St. Valentine had nothing to do with all this cake and romance stuff, far as I can tell. All he did was instruct couples on marriage. God's laws. There's far too much of this lovey-dovey nonsense, if you ask me."

Sister Cilla sniffed more vigorously, and Sister Bernadette huffed, "No need to take your bad humour out on us, Sister Margaret."

Mother Grace, breathless from the long climb upstairs, listened to them from the entrance of the dorm. So it was St. Valentine's Day. She had forgotten. In truth, there was no reason for her to remember it, though for a fraction of a second the image of Father Patrick, young and strong, popped into her mind.

"Let's not air our dirty laundry in front of the students, sick as they are," she scolded as she made her way to the infirmary, opening the door on a barrage of retching. *Vieilli*, things were worse than she had thought. "Water," she announced. "I'm going to get you water, and I want you all to drink it. Sister Cilla," she called out the door. "Bring a pitcher of water and glasses for these girls. Chicken soup, Sister Bernadette."

They would do the best they could. *Aie foi en Dieu*. Though sometimes it wasn't enough.

Both Anataki and Rose Marie suffered a low-grade fever, watery eyes, and scratchy throats, but it didn't slow them down much. Even though she was achy-boned and yawning, sleep was a problem for Rose Marie. At night the lightbulb hanging over the entrance cast shadows that kept her awake. She shifted in her bed, clutching her thin blankets and turning this way and that.

One night, the dormitory was unnaturally quiet. No snores or squeaking bedsprings. She couldn't even hear the girls breathe. It was like no one was there. "Mama, Papa," she whispered over and over, until she was able to wade into the sleepy grey river and float away.

The scrape of an opening door jarred her back to her hard bed in the dormitory. Raising herself on one elbow, she looked behind her to see a girl slip from the infirmary. Ruth Crier. Smarty-pants Rude, as she had taunted her. Oh, but now Ruth's face was swollen, her eyes puffy, lips cracked. She was sick, too sick to be out of bed.

"Ruth," she hissed.

Ruth walked towards her, looking to the far end of the dorm. For her big cousins, probably.

"Ruth, are you okay? You're not supposed—" Ruth was right beside her, and, oh, Rose Marie's skin turned to ice. She could see right through her!

"Ruth. I'm sorry, you know, about our fight, that time I—" Tears smeared her vision. "Don't go," she sputtered. "Get back to that hospital room. Get better."

She tried to say more, to ask Ruth to forgive her, to beg her to stay, please stay with her in the dormitory, at the school, in the world, but her words were sinking under a sea of sad, and all that came out were sobs.

Ruth wasn't listening, anyway. She couldn't hear. She was already gone, a ghost, a shadow.

13

The Prodigal Son

STANDING BEFORE the nuns in the dining hall, Mother Grace waited for Sister Bernadette to deliver what appeared to be one of her more successful attempts at an omelette and take a seat. "Sisters," she began, "I don't need to remind you that three students died from fever in the past week: Lydia Weasel Foot, Ruth Crier, and Maryanne Little Horse. Close to a dozen girls are still ill. Keep them in your prayers."

Wimples bobbed wearily.

"I have an important announcement. Father Damien, now going on four years deceased, may he rest in peace, will be replaced by Father William, arriving at the school at the beginning of next week. Some of you may recollect William," she added, carefully draining her voice of any telltale scorn. "He served at St. Mark's when the boys were still in attendance at this school, as a dorm supervisor—was it eight years ago? Then he went to St. Gerard's for—what was it, three, four years?"

"Five," Sister Joan snapped decisively.

"No matter. He then returned to Montreal to complete his education and take his vows as a priest." That Father William, then Brother William, had not left under the best of circumstances she would not mention.

As the dining hall buzzed with speculation, she removed her glasses and pressed a finger and a thumb against her eyelids. She reminded herself that though she had been disturbed by the rumours surrounding William when he left St. Mark's, her knowledge of them could very well give her a certain power over the man, one she might be forced to use if he should decide to wrest control of St. Mark's from her grasp.

"Be sure to welcome Father William back to the fold," she added, sitting.

The next morning after Matins, she motioned Sister Cilla to her office. The previous evening over three fingers of brandy—certainly no more than four—she had come to the conclusion that if God wouldn't show her the way to fulfil her destiny, then she must find it herself. The pompous voice of Sister Joan had clanged through her mind, declaring, *God helps those who help themselves.*

"Your new assignment, an additional assignment," she told Cilla, "is to assist Sister Joan in the classroom."

"Oh my, yes, Mother Grace," Sister Cilla replied, looking both pleased and flustered. "That will be along with—"

"—your assignment of assisting Sister Margaret in dormitory supervision? Yes, Sister Priscilla. Unless you feel that is too much responsibility."

"No, dear, oh law, I didn't mean that, Mother Grace."

"I'm relying on you, Sister," she confided, "to bring young Rose Marie Whitewater to me, should she . . . upset Sister Joan or try to escape her class. It's part of my plan . . . I don't want any more . . . untoward incidents. Do you understand me?"

"Yes, Mother Grace." Priscilla nodded enthusiastically.

Mother Grace was pleased. Perhaps all would work out for the best. Sister Cilla had a certain melancholy that had not been alleviated by dormitory work, and by giving her this new assignment, she could very well be killing two birds with one stone. *Vieilli,* what a terrible expression. Another one popped into her mind, one that Father William had bandied about years ago: *Idle hands are the Devil's workshop.* And if anyone should know, it would be William.

Father William arrived at the end of March, two days after Mother Grace's birthday, one she again passed without mention. The temperature had risen from thirty-four below to "a balmy minus-nineteen," as Brother Abe announced before lunch. Father Alphonses met William at the Hilltop station as he stepped from the train into a gust of wind that, according to Alphonses, very nearly swept him off the platform.

"Welcome back," Mother Grace greeted William as he entered the dining hall. Father Alphonses excused himself and went upstairs to visit Father David in the priests' suite. "And congratulations, *Father William.*" As he sat on the bench across from her, she reached over, touched his shivering hand, and whispered, "We're all very proud of you."

Father William looked tentatively at Mother Grace, a hint of gratification in his eyes. But before he could open his mouth, she hurried on.

"I'm sure you'll find yourself very busy. Father David, you'll see, is very old now, and not always"—she paused—"sound. More provocative than ever, but at least he still remembers how to say Mass." She forced a chuckle. "But I'm sure you'll be taking that over from time to time. My, what with serving as our spiritual guide, preparing sermons for your flock, giving Mass, and hearing confession for all the intermediate and senior girls—Father David will still hear the sisters' confessions—you'll be run off your feet. It's a heavy load, to be sure, William." She was careful not to mention the school administration, which was considered by the Church to be the job of a priest. "I certainly don't envy you your new responsibilities." She patted his hand again, smiling warmly if disingenuously. She had not mentioned the name of the young boy.

14

Works of Mercy

ROSE MARIE, SITTING in class, felt an itch in her tummy. Ruth and two big girls dead and now the shadows and sickness of the school were seeping inside her, making the fire worms wriggle and burn. She couldn't stand it! One foot shook, her fingers twisted, and as soon as Sister Joan turned to the board, she slid out of her seat.

No sooner was she out the classroom door than Sister Joan was screaming her name and Sister Cilla was on her tail. Before she could pick up speed and run through the front door, Sister Cilla had her skirt in her fist and was hauling her in like a fish on a line.

"Let go of me!"

One hand squeezing her upper arm, Sister Cilla dragged her down the hall.

"Let me go!"

Dropping to a crouch, Sister wrapped her long arms around her, wiry and warm. "It's all right, Rose Marie," she said. "God will show us the way."

Us? She was too surprised to say anything.

Sister Cilla stood up, just like she had never hugged her. "Come on," she said, and they walked to Mother Grace's office.

"Were you misbehaving in Sister Joan's class, Rose Marie?" Mother Grace asked, her sharp blue eyes digging in and holding her.

"No." She blinked away the blue, her heart banging. "I mean yes."

Mother Grace almost smiled. Rising from her chair, she plucked a book from her shelf. "Follow me," she ordered, sweeping from the room.

Rose Marie trotted behind.

Entering an empty classroom, Mother Grace pointed at the first front-row desk. "Sit," she ordered, opening the book. "Catechism," she said, and placed the book in front of Rose Marie. From the teacher's desk a few feet away, Mother Grace snatched up three sheets of lined paper, a pencil, and an eraser. "You will copy out the *Corporal Works of Mercy*," she said sternly, leaning over and sliding her index finger down the page. "Start here." She creased the spot with her fingernail. "Copy as many lines as you can before I return in—let's see—an hour. Do you understand me?"

Rose Marie nodded.

Mother Grace cleared her throat.

"Yes, Mother Grace."

Back in her office, Mother Grace put the classroom keys back on the hook. This was the chance she was giving the child. She thought she had seen something in her: a quickness of mind and not just of body, a certain understanding that was beyond her years, those dark, inquisitive eyes darting everywhere. *Oui*, she could recognize acuity when she saw it. Perhaps. She sighed. Perhaps not. After all, Sister Mary of Bethany had been an intelligent young woman, one she had believed capable of redirecting her young woman's passion to a deep and abiding love for the Lord, a practice she, herself, was more than familiar with. *Mon Dieu*, she had been wrong.

This girl, Rose Marie Whitewater, was not Sister Mary of Bethany, she reminded herself, not a young woman of twenty, but a mere child of seven, and one, she had heard from Sisters Priscilla and Margaret, who had difficulty sleeping. She knew from Sister Joan that the girl had an egregious lack of self-control. "Though her wild nature is accompanied by a good memory and a superior vocabulary," Joan had acknowledged grudgingly.

No doubt Rose Marie had never been taught discipline or given religious training before arriving at the school. If she could not control her agitation and perform the task, or if it was more than she was capable of, *ça ne fait rein.* But if she could make herself sit still long enough to copy out at least three of the seven *Corporal Works of Mercy* before she had learned to print much more than twenty-six disconnected letters and her name, then clearly she had the determination necessary to succeed in the world. The Christian world.

Mother Grace rubbed an aching finger joint and smiled. The girl might have prospects. After all, she, herself, had been given an opportunity for a better life when she was young.

Mother Grace recalled how the Sunday before her thirteenth birthday, she had sat at Mass in the Église Jeanne d'Arc and noticed a young man looking her up and down with an intensity that had frightened her. As she glanced around at the farmers, labourers, and merchants, she recognized, for the first time in her life, the hard work, large family, and grinding poverty that most surely were her fate, and while the rest of the congregation rose to sing, she collapsed on the prayer bench and beseeched the Lord for rescue.

He in His mysterious way had provided. *Dieu soit loué.* First had come an unexpected endowment from dear Uncle Gabriel, who had witnessed her birth. She had come into the world suddenly, the story went. Her parents' third child and first daughter, she had torn from her mother's womb with such force and protruding limbs that Maman, washing dishes and speaking in comforting tones to her younger brother, doubled over as watery blood gushed from her womb.

Gabriel, the only one to witness the violent birth, was so shocked that he vowed to God that if He saved the life of his favourite sister and her emerging child, he would devote himself to His service.

Once he was ordained as bishop a mere thirteen years and one month later, Uncle Gabriel decided to remember the child whose traumatic birth had caused him to enter the priesthood. He had provided his niece with the means to receive a convent school education. He had intervened and changed her life. As perhaps God intended her to change Rose Marie Whitewater's life.

How hard those strings of letters were for Rose Marie to form! She stared down at the lines, curves, and dots that meant sounds and pauses, but so many, all jumbled together in lumps!

Her tummy grew hot. She closed her eyes and tried to will the heat away, but instead it built, the fire worms itching and burning and crawling. She couldn't stand it! She dashed to the door, turned the knob, and pulled. It didn't budge. Again she turned the knob and yanked with every bit of strength she had. Locked.

She ran around the room. She smacked into the far wall. She ran back to the door, turned and pulled and kicked the door jamb. She beat her fists and stamped her feet. She jumped up and down and up and down until her legs were jelly and her eyes ran. She crawled to the row of narrow windows and pulled herself up on tiptoes to look outside. Already the sun was fading. A dark snake slid down the sky.

She went back to the wooden desk, climbed into the seat, and picked up the pencil. At first she couldn't find Mother Grace's fingernail line. She banged her head on the desk, but that made the sore spot above her left eye hurt. She looked back to the blotchy page, found her place, and started to print. One letter, two letters, a short word. She lost her place. She stood up, jumped up and down, then sat. Another line, her insides jiggling hot. She ran around the room. She picked up the pencil and started another sentence. Over and over, until the

pencil felt firm in her fingers and forming the letters made the worms
settle down and sleep.

After an hour and ten minutes, Mother Grace surveyed the clumsy
letters pressed into the damp paper, its blue lines bleeding. Rose Marie's seven *Works of Mercy* were more than she had expected. "Good,"
she said, trying to keep a note of triumph from her voice. "Very good,
child." Rose Marie smiled shyly up at her, and, despite or because of
the girl's damp eyes and missing front tooth, she was charmed. Almost.
"Don't count your chickens before they're hatched," Sister Bernadette
often warned.

"Off you go to class. *Va t'en,*" she ordered, but softly.

Once Rose Marie was gone, Mother Grace grinned to herself.
Clearly the child could overcome her rambunctious nature when required. Now she would take her under her wing, helping her grow
and flourish, just as God most assuredly intended. But timing was
problematic. The school year was almost over, and there might not
be much point in starting the necessary private lessons. She'd have to
wait until September to work with the girl, missing precious months.

Unless . . . Rose Marie were to stay at St. Mark's all summer. An
interesting thought, and not one impossible to implement. It was likely
in Rose Marie's best interests to remain at the school in a stable, spiritual environment, both body and soul nourished. She would check to
see if the girl's home living situation had changed. *Oui,* she'd write a
letter to the Charles Camsell Hospital in Edmonton and learn of Mrs.
Whitewater's condition.

Opening her desk drawer, she found she still had had two pages of
linen stationery and a bottle of quality black ink. Perhaps things were
finally falling into place.

15

The Mystery of Godliness

THE DORM WAS finally dark. Even the senior girls had finished whispering and were sleeping quietly, except for Abby First Eagle, who, as usual, made little piggy snorts. Unable to find the grey river and drift down it to sleep, Rose Marie opened her eyes. A hazy shape hovered at the foot of her bed, so she quickly shut her eyes again.

She smelled smoke. Raising herself on one elbow, she was ready to scream "fire," to wake Taki and Martha and Maria and to run down the stairs and out the front door, because that shadow sister must be trying to burn them alive!

Instead, a downpour of daylight. She sat up, letting it soak through her, warm and delicious.

"Mama!"

Standing over her, Mama held a braid of burning sweet grass in one hand. With the other hand she pushed smoke over her daughter, clean and warm.

"Oh, Mama, I been thinking of you." She reached for that soft, familiar body, leaning into it.

"*Nitan.*"

"How did you get in the school, Mama?"

As Mama smiled, shimmering smoke blew through Rose Marie's sparrow bones, washing her.

"Sinopaki," Mama whispered, the name a robe of fresh air, and she heard her creek splash over smooth rocks at the edge of Mama's voice. Just over Mama's shoulder, on the bank, a breeze billowed the damp clothes hanging on the bushes to dry.

"We're home, Mama."

"*Aa.*"

"I love you," she said, and Mama said it back in a way that was wide and warm and free as summer. Sunlight fell from Mama's eyes, skittered over the surface of the creek, and flashed back at them. "I'm so glad you're here!"

Mama held her until she drifted off to sleep.

On the way down for breakfast the next morning, she told Taki about the visit. "Everyone was asleep except me. Mama snuck in."

"How did she do that, Rosie?"

"I don't know."

"You sure you weren't dreaming?"

"It was real! Never mind, if you don't believe me." She stamped ahead of Anataki biting her lip against the sudden sting of tears. Mama had been at St. Mark's. She *had*!

At the end of that week came the longest day. The following week, the students were herded outside after breakfast to await the yellow buses that would take them home.

Rose Marie was playing tag with the other first-years when Sister Cilla rushed up to her. "There you are. Dear, oh law, Mother Grace wants to see you. Come with me."

As soon as Rose Marie entered the office, Mother Grace, her face pulled tight, motioned her to sit down.

"I just got a letter from the Charles Camsell Hospital, the sanitorium. I have some terrible news for you, *chérie*. God rest her soul, your mother has passed away."

Mother Grace reached over and patted her hand. Rose Marie saw her do it, but she didn't feel it.

"You won't be getting a bus home today, *chérie*. There are other arrangements in place for you this summer."

"No, I don't think so, Mother Grace," she said. The bump above her eye throbbed.

"I'm very sorry, Rose Marie."

Now Mother Grace was coming around the desk towards her, stretching her hand out to pat her shoulder. This time she felt the woman's palm right through her dress, and it was dry as a stale bread crust. A hankie squeezed into her fist.

"The buses are here," Mother Grace said, looking out her window. "Would you like to go out and say good-bye to your little friends?"

"Anne!" She ran down the hall and out the front door.

The first-years were chattering in a group, talking about everything they were going to do that summer.

"Horses!" Taki yelled.

"Ride in my uncle's car!" whooped Martha.

"You sound like a bunch of squirrels," Rose Marie shouted at them.

"Come 'ere, Rosie," Taki said.

She started to shake.

"What's the matter, Rosie?"

"My . . . my mama's dead!"

"Oh, Rosie!" Taki put her arm around her waist and pulled her close. "It's like the worstest thing."

Clamping her teeth down on her lip, she pulled away. "Have lots of fun riding your stupid horse with your stupid brothers!"

A few feet away, the doors of the first bus huffed open and the driver yelled, "C'mon!"

Anataki shifted towards it, glancing back.

"Just go," Rose Marie cried. "I don't care!" She turned and ran back to the school, up two flights of stairs, and into the dormitory.

Sister Cilla had already unlocked the shutter on the low window, but it didn't want to budge. Rose Marie squeezed her small fingers into the crack and pried it, splintering the dry wood, and, *ow*, getting a sliver. Below, three buses sputtered down the road, away, far away from her. Sucking her finger, she watched the dust settle. It plugged her nose and clogged her eyes, making the world runny and sore. There had been buses and Taki and Mama. Things had been—and just like that—they were gone.

After a while of trying to see and breathe and suck blood from her finger and bitten lip, she spotted a plume on the horizon. It was coming towards the school. Forest Fox Crown's truck! She pounded down the stairs, ran through the front door, and flew to the road as fast as she could go.

Squinting, she could make out Papa in the passenger's seat, Aunt Angelique beside him, driving. She ran towards the truck, shouting. It ground to a stop just a few feet from her, and Papa jumped out. She flung herself at him.

"I've come to get you." He wrapped his arms around her. "To take you home"—the words she had wanted forever and ever to hear.

"Oh, Papa."

He crouched and spoke, his voice suddenly slack as an old rope. "Mama's gone, Sinopaki. To the Sand Hills." He hugged her tight, but she was too stuffed up with dust and sad to hug back. Papa kept talking, the words English and Blackfoot, all mixed up. Then he stood up.

"I'm going to see that Mother Grace. I have to tell her you can come up north to Aunt Katie's house with me." He held out his hand, and she grabbed it tight.

Inside, Mother Grace was working at her desk. Her mouth folded when she saw Papa at her door.

"I've come for my daughter," he said, looking down at her.

Mother Grace lifted her chin. "I'm sorry, Mr. Whitewater, but you won't be able to take Rose Marie with you today."

"What?" Papa stepped forward, so she did too, still clinging to his hand. He was Medicine Man. Blessed Wolf. Nothing could stop him.

Don't let Mother Grace stop him, Rose Marie prayed to herself.

"I'm afraid, Mr. Whitewater, it's come to our attention that you no longer have a proper home for your daughter. We're very sorry about your recent loss. Great is the mystery of Godliness." Mother Grace glanced at her, eyes softening as if she were doing something nice, not something mean, but when she looked back up at Papa her eyes turned to glass splinters. "It's in the child's best interest for her to stay with us at the school until . . . your situation changes. Naturally, you can visit every Sunday during the regular visiting—"

"No," Papa interrupted. "She is my daughter. Mine!" He let go of Rose Marie's hand and thumped his chest with his palm. Mother Grace winced. "You can't keep her from me."

Oh, her papa was strong. He would take her home for sure!

"That's where you're wrong, Mr. Whitewater," Mother Grace said in a low voice. In that moment, Rose Marie hated-hated-hated her!

She slipped behind Papa, peering out.

"What did you say?"

"I've discussed the matter with Father Alphonses, the priest at Hilltop who also presides over the Reserve. You must know him, Mr. Whitewater. In addition, I have written a letter to Indian Affairs and received a reply. I have instructions to keep Rose Marie here at the school for the summer. I can show you the letter, if you like."

"Show me," Papa demanded, stepping forward.

Mother Grace rustled through the papers on her desk, then stood, handing one to Papa. He looked at it, his eyes going over it one, two, three times. Rose Marie pressed harder into him.

"You have no right," he said. A vein throbbed through his voice.

Mother Grace's eyes flickered. "I have every right." Raising her chin, she fixed him in her hard glass gaze. "It is my duty and the duty of the residential school system to make sure our students receive adequate care." Her words sounded clipped from her mouth with pointed scissors. "We would be remiss in our duties if—"

"Adequate care, eh? Beatings and sickness and self-righteous—"

"Not at this school, Mr. Whitewater. I don't know what your experience might have been at another school, but here at St. Mark's, everything is sanitary and—"

"She's my daughter, and she belongs with me!"

"Nevertheless, I assure you that should your daughter be taken by you or anyone else, the authorities will be notified forthwith. Kidnapping is a most serious offence."

Rose Marie took a backwards step from Papa, and another, but she didn't rush. She wouldn't do anything to attract Mother Grace's attention. She inched to the door.

"She is my daughter!" Papa cried, his voice spraying a dark cloud through Mother Grace's office.

Softly, Rose Marie stepped into the hall. She crouched. She would slip off her shoes and run soundlessly to the front door and down the steps to Aunt Angelique's truck. She'd get inside and lie on the muddy floor. Then Papa would come out of the school, jump in, and they'd drive away.

"Rose Marie." A hand pressed her shoulder. "Dear, oh law, what are you doing?" Sister Cilla asked.

After Papa left, his shoulders hunched, Sister Cilla held her by both arms. But as he swung open the front door to leave, she broke away, running after him. She could hear stupid, ugly Mother Grace and stupid, ugly Sister Cilla following her down the hall as she burst outside. The truck had started up, and she watched it toss dry stones and hot dust as it roared away, filling her up with grit.

Mother Grace came out and bent down beside her on the top step. "*Chérie*," she said, "it's for the best. I have plans for you this—"

"No," she screamed. "I hate you!"

She ran inside the school and back upstairs to the dormitory. Finding her towel, toothbrush, and clothes gone, she thumped back down to the second floor and pushed into the room they kept her in when all the other kids were gone. The jail cell. Where that shadow sister used to live. Sure enough, Sister Cilla had already moved her things there, just as if she had known for certain, as if Mother Grace had told her to before Papa even came to the school.

She climbed on the bed and started jumping. The bedsprings shrieked, and she did too. She bounced hard and high. Reaching out, she grabbed the end of the crucifix that hung over the door. Yanking it off, she flung it against the opposite wall. Her feet hit the bed's metal frame, and she crashed to the floor. "God damn, God damn!" she screamed.

"What's going on up there?" Sister Margaret hollered.

Rose Marie got up and climbed back on the bed. Jumping, bedsprings screeching, she pulled the small palm crosses from above the bed. She broke the dry fronds to pieces and threw them around the room. She kept jumping on the bed until the springs sagged and the mattress slumped, belly down, to the floor.

"Should I come up there with my stick?" Sister Margaret bellowed.

She crawled under the saggy mattress and lay in the shadows. Everything hurt. Her eyes were burnt-out holes; her ears itched with tears; her forehead, skinned fingers, scraped knee, and stubbed toe throbbed.

"Mama," she whispered. She closed her eyes, becoming very young again—her before-being-born self. *"Na-a,"* she moaned, the word she had once called silently to Mama's body, her whole wide world. *"Na-a,"* now to the hard floor, the stale school air, all the sharp corners of this dead sister's room, the stark space around her, sinking through her, a world of emptiness. *"Na-a,* please come back from the Sand Hills. Come back and take me with you."

I've come to get you, Papa had said as he knelt beside her in front of the school. With Mama gone, he and her baby brother were all she had left. He had told her he had come to get her, and it was exactly what she wanted, everything she had hoped for.

But he had lied, lied, lied!

PART TWO

16

Womanhood

ON A PLEASANT day in June, Mother Grace watched the twelve-
and thirteen-year-olds in the schoolyard. From the shadowed
doorway, she could discreetly observe the girls, and she spotted Rose
Marie walking with her friend Anne.

Anne Two Persons, at average height, was taller than tiny Rose
Marie by about four inches. Mother Grace had always considered Anne
nondescript, not pretty and not plain, almost invisible, in fact, though
on the few occasions she had seen Anne laughing, it was as if a mask
had been pulled from her face. Once she had been sure that Anne was
boldly imitating Sister Joan's stern stride, but when she looked back,
she thought perhaps she had been mistaken. Sister Margaret liked her
well enough, though she unfailingly declared at the start of each new
school year, "The Indian's on that Anne Two Persons like a brand."

Mother Grace set her cane against the door and kneaded her left
shoulder. She would have chosen a different girl to be Rose Marie's
best friend, if it were up to her. Someone more pious, more studi-
ous, more—well, évoluée. Yet the two were inseparable and had been
since virtually their first day at St. Mark's, six years before. Anne kept
Rose Marie from being alienated, as special children so often are. As

she herself had been, to a degree. Indeed, the Lord knew best. She glanced towards the bottom of the steps, where a clatter of voices had started up.

"I was the one who said it first," Maria Running Deer insisted. "I said, 'I'll do the folding,' but Sister Margaret didn't hear me, and Becky said, 'Sister Margaret, I'll fold. Pleeeeease,' even though she knew I wanted to, and I never get folding. I always get ironing, and—"

"I never heard you!" Rebecca Old Bear cut in.

"Did so!"

"I did *not!*"

Vieilli, yet another shrill argument. Retrieving her cane, Mother Grace realized she was simply too tired to make her authority known. As she looked back to Rose Marie, she allowed herself a small surge of pride. While Rachel Useful was becoming alarmingly voluptuous, while poor Susanna Big Snake grew taller and knobbier by the day, Rose Marie's small frame simply softened. She had to admit that she had detected a despondency in the girl during some of their private lessons that term. Perfectly natural. The difficulties around *les règles*, maybe. Hormones, or whatever they called them these days. Surely the dormitory nuns mentioned something to the students about the changes of womanhood. It wasn't her role.

She met with Rose Marie once a week, for what she termed "advanced catechism," no longer just catechism. Beginning next year, she planned to increase their lessons to twice a week. Rose Marie learned quickly, and she knew more about the sacraments and obligations than most of the sisters. Gone was the wildness that had tainted her first years at the school. The girl's future was in the Church, she was almost certain. She pressed her fingers to her mouth to stop from smiling. *Let's not get ahead of ourselves.* Rose Marie must come to that conclusion herself.

In just a few weeks, the girl would move down from the dormitory and take her place on the nuns' floor. During the summer months, she truly became part of the religious community of St. Mark's. *Oui,* all was proceeding as it should. Easing herself down on the cement balustrade, Mother Grace retrieved a bottle of aspirin from her skirt pocket and shook out two. As she swallowed the pills, she already felt lighter, as though she had escaped the rusted machinery of her mortal body.

17

Blue

TWO DAYS AFTER every other girl had piled into a yellow bus and left St. Mark's for the summer, Rose Marie sat on the toilet staring at the discharge on her underdrawers. Old blood, it looked like. She tugged a piece of toilet paper off the roll and dabbed at her thighs, checking for a cut. Nothing. And no pain. Quickly, she pulled up her underdrawers, washed her hands, and went back to sweeping the hallway. It would probably just go away.

She wondered if Anataki had crossed the border into Montana with her family yet, if they were getting close to their summer camp. She imagined Taki and her brothers on galloping horses, squinting as the midday sun sprayed over their foreheads. She could see them clearly in her mind, sage and wild rosebushes rushing by their feet. Behind them, a little slower and more watchful, Taki's father and uncle swayed on their horses, and to the southwest, a plume of dust trailed from the old truck her aunt drove down the dirt road. In the back of the pickup, head scarf blowing in the hot wind, Taki's mother sat among skins, poles, blankets, pots, and pans, her hands dancing from one to the other, trying to keep them from bouncing out.

Longing punched Rose Marie in the belly, and for a moment she stopped sweeping. She would give anything to be with Taki and her relations. Especially her brothers. Taki spoke of them so often, Rose Marie had dreamt of them. As if they were her brothers too. Or cousins. Maybe even boyfriends.

By supper there was more discharge on her underdrawers. It was a mourning of sorts, she decided. Without Taki, she was bereft. *Bereft*: she liked that word. At Easter, Sister Joan had used it to describe the Madonna's reaction to Jesus' death. "Mother Mary was bereft," she had said. Well, this stain was bereavement's outward sign, just like the stigmata on the palms and feet of St. Francis of Assisi. Still no pain, so big deal.

The next evening, the blood was gone. *Thank God.*

Day by day, she grew more lonely, more—what was the word Maria Running Deer used? *Blue.* A good word, because she had seen the colour blue slink around Papa, bruising the air when he was worried about Mama, and after she died, when he missed her so much. And the first time Mother Grace told him he couldn't have her, his daughter, anymore. Sometimes, if he wasn't feeling well. His cough, for one thing.

This *blue* soaked into her and dragged her down. Maybe it came from the shadow nun. Oh, she didn't want to think about that. Dull and dazed, she felt like she was crawling through prairie gumbo. Even the bright summer sky winking through the classroom windows couldn't wash the film from her eyes, the weight of blue clinging to her legs and arms.

By the end of that first week, she found herself once more immersed in the summer routine. She slept in the little room on the nuns' floor, attended evening Compline, and sometimes, if she awoke to Sister Joan's clanging bell, Matins, though Mother Grace didn't require it of her. "Girls your age need their sleep," Mother Grace had said.

"Sure wouldn't do her any harm," Sister Joan had muttered.

Once again, she was eating her meals in the dining hall with the sisters, where they were usually joined by Brother Abe and Father William, often Father David too. Sure enough, she slipped back into a slot, just her size, much more easily than she liked to admit.

Twenty-two days after the students had gone home—St. Benedict's Day, Father David had announced at Mass that morning—Sister Joan came to fetch her from the garden, where she was thinning radishes. As she followed Sister's stiff back to the visiting room, her eyes not yet adjusted to the dark interior, a shape rose from one of the chairs, buttercups blooming along its shoulders.

"Oh, Papa!"

His arms enclosed her, wrapping her in a memory of metal traps, fresh meat, and the mixed feel and smell of his medicine bag: hide, plant, stone, feather, tooth, and bone. She was caught up in a rush of old sensations—the touch of Mama's hand on her forehead, the baby's chamois skin, *katoyiss* scent pricking her nostrils, moose stew, the creek gurgling, the wind singing, and raven wings whooshing through it. For the briefest of moments, her Sinopaki self fit into her St. Mark's uniform and she was whole. She clung to Papa, did not want that feeling to leave, did not want him to leave her ever again.

Then Papa shifted away from her, and just as quickly as it had come on, the feeling vanished. She was left with nothing but Papa's buckskin vest in her fingers and a poke of anger in her belly.

She looked up at him. "Where have you been?"

"Just got in yesterday at Angelique's. Took me more than two days to get there. Today I caught a ride with Sam First Rifle."

Sister Joan cleared her throat, her face scratched with impatience. "This visit wasn't planned, but Mother Grace is allowing you half an hour," she said, checking her watch.

Papa backed up to the row of chairs against the wall and sat down. She sat beside him.

"It turned out Sam was delivering hay to a farm two miles south. Horse and cart, eh?" He shook his head, eyes twinkling. "Those big horses, Clydesdales. Two real old ones. They walked so slow, we were going backwards. I thought I'd get here yesterday."

She laughed, her anger gone.

Sister Joan leaned back in her chair, surveying them. Obviously she wasn't going to leave them alone.

Rose Marie grabbed Papa's hand. "How is my brother?"

"He's good. Growing like crazy. Going to be bigger than his papa." He raised his hand to her shoulder. "Up to here, I'd say. He'll be bigger than his big sister too. He'll call you his little-big sister."

She smiled, but there it was again, that *blue*, the sense of being alone, even with Papa beside her.

"Always, my girl, I miss you every day."

There was sadness in his eyes as he spoke, and she wondered if it had always been there. Was sadness part of the world and its people, a secret grief you never even learned of until you were all grown up, or at least starting to be?

"Once we're out of St. Mark's, we can make our own lives," she and Taki were always saying. But now, sitting in the visiting room, she couldn't imagine what that life would be. Could she live like her mama and papa had in the bush, hunting, trapping, picking, and digging for food? Like Grandfather Whitewater and Grandmother Tallow before them? Would she ever be a wife, a mother? All she could imagine were the walls of the colourless school and her body dissolving into them.

"That Reserve's where my relatives are, Sinopaki, but it doesn't feel like home to me anymore; for one thing, you aren't there. But Kiaa-yo—Joseph—is only six. He needs looking after when I'm hunting or doing healing. I need my relations."

She nodded dully.

"Tomorrow I'm going west to our old house, see if it's still standing. Then on to visit Whitewater and Tallow. I'll get some plant medicine while I'm there."

She knew that the healing ceremonies Papa performed were "heathen." That's what Sister Joan had said. And the Sun Dance was "shameful in the eyes of God. A grisly profanity!" Moments after she made that pronouncement, Sister jumped up, grabbed the pointer from the blackboard ledge, and smacked Susanna over the head to make her "stop giggling like a baboon, missy!"

"Mumbo jumbo" is how Sister Margaret referred to the ceremonies. "Witchcraft" was what went on at powwows, the dancing "disgraceful."

But Papa was a dancer, the best wolf dancer ever. She thought of her life without dancing or feasts, forever surrounded by the dark wood and white paint of the school. There would be only boring church ceremonies in her life, and no feasts—just the thin dry crackers, often burnt, that Sister Bernadette baked for Eucharist.

Papa talked about the winter, about getting caught in an *ahki-tsimii* storm during the eagle moon. He showed her his fingers, the tips of two of them white. "Froze a bit. Can't feel 'em still, but that might come back." He kept talking as if his stories could fill all the time lost between them.

She nodded, her thoughts limp rags hanging in the airless room. Maybe happiness came for only a minute or two, just as she had felt it when Papa had hugged her. Maybe sometimes for an hour, like when she and Taki held hands and walked around the schoolyard or whispered in bed after lights-out. Just small bright pockets in the gloom.

She kept nodding at what Papa was saying, but she wasn't really listening. Everything he did was wrong. All her relations were wrong, and Anataki's too. Last summer, Taki's family had to move their camp to the other side of a river because a white man with a rifle came and said he owned the land and he'd shoot anyone on it.

"Kiaa-yo starts school next year," Papa told her, "but he doesn't have to sleep there. Only kids from big families that don't have enough money. They changed everything."

"What?" She was angry. "I should be at that school with him!"

"Sinopaki—"

"I know, I know. Mother Grace won't let me." She rubbed her nose to the back of Papa's hand and looked up at him. A few sparks, but the bright colours that had escaped his wiry body for as long as she remembered—his giant spirit—had dimmed first with his cough and then Mama's death. Since his fight with Mother Grace, since he lost that fight, his colours had all but faded away. He was wrong, he was weak, and she was stuck at St. Mark's forever.

Sister Joan stood up. Papa rose too, and Rose Marie dragged her heavy blue body back to the garden.

After supper, Rose Marie hurried down the hall from her bedroom to the nuns' bathroom. Her underdrawers felt hot and wet, and as she pulled them down, she saw blood soaking the bleached cotton. Was this a sign of more loss? Papa, whom she hardly ever saw, gone until next Sunday, then gone again until the Sunday after that. Then the Sunday after that one. *If* he could get a ride. And *if* he didn't leave for the north again. The blood was fresh, darkening only at the edges. As if her life was draining away. Tears boiled in her eyes. Everything, everyone, went away. She was being bled dry.

She pressed toilet paper to the gusset of her underdrawers and washed her hands. She wondered if she should tell someone about this wound. The next day she would see Mother Grace for advanced catechism. She could tell her then. If the blood was simply coming from an arm or an ankle, she would tell Mother Grace for sure.

After evening prayer, she took her washbasin to the bathroom, filled it with cold water, took it back to her room, and scrubbed away the stains on her clothes. As she lay in bed, her wet dress and underdrawers stretched on wire hangers in the closet, she realized she couldn't tell Mother Grace about the blood.

Despite making her stay at the school against her wishes, Mother Grace was always good to her. And she had saved her from her own rash nature and Sister Joan's rage by removing her from class and giving her special lessons in her own office. Mother Grace was smart too. She knew everything about the Bible, and she could say long words no one else even knew. She even had another language, one that wasn't against the rules to speak. And she had chosen her, Rose Marie Whitewater, out of all the girls at the school. But if it was love she felt for Mother Grace, it was the same kind she had for the Virgin Mary, Mother of God. Love for someone removed and not completely human, not made of flesh, not really. As she searched with her fingers, she found blood was still flowing from *there*. Just as if she was wounded, and, *God help me*, she must be.

She rose from bed and crept to the bathroom. In one of the cubicles, she stuffed her underdrawers with more toilet paper. When she heard a noise from the hallway, she froze. The long strides of Sister Cilla. If Sister came into the bathroom, she decided, it would be a sign to tell her about the blood.

Sister Cilla's footsteps splattered past the bathroom door and down the hall. A door whined open and clicked shut.

Maybe she should run down the hall and knock on Sister Cilla's door. When Sister answered, she would say, "I think something must be wrong with me."

But Sister Cilla seemed flustered these days, rushing around with sheets and pillowcases, mad at Sister Margaret, she could tell, then tromping off to help Sister Bernadette unload bedding plants or even the sides of pork Scarecrow Olaf delivered. Half the time, Sister Cilla had a faraway look in her eyes, like she was thinking of something that had nothing to do with St. Mark's. No, she couldn't say anything to Sister Cilla.

When Rose Marie awoke to Sister Joan's clanging bell, she saw that the blood had not stopped. The toilet paper in her underwear was soaked. And even though she had slept like a stone, she was tired. Tired and heavy, but not sick. She knew that TB caused blood to erupt in coughs through the mouth, not between the legs. It drew fevers and sores as it had with Mama, and it did not come on so fast. TB was a slow, creeping thing. She was not dying. Not yet. As soon as the sisters had gone down to Matins, she'd clean herself up.

"Rose Marie, what is it?" Mother Grace asked at breakfast when she saw the girl squirming in her damp dress and stuffed underwear.

"Nothing, Mother Grace."

"All right, but sit still, *chérie*. The first thing I'll have you do this morning is go up to the dormitory and see if last night's wind blew things around. You know how Sister Cilla opens all the windows at the end of the school year to freshen the dorm." She smiled indulgently at Sister Cilla, sitting farther down the table and a million miles away.

"What? Beg your pardon, Mother Grace," Sister Cilla stuttered.

"Just give it a sweep, *chérie*," Mother Grace told her, ignoring Sister, who was already returning to her own bewildered world.

Back in the dorm, Rose Marie felt a prick of curiosity. She walked over to one of the senior girls' wardrobes. Even standing on tiptoes, she could not see the top shelf, had to reach in with her hand and feel around. There. She brought out two—those cotton rectangles the older girls were always sewing in domestic science classes from laundered flour bags and worn bedding. She had never known what they were for, and like the other girls her age, she knew better than to ask. "Wouldn't you like to know," they always said. "That's for me to know and you to find out." She turned the pad over, examined its brown stains, the thick, layered construction and hurried stitching. Right there in one corner, she spotted the number of the girl it belonged to, sewn in red thread.

Over the years she had seen bigger girls wrap these cotton rectangles in their towels or clothing, trying to hide them as they hurried to the bathroom. She remembered Maria Running Deer crying that spring, and her older cousin, Judith, throwing an arm around her shoulders, whispering, then taking Maria to her wardrobe and reaching up to the top shelf.

Maybe she wasn't hurt or sick. Maybe these cotton rectangles had to do with the "fall of Eve" and "God's punishment" that Sister Joan often mentioned but never fully explained. "The temptress," Father David had called Eve more than once during Mass. Maybe her bleeding was a sign of woman's sin, of shame, something not to be spoken of, to be hidden away and suffered through silently. After she finished sweeping the dormitory, she would go quietly downstairs, slip into the sewing room, and make her own cotton pads.

18

A Very Good Age

MOTHER GRACE ROSE from the table, leaving her dishes for Sister Cilla to take to the kitchen. With her cane in one hand, it was too difficult to carry a bowl, cup, saucer, and cutlery. A few weeks back, she had broken an entire place setting.

Breakfasts were the worst, her joints still locked in a stiff repose, unwilling to flex and bend. She had to rely on Sister Cilla more these days, but that was as it should be. In fact, she really had to introduce Priscilla to the administration of the school. She had plans for her, plans that would keep Sister Joan far away from a position of power at St. Mark's.

"Could you stop by my office this morning, Sister Cilla," she called out. "There's something I need to discuss with you."

Sister Cilla straightened. "My! Yes, of course, Mother Grace," she said, cheeks flushing.

Just what was wrong with Sister Cilla these days? she wondered as she made her way to her office. She had seen her going in and out of chapel on a few occasions. To pray, no doubt, but for what? Mother Grace was checking her calendar when she heard a tentative rap at her door.

"Come in."

Her eyes a little wild, Sister Cilla sat down.

"You don't seem yourself, Sister."

"Dear, oh law." She pushed the door shut with one long foot. "I'm sorry. There will be no more of that, Mother Grace, I promise. I haven't broken my vows or anything, but—" A sob escaped her mouth. "Oh, Mother Grace, I have a sinful nature!"

"Don't we all, Sister Cilla. Now, what in heaven's name are you referring to?"

"Dear . . ." Sister Cilla closed her mouth. When she opened it again, she seemed more composed. "Well then, it's my birthday, I suppose. You see, Mother Grace, this Thursday I'll be thirty."

"A very good age."

"But you see, Mother Grace, at thirty, I thought I'd be . . ." Her voice trailed off, and her eyes had that wild look again.

"Yes?"

"I guess thirty isn't that old, but, you know, when I joined the Sisters of Brotherly Love, it was just after . . . I don't know if you remember, but I had been engaged to be married."

"I do recall, Sister. The young man in question betrayed you."

"Yes." She blushed. "Well, after all that, I didn't know what to do. I decided to enter the sisterhood, but I wasn't exactly sure. I didn't really hear a calling, you know?"

"*Calling* is just a word, Sister."

"Well, yes. But I wasn't sure, Mother Grace."

"Are you now?"

"Uh, maybe." Her eyes darted from the cross above the door to the bookcase. "I don't think that's it."

Time for patience and empathy. Mother Grace softened her expression and leaned across her desk. Patting Sister Cilla's hand, she asked, "What do you think is the source of your confusion?"

"Kids," she blurted. "Children. I always wanted them. I thought I would have them."

"That desire is fulfilled at St. Mark's, is it not? Here you have children, dozens of them, children whose lives you influence and enrich in the name of the Lord."

"Thanks be to God," Sister Cilla intoned faintly.

"We all have our moments of doubt, Sister Priscilla. It's important that you came to me." The fact that she had bidden Sister Cilla, that Cilla had not come of her own accord, was a mere technicality, she decided. "Ours is a life of sacrifice and devotion, *oui*, but also one of self-examination and prayer."

"Yes, Reverend Mother. I have been praying. I've been praying all the time." Sister Cilla paused, glancing at her lap. When she looked back at Mother Grace, she seemed calmer. Their conversation turned to other things—linen counts and the number of nightdresses needing mending or replacement.

"Do you have time for the garden in addition to the dormitory preparations, Sister?"

"Absolutely. In fact, it does me good to be outside. I think I need some time away from—" She stopped.

"Sister Margaret?"

"Dear, oh law. We don't always see eye to eye. I try, Mother Grace. I really do. It's just that—she's, um, a little bit cranky sometimes and—"

Mother Grace raised a hand to silence her. "I believe a young strong woman such as you needs more physical work and less time fussing over dormitory maintenance." And listening to the complaints of the increasingly crotchety Sister Margaret, she thought to herself, *la vieille mappe*. As if Margaret were the only one who suffered. "Perhaps you'd like to work with Sister Bernadette over the summer?"

"Yes, Mother Grace, I would."

"I'm going to assign you to help in the garden, in the kitchen, and with food acquisition over the summer."

Sister Cilla flushed with pleasure, and when she left, her steps down the hall sounded lighter. Even if it had been a quick decision,

it was a sound one. Sister Lucy, who usually assisted Sister Bernadette during the summer, was becoming more of a hindrance than a
help. Getting deafer by the day. And, Mother Grace was beginning to
realize, blinder. Why Sister Lucy refused to go east to the perfectly
nice retirement home in Montreal was beyond her comprehension.
Of course, Lucy couldn't speak much French. But then, most of the
sisters from the west couldn't, and there would surely be at least
one or two of them at the home. Sister Lucy would have company.
Then again, they'd all have to holler in order for her to know they
were there.

Vieilli, with her new assignment, Sister Cilla would not have time
to learn how to keep the books, the main reason she had asked her
to the office in the first place. Well, there was no rush. Cilla had lots
of time to learn administration—years, in fact. She, herself, was not
going anywhere.

As far as Mother Grace could tell in the following weeks, Sister Cilla's
new assignment was working well. Though broomstick thin, Priscilla
was strong as an ox and ten times as fast. Brother Abe appreciated being
called on less for lifting and carrying; that was plain as the nose on
his face. But Mother Grace wasn't going to let him get away scot-free.

"When are you planning to start the repairs, goodness, so long
overdue, Brother Abraham?" she demanded at breakfast the next day.

He looked a little dismayed, but nodded nevertheless. "I'll get on
them real soon."

When Olaf dropped by that afternoon to do the meat cutting, she
seized the opportunity to employ him as well. The man was obviously
lonely or he would be cutting the meat at his farm.

"Mr. Johanson," she called as he pulled out a set of battered knives.
"If you're not terribly busy with your pigs, perhaps you could help
Brother Abraham with some very necessary repairs to our school."

His face actually lit up. "Yah. I can do that."

"Bless you," she allowed.

Sister Cilla, though busy, was cheerful once again, at times to the point of giddiness. Was there no happy medium? The young nun seemed to have an excess of energy, despite her late-night forays to chapel. She was constantly running out to the garden, down the basement steps to the cold room, or out the front door to greet the farmers with their deliveries, often with poor Sister Bernadette struggling on her short legs to keep up.

Things would be back to normal once the students returned. Then Sister Bernadette could explore new ways to ruin perfectly good food, and Sister Cilla would be back to the dormitory listening to Sister Margaret's litany of complaints and very likely becoming discontented once again. An endless cycle, spinning them all into old age. *I am weary of my life.* Genesis. She sat at her desk and pulled out a sheet of paper and a bottle of ink.

Dear Patrick,

I received your awaited letter three days ago. May God bless and keep you.

Our summer is half over, but instead of appreciating each day, I find I am already anxious about the return of autumn. What is the matter with me that I cannot enjoy the moment without regretting its future?

I have just spoken to the young sister I have put much stock in, Priscilla. Her warm heart and concern for the children in her charge were a welcome relief in the penury of the war years. Even with the war over, praise God, the sisters at St. Mark's are sometimes poor of spirit. Sister Cilla has always been an exception. Yet now, despite her exuberance, something is off-kilter. I have plans for her in the running of the school, as you know, and I pray for the insight and wisdom to guide her appropriately.

Great is the mystery of Godliness: I have told myself that for years, and yet now the phrase no longer comforts me. What am I missing? What besides my life is slipping away?

How I miss you, Patrick.

Yours in Christ,
Grace

19

Heat

DESPITE AUGUST'S HEAT and Papa's Sunday visits, *blue* still crept up on Rose Marie. It clutched her and hung on, sometimes for days at a time. Rose Marie felt as if she were carrying a deadweight, someone dead who could not be thrown off. Like that stupid shadow nun. Could she, should she tell Mother Grace about the shadow sister and the shadow students she sometimes saw? Alone in her bed at night, she thought she could, believed she must. Or else go completely crazy. And possibly to hell.

But the next morning, it didn't seem right. There was Mother Grace's reserve, the reserve of all the sisters, except Sister Cilla, and every now and then Sister Bernadette. It was as if there were unwritten, unspoken rules among the sisters about sharing secrets the way friends did, the way Mama and Auntie Constance and Auntie Angelique had, the way she and Taki did—a kind of formality, stiff as their wimple bands. No, she could not tell Mother Grace or any of the sisters about the ghosts.

Again, a week later, blood seeped onto her sheets, and flowed for five days. Unexpectedly, tears pressed against her eyes, ready to spill.

Mother Mary, she prayed to the picture on her small bedroom wall, *help me*. But the Virgin was shocked by the appearance of the Holy Ghost, and just like Sister Cilla, was preoccupied, of no help at all.

Washing her face before bed, she peered at herself in the bathroom mirror. Was she pretty? Some of the girls were. Judith Shot One Side, for example. And Maria Running Deer. Holy moly, and Judith's boobs—her cousin Rachel's too! She surveyed her own chest in the mirror, turning from side to side. Both Judith and Rachel had arrived at school the previous September with two brassieres each, but by the time they left for the summer, they were spilling out of them. "They got four boobies," Taki had whispered. "Two little ones pushed up on top of two big ones." They had jumped up and down, chortling, happy to get back, even secretly, at the smug relatives who frequently referred to her chest and Taki's as "raisins on a breadboard."

She squinted at the mirror. She wished her skin was lighter—gold, not copper. But not sunburnt or freckly like the sisters'. Or with those thin red lines that ran across Sister Lucy's cheeks, cracks in a china cup. She pulled up her bangs and examined the bumps on her forehead. "Pimples," some of the girls called them. Maria, always trying to be ladylike, said, "I wish I didn't have these *blemishes*." La-di-dah.

Watching her reflection in the series of small mirrors hung over the sinks, she walked the length of the bathroom, swaying from side to side just like Adele Fox Crown and her friends, chest pushed forward, hips weaving. "Fancy wiggle-walk," Anataki called it, exaggerating the motion, limp-wristed, lips pouting, making everyone laugh. And yet it felt good; it made her think about dancing in the arms of a handsome man, like the one she'd glimpsed in Maria's magazine. She glanced around, but no one was there to see her, not even the shadow sister.

That night she wanted dreams, lazy ones of her once-upon-a-time trees and creek, the beaver she had seen one time with Papa, pushing her baby upstream with her nose. *Close your eyes, Sinopaki*, Mama whispered, and she settled under her sheet.

Land burst open. Her legs stretched around a warm, broad back. Pounding hooves, a blur of yellow grass whizzing by, and sunlight, thick as honey, pouring down her back as her horse raced over the prairies. Ahead, two young men rode painted horses, their black hair flying, bare chests slick with sweat. One slowed and turned his horse to face her, his grin red and white and wild, eyes spilling mischief. He stretched a muscular arm towards her. Her horse slowed and sauntered over to his, nuzzling its neck. He reached across his saddle and drew her to him. He held her and his sweat dripped down her breastbone, down her belly, down between her thighs, their bodies bannock-wrapped around a willow branch . . .

A bell clanged. "Time to get up!" Sister Joan yelled from the hall.

Pulling the blanket snugly to her chin, she curled around the moment still singing in her skin. In her nightdress, the shadow sister leaned against the opposite wall, her eyes lazy, her hand falling to her breast. She cupped the flesh, squeezing the tip. Rose Marie felt fingers on her own nipple, a tickle. A spurt of warmth ran down from her stomach, then the static shock of sock feet rubbed along carpet. In her ears, the whimper of an injured animal.

"Rose Marie, is that you in there?" Sister Joan demanded from the hall.

"I just have a charley horse, Sister." It was all she could think of.

"Well, get dressed. Snip, snap." The shadow sister melted like candy, but Rose Marie stayed in bed until it drizzled away—her beautiful, sinful dream. Then she pulled on her uniform and ran down for Matins.

20

Juggling

IN THE KITCHEN, Rose Marie took the cup from Sister Bernadette, dried it, and handed it to Sister Cilla, who placed it on the counter with three other cups.

"Watch this," Sister Cilla said. Rapidly, one after the other, she threw the cups in the air.

Rose Marie gasped, just as Sister Bernadette pulled her hands from the dishwater, demanding, "What are you doing, Sister?"

"Juggling. You're juggling!" Rose Marie cried.

With the cups flying through the air, Sister Cilla kicked out her feet in an awkward dance, black skirt flapping.

Rose Marie giggled. "Sister Joan would have a fit if she saw you!"

Sister Cilla blew a raspberry, Rose Marie guffawed, and Sister Bernadette clapped her hands. Face flushed, legs kicking, cups soaring, Sister Cilla kept spinning around, catching and throwing.

As Rose Marie hooted and joined Sister Bernadette in clapping, Sister Cilla's dance grew wilder, more energetic, cups flying overhead like dizzy doves. The three of them were suddenly caught up, a procession of chaos whirling through the kitchen. Sister Cilla jumped, then lunged again and again, her hands a blur. Around the butcher block all three of them turned and swooped, their whoops rising and falling with the cups.

Off balance, Sister Cilla missed a cup. With a loud crack, it hit the floor. The handle hurtled across the room, and Sister Bernadette shrieked. Laughing so hard she could hardly stay upright, Sister Cilla managed to jerk to the left, plucking the next cup from the air. As Rose Marie and Sister Bernadette clapped, another cup hit Sister Cilla's knuckle, and she yelped. The cup flew to the counter, smashing on the edge, and white porcelain ricocheted around the kitchen. The three of them doubled over, gasping for air.

"What's going on in there?" Sister Joan's voice called from the other side of the kitchen door.

All three froze.

"I said, 'What's going on?'"

"Nothing to worry about," Sister Bernadette called.

"Didn't sound like nothing to me!"

"I dropped a cup," Rose Marie announced.

"Figures," snapped Sister Joan. Her exasperated footfalls pounded down the hall.

"Figures," Rose Marie repeated, drawing her lips in as Sister Joan did. She had seen Taki imitate the sisters so many times she was almost as good at it as her friend.

Sister Bernadette and Sister Cilla looked over at her, eyebrows raised.

"Oops." She clamped her hand to her mouth, but a giggle erupted through her fingers.

Sister Bernadette snorted, and all three, once again, broke into laughter.

By the time they were able to stop, they were weak-kneed. Propping themselves against the cupboards, they finished the dishes, not daring to look at one another. Rose Marie drained the dish tray in the sink just as Sister Bernadette turned on the tap, and water sprayed them both. Oh my, that started them off again!

"Sister Cilla, where did you learn to juggle?" she was finally able to ask. Her stomach ached, and she felt limp as an old sheet, but happy—as she hadn't felt since Taki left. "I've seen you toss rolls of socks in the air for the first-year girls, but never cups. I didn't know you could juggle cups!"

"Dear, oh law," Sister Cilla panted, untying her apron. "My big brother and his friend learned to juggle in high school, from a library book, believe it or not. They practised all the time. Someone gave Sean, my brother, a unicycle, and his friend chopped down an old bike and made his own. They juggled and rode unicycles at the same time. His friend taught himself to walk tightrope too." She paused. "Bernard." The name stuck on her tongue as if she didn't want to let it go. "Six foot four. Wavy hair. I was fond of him, and he of me." She gazed out the window at the long shafts of light on the horizon. "Or so I thought." The mood in the kitchen had changed, and *blue* drew like curtains between the three of them. Rose Marie hung her dishtowel on the hook and slipped out the door and down the hall to the sewing room.

Reaching into the fabric cupboard, she pulled out the bag of cotton pads she had sewn the previous week. She crept upstairs and deposited a handful in her bedroom closet. The rest of the bag she took up the next flight of stairs to the dorm. They would be in her wardrobe when she needed them in the fall.

She was turning to go back downstairs when she saw it pulling from a dark corner of the room. Oh, a blunt shadow head and thick, short arms! Not the shadow sister. Slowly, she backed away until her back hit the cold metal of a bedframe. Squeezing her eyes shut, she crossed herself. *Blessed are the poor in spirit, for theirs is the kingdom of heaven.* When she opened her eyes, the shape was gone. She dashed out the dormitory and down both flights of stairs, back to the safety of the kitchen.

"Since you're back, you can help me roll oats for tomorrow's breakfast," Sister Bernadette said, turning to her. "Rose Marie," she exclaimed, holding out a rolling pin. "You look like you've seen a ghost."

21

Happy Birthday to You

MOTHER GRACE FOUND Sister Margaret on the back porch instructing Rose Marie on how to shuck corn.

"Not like that," Sister Margaret objected, her chins jiggling. "Grab it by the top. Pull two or three leaves at once or you won't get all that silk stuff. No, pull harder! Heavens to Murgatroyd, if my lumbago weren't so bad, I'd do it myself!"

"I've been looking for you, Sister Margaret." Putting a hand on the woman's shoulder to distract her from Rose Marie's half-hearted efforts, Mother Grace wished her a happy birthday. "Rose Marie, did you know it is Sister Margaret's seventy-fifth birthday today?"

Sister Margaret's scowl deepened as Rose Marie mumbled an unenthusiastic "Happy birthday, Sister."

"I'd like to speak to you before we eat," Mother Grace said, and Sister Margaret turned, giving her such a baleful look, she had to wonder if the woman didn't know exactly what she was about to say.

"Now, if you're not busy, Sister. In the dining room."

As they passed through the kitchen, Sister Margaret looked longingly at the cake Sister Bernadette was icing, and Mother Grace contemplated whether a chunk of it might sweeten Margaret's mood. But lunch was almost ready, and she shouldn't jump to conclusions. Sister

Margaret might very well be relieved to hear what she had to tell her.

Once they had sat down, each of them grunting softly at the effort, she got right to the point. "Sister Margaret, due to your venerable age, I'm going to lessen your workload. Sister Cilla will take over as senior dormitory supervisor. Of course, you'll still have your duties in the dorm, but you can leave a lot of the running around to Sister Cilla."

Outrage bubbled across Sister Margaret's face, and despite herself, Mother Grace felt herself blanch. Sister Cilla, of all people, stepped into the room with a handful of cutlery.

"I guess I'm too old to be useful," Sister Margaret bawled. Sister Cilla had the good sense to freeze in her tracks. "I'm not the oldest one here, you know. Sister Lucy is. And I'm sure not sick. Just a little lumbago is all. No appreciation. All my hard work, and now I'm not good for anything!" Sister Margaret's bottom lip quivered. She looked over to Sister Cilla, who was slinking back to the kitchen. "I guess someone less experienced can run things better than me. I guess I'm just too feeble—"

"Nobody thinks you're feeble," Mother Grace cut in. Now Sisters Joan and Bernadette were coming into the dining room. *Vieilli*, and Rose Marie right behind them. She raised her voice to include them all. "We more senior women need to allow the younger, more energetic ones to contribute, Sister Margaret. It's time to take things easy before we wear ourselves out." She attempted a lighthearted chuckle as she struggled to her feet. "Now let's eat, everyone. This is a celebration."

All during supper, Sister Margaret was pouch-eyed and silent, saying nothing, not even to Sister Joan, except "Pass the butter."

After the meal, Sister Bernadette brought in the birthday cake with a large 75 inscribed in blue icing. Everyone clapped, and Mother Grace led them in "Happy Birthday to You" while Sister Margaret glowered.

Sister Bernadette handed a large corner piece of cake to Sister Margaret. As soon as it was in front of her, Sister Margaret grabbed a fork in her meaty fist and plunged it in, metal tines screeching against the porcelain plate.

22

Dead Chickens

ROSE MARIE HAD learned how to make the most of summer. Sure, Taki was gone, but Papa visited her Sundays, and sometimes she was able to sneak off during the day and walk to the marsh to see the young ducks diving in the reeds or trying out their wings. She could sleep in once in a while, and the sisters were more relaxed than during the school year. But this summer wasn't the same as usual. The sisters were different, less fixed somehow. Or was it her? She wasn't entirely sure anymore what was really happening and what she imagined. Sometimes her dreams seemed completely real. And those awful ghosts. The shadow sister touching herself. That new thick shape. A man.

When she was little and saw the spirits of trapped and snared animals fly out of their bodies, Papa said she had power. Mama said she could see the world in all directions—forwards and backwards. Now, she just wanted to see it the same way everyone else did.

She was sitting at the breakfast table staring at her doughy waffle and pondering all these things when Mother Grace leaned towards her. "There's still a lot to do before the school year starts, Rose Marie."

More chores, no doubt. She nodded dully.

"What it means, *chérie*, is that we'll have to cancel at least two of our catechism classes."

"Pardon?"

"Preparations have fallen behind. Surely you don't mind having time off from your studies?"

"But, Mother Grace, you've never cancelled catechism before. Ever."

Mother Grace patted her wrist. "I'm afraid I need you to help Sister Lucy," she whispered, looking over at the old woman at the table behind them.

Rose Marie turned to see Sister Lucy tilted in her seat, her face as blank as her apron.

"Rose Marie will take you up to your room, Sister Lucy," Mother Grace shouted. "You need to rest."

Rose Marie took her arm, and they climbed to the second floor, Sister Lucy moving at an alarmingly slow pace.

"Are you okay, Sister?"

Abruptly, Sister Lucy stuck a crooked index finger in her face and shook it. "You are one shameful girl, Sister Mary of Bethany. It's disgraceful, the way you prance around here. I have eyes, you know. I can see what's going on with you, with you and, and that so-called—" She waved at the floor below.

For no reason at all, Rose Marie was stung with guilt. Who was this Sister Mary? She opened her mouth, but she was stopped by Sister Lucy's expression of outrage. She couldn't think of a thing to say.

After Mass on Sunday, Rose Marie spotted Papa going to Mother Grace's office rather than the visiting room.

She waited for him in the hall. "What is it, Papa?" she asked him as soon as he emerged.

Facing her, he cupped her shoulders in his hands. "I have to go back up north."

"No, Papa. Just one more Sunday."

"I can't wait any longer. Joseph has to start school. Day school." A pleased expression glanced over his face. "He will come home on a bus every day."

"Fine!" She sounded just like Sister Joan. "You're leaving me after only—what?—six or seven visits? So you can see him every single day, all year round. That's just fine."

Sister Lucy limped in and sat on the other side of the visiting room. As if they needed a guard. As if this were a prison, a goddamned prison—and it was. It most definitely was!

Rose Marie stamped her feet, trying to stop the heat darting up her calves.

"Sit down, my girl."

"I'm not your girl!"

Sister Lucy squinted at her. How could the old bat hear only when she didn't want her to?

"You don't even love me," she flung at Papa. She was about to run, but he caught her arm.

"I talked to that Mother Grace again," he said. "She won't let you come with me." His hand gripped her arm more tightly as she tried to shake him off. "Stay still, Sinopaki. That Mother Grace got another letter from Indian Affairs. *Kiikaa!* I seen it myself. Just now, she shoved it in front—"

Papa started to cough, and she broke free. Down the hall to the kitchen she ran, Papa coughing and waving his arm at her. She banged through the back screen door into the blinding afternoon.

Papa had Joseph. Why would he want her? No one cared. She raced past the garden, past the shed, down the path to the barn, where no one would look. She hated them, hated the school and all the nuns! She hated Papa and Joseph.

The stink of chickens. Oh, at her feet, a flock of headless birds! Pulpy-necked, their feathers slick with blood, they staggered around her. A scream hatched in her throat. Headless chickens lurched and stumbled, smearing her with their blood and feathers and stink. Just as the scream flew through her mouth, the birds faded, disappearing in their own deaths.

She ran faster, past the wire-mesh fence and into the barnyard. No one but Brother Abe was supposed to go near the barn. The chickens wouldn't lay if they got scared, he always said. She didn't care, not even if it was true that any little noise made them start pecking one another. She didn't care if they all moved in for the kill at the first sight of blood. She didn't care, she didn't care, she didn't care!

As she raced around the barn, she could hear the chickens start up, the pound of her feet driving them into a loud squawk. In her mind, she saw Papa and Joseph having supper together in Aunt Katie's kitchen. The squawking and flapping in the barn grew frantic, her breath coming hard. She would run them all away—the birds, the sisters, Papa, Joseph, and Aunt Katie—beat them into the ground with her beating feet.

She ran until her eyes blurred and her breath caught on fence wire. Gasping, choking, she stumbled through a chaos of flaps, pecks, and *blue*; through straw, dirt, and chickenshit. She fell against a fence post.

Up, way up, at the very top of the barn, a flicker of movement caught her eye. There, near the overhang of the roof, at that small door, was a thick man's shape. Then a hand outstretched, pushing.

The black shape plummeted against the blue sky, the flaring afternoon sun. *You bitch!*

Oh God, *she* was flying, falling, cursing! She smacked the earth with a bone-crushing thud. Pain ripped out her breath and drove through her head, her chest, her splintered ribs.

Forgive me. A guttural voice bubbled in her throat, words grinding in her jaws like broken teeth. A man's voice: *For I have sinned. In te, Domine, speravi, non confundar in aeternum.* A priest's language. A cold wave of fear surged from her belly. *Forgive me, oh my God.* She/ he was dying.

Her body was a bag of sand and splinters. Everything else had seeped away. She opened her eyes, unsure of where or who she was, what had happened.

In the barnyard, yes. Hurting, retching, she crawled. Like tape pulled from a window, the priest's broken body separated from hers. She crumpled against the garden shed and sucked in barbed air. She'd stay here until death had folded itself back—years, lives away—from that terrible time.

"I don't know where Sister Cilla got to," Sister Bernadette huffed as Rose Marie dried the supper dishes. "You'll have to put them away tonight, dear."

"Sister Bernadette, I was just wondering," she began. She bit her lip to stop her voice from trembling.

"Yes?"

"Who is Sister Mary of Bethany?"

Sister Bernadette's hands shot out of the dishwater, one falling to her breast. "Where did you hear that name?"

"Sister Lucy called me that."

"Well, she shouldn't have!" Sister Bernadette slipped her hands back in the water, her brow furrowed.

"Is she the sister who died?" It was just a guess, but she had to know.

"A terrible tragedy." Sister Bernadette sighed. "How did you hear about it?"

"Mother Grace." She crossed her fingers behind her back. At least she wouldn't have to invent anything to confess to Father William that week.

Sister nodded. "We never found out why exactly, what claimed her. Father Alphonses brought old Doc McDougall from Hilltop—that was the year before he retired—but there were no visible signs. And not a month after that *other* death." Her voice fell to a whisper. "No one wanted a fuss made. Dr. McDougall put it down as a heart attack, young as Sister Mary was." She rubbed a forearm over her brow and sighed. "It may very well have been a heart attack, for all any of us knows."

"Sister Mary of Bethany slept in my room, right?"

"Yes. Why? You haven't seen—"

"No," she said quickly. The lies were slipping from her mouth as easily as prayers.

"It's just that there were some silly stories afterwards, that's all."

"But did she—Sister Mary of Bethany—stay in the dormitory sometimes?" She had seen her there countless times.

"Yes." Sister Bernadette grabbed a clump of steel wool and started scouring a pot. "Sister Mary was not always dutiful, and she was required to do penance in the dormitory one summer once the students left. She was, well . . . she liked to flirt. You know, with the volunteer painters from the community, farmers bringing food, anyone. Harmless enough, but not suitable for a servant of God. I shouldn't be telling you any of this, but Mother Grace said that if she wasn't acting as a sister should, then she couldn't sleep on the sisters' floor."

"The other death, Sister—"

"I'm not saying another word!" She rinsed the pot under a torrent of water and banged it into the dish rack.

"Was it a man, a pr—"

"Enough, Rose Marie!" Sister Bernadette scuttled over to the stove.

"Please, Sister." Oh, she had a million questions, but Sister Bernadette's unyielding back told her their conversation was over.

23

You Make Your Bed

THE BUSES WERE scheduled to come back to St. Mark's on Monday, the fourth of September. Classes were to start the following day.

Right after breakfast, Rose Marie helped Sister Cilla carry the ladder from the tool shed up to the dormitory. They set it under the first window, and Sister Cilla, climbing to the top, instructed Rose Marie to sit on the second rung from the bottom. "For stability, dear."

Rose Marie was anxious for Taki to arrive. Already bored with helping Sister Cilla, she slouched, resting her chin in her hands.

"Dear, oh law," Sister Cilla panted from above as the ladder quivered. "This one's stuck."

Rose Marie got up and turned sluggishly around, kneeling on the bottom rung and placing a hand on either side of the ladder. She found herself staring up Sister Cilla's long stockinged legs, oh, and white drawers! Quickly, her face burning, she looked down at the floor she had spent most of the previous day washing and waxing. This summer she was seeing all sorts of stuff she wasn't supposed to see and didn't even want to! She closed her eyes, braced her feet, and held tightly to the ladder rattling under Sister Cilla's tugs and jerks.

As Sister Cilla descended, they both heard the popping slide of wheels coming to a stop on gravel and the huff of a bus door opening. They ran to the one low window in the dormitory, shuttered and locked during the school year "to keep busybodies in their beds," Sister Margaret claimed. Sister Cilla kept it open all summer just as she did the high windows. Now she and Rose Marie stared down at the first group of girls spilling into the schoolyard.

"There's Rachel Useful," Sister Cilla pointed out. "Dear, oh law, look at those little first-years. One, two, three; looks like four from that bus alone. And there's Judith Shot One Side looking more . . . mature than ever."

"Yeah." Rose Marie, surveying the outline of Judith's large, high breasts and long legs, had to agree. "She looks like a grown-up."

But it wasn't Taki's bus, and Judith's figure couldn't hold her attention for long. She went back to the ladder and waited for Sister Cilla to take hold of the other side. Together they carried it to the next window.

A window later, they heard the second bus arrive and scurried back to the low window. Looking down on the girls, Rose Marie quickly established that this wasn't Taki's bus either, but Sister Cilla wouldn't budge.

"Becky Old Bear isn't on that bus," Sister Cilla said. "Ager Many Guns wasn't on the first one. What will the older girls do if they don't come back to school, Rose Marie?"

"Stay on the Reserve, most of them, I guess, Sister." She really wasn't sure. She hadn't been to the Reserve for years. But she had heard the senior girls chatter about their plans, and often the intermediates and juniors had gossip to share. "Some might go work in the city," she added.

She dimly recalled her grown-up boy cousins Elias and Charles, who had left for jobs in the mines just before she was taken away to school. Soon afterwards, Auntie Constance had followed them. She hadn't thought of those relatives in years. Was Auntie Connie still in Coulee? Had the boys married?

"Some might get married," she added.

"That's what I'm afraid of! They're far too young for that kind of responsibility. It's a very big decision for a young woman to make. For any woman. She has to know what she truly wants and what kind of man her husband-to-be is." Sister reached down and placed long, warm hands on her shoulders. "Promise me you won't do that, Rose Marie. Leave the school at fifteen or sixteen. Promise me now."

"No, I won't."

Sister smiled. "You seem very sure of yourself."

"I am. It's because I have nowhere to go. I'm stuck here." Her words surprised her, but yes, that was it.

Sister Cilla gave an abrupt laugh. "It's all right. I'm stuck here too." She paused. "You make your bed, you lie in it."

Moving slowly, they set the ladder beneath the last window. The sky had turned dull and gloom seeped into their limbs. Rose Marie was heavy with it, and she could tell that Sister Cilla was as well.

"When they were done, they went downstairs to help out with the students, but Rose Marie couldn't seem to shake the *blue* that had come over her, and she plodded back and forth with piles of nightdresses, towels, and face cloths, ignoring the sisters' orders to "Hurry, hurry, hurry!" She filled and dumped basins, threw piles of severed braids into the garbage can, and guided snivelling first-year girls in and out of the bathroom, but she was doing it, Sister Joan complained, in an "irritatingly unhurried fashion!"

"Slow as molasses in January," Sister Margaret agreed.

She heard girls' voices coming from the front hallway. Within seconds, she was at the front doors under Our Lord Jesus Christ, hugging Anataki.

"The bus kept breaking down," Taki explained, squeezing her.

Taki's hands were cold, but her eyes held the light that sometimes seemed to fill her to the brim.

"Hey, you're taller," Rose Marie gushed, noticing how her friend had changed over the summer. "You're so tanned, and your hair's sun-streaked." As they hugged, she could feel Taki's body—substantial, with no poking bones, and, jeez, her boobs seemed to have sprouted as well.

"I sure missed—"

A whack across the back of her head.

She spun around to find Sister Joan standing over her, lips pursed. "Stop that!"

Hugging was forbidden, as far as Sister Joan was concerned. But Rose Marie couldn't care less what Sister Joan said or did. "The old rhymes-with-witch," she whispered to Taki, and the two of them giggled into their hands.

At supper she announced, "This year'll be better," to Anataki, Maria, Susanna, and Martha, all sitting at her end of the table. "Sister Cilla's in charge of the dorm now. We won't have to worry about old Sister Margaret coming up after lights-out, swinging her stick."

She and Taki stayed up late that night. Like several of the other intermediate and senior girls, they comforted the sobbing first-years long after lights-out, stroking their newly cut hair and reassuring them. "Everything will be fine in the morning. Don't worry, your mama and papa will come visit before you know it."

"Lies," she told Taki, who nodded vigorously. "But what else can we say?"

"It won't do them any good to cry their heads off all night long, scared half to death," Taki reasoned.

Once the last little girl had whimpered herself to sleep, Rose Marie and Anataki stuffed their pillows under the covers of their beds and tiptoed to the bathroom. Inside, Taki snatched Rose Marie's hand.

"I got something to tell you, Rose Marie, since you're my very best friend in the whole world."

"What?"

"*Oh-kioysi,*" she said. "My moon cycle started over the summer."

"What do you mean, your 'moon cycle'?"

Taki didn't answer. As she turned her chin to the door, she looked grown up. And smart, like she knew things. That old burning sensation in her belly again. She wondered if Taki was growing up faster than she was, growing away from her—if she wouldn't want to be her friend anymore. And if she ever lost Taki . . .

"Mama told me about it. It's like when a girl gets old enough, and one day she'll get married and she'll be able to have babies because when she was younger, like we are now, her body got ready for it by building a nest for the baby to grow in like when she's with her husband, you know"—Taki, grinning broadly, reached over and slapped her on the upper arm—"*with* her husband."

"What?"

"You know, *kyak*."

But Rose Marie didn't know the word. Not anymore.

"You *know*!" Taki insisted, rolling her eyes. She pressed the palm of one hand against the tops of the fingers of the other and pushed back and forth with a springing motion. "Getting a baby."

For a moment, Rose Marie felt completely stupid. Then, "Oh." The ritual of strut and pose, chase and flee, offer and accept. She had seen it with elk, deer, and even frogs around her home so long ago. Had heard it with Mama and Papa a few times when she had woken in the night. The first part of the dance with Aunt Angelique and Forest Fox Crown down in the bush behind the house one time they stayed with them. That had made her laugh out loud from her hiding place in the willows, and hearing her, Forest Fox Crown got real mad and shouted, "Get lost, *pokaitapi*!"—scaring her silly.

Now she thought of the shadow sister with her snaky hips.

"And when a woman's not, you know, like going to have a baby," Anataki continued, "the baby-nest all comes out, like in blood between her legs, when the moon is in the right phase, at least the right phase for her, because it's different for each one of us, and that's why it's called *your* moon cycle."

Rose Marie didn't know what to say.

"And when you have your monthlies," Anataki continued, "it

cleanses you and puts you in harmony with the world. That's why women can't do sweats or ceremonies four days before and four days after the blood cleansing. We're way too powerful, can make others sick, even." She grinned. "Now we can make new life. Powerful," she said, striking her chest with a fist, her voice thick with pride. "We're powerful, Rosie!"

"But—but the blood," Rose Marie stuttered. "It's like a bad thing." She was confused. "You know how the seniors always hide their cotton pads under towels when they go to the bathroom so no one can see, and how they all keep it secret. And what about the time I heard Bertha say, 'I have the sickness today,' like she hated it or was kind of ashamed or mad even?"

"Yeah, I know, but really, it's a good thing, Rosie. My mama told me." She felt the last trace of her *blue* slip away. Maybe it wouldn't be gone for long, and maybe Taki was wrong that the blood was a good, a cleansing thing, but she felt happy just the same. She grabbed Taki's hand.

"Me too." She laughed. "I got my moon too."

"Really?"

"Yeah."

"Rose Marie," Anataki said, frowning and folding her mouth into Sister Joan's expression of disdain, "you are becoming a young lady, and it's about time you acted like one!"

Snickering, they fell against each other.

Oh, it was so good to have Taki back.

24

Iikss-tah-pik-ssi-wa

ANATAKI HAD IT every September—nausea and vomiting caused by the residential school food. By October, she usually had recovered and was once again accustomed to the meals, though thinner. Even though Sister Margaret did little in the way of cooking, for some reason, she took Anataki's reaction personally every single year.

Rose Marie, returning from Mother Grace's office after her first advanced catechism class of the new school year, heard Sister Margaret declare from the sisters' dining room, "Good gracious, it's not our fault. Whatever they give that poor Anne at home—dog eyes or gopher brains, I can just imagine—it's turned the child right off the *sensible* food we serve here at the school."

Sister Marg, tub of lard, Rose Marie thought to herself. The "sensible" food Sister was praising was what Taki called *makapii*, really bad. Once Taki had even called it *tistaan*, poop, then made a barfing noise that almost made her really, truly barf. Rose Marie scurried to the kitchen to join her class for what Sister Bernadette called "cooking lessons" and the girls called "making everyone's damn lunch."

This year, her seventh at the school, Anataki's illness lasted not much more than a week, yet she had very little appetite throughout

September, and by the end of the month it seemed to Rose Marie that her friend had lost all the weight she had gained over the summer. Once again, her eyes looked too large for her face, and her hair, chopped short by Sister Joan, hung limp at her ears.

"I'm sort of tired, Rosie," she told her the first week of October, when Sister Cilla took a group of them east to the frozen-over marsh to skate and slide. "Not puky sick. Just yucky."

After the tramp across the prairie through a skiff of snow, Anataki could barely catch her breath, and when they started Crack the Whip, a game she loved, she coughed so hard she collapsed on the ice.

"Anne, that's a terrible cough," Sister Cilla scolded, peering down at her. "I daresay you need a day or two of rest in the infirmary. Lots of liquids." She fixed Rose Marie in her gaze. "And no visitors sneaking in, keeping you awake."

Anataki shook her head. "No, I'm fine, Sister Cilla. Just a frog in my throat."

A few days later, her cough was even louder and lasted longer, her cheeks were flushed, and as she tried to get out of bed in the morning, she staggered and fell to the floor.

Rose Marie rushed over. "Hey, you okay?" Crouching beside Anataki on the cold floor, she laid her hand on her forehead. "Holy moly, are you ever hot! Is she ever hot, Sister!"

"Rose Marie," Sister Cilla said quietly, "help Anne into the infirmary. I'll be there as soon as I get the morning shift moving." She clapped her hands. "Those on kitchen duty should be downstairs by now. Let's go, girls!"

Even though her face burned, Taki whimpered that she was "freezing." Rose Marie fetched the blanket from her bed and took it to her friend. Holy mackerel, as she tucked it under Taki's chin, she noticed how dull her eyes were.

"Get better," she whispered, grazing Taki's cheek with her chin.

"Make sure you come visit me, eh, no matter what Sister Cilla says."
Taki's eyes fluttered closed. "Promise, Rosie?"

"I promise."

At noon, Rose Marie glimpsed Sisters Cilla and Margaret in the sisters'
dining room, so she dashed up the stairs to the top floor. When she
stepped into the infirmary, she saw that Taki was perfectly still. The
door clicked shut behind her, and suddenly the heap of bedclothes
shook, and Taki shrieked, "Get out of here!"

The words slapped Rose Marie in the face. *You get out of here*, she
was about to yell back. *I waited for you all summer, and now you don't
want me? You can get the hell out of here and stay away from me!* But
then Taki turned and squinted through the darkness.

"Rosie? Thank goodness it's you. Come here!"

As Rose Marie neared the bed, Anataki reached out, grabbed her
hand, and clung. "I think it was her," she choked out, shuddering. "That
one you told me about, *sta-ao naatowa-paakii*."

"What?"

"You know, that ghost nun. I woke up and there she was. Oh, Rosie!
Then she just like, jeez, disappeared! Please, get me out of here!" She
coughed until her eyes ran.

So Taki had seen her too. And Taki believed her, had always believed
her. "But Sister Cilla will kill us," she hissed back. "She doesn't want
you to have visitors even."

"I don't care. Please, Rosie," Taki begged, squeezing her hand.

"She goes in the dorm, anyway, that shadow sister. You'd see her
there. She won't hurt you, you know."

Shivering, Taki closed her eyes, tears welling behind her lashes.
"Then you have to stay with me, Rose Marie!"

"I will."

She sniffed the chicken broth on the night table. Sister Cilla must have brought it up, but it didn't smell right, and she didn't want Taki drinking it, not with her stomach. She carried it into the bathroom and flushed it down the toilet, then poured Anataki a glass of water.

"Drink it," she ordered when she returned, snatching a pillow from the next bed. Setting it by Taki's head, she took off her shoes and climbed in beside her. The heat from Taki's body burned right through her uniform. "Now go to sleep." She curled against Taki's back. "Snug as a bug in a rug," Sister Cilla sometimes said to the first-year girls. She closed her eyes and drifted.

A warm wind rippled the horse's mane, its broad back swaying beneath them. She tightened her grip on Taki's waist. Everything was warm: the horse, the breeze licking her hair, and Taki's tummy beneath her sweaty palms. They were headed for the border. In another day, they would see Taki's family's camp and the great ii-nii *grazing in the distance.*

The following day and the day after, other girls came down sick: three first-years, two juniors, and stupid Bertha Bright Eye, now a senior. There were only six beds in the infirmary, so Anataki took the opportunity to tell Sister Cilla she was feeling better. "Let a little one have my bed. I can go back in the dorm."

"Oh dear." Sister Cilla looked pained.

"You look good, Anne," Rose Marie said. "She looks almost better, Sister."

"All right, then."

"I hate that hospital room," Taki whispered to Rose Marie as they rushed back to the dorm. "I'm glad I never saw her again, that shadow sister, and I was always scared she'd come back, but I think I saw someone else, someone worser! Listen, this morning while the other sick ones were sleeping, this man, this—"

The entrance door swung open and the first-year girls spilled into the dormitory. Rose Marie, not wanting to be sent to the kitchen for washup duty, dropped to the floor, crawled to her wardrobe, pried the door open, and hid inside, oh, forever it seemed, all cramped up, while Sister Cilla got the little ones washed up and in bed.

Taki didn't have a chance to tell her what she had seen, and later, cranky after her long wait in the wardrobe, Rose Marie didn't ask.

25

A Burning Bush

NOT TWO HOURS from St. Mark's, fires burned beneath the soil. Every once in a while, someone reported seeing flames that reached up from the very bowels of the earth.

"Overactive imaginations" was what Mother Grace had put the stories down to when she first arrived in the region decades before. Fanciful tales dreamed up by some drunk stumbling home three sheets to the wind or an Indian recalling a heathen tale. Perhaps the fancies of a bored farmwife or the delusions of an overzealous Presbyterian. But the stories had persisted—a new sighting every few years.

Then word came down in a letter to Father David from the Anglican priest of the Sarcee—a Dene tribe near Calgary—of a bush bursting into flame.

"Hear this, Sisters," Father David cried in his trembly voice as he shuffled into the dining room at suppertime. In a scrawny hand, he had a letter, which he held up not an inch from his milky eyes. "*Something out of the ordinary has occurred five miles east of the Reserve here. Two of my parishioners, both solid Christians, witnessed a bush bursting into flame on the prairie. Let me assure you, no cause was apparent. There have been no lightning strikes recently, only cool, clear weather. I myself witnessed the bush burnt to a black stump, while no other vegetation was affected, save a patch of weeds at its base."*

"Father Winston thinks it's a sign from God. What do all you holy women think?" Father David demanded, squinting around at them.

"Heavens," Sister Bernadette said, dropping her fork. "It must be a sign from God!"

"Not coal burning under the surface?" Father David demanded, once again revealing his perverse nature.

"And the Lord appeared unto him in a flame of fire out of the midst of a bush," Father William cut in just as Mother Grace was contemplating the same verse.

"Yes, Father William. The Lord or the Devil." Father David smirked, enjoying himself. "As you know, the Devil often mimics God."

Sister Joan huffed, Sister Margaret snorted, but other than that, no one responded. Father David, clearly disappointed at not being able to spark an argument, speared a pork chop onto a plate, snapped it up, and shuffled back upstairs to his suite. He ate in his room most of the time these days. No great loss, was Mother Grace's opinion. The man did nothing more than give Mass once a day and attempt to provoke the sisters. And Mass was becoming more abbreviated by the week.

"It's God," Sister Cilla said as soon as Father David had left. All the sisters nodded in agreement.

That night, picturing a dry little bush erupting in flame in the midst of the bare prairie, Mother Grace couldn't sleep. Signs from God had been scarce of late, and she wanted, no, *needed* a sign. *Assist me, O Holy Spirit, strengthen me in my weakness, help me in all my needs.* She envisioned coals smoking, turning from black to red beneath the surface, then flames leaping forth—a miracle, *certainement.* Or perhaps a catastrophe.

There had been a time when she felt fire within her own bosom, an unruly, unmanageable fervour. There was a time when being close to Father Patrick, her professor, seemed to give credence to that fire, to both feed and control it, to turn it from a volatile blaze to a powerful furnace.

As a student, she would see him on campus during his office hours, and they bantered about matters of theology that suddenly became exciting, essential even, igniting her brain, while Catherine, her companion, waited, impatient and cranky, to walk back to the Mother House with her. A brief question about the story of Susanna and the Elders in the book of Daniel had turned into a discussion about the diminishment of female figures in doctrine, she recalled, that lasted two riveting hours. After that, Catherine, despite the regulations for novices of their order to travel in pairs, had taken to waiting in a cubicle down the hall, her head on the desk, her snores discreet.

Oui, and one day while Catherine dozed, Grace had realized that being close to Father Patrick no longer checked her fervour, but made the fire leap higher and burn hotter within her. That day she had reached out and touched his hand. Abruptly, he had stood, and, stunned, she rose too. As Patrick strode around the desk towards her, she found herself leaning into him, ready to be caught up in his arms. She would not resist, she knew, could not. There was nothing she had wanted more.

Out of the corner of her eye, she saw movement in the doorway. She gasped, Patrick turned and dropped his arms, and both of them faced Catherine, who was peering in, her face creased with sleep. Seeing her companion, she had felt not relief, but disappointment, God forgive her. And she knew it was disappointment she had seen on Patrick's face too.

After her course finished the following week, she would see Patrick only by accident. That was when they had begun to correspond. And in the end, she had given all her passion back to the Lord. She looked up at the wooden cross hanging over her door, the one Patrick himself had made her.

Rose Marie was now a young woman. Would she succumb to a similar disturbance of the heart? Would the fire within her burn faithfully, a beacon to the unholy world from which she had sprung? Would it blaze up erratically, dangerously, as it had for a few months with her? Could it engulf her as it had engulfed Sister Mary of Bethany, destroying all potential?

"Lord, allow me to help, to guide her, to fulfil Your purpose here on earth. I am Your instrument." She longed for an event, a cause, an epiphany—something important to direct the rest of her life—a burning bush, a sign, a miracle. *Dieu soit loué.*

26

Jam

AFTER RECOVERING IN late October, Anataki took sick with a fever and that terrible cough again in early November. On St. Elizabeth's memorial day, she was in bed when a snowstorm closed the roads and brought down telephone lines.

At the start of their catechism lesson, Mother Grace complained to Rose Marie that with the damage done by the "inclement weather," she was unable to get Dr. Stanton's advice by phone or medicine brought in by car. "Though why he refused to drive out here and check Anne and the other sick girls earlier, I don't know." She did, of course, know, but she wouldn't tell Rose Marie how little most of the outside world thought of residential schools and their students. "I called the man every single day for a week. The next week he had the nerve to have his nurse tell me he was 'indisposed.' Indisposed indeed!" Mother Grace's blue eyes narrowed. "And now it's too late. No one can get through. We'll just have to make do."

Poor Taki had to be helped to the toilet, her arms looped over Rose Marie's shoulders or wrapped around Sister Cilla's waist. She was scalding hot and thin as a reed.

"She's really, really sick, Sister Cilla," Rose Marie said. "What can we do?"

"Anne really should go back in the infirmary as soon as a bed comes free."

"Don't put her there. Please, Sister. It gives her the creeps."

The next day Sister Cilla had Rose Marie, Beth, and Susanna help her lug Anataki and her bed to the west side of the dormitory. "Now her coughing won't disturb the other students, and we can keep a close eye on her."

"Jam," Rose Marie heard Taki whimper to Sister Cilla, who instead brought her chicken broth from the kitchen. Watching Taki's nostrils quiver, she knew the broth had been sitting warm on the stove far too long, that it should have been outside in the cold. Why was Sister Bernadette so careless? Most of the girls' stomachs were used to sour broth by now, but not Taki's. She watched as Sister Cilla raised a spoonful to her friend's lips.

"No, Sister," she cried, running over. "The chicken broth isn't good for Anne."

"Rose Marie, it's exactly what Mother Grace ordered, and she used to work in a hospital, you know." Sister Cilla continued spooning the broth into Anataki's drooping mouth.

Ten minutes later, Rose Marie held Taki's hair off her face with one hand and grasped the back of her nightdress with the other as she bent over the toilet bowl, vomiting. More than the chicken broth, she noticed. Something greenish-black.

"Jam," Taki pleaded to her that night when she snuggled in beside her. "Bread with jam," she croaked once before falling asleep.

The following day, Rose Marie spread her bread with the dollop of jam on the side of her plate and put it on the bench she had always shared with Taki. Then she was on her feet again, squeezing herself back in the cafeteria line in front of Abigail and Leah, who were too busy talking about putting their hair up in pins to even notice.

On her third try, Sister Bernadette looked her full in the face. "Just what do you think you're doing, Rose Marie? I already gave you lunch."

"Anne," she whispered. "She's so sick, and all she wants is jam, Sister."

"Mother Grace said that the sick girls are to be given water and broth only, things easy on the stomach."

"But, Sister, she won't eat broth. All she'll eat is jam."

"Heavens to Betsy. Well, I guess it won't do her any harm." Sister Bernadette retreated to the back of the kitchen and returned with a jam sandwich wrapped in wax paper.

My, oh my, the smile on Taki's face when she saw those two slices of bread with jam and one jam sandwich! By noon the next day, Taki had eaten them all, and she didn't even throw up. She slept all afternoon, and sleep was good, Rose Marie knew. But not that cough. Different from Mama's or the one Papa had. "Whooping cough," she heard Mother Grace whisper to Sister Cilla. Rose Marie didn't like the tone of her voice one bit.

Late that night, sitting on the toilet, Rose Marie opened *The Magnificent Prayers* she had borrowed from Mother Grace and flipped through the book. She had always said her prayers, she had to, but like the other girls, she muttered them mainly out of duty and habit. Now, she decided, she would take them seriously. She used to take the medicine of Papa and Tallow, her grandmother, her Naasa, seriously, but what good had that done? Mama had died, Papa caught the bad cough, and she was stuck at the school all summer, Christmas and Easter too. She would find the very best prayers in this book and memorize as many as she could. She'd see if they worked on Anataki.

Tiptoeing through the dark dormitory, she knelt by Taki's bed. *Through torments and insulting words, I beg Thee, O my Saviour, deliver Anataki and me from all enemies. Including sickness,* she added, climbing in beside her friend. Taki was light in her arms, like a bird, a baby bird struggling to fly. "I won't let you go," she whispered as she threw a leg over Taki's shivering body. "You have to stay here with me."

Gradually Anataki's shivering fits lessened in the night. She was barely trembling when Rose Marie, her arms and legs still locked around her, floated down the grey river to sleep.

They were lying against the walls of a tipi: she, Anataki, Taki's mama and papa, and two big brothers, each of them wrapped in a skin, ready for sleep. She could hear Taki's breath slow and deepen, feel the shift of her body as she curled in on the night. Up through the smoke hole, summer stars blazed like hope in the black night.

Early the next morning, as she crept from Taki's bed to her own, she prayed. *Merciful Jesus, who art the consolation and salvation of all who put their trust in Thee, I humbly beseech Thee by Thy most bitter passion, grant the recovery of Thy servant, Anataki Two Persons.*

Wind howled outside the school and shrieked threats through door and window cracks. The roads were still closed, and no visitors or supplies had reached the school for weeks. There was no medicine for Taki, and Sister Cilla kept bringing her sour chicken broth from the kitchen.

"She's too sick for bread and jam now," Sister Bernadette told her at lunch. "I'm sorry, Rose Marie."

That night, snuggled beside her friend, Rose Marie drifted into sleep, dreaming of Taki's summer camp.

As the morning sky turned from pink to egg-yolk yellow, Taki helped her aunt and mother clean up after the morning meal while Rose Marie, in the meadow close to the tethered horses, watched Sik-apsii creeping towards her. Suddenly Awa-kaasii was behind, pulling her braids. She cried out, spun around, and ran after him, the three of them laughing and sprinting through the long grass, dodging, calling out, and backtracking. They darted between the horses, past the two older women and Taki, who looked wistfully after them as they chased each other over the long, loping plain.

Rose Marie awoke. Sweaty, lips crusted, Taki mumbled in her sleep. "What? What did you say, Taki?" But she couldn't make it out.

Heal her for her soul's welfare, that with us she may praise and magnify Thy holy name. My Taki.

Another night, another dream.

She and Anataki, on one horse, her two brothers on another, rode along the cricket-buzzing bank. "There," Sik-apsii said, pointing. Down in the creek bed, a frantic calf nosed the bloated corpse of its mother lying in shallow water. Glancing around, Rose Marie noticed two coyotes slip through the grass. Awa-kaasii and Sik-apsii urged their horse to a gallop. Awa-kaasii raised his arm and swung a rope in a loose circle. It flew towards the skittering calf, flopping in the water beside it. Cursing, Awa-kaasii pulled the rope back and tried again. This time the lasso landed on the calf's woolly back, but he bolted away, shaking it off. Damn! The coyotes slunk closer.

Rose Marie prayed: *Look upon Anataki in Thy lovingkindness, preserve her in danger, give her help in this time of need.*

She dabbed Taki's burning cheeks with a damp face cloth, and Taki's eyelids fluttered. She grunted, then waved a hand in front of her face, knocking the cloth away. A sound trickled from her lips.

"What?" Rose Marie leaned closer. "What did you say, Taki?"

"If should die before I wake—"

"No. No, don't say that."

Taki coughed, her torso heaving and crumpling on the bed, her hair dry twigs scattering over the pillow.

Through the Immaculate Heart of Mary, I pray, I beg, please make Anataki better.

Rose Marie ran to the bathroom and held the face cloth under the tap. Returning to the bed, she squeezed a little water into Taki's mouth, then gently pressed the cloth to her cheeks, throat, and forehead. She took Taki's hand and held it tight—a burning coal. *Soul of Christ, be her sanctification. Body of Christ, be her salvation. Save her life here, on earth.*

She went to her bed for nightly prayer, then lay down, closed her eyes, and waited. As soon as the dormitory was quiet, she stole over to Anataki and climbed into bed beside her. Curled into her friend's warm back, she fell asleep.

The next day at catechism, Mother Grace said, "This is what Esther prayed in her time of trouble: *O my Lord, who alone art our king, help me, a desolate woman, and who have no other helper but Thee.*"

That night Rose Marie prayed by Taki's bed, ending as Esther had, but with a small revision: *O God, who art mighty above all, hear the voices of we who have no other hope, and deliver Anataki from illness.*

She and Taki were riding their horses in the summer afternoon heat, racing through goldenrod and broomweed, the haunting scent of sage. As the western sun dazzled their eyes and licked their shoulders, joy gushed from their mouths. Just then, Taki's horse cut in front of hers, and turning, Taki whooped, waving crazily.

"Wait for me, Taki," Rose Marie shouted, giggling and spurring her horse on. Ahead, Taki's hair whipped from side to side, black as midnight, white as summer stars. The wind, the grass, the horses' manes, even her own hair flew wild and free through the heat and grass and insects.

Jesus Christ, do not forsake Anataki in her needs and afflictions, she prayed when she awoke later that night.

Ahead, Taki's horse charged forward in a lightning flash of speed. Rose Marie lowered her head and urged her own horse on, "Go-go-go . . ." her heels tucking into the horse's flanks. Below, hooves stitched a carpet of gold to the golden light and the golden rope of the horizon that went on forever and ever, amen.

Holy Trinity, one God, have mercy on her.

Beside her in bed, Taki burned like a candle.

Far ahead, Taki rode into the vivid setting sun. Her horse's hooves flicked light as he reared.

Rose Marie pressed a cold cloth to Anataki's forehead and temples. "Come back, Taki."

Maybe there was mud under her horse's hooves. Maybe that's why he couldn't sprint as fast as Taki's horse. The harder she kicked, the slower he moved and the farther they fell behind. "Taki, wait!" she cried, but the earth was holding them. She dropped her head along the horse's long, sinewy neck, whispering, "Go-go-go," but her voice was waterlogged, heavy, sinking in prairie gumbo. Around her, the clouds shuddered to a standstill.

Anataki, on her lightning horse, leapt into the sun.

When Rose Marie awoke, Sister Joan had not yet snatched up her brass bell and marched down the nuns' hallway, clanging it to signal the start of another day. The dorm was dark and silent. She knew it was very early.

A first-year girl whimpered in her sleep from the back of the dorm, but other than that, it was quiet. Rose Marie glanced at Anataki beside her, one arm reaching out to the cold wall, her head slumped on a hollowed shoulder, and her mouth open, revealing a row of shiny teeth. In the thin winter light, she looked peaceful, no longer burning, coughing, and wheezing. God had answered her prayers. Taki's fever had broken! She reached over to touch her forehead.

"Sister Cilla!" she cried, springing out of bed. "Sister Cilla!" She pushed through the door to the hall. Gripping the rail, she hung over the banister. "Sister Cillaaa!" she screamed.

Behind her, sheets shuffled and mattresses creaked. "Who's yelling?" a sleepy voice complained.

"Sister Cillaaa!"

She raced back to the bed. Gazing down, she slid one arm deftly under Anataki's head and her beautiful face fell towards her. With the other hand, she made the sign of the cross on Taki's forehead. "I claim you for Jesus," she whispered. She could hear Sister Cilla's big feet pounding the stairs, and she threw herself across her Taki.

From Thine anger, O Lord, deliver her. From the peril of death, from an evil death, from the pains of hell, from all evil, from the power of the Devil, by Thy Nativity, by Thy cross and passion, by Thy death and burial, by Thy glorious resurrection, by the grace of the Holy Ghost the Comforter ...

She felt Sister Cilla's hand on her arm, but she shook it off. Someone close by started wailing in her ears, the sound of broken wings and suffering animals.

"She's gone," Sister Cilla whispered. "There's nothing we can do. Stop, Rose Marie, please stop making that noise."

The day thickened to clay. She tried to move her limbs through it, but she couldn't. She was hardening to stone. At night, she lay petrified between cold grey sheets. Time shifted around her and compressed.

"Rose Marie," Sister Cilla said, kneeling by her bed. "All the other girls have gone to class. You must get up."

Oh God, what have You done?

"Rose Marie," Sister Margaret barked, "I won't have this!" She grabbed a handful of hair and yanked, dragging her from the bed. Head wrenched back, Rose Marie hung by her hair until Sister Margaret let go. She dropped to the floor.

Grant that I may die in Thy love and Thy grace. Grant that I may die.

"You have to eat, Rose Marie."

She pried her eyes open a crack and saw an angel in black standing over her, a bowl in her hands. The angel of death. *Let me die too.*

"Try a little food, Rose Marie. Please."

Jesus, Mary, and Joseph, assist me in my last agony.

The Virgin took one hand and Joseph held the other. They led her away from the dark angel and her bowl of oblivion.

No. Grant me death!

"Rose Marie, I brought you a little supper." Mother Grace slid a hand over her head of stone. "Wake up, *chérie*. Just mashed potatoes. You can eat that."

Oh Lord, make no delay.

"Rosie?" Susanna perched her bony bum on the bed. "Are you gunna be okay?"

Don't call me "Rosie." Don't say the name Taki called me.

May the body and soul of Anataki be made flesh again. May she rise from the dead as Lazarus did. Raise her up. Or else take me too.

"She said something!" Susanna yelled across the dormitory.

Kneeling on the floor by her bed, the shadow sister raised her head.

Sweet Jesus, make sure you take Taki to heaven. Don't leave her here with the shadow nun!

Taki came to her. She smiled, sun glowing through her skin, her brimming spirit flowing. Behind her, the ii-nii grazed and faded into night.

The release started with Rose Marie's fingers. The top joint curled. Then the second joint. Her fingers folded into her palms. She could wiggle her wrists and turn her forearms. She struggled against the stone until it freed her shoulders, her back, vertebra by vertebra, her hips. Then her legs, ankles, and feet. The slate around her face cracked, and she opened her eyes. She was in the dormitory, and it was empty.

She would do one last thing for her friend.

Stiffly, she climbed out of bed and tottered to the bathroom. The stone in her belly was shattering, water rushing through, a hot river. She sat on the toilet and pissed while the world trembled and slowly began to turn again. She pissed forever, it seemed.

One foot in her stocking. The next foot. Pull them up, over her knees, her thighs. Dress over her head. Arms in. Shoes on. Walk. Then run to the chapel.

"For the repose of the soul of Anne Two Persons, we ask you," Father William sang, stretching one hand out to the congregation.

"Lord, hear our prayer," the first-years, the juniors, the intermediates, the senior girls, Brother Abraham, Mother Grace, and all the sisters chorused. Rose Marie joined them.

The next morning, Rose Marie got up with other students and went downstairs to the dining hall. She stood in line for breakfast and sat where she always did, the space beside her, Taki's seat, empty.

"Heartsick," Mama had said when she told her the story of Auntie Constance, how she hurt and moaned, clutching her sides, and Father Alphonses had to drive her to the hospital in Fort Macleod so she wouldn't die.

The problem was a baby growing in the wrong place. "The doctors gutted Connie like a fish, took everything out," Mama said. "No more babies. She was heartsick."

Rose Marie felt like she had been gutted. She was heartsick too.

A hand on her shoulder. Turning, she saw Sister Cilla gazing down at her. "How's Rose Marie?"

She couldn't speak.

After roll call, Sister Joan ordered the class to the sewing room. The girls stood up, filed through the door and down the hall. Rose Marie's body moved with them. Air leaked into her lungs, seeped back out. In, out. One foot, two feet. As she neared the front entrance, two people pushed through the door, cold spilling in behind them.

Anataki's parents. She knew them from her dreams. Someone must have told them. She heard Sister Joan walking behind her, so she turned the corner and pressed herself up against the wall.

"May I help you?" Sister Joan demanded, her words breaking from the stale biscuit of her voice.

"We've come for our girl's body," Taki's father said.

So they weren't going to let her be buried out back with the others, the dead ones whose names were forgotten as soon as they were in the ground with a wooden cross planted by Brother Abe. A cross that got buried by snow and splintered by drought, that fell apart and blew away. But if they took Taki's body, she wouldn't be able to sneak out to her grave. She wouldn't ever be able to visit her.

"Yes, the Two Persons." Sister Joan's voice softened in pretend sympathy. "Come with me." She started off towards Mother Grace's office.

As Taki's mama took a step forward, her eyes found Rose Marie flattened against the wall. For a fraction of a second, they traded looks like arrows, each shuddering into the other's heart with piercing pain. Then Rose Marie slipped down the wall and crumpled on the floor.

27

Mould and Charcoal

A T MEALTIME, SITTING at the table she had once shared with Taki, Rose Marie tried to eat. Porridge, bread, peanut butter, mashed potatoes—everything stuck to the roof of her mouth and wouldn't go down. In class, her mind floated and refused to light on any of the lessons. Her eyes stung, full of grit.

"Rose Marie, stop daydreaming!" Sister Joan yelled. "Wake up. Snip, snap."

At night, she tossed and turned.

"Rose Marie, I'm going to speak to Sister Cilla about putting you to bed at the same time as the first-years, since you're so dozy."

When all the girls were asleep, the shadow sister slunk through the dormitory, and behind her crept a shadow man. Goose pimples and ice danced up and down Rose Marie's arms. She pulled the covers over her head, squeezed her eyes shut, and bit her lip to stop from crying or screaming or jumping up and running for the door. Slowly, she climbed out of bed and crept over to the empty bed where Anataki used to sleep. No one had removed the sheets, so she slid inside Taki's smell of sweat and sick. As she closed her eyes, she finally felt the grey river of sleep lap the shore of her body. She tried to plunge in, to sink to the bottom, but the river withdrew, and she was left awake and aching. She tasted blood on her lip and sucked, trying to shift the pain from her head and guts and bones to that one small cut. No dreams. No Taki.

In class, her eyes watered. She yawned.

Sister Joan smacked her across the head with the rolled-up student roster. "What's wrong with you? I asked you a question, missy!"

In advanced catechism, Mother Grace told her about the imperfect sacrifices of the Old Testament and God's desire for one clean sacrifice to be offered throughout the world. Rose Marie wriggled.

"Have you no respect for what our Lord endured?" Mother Grace demanded.

"I'm sorry." Her eyes filled.

"Anne is now with God, dear child." Mother Grace's papery hand folded over hers. "Pray for her soul. You can do no more." She straightened in her chair. "I don't think either of our hearts is in the lesson today. *Va t'en*, and take the Bible with you. Read the book of Malachias for your next lesson. God willing, it will put you to sleep."

That night, Rose Marie watched the stocky man break from the darkness and trail the shadow sister. As he crept by her bed, his odour of mould and charcoal made her stomach lurch. She pulled a blanket over her nose but could not shut her eyes or look away. He wore black with a white stripe at his throat. A priest's collar.

His meaty hand leapt to the sister's shoulder, and turning, she gasped. His hand moved to her neck, and a ray of moonlight from one of the high windows caught a ring on his finger—gold, engraved with an *X*—making it flare. The sister opened her mouth to scream, but his thumb pressed her throat and only a gurgle spilled out. His other hand fumbled with her long skirt. Her fingers tore at his wrist. He pushed her hard, and she crashed into the wall.

"Stop!" Rose Marie cried. She shoved her fist in her mouth as the two fell against each other and plummeted to the floor, the sister flailing under the thump of his body, the priest grunting. She would suck her fist down her throat. She would suffocate.

A flash of metal. It was the kind of knife Sisters Joan and Lucy used for cutting out paper crosses, stars, and lambs to tape on classroom windows. Rose Marie saw it clearly, pulled from the sister's skirt pocket and clutched in her hand. She saw the blade tear into the priest's face, heard him bellow.

Lights flashed on, then off again. Abby First Eagle snorted, and a mattress creaked. Someone came through the entrance and strode towards her. The angel of death. *I pray the Lord my soul to take.*

"Rose Marie, is that you? Are you awake?" Sister Cilla bent over her bed. "What was that noise? Are you crying?"

Wiping her nose with the back of her hand, Rose Marie couldn't stop the flood of tears and snot and sobs. Sister Cilla stroked her shoulder. Two rows ahead, Abby was making piggy snorts.

"It's Anne, isn't it, Rose Marie? You miss her."

She shook her head. "No, that's not it." Then she nodded, choking. "It is, but it's so much more!" Everything was terrible, the school, the whole, wide world. Sobs shook her body. The more she tried to stop, the harder she cried.

Sister Cilla's hand patted her back. "There, there," she comforted, now drawing circles as she made soft, reassuring sounds. Just like Mama used to do.

One of the junior girls sat up, said, "Oh," and sank back to sleep.

As her sobs subsided, Rose Marie was overcome by embarrassment. "I'm sorry, Sister," she muttered. As she looked up at Sister Cilla, she noticed her nightcap was askew.

"Sister," she whispered. "Your hair. It's almost long."

28

The Confessional

R OSE MARIE SAT in Mother Grace's office. They were about to start her catechism lesson when Father Alphonses knocked on the door. Mother Grace struggled to her feet.

"I'll be right with you, Father." Turning to Rose Marie, she told her to read ahead. "I won't be long."

Rose Marie pushed her chair closer to Mother Grace's desk and leaned heavily on her elbows. She knew Mother Grace would pester Father Alphonses with a million questions, as usual. *"What's new in the parish, Father? Tell me everything. Did you bring a newspaper?"*

Rose Marie pressed her palms to each side of her head, trying to squeeze out the ache and grief and ghosts. All morning in class, she had worked hard to concentrate.

"I see you're with us today," Sister Joan had announced. "How nice."

She picked up *A Child's First Confession: Its Fruitful Practice,* but the book slipped from her fingers and tumbled back on Mother Grace's desk, pages splayed. Folding her arms on the top of the desk, she laid her heavy head on it. She had been nine at the time of her first confession, she recalled.

* * *

"Remember when I put a tack on Sister Joan's chair?" Beth had asked as they huddled around her in the dorm just before lights-out.

"Yeah, Sister never even noticed," Taki quipped.

"So much the better," Beth retorted. "I never got caught *and* I've got something to confess now."

"Eww, that's good!" Martha Buffalo squealed. "Should I confess stealing food?"

"No, stealing breaks one of the Ten Commandments," Beth warned. "A mortal sin. Sister Joan will make you pray on your knees down the whole chapel aisle. Probably the Commandments to copy out too. Unless you can get Rose Marie to write them for you." Beth had glanced over at her, sniggering.

Rose Marie retaliated. "As everyone knows, E-liz-a-beth"—she pronounced the name just as Sister Joan did when she was mad—"the priest can't tell the nuns what you confess. Only God."

Just then, Sister Margaret snapped out a warning and switched off the lights. Lying awake in her bed while the other girls, one by one, stopped whispering and fell asleep, Rose Marie decided to take her first confession—*her reconciliation with God*, Sister Joan had told them in class—seriously. She was fed up with being awake at night with no company but ghosts no one else ever saw. She would tell Father David what she had never told anyone but Anataki.

Next morning, inside the confessional it was dark, almost as dark as the dormitory at night. The prayer bench was low, and she had to raise her head to speak through the screen. They had practised what to do in Sister Joan's religion class, and Sister Cilla had gone over the procedure with all the girls in third year for a few nights just before bed, but still, she felt small and bewildered.

"Good afternoon, my child," Father David greeted her, but no light flooded down from heaven, no flame ignited her heart, no wings of deliverance had lifted her spirit.

"Have faith in the Lord, my child."

"Amen."

"Blessed is he whose transgression is forgiven, whose sin is covered."

"Forgive me, Father, for I have sinned," she muttered. "This is my first confession, and I'm not sure if God is really here."

She had been so ignorant.

"The Lord thy God is with thee whithersoever thou goest."

"I confess to Almighty God and you, Father, that I hate those people at night!"

"Speak up!"

She raised her voice only slightly, afraid the other girls waiting their turn outside the confessional would hear her secret. "Father, something happens at night, things I see, things that no one else knows about."

"What is it you see?"

She leaned on her elbows to raise herself closer to the screen so Father David would hear. "They come out of the shadows. They walk all around the dormitory. That nun, a young one who isn't even here in the day. She talks to me."

"A nun?"

"Sick girls too." She stopped. She thought she heard something—a scoff in Father David's voice—and she wondered if he believed her. She wanted him to lift the edge of her fear, to pull it from her with his old fingers, then explain it, pray it away.

"Dead ones," she said. "Lydia, Ruth, Maryanne. I see them when they leave. But mostly, it's just the nun." Her voice became a whisper, but Father David, his ear pressed to the screen, didn't ask her to speak up again. He didn't speak at all.

"Child," he said finally, "I believe you're dreaming. *May the Almighty God have mercy on you, forgive you your sins, and lead you to Eternal Life. Amen. May the Almighty and Merciful Lord grant you pardon, absolution, and remission of your sins. Amen. May our Lord . . .*" He went on forever before muttering the words she expected to hear: "*I absolve you of your sins in the name of the Father, and of the Son, and of the Holy Ghost.*"

She would never confess to seeing shadow people again. He thought she was dreaming.

Now she raised her head and stared at the books on the desktop, Mother Grace's chair, the cross over the door, disoriented by all the years that had passed at the school. But one thing she knew for certain: she couldn't stand it, couldn't stand *them* anymore. The ghosts. She shoved *A Child's First Confession*, and it thudded to the floor. Hearing Mother Grace's footsteps coming down the hall, she quickly retrieved it.

"Rose Marie!" Mother Grace exclaimed as she entered, as if she was surprised to see her. One of her hands was locked around a newspaper, and her tongue flicked nervously over her bottom lip. She looked different, older than ever. "We'll have to leave things for today." She dropped the newspaper on her desk. *"Mon Dieu, Mon Dieu."*

On Saturday, Rose Marie went to confession even though she didn't want to. She tripped through a list of dumb venial sins but didn't say anything about the shadow people. Father William probably wouldn't believe her any more than Father David had. "Dreams," she was almost certain he would mutter through the confessional screen. Or "lies." "Say the rosary. In the name of the Father, of the Son and of the Holy Ghost." Blah, blah, blah. If only she *could* dream. Taki had taken her beautiful summer dreams with her.

On Monday afternoon during free time, she walked around the school grounds with Susanna Big Snake and Maria Running Deer, listening to them chatter about some singer named Elvis Presley.

"I think he's part Indian," Maria said. "You can tell."

Susanna nodded. "What a dreamboat!"

Blah, blah, blah.

She knocked on Mother Grace's office door. "Do you think I could attend evening Compline with the sisters like I do in the summer?" Perhaps if she were around the sisters more often, the ghosts would stay away.

Mother Grace examined her closely. "All right."

That evening she went to chapel with the nuns. After prayers, as the sisters rose to file out, she followed at a distance. Before she reached the font of holy water by the door, the new nun, Sister Simon, who was now the youngest, younger than Sister Cilla, turned off the lights.

Rose Marie made the mistake of looking back at the altar.

Moonlight drifted through the stained glass and revealed the thick outline of the ghost priest as he dropped to his knees before the crucifix.

"*Loathe*," Sister Joan had pronounced that day in class, drawing the word out and making Rose Marie remember maggots wriggling through a deer carcass. "The people loathed the lepers. Everyone loathed them but Jesus."

The shadow priest loathed himself, but watching him, she thought he was taking pleasure in his loathing, working at it like it was his sacred duty.

She needed her Anataki back. Who had always listened. Who had believed her, had even seen the shadow sister herself. She crossed herself with holy water and left the chapel.

As she climbed the stairs to the dorm, she remembered what Mother Grace had said to her that afternoon. Mother had been upset, still upset, and that newspaper on her desk was folded so tightly she couldn't read the headline. "God doesn't always answer our prayers in the manner we expect, Rose Marie. He provides answers, but we don't necessarily understand them. Not at first. We have to use this—" She had tapped her temple with a forefinger.

But Rose Marie's brain wasn't working. Her skull had cracked, and if she went up the steps too fast, pieces would break off and shatter. Yet she wasn't dying. All this *blue*, all her *heartsick*, and yet she just wouldn't, couldn't seem to die.

29

Paperwork

MOTHER GRACE ASSUMED that Father Alphonses had told William about Tom Two Horse's death firsthand, though he had informed her by simply muttering "terrible tragedy" and shoving the newspaper in her hand. *Body Found Behind Hilltop Catholic Church* the headline screamed, as she opened it on the kitchen table.

Since reading the article, she had tried not to think of Tom, yet thoughts of him kept dropping into her mind like black rain. *Aie foi en Dieu*, she told herself, pressing her fingers to her eyelids. Trust in the Almighty. Piled in front of her on the desk was the bookkeeping she should be doing, would be doing if she could stop the memories of Tom. She hadn't thought she remembered what he looked like, but *Mon Dieu*, there he was—a first-year boy, small for his age, his eyes as large and soft as those of a new calf, an immature and vulnerable child with no brothers or cousins to protect him.

Hearing footsteps in the hall, she glanced up in time to see Father William hurry past her door, a cup and saucer clattering in his hands.

"Father William," she called, but he didn't so much as slow down.

He was taking all his meals with Father David this week, carrying them up to their suite on the second floor rather than sitting in the dining room with Brother Abe. Perhaps he was afraid he'd miss Father

David now that the old man had finally decided to retire to the Oblates' facility in Toronto.

The first Thursday of Lent would be St. David's Day, and while honouring his namesake, the religious community of St. Mark would also celebrate Father David's service to the school. On the Saturday, Father Alphonses would drive Father David and his boxes to Hilltop to catch the train.

She wanted to ask William about Tom's death. Did he have any insights; indeed, any guilt? She could think of little else, and since Father William was avoiding her, she would have to find out the details from Father Alphonses. Despite not having money in the budget for unnecessary calls, she reached for the phone and dialled the rectory in Hilltop.

"Well, Grace," Father Alphonses impertinently addressed her. "It was snowing and the walk needed shovelling. I went around the back of the rectory to retrieve the shovel. Nothing clears the mind before Sunday services like shovelling snow."

Such false levity, she thought.

"I was breaking ice from the top stair when I noticed something grey hanging from the big elm at the back of the yard. I couldn't tell what it was." There was a pause, and she heard the muffled sound of popping joints. Father Alphonses had an annoying habit of pulling at his cold fingers when nervous.

"He had hung himself," Father Alphonses said finally. "I hardly knew the young man, but he was a drinker. Hadn't made much of his life since he left school. Why he chose the churchyard to do his dirty deed, I can't say."

"Well, I can. Unless he was about to hitchhike to St. Mark's or St. Gerard's, there wasn't a more appropriate place. Both church and school were the sources of his suffering, and if you don't know that as well as I do, you can guess."

Her outburst startled her, and she pressed her fingers to her lips. Normally she held her tongue until she could think of a way to approach controversial topics diplomatically. But her jaw was sore with all the tongue-holding she'd been doing for the past four decades.

"Well . . . why . . . Mother Grace, I'll have you know—" Father Alphonses stuttered, but she had no time for his attempt at righteous indignation.

"That's all I wanted to know, Alphonses." And she hung up.

Just before supper, she heard Father William quietly making his way down the hall towards the kitchen. As quickly as she could manage, she got up from her desk and moved to the door.

"Father William." She stepped neatly in front of him.

"Oh." As she caught his eye, he looked down.

"I was just recalling when you were Brother William, before you returned to the seminary to become a priest."

He was clearly uncomfortable. "I'm afraid I, um—"

"The school was coeducational then. Remember?"

"Yes, Mother Grace, I do. I'm sorry, but I really must—"

"Of course, that was before the fire that forced the Antelope Hills students to attend St. Mark's. My, but it was crowded, wasn't it, Father? St. Mark's nearly burst at the seams. What did it take? Two years before we finally got money to build St. Gerard's and make it the boys' school? Another year before the doors opened. And it wasn't finished then. You went to St. Gerard's with the boys."

"Yes. Now I, um, really must get Father David his dinner." He ducked around her and rushed away. As if he knew exactly where the conversation was headed.

Mon Dieu, she could see now that so much of what had gone wrong at St. Gerard's and St. Mark's had been unnecessary. She was so naive back then. She should have opened her eyes. Instead, she did as she had always done: she had trusted her superiors and prayed to God that things would improve. Just as she was always advising the sisters to do.

And what good had it done? Father Damien, a man subject to

temptations of the flesh, had been sent to St. Mark's from St. Gerard's after he beat poor Tom Two Horse so soundly. None of the sisters had been unduly concerned when Damien arrived, because no one had informed them that he had been transferred to St. Gerard's from a school up north due to unseemly allegations involving senior girls. She still wondered if Father Matthew had told Father David, who simply hadn't passed on this "trivial" piece of information to Mother Paul Pius, or if Matthew had kept Father Damien's shameful conduct to himself.

To make matters worse, Father William, with his own proclivities, had remained at the boys' school. Why hadn't Father Matthew reprimanded Father Damien for his violence against Tom and then placed him under his watchful eye? If the man had a watchful eye in his empty head. Conversely, an all-girls' school would have been a much better place for Brother William, who had grown too fond of certain male students, the ill-fated Tom Two Horse for one. The beating administered to Tom by Father Damien had been the act that had started even more trouble.

She wished William hadn't run off just now. She wanted to be absolutely certain he knew about the death of Tom Two Horse. *Non*, he knew. She was certain of it. She turned back to her office and her accounts.

But she couldn't concentrate. Little Tommy was watching her.

He must have been ten years old when he went off to St. Gerard's with the other boys. And encountered the wrath of Father Damien, as it turned out. She remembered Brother William, while delivering supplies to St. Mark's, in a breathless recounting of the crime, describing the marks Damien had left on Tommy's back as "terrible welts on the boy's flawless skin." That was the beginning, she supposed, of Father William's subsequent fixation on young Tom.

And now the young man had hanged himself in the Hilltop churchyard. She folded her hands on her chest and closed her eyes. *Sweet Jesus, be not his judge, but his Saviour.*

Perhaps this third terrible death would signal the end of the monstrous cycle that had begun with the mysterious deaths of Father Damien and Sister Mary of Bethany—what was it, ten years previous, now? She must believe that. *For with Thee there is merciful forgiveness.* She hoped.

Crois en Dieu, she admonished herself. She had trusted in the Lord since she was a toddler nestled between her two big brothers as Maman read them Bible stories. Throughout her childhood, the family had never sat down to a meal, no matter how meagre, without a prayer preceding it. She had been raised to believe that through God's infinite mercy, anything was possible.

Maybe it was. The war had ended, after all, and the school budget had been modestly increased. And though the residential school system had its critics—she herself at times, she had to admit, and *oui*, Father Patrick certainly—though she had devoted a large part of her life to St. Mark's Residential School with its illnesses, deaths, and chronic despondency, though there were grumblings among politicians about closing the schools—the Lord would surely reclaim her years of service—often frustrating, always challenging—and redeem them. *Crois en Dieu.* In due time, He would reveal her true purpose to her.

She opened her eyes and looked around. She could almost see how it would happen: a younger, more vigorous woman with love in her heart to take over the running of the school as she aged. And someone else—a younger woman appearing, as if out of nowhere, a guide of sorts, someone to set things right. She, herself, would contribute as mentor and superior. She had her role to play, most certainly.

The books. She had to finish the first half of the fiscal year if it killed her. So far the school year had been a difficult one, and something concrete had to be salvaged, if only neat paperwork and a balanced budget.

30

The Visitation

ACH NIGHT, THE sun trimmed a piece of dark cloth from its hem. Ice melted in the schoolyard, and streams trickled by day, freezing at night. Rose Marie's body diluted, seeping into the wood, brick, and plaster around her. Each season, it seemed, the school absorbed more of her.

One morning, just after Sister Joan's clanging bell had broken her sleep apart, Rose Marie looked over to Susanna's bed and saw the shadow sister collapse beside it, hands pressing the side of her belly. *"He did this to me,"* she moaned.

She was everywhere now—Sister Mary of Bethany, or the ghost of Sister Mary, or *sta-ao*, whoever, whatever she was—always hovering in the dark corners of the dormitory or the bathroom, clutching her side as if in pain, muttering. But she was different too, less solid-looking than before, less human and active, but pervasive, ubiquitous. Rose Marie had to smile as she sank back into the mattress. There was no doubt that she was picking up Mother Grace's vocabulary. As she closed her eyes, she heard Sister Mary's voice drifting like a lost line: *He's killing me. Now I'm going to kill him.*

Her eyes flew open. She was about to hiss to the shadow sister, *"Go away!"* The words *you bitch* were stones falling through her brain and taking her back to that day in the barnyard with the chickens squawk-ing and the man falling through the blue summer sky. As she looked over to Susanna's bed, she saw the shadow sister's form—little more than graphite lines wavering over the floor, a pathetic sketch of a life. Oh God, oh God, oh God.

She just couldn't take any more. Not without Taki. She couldn't put it off any longer. She would tell someone. She had to.

Instead of filing to chapel with the other girls after lunch on Satur-day, Rose Marie ran up to the dormitory and opened the door to the wardrobe at the end of her row. She still wasn't sure if she was ready to tell Father William about the shadow priest and nun, how the priest followed the nun, what he did to her, and what the nun was about to do—no, already had done years before—to him. She needed a private place to think. As she crawled into the cupboard, she heard two girls come into the dorm.

"So, what are you going to confess this time?"

"I'm going to admit that I'm in love with Peter Gift to the Sun," a girl answered decisively. It must be Rachel, a senior who was always falling in love. Rose Marie was sure she recognized the characteristic thickening of her s's.

"No, you can't tell him that!" the other voice cautioned. Prissy First Rifle, Rachel's best friend. "He'll want you to quit him. Tell him you're worried about your immortal soul."

"My what?"

"Well, that's what the crazy one tells him, that Rosary Mary, what-ever her name is. I heard her once. Everyone else had gone and she went inside, so I put my ear against the confessional—"

"It's Rose Marie, stupid. And shut up. She's related to your cousin Esther."

"By marriage only. And her dad, you know, he's that medicine man, the one they call Blessed Wolf? Well, he moved away after her mum died and didn't even take her."

"Why don't you confess you listened at the door of the confessional?"

"Yeah, sure. Father would kill me. Hey, I know, I'll tell Father William I'm having impure thoughts."

"About who?"

"About him!"

Rachel started laughing. "And what will I tell him?"

"Tell him you're having impure thoughts too."

"About him?"

"No. About Sister Margaret."

Rose Marie, huddled in the closet, thought the girls would choke to death, they were giggling so ferociously. Even though they had stated plainly what she already knew—that many of the students thought she was nuts—she didn't feel the usual sting of rejection. In fact, she had to bite her hand to stop from laughing out loud. It was way too long since she had heard any of the girls laugh like that. The way Mama had laughed, making Papa laugh, and then her, all three of them. The way she and Taki used to laugh, jumping and snorting, tears running down their cheeks.

"Girls, get down here now!" Sister Cilla's voice blasted from the staircase.

Rose Marie could hear them rushing away, trying to muffle their giggles.

She'd wait a minute, crouched in the dark wardrobe. Then she'd go downstairs to chapel. She breathed deeply, smelling the musty stockings and underwear in the drawers under her, the nightdress hanging over her head. The toe of a shoe dug into her bum, but despite it all, she knew what she had to do. She'd tell Father William.

* * *

In the confessional, Rose Marie opened her mouth and let her words fall into Father's ears. She told him about the shadow sister, how for seven years she had witnessed the young nun on the top two floors of St. Mark's.

She heard Father William shift in his seat and scratch his beard. "Why have you never confessed this before?" he asked.

She smelled his sweat and his doubt.

"I *have* confessed it before," she told him. "Father David didn't believe me about Sister Mary of Bethany. But, Father William," she rushed on, "now there's someone else."

"Yes?"

"A priest, a terrible priest!" Her voice quavered. She saw someone through the screen, not Father William, but a young man, face bloated, his neck raw, a rope—"Oh, God help me," she murmured.

"Of course God will help you, child," Father William said. His voice was soft, almost tender, and the young man faded away. "But you know, now that Father David has retired to the east, I am the only priest here, and I assure you—"

"No, not you." She peered through the screen. It really was just Father William sitting in shadow, the edge of his beard half lit by the dim light on his side of the confessional. She was seeing too much, too many of the dead. Maybe she was imagining half of them. She had to get at least Sister Mary of Bethany's story off her chest, and Father Damien's too. Maybe that was her role. A witness to the dead. And maybe the discloser of secrets. "It wasn't Brother Abe either. It was a ghost priest," she whispered.

"A ghost priest." He snorted. "Well, what can you tell me about this, this . . . ?"

"Black oily hair brushed straight back." She closed her eyes to concentrate. He was slightly taller than the sister, but how tall was that? "Rusty eyes. He wears a ring with an X on it. And he has a cut on his cheek." She swallowed. The words, which had come easily when she started the confession, were now clogging her throat. "Something ugly happened," she said. "Disgraceful," a word Sister Joan liked to use. She wouldn't tell Father William that she wasn't exactly sure what it was. She could hear him wheezing through the screen.

"I'm listening," he said, suddenly intent.

"He jumped on Sister Mary of Bethany." She pushed her words over the lump in her throat and kept her eyes lowered so she wouldn't see the man with the swollen face and raw neck if he appeared next to Father William again. "He did something to her. She was in pain."

A voice whispered in her ear, Mama's voice. *Auntie Connie,* she said. And then Rose Marie knew.

"She had a baby growing in the wrong place. He did that to her, and now she wants to kill him. I think, Father William, she might have, well . . . asked him to meet her there, in the barn." She remembered the small, high door on the side of the barn and a hand outstretched. "I think she pushed him from the top of the barn."

Finally, she had said it out loud.

Silence.

She was afraid of what would happen now, but she had heard Mama's voice. Mama was with her. From time to time.

Mother Grace didn't look up when she heard the rap on her door. The faltering knock of a faltering man, she thought as she signed her name in a flourish to the supplies order. Surprisingly, today her hands didn't ache at all.

"Come in." Two tentative footsteps came across the floor. She looked up—into the face of Rose Marie Whitewater. "I was expecting Father William."

"Father William told me I should come tell you, Mother Grace. What I saw. What happened."

"Yes, Rose Marie?" The girl looked different, Mother Grace thought, though she couldn't put her finger on how, exactly. "Don't be nervous, *chérie*. Sit down and tell me what on earth you are talking about."

"Father William said I should tell you about my *Visitation*."

The last word was forced, louder than the others, a word Rose Marie obviously was not familiar with. One Father William had, no doubt, supplied.

Rose Marie studied her small hands, and when she looked back up, her expression was calm, though her sentences were rushed. "Sister Mary of Bethany is always in the dorm and now Father Damien is too. They were dead, but they couldn't leave."

Heavens! Mother Grace blinked. The dear girl must have heard about the events of that terrible summer ten years before! *Mon Dieu*, she had done everything she could to prevent rumours and speculation. If any of the students returning in the fall asked where Sister Mary of Bethany was, she had instructed the sisters they were to be told she had gone east. Other than that, there was to be no further talk of the incident, lest the students overhear.

"What, dear child, do you mean?"

"Please listen, Mother Grace. Father William wants me to tell you what I told him in confession."

"All right." She sighed impatiently, yet she had to admit, her curiosity was piqued.

"The sister and the priest wander through the dormitory. I see them and others too—girls mostly, who died here. I've seen them so many times and—"

"Ghosts?"

"Yes, Mother Grace."

Mon Dieu! After Sister Mary of Bethany's mysterious death, several students and two of the sisters had sworn to seeing her in the dormitory, Sister Lucy being one of them. And poor Lucy had never been the same since. *Nom d'un chien,* wasn't it enough to endure the unexpected deaths of two religious without having ridiculous stories to contend with, she had thought at the time. "Surely the figure of Sister Mary of Bethany is nothing more than the product of fear," she had cajoled Sister Lucy.

She pressed fingertips to her temple. Was this the beginning of a blasted headache? To this day, Sister Lucy refused to enter the girls' dormitory. At first Mother Grace had tried to reason with Lucy, then to shame her. Finally she had admitted defeat and given her only duties that could be performed in the laundry room, the sewing room, the kitchen, or classrooms.

"Maybe Sister Mary of Bethany was supposed to meet Father Damien in the dormitory," Rose Marie continued. "I don't know, but she was there and, oh, Mother Grace, he snuck up on her. He attacked her! She slashed his face with a paper-cutting knife. She had a baby growing in the wrong place."

"What a tale!" *What nonsense*, she thought. Wincing, she opened her mouth to say more, to dismiss Rose Marie's story as "silly superstition," to admonish her. While very bright, Rose Marie was also highly strung. *Oui*, and at one time she most certainly would have been convinced that Rose Marie was delusional. But a full year after the deaths, on a late-summer evening when she was checking supplies in the dormitory, a sister had slipped behind her, quick, moving only as the young do, and she had turned and—*Mon Dieu!*

Later that night, as she sipped brandy in her office, she had wondered what exactly she had witnessed. The white apron, drawn-up skirt, and familiar face made wretched by despair were still sharp to this day, far too sharp in her mind. At the time, she had wondered if her vision was merely the manifestation of her own disillusionment, her spiritual fatigue. Eventually that's what she had convinced herself. Now she examined Rose Marie's expression, and the girl looked her straight in the eye.

"It's true," Rose Marie said evenly. "She pushed him from the barn."

Right then, Mother Grace realized that her spiritual fatigue had lasted until this very moment. As her heart skipped a beat, she was overtaken by another thought, a surprising one, thick, heavy, and intractable as stone: *What a revelation!* She could feel herself smiling.

But she had a question. Looking at Rose Marie, perched in the same chair she occupied twice a week as she learned of God's word and the Church's ways, she asked, "If indeed you saw ghosts so many times before, why then did you never mention them to me, dear girl?"

But she knew the answer before she had finished the question. She wouldn't have listened. While she was always talking about "the mystery of Godliness," she hadn't believed her own words. She had thought everything had a reason, and, *bien sûr*, that she knew most of them. A phrase from Daniel jumped into her mind: *Children in whom there was no blemish, well favoured, and acute in knowledge.* Was God offering His wisdom through this girl? *A little child shall lead them.*

All doubt fell from her. Like scales, she reflected after supper as she made her way to chapel. Heavy metallic scales that had held her together in pride and in fear. Cold scales, impenetrable, an armour. All the times she had prayed to God for a sign, she had not believed it would come. Now she was experiencing the same kind of marvel of faith God had worked on St. Joseph in convincing him of his betrothed's purity. On her uncle Gabriel as well. God's hand was in this Visitation, most certainly.

Her eyes found Jesus on the huge cross at the altar. *Lift up your eyes on high and see who hath created these things.* Kneeling, she felt weightless, gloriously incandescent, and completely free of pain. *Praise God from whom all blessings flow. Praise Father, Son, and Holy Ghost.*

Later, as Mother Grace sat in her office feeling nothing less than *merveilleuse, incroyable, joyeuse, bénie*, there was a knock at the door. Before she could say anything, Father William stuck his head inside.

"Did the girl come see you?"

"If you mean Rose Marie Whitewater, Father, yes, she did."

Father William slipped inside. As he scratched his beard, his eyes flickered from bookshelf to desktop, avoiding hers. "I instructed her to tell you, if she chose to . . ." His fingers dug under his collar. "Of course, I can't reveal a confession, but—"

"Something amazing has happened, Father William."

"Yes!" He looked at her, jubilation on his face. "I agree, Mother Grace. There are simply too many things the girl couldn't know. Father Damien and Sister Mary of Bethany: she described them to me in detail. Even their . . . what happened . . . the terrible—"

"Behaviour," she put in. "And consequences."

"Absolutely. She *knew* . . . everything. Her confession is no joke. I know these girls and their little games. Rose Marie was sincere. The school has been acknowledged by the Lord, our God. He has given us a sign—"

Mother Grace wasn't sure where this was going. "One we must reflect on," she interjected.

"Yes, of course." Father William was animated now, his bobbing head and flying hands against his black cassock making him look like a puppet.

But Mother Grace didn't smile. She was entranced.

"Given that this Visitation is a sign to the religious of St. Mark's," he continued, "we must ask ourselves, of what? I offer to you that it may very well be one of renewal. Our Lord has chosen to show us, *explain* to us, if you will, what took place so as to cleanse us of doubt and guilt."

"Guilt, Father?"

"Um, yes. For their deaths, I mean. But, Mother Grace, this vision, this Visitation, signals so much more. I suggest that the Lord is giving us a sign of forgiveness for that which has . . . um, transpired at our school, any . . . um, *missteps*. Most importantly"—his words began to gallop again—"not just for Sister Mary of Bethany and Father Damien, but divine forgiveness for all of us. The incredible love and mercy of our Lord has been revealed through this innocent's vision!"

Vieilli, the evening was taking on an air of unreality. Was he right? she wondered. Is God pardoning William for his misuse of Tom Two Horse? For all the mortal sins he may have committed with other boys? Does this Visitation absolve the transgressions of each of us?

Including her own in denying Rose Marie her father? And a hundred other things, from small omissions and inappropriate desires to major acts of cruelty?

"Don't you agree, Mother Grace?"

She was tempted. It would be so easy to believe, so beautifully freeing. "Perhaps you are right, Father William," she said finally, a grin warming her face. "Great is the mystery of Godliness."

31

Destiny

THE NEXT MORNING, cane gripped in her hand, feet slightly apart, Mother Grace stood before the tables in the dining hall, Father William beside her. Feeling nervous flutters in her breast, she took a deep breath and waited for the sisters to finish shuffling into the room.

In the darkest part of the night, she and William had decided to call a morning meeting before Mass. Since it was Sunday, they wouldn't call it a meeting but a "spiritual obligation." The plan had seemed sound then, but now, four hours and the briefest of sleeps later, she wondered if Father William still found it so. His eyes were bloodshot and his skin had a greenish tinge. Clearly the man was hungover, and no wonder. Together they had consumed her bottle of brandy and had started on the mickey of rye William retrieved from the priests' suite. She was feeling a little the worse for wear—tired, and her arthritis was, again, bothersome. Fortunately the three aspirins she had chewed as soon as she awoke were starting to do their work.

They had been in fine spirits last night, overwhelmed by what they now conclusively termed the Visitation. As always, William had liked the way his voice sounded as he spoke and gesticulated in her shadowy office.

"God answered our prayers," he had said, sliding his chair back from her desk and draining his cup. "I can't say I understand it. All I know, Mother Grace, is a miracle has taken place."

"Something monumental, at the very least," she agreed. She had stopped drinking by then, encouraging William to pour himself another rye. Though she felt exhilarated, she was also anxious. There was more she had needed to know, and something she had to ensure. "What else, William, aside from divine forgiveness, might we glean from this vision?"

"Recognition," he retorted promptly, and she cleared her throat.

"Well, no, Mother Grace. I didn't mean just me. Recognition for yourself . . . um, and the sisters too, of course. For all you've done. Your—"

"Our part in raising Rose Marie? After all, William, the revelation came to a child brought up by the Sisters of Brotherly Love. Under my supervision."

"Yes, certainly, but let's not forget that I was . . . I *am* the girl's priest and confessor. Not that I alone can take credit—"

"Of course you can't. Nor would you try. The Visitation comes ten years after the terrible deaths that blackened the reputation of St. Mark's. Once word gets around, it may very well release us from the stain of those deplorable tragedies. If handled properly. The religious community of St. Mark's, who have devoted their lives to the doctrine of miraculous events and graces, needs it. We all—every one of us—need it."

I especially need it, she had thought.

This morning, scanning her audience, she noticed Brother Abe was not in attendance. Probably in the barn with his damn chickens. The faces of the nuns puffed from their wimples like grey pussy willows, and she wondered if she had misjudged. Would they look first incredulous, then askance, at the strange news? Would Sister Joan laugh outright?

She cleared her throat, and the sisters' cups clattered to their saucers. That's when she knew that "God's hand was in it," as she was to write to Father Patrick later. Indeed, she read a flicker of anticipation in the eyes of every one, save Sister Joan.

"Colleagues," she began, "we have been through much together. Our path is often difficult, but we did not choose the service of God because it is easy. We chose this life"—she paused, suddenly overcome, then began again, her voice trembling—"because, though difficult, though trying, tiring, and just plain hard work, it was right. It was what each of us was called to do."

Wimples bobbed, and the sisters smiled wearily.

"Sometimes it seems that we try and try but have little compensation," she continued, the words pouring forth with little thought and no effort, *Dieu soit loué.* "Often our best attempts are met with anything from ingratitude to defiance. Though we do not work for material gain but for God's glory, we sometimes become discouraged, even bitter. We are only human, after all."

The sisters gazed at her. Hungrily, she realized.

"But every now and then we receive a smile, a thank-you that warms the heart, and we are reminded that our work is worthwhile. A smile, a thank-you—that's all we ask, more than we expect. And usually it's enough to keep us going for another day, another week, another month." She lifted her arms, and her voice rose. "We do not expect miracles. *Non.* We do not even hope for them." One by one, she gazed at her audience. "Yet miracles come unbidden. A miracle has come to St. Mark's, dear sisters!"

She noticed that even sour Sister Margaret was listening intently. Only Sister Joan was indifferent, peering out the window.

Mother Grace announced, "A sign from our Lord and God has been received at this humble school on the barren prairie!" She heard herself quote the Psalms: *"Bless the Lord, all ye Thy angels. He makest Thy angels spirits."* She spoke of the difficulties they had all endured teaching the precious word of God to little ones "ripped from the bosoms of their families," much to her own surprise. "Rose Marie Whitewater was one of those children. Rose Marie is the one through whom the Lord God has summoned us."

Grace à Dieu, you could have heard a pin drop!

"Jesus told us, *Learn what this meaneth: I will have mercy and not sacrifice.* Too often, Sisters, we focus on our sacrifice and not on mercy. Too often, we fail to demonstrate our love. But the Lord has offered a truth previously hidden from us. Through His revelation, He has absolved us of blame for the deaths of Father Damien and Sister Mary of Bethany."

She went quickly through the important information about the demise of the two religious. She wasn't about to get caught up in the sordid details, so she emphasized a sentence from the Act of Faith: *You have revealed them, who can neither deceive nor be deceived.*

"The Lord our God has verified His love and forgiveness to all at St. Mark's through Rose Marie's Visitation," she assured the sisters. *"Forgive if you have ought against any man, that your Father also who is in Heaven may forgive you your sins."* All her bodily pain fled; her voice soared and her eyes fixed on the crucifix over the door as she reminded the sisters of Jesus' words: *Unless you see signs and wonders, you believe not!* When she looked down at the sisters, she saw they were spellbound. All but one.

Sister Joan cleared her throat noisily. "Mother Grace, I can't help but wonder why the Lord God in all His wisdom chose Rose Marie Whitewater, one little Indian girl among so many, and every other one of them asleep, so there were no witnesses to His glory." Her tone was ironic. She looked over to Sister Margaret for support, but Margaret wouldn't meet her eyes. She tried again: "I only wish the Good Lord had seen fit to guide *me* in the same way Rose Marie supposedly was."

"Not surprisingly," Mother Grace answered severely, "God has seen fit to give us a sign through the student we rescued from the depths of heathenism, schooled and raised ourselves in the Word of the Lord."

"Thanks be to God," all the sisters uttered, all but Sister Joan.

Sister Bernadette turned to Sister Joan. "Think of my namesake, not to mention your own," she scolded. "Joan of Arc was visited and counselled by saints and Bernadette by the Blessed Virgin herself! As were so many others. I've been reading about Petruccia de Geneo, the widow of Genazzano in Italy. There are hundreds of instances of divine intervention."

The other sisters nodded wisely. Clearly, Sister Joan was alone in her doubt.

Then into the silence came a question. "Since the, uh, the Visitation happened to Rose Marie," Sister Cilla asked, flushing, "does that mean she has been chosen by God for a reason?"

Mother Grace paused. The question, an obvious one, hadn't occurred to her. Glancing at Father William, she could tell he had not anticipated it either. They had both been too caught up in what the event meant to each of them, how it defined their own lives. But she recovered quickly. "Why yes, Sister. Rose Marie is destined to join the Sisters of Brotherly Love, to serve the Lord and help her people. She has been chosen!"

"I knew as much," Margaret loudly declared. "That's why I've been a little hard on the girl at times. Something told me more would be expected of her. Why, I had a hunch the first time I laid eyes on her. I told Sister Joan as much."

Beside her, Sister Joan nodded sagely. "Yes, of course. Both Sister Margaret and I had a premonition, but we also had concerns. I was simply trying to establish the facts of the situation just now."

Was Sister Joan truly won over? Mother Grace wondered. Or was she aware that hers was an argument she could not win? In the end, it probably wasn't important.

"Why else would I give Rose Marie the necessary discipline right from the start?" Sister Joan continued, her voice growing more authoritative. "Of course, not everyone agreed with me."

Father William raised his arms over his small congregation. "Let us bow our heads in prayer. Let us praise the Lord, our Redeemer, the Light of the World, who died for us sinners."

"Our Father . . ."

"Who art in heaven . . ." the sisters joined in.

"Hallowed be Thy name . . ."

"Thy kingdom come, Thy will be done . . ."

"On earth, as it is in Heaven."

Soon, Mother Grace knew, she must inform Rose Marie of all this.

The next morning, Father William walked into Mother Grace's office, his face shining with oil and enthusiasm. Did the man never wash?

"Mother Grace, we must take steps to gain official acknowledgement for the miracle at St. Mark's!"

"Although we've been terming the Visitation a miracle, William, that must be decided by the Church and overseen by the Congregation for the Causes of Saints."

"It's miraculous for us. And it must be given the attention it deserves."

"Oui," she admitted.

"I'm thinking of a speaking tour," he continued. "Father Alphonses has agreed to come in Sunday afternoons to say Mass while I'm gone."

"Aren't you getting ahead of yourself, Father?"

"Of course I'd like your input, Mother Grace. Perhaps you could notify the various parishes."

"Perhaps," she allowed. "Now let's plan this properly. Sit down, Father. As I see it, you should travel as far as Fernie in one direction and Lethbridge in the other. It's impractical to go farther at this point. I have a feeling that at this particular time, with criticism of the residential school system in the news, the Church will seize upon the Visitation as a consolation if not a victory," she said, her cynicism shaming her. But only slightly.

"Yes, Mother Grace. Brilliant!" Father William pumped his fist in the air. "Could you also write a letter to the parish bulletins? You have such a talent with the written word."

"Flattery will get you nowhere," she responded, knowing it already had.

Far-reaching implications, she decided, would be a phrase to use that afternoon during her talk with Rose Marie. *Faith* also. *God's glory*, and especially *destiny*. Rose Marie would welcome the news, she anticipated. The girl needed encouragement as much as the rest of them.

Not quite a month later, Mother Grace had to admit that Father William, bless his small soul, had been right. The reputation of Rose Marie, humble, pious, *Indian* Rose Marie, grew like winter wheat over the prairies, thanks in large part to William's speaking engagements, and perhaps, a small share to her letters.

She was finishing an order for four new beds at the school when she looked up to see Father William standing at her door.

"*Show me, Lord*, I prayed when I was most uncertain," he cried as he plunged into the office, a letter in his hand. "And the Lord affirmed the miracle!"

"William, you're becoming more of an evangelist by the day."

"Not unlike St. Mark, Mother Grace. It all began with a note of enquiry from the Reverend Josepha Paul of Edmonton, which you answered for me. Then a letter of congratulation signed by Father Josepha and several other proponents of residential schools, all who found my news uplifting." Father William waved the papers in his hand at her. "And here is a letter of satisfaction from the Right Reverend Jacques Morin of the Oblates! My message is being heard."

She cleared her throat.

"The message, um, of the Sisters of Brotherly Love."

PART THREE

32

A Wolf Paw

SIIIIN—OOOO—PAAAAAAAA—

Ears pricked, Rose Marie lay unmoving in her bed. It was as if the wind and trees from her long-ago home were calling her name, an old chorus she knew, she used to know so well, many, many years ago when she was a child and not the most senior-senior of St. Mark's, a young woman just-turned nineteen, the only student to complete her high school matriculation, *Miracle Girl*, as she had heard some of the younger ones call her, their voices a mixture of reverence and disdain. She opened her eyes.

Two pinpoints of light, two distant stars moving closer, their rays pricking her skin. She could just make out a shape.

"Mama?"

No, the eyes of some kind of animal. A wolf, its coat luminous. And behind the wolf, something else. No, someone else. A man, his every step a dance, his right foot graceful as a spruce bough sweeping the ground, his left foot, uneven rain. He came towards her, his long black hair swinging through the night.

"Papa?"

He wore the shirt Naasa Tallow, Grandmother, had made for him, the one he always put on when he did his medicine—his power shirt. It was sewn from a wolf hide with a fur collar, but new now, not chafed and stained as it had been when she was a little girl. Beads rippled across the chest in bright patterns, shooting small moons against the wall. In his hand, an eagle feather.

"Papa!" she cried.

His spirit, too big for his body, flared from his skin, and a smoky updraft carried her high. Below was her bed, and beyond that, all the other beds with all the other students collapsed in sleep. In just three days, they would be gone for the summer.

Heavens, there at the edge of the room hovered the shadow people, that nun and that priest who still slunk through St. Mark's, but since she had told on them—her confession that became the Visitation—just ghosts, like the students who had died—shapes at the edge of her sight, sometimes milky, sometimes simply smoke in the process of dissipating.

"Take them, Papa. Those shadow people."

Papa stretched out his eagle feather, and from the side of the dorm the shape of Sister Mary of Bethany straightened. She took the form of flesh in a black habit, a bunched-up white apron, almost real again. As the priest raised his dark head, the wound on his cheek, a ragged red crevice, caught the light and burned to a thin white scar. Sister Mary of Bethany and Father Damien crept to the pool of starlight around Papa—Blessed Wolf—and the blessed white wolf beside him.

Right through her, Rose Marie felt light shoot, flooding all the dark twists, nests, and tunnels the fire worms had burrowed over the years. It incinerated their small corpses.

Now the wolf grew through the dormitory, and Papa did too. They took over the large dark room, the dissolving shapes of the shadow sister and priest, shimmering through the walls and ceiling, falling upwards.

Warm, euphoric, and sleepy, Rose Marie closed her eyes and drifted down to her bed. *Good night, Papa.*

The next morning she wondered what, exactly, had taken place. The dorm felt different, as if a warm wind had blown through it, sweeping dust, tears, sickness, and death away. The shadow nun and the shadow priest were gone. Banished. Her restlessness and *blue* were gone as well. *Dear Lord, let this last forever.*

At the start of class, when Sister Joan instructed her to lead the senior girls in the Lord's Prayer, she made a choking sound and pointed at her throat. In fact, she felt a pressure on her larynx just the size of a wolf paw—a sign, she decided, to remain silent. Besides, she wasn't sure what her dream, or whatever it was, meant.

If it was bad, if Papa had died and come to her as Mama had done so many years before when she died, then Mother Grace would be notified by the priest on Papa's Reserve. And Mother Grace would tell her. *God Almighty, let it not be that.* But then, if it were possible that Papa *had* died and Mother Grace hadn't yet been contacted, would she feel this reassured and loved, so whole?

She did not attend confession that Saturday. The practice had become unsettling rather than comforting ever since a young man with a rope at his neck had started to trail Father William, sometimes appearing next to him in the confessional. That had begun when she confessed to seeing Sister Mary of Bethany and Father Damien—the Visitation—what, four and a half years ago now? Oh dear, on occasion the young man appeared as a boy, small-boned with enormous eyes. Brown eyes bleeding *blue.* For the past few years, during confession, she had simply gone through her list of venial sins as quickly as possible and left. Father William didn't seem to expect anything more.

But to do that now, right after Papa's visit, seemed dishonest, and she didn't want to disturb the sense of calm that enveloped her ever since that night. It came to her that if seeing Papa was just a dream, then it was a *healing* dream. In removing the shadow sister and priest, he had restored her. *Thank you, Papa.*

* * *

As usual, she took advanced catechism with Mother Grace, whose mind seemed to be elsewhere. If Papa had died, Mother Grace would look at her differently, and, of course, tell her. Instead, she was preoccupied, forever glancing at the pile of growing and shifting correspondence on her desk. Rose Marie could see from the letterhead that most of it was from the Mother House.

The students went home for the summer, but she wasn't envious of them. In fact, she felt light and strangely worry-free, the debris of the past—fire worms and shadow people—swept away. Soon Papa would visit. Soon Mother Grace would tell her what was in store.

Content and confident, she went about her duties and did her chores without being reminded. Instead of sleeping in, she rose at first light and the second clang of Sister Joan's bell, going downstairs with Sister Simon the Silent, as she had begun to think of her, for Matins.

33

The Assignment

GOOD, YOU'RE HERE, Rose Marie," Mother Grace remarked as she entered the office. The reverend mother's face was damp, and her sharp blue eyes darted nervously from her hands to the clock to Rose Marie, to the cross over the door, and back again.

"Please sit down. I have just sent Sister Simon off to borrow Sister Lucy's suitcase for you. Father William is offering confession this evening. Then pack your things. Tomorrow you will be catching the Greyhound bus to a small parish west of Two Raven Pass, where you will serve."

"Pardon me?"

"*Oui, chérie*, it's all arranged. Sit down. Sister Simon also has some gumboots for you, Sister Bernadette a raincoat. They're closest in size to you, though I don't doubt their things will still be large."

"I don't understand, Mother Grace."

"I'll explain, *chérie*." Finally Mother Grace looked right at her, sighing deeply. "There's a procedure you must follow—a formality, really—in order to realize your destiny as a Sister of Brotherly Love."

"Procedure?" She could feel her newfound calm crack.

"Before going to the Mother House as a novitiate, it is required that you work in a parish for three months." Again Mother Grace sighed deeply, her eyes clouding. "You will be under the guidance of Father Patrick, a dear friend of mine and a true man of God. You'll be helping out. He has a housekeeper, I understand, but you will, no doubt, be called upon to assist—"

Oh dear. Something was wrong. Mother Grace's words had started to balloon from her mouth like wreaths of smoke. "Mother Grace?" Her eyes burning, Rose Marie blinked rapidly, overcome by a wave of panic.

"After the three-month period, you will return to us. Then you will travel to the Mother House—"

The sound was breaking up. Grey letters spilled from between Mother Grace's lips.

"I can't hear—"

A stream of letters. Oh, and Rose Marie tried to read those letters, but she couldn't keep up, her heart pounding, the shapes blackening like burning matchsticks, colliding and breaking apart. "What did—"

More burnt matchsticks.

"—you say?"

Mother Grace closed her mouth, a look of alarm on her face.

"Something's wrong, Mother Grace. I can't hear!" Oh, not even her own voice! She clamped her teeth down on her lip to stop the tears.

Mother Grace touched her hand. The rustle of her habit was soundless black splinters, but she felt the old fingers. Like paper, thin and crinkly as always, with that whisper of warmth. Yes, comforting. She choked down a mouthful of air.

"Rose Marie, are you all right?"

"Oh. Thank goodness, I can hear again!"

"I'm sorry, *chérie*. This is a shock, I can see. I should have said something before, but I was hoping you could go straight to the Mother House. Most orders don't have such a long waiting period. I'm afraid this is one I suggested myself years ago, after Sister Mary of Bethany—" Her eyes glittered. "It was a mistake! At the time, I thought such a

practice would stop young women not suited for the religious life—
Mon Dieu, the Mother House adopted it as policy." Mother Grace's
eyes fluttered closed.

"For the past six months," she continued, patting Rose Marie's hand,
"I've been seeking an indulgence for you. I didn't want to upset you, so
I didn't mention the matter, but truly, I thought our Mother Superior
would grant one, given your *special circumstances*." She opened her
eyes. "*Non*, she made it very clear it was not to be. You must think of
your separation from St. Mark's as your *assignment*. When it is done,
God will return you, and you will follow your destiny. Have faith, Rose
Marie. This is, as I've said, just a formality. The Lord provides. Not
always in the manner we expect, but *the Lord provides*."

"Y-yes, Mother Grace," she stammered, no longer the self-assured
young woman who had, minutes before, walked into the office.

"You're all right?"

She nodded uncertainly.

"Now listen. Tomorrow, once you are on your own"—Mother
Grace's voice wavered—"on that Greyhound bus, you must sit near
the front where you can see the driver and he can see you." She looked
directly at Rose Marie, studying the pillowcase she had cut, bleached,
hemmed, ironed, and tied behind her ears. "A white headdress. *Mais
oui*, the sign of commitment I've been waiting to see. Now, *chérie*,
there isn't much time, so pay attention. There are often 'undesirables'
at the back of the bus. If you must share your seat, sit next to a woman,
preferably an older woman."

"But why do I have to leave St. Mark's? Do you want me to go?"
Her lip was bleeding, the taste like an old penny.

"*Non*." Mother Grace pulled a hanky from her sleeve and dabbed
her nose. "I'm afraid there's no getting around it. Now, there's something else I must tell you."

"Mother Grace?" She hated the childish whine of her voice, the
tears burning her eyes.

Promptly Mother Grace closed her mouth and struggled to her

feet. As she made her way around the desk, Rose Marie rose too. For the first time in her life, Mother Grace wrapped her wiry arms around her. How thin and bent the old woman felt, so much smaller than she really was.

"*Dieu, aidez-moi,*" Mother Grace whispered, squeezing. "You must be careful while you're away, child. Be good. Don't let any man"—she swallowed—"get close to you."

"I don't want to leave," Rose Marie sobbed like a first-year girl. It took all her will to withdraw her arms from Mother Grace's brittle waist, her familiar scent of soap and age.

Sister Lucy, looking bewildered, wobbled out of the confessional, and Rose Marie stepped in. It was good practice, she knew, to take confession before any trip, any change, any danger. Just in case. *Come Light of the World and enlighten the darkness of my mind*, she prayed as she knelt. She had no idea what might be lurking past the prairie, over the rolling foothills and in the crevices of the mountains hovering at the edge of the western horizon so very far beyond St. Mark's Residential School for Girls, her home for twelve years.

"Forgive me, Father, for I have sinned," she muttered. "This is my first confession since school ended. I'm sorry about that, Father William, but right now I am fearful of what lies ahead. It's me, Rose Marie, and Mother Grace has told me that I must leave St. Mark's for three months." She tried to steady her voice. "I'm having trouble trusting in God Almighty."

"As you know, my child, the Lord thy God is with thee whithersoever thou goest," Father William said. "Even to the parish of Black Apple."

"Yes, Father," she began, but he was moving. Through the screen, she could see him turn his back to her until she could spot every nub running down the back of his black cassock.

On the other side of Father William stood a boy, his hands on a small priest's bed in a small priest's bedroom. The boy's back was also turned to her, striped and bloody, just as hers must have looked when Sister Joan beat her with the electrical cord, so many years before.

"This may hurt," Father William murmured to the boy as he poured liquid onto a cloth. "I'm afraid, son, it's necessary to avoid infection." The boy jerked as Father William applied the cloth. "There, there," he said, his voice as tender to the boy as it had been to her on the day she had revealed the truth about Sister Mary of Bethany and Father Damien.

Lower down the boy's back, Father William dabbed with the cloth. The boy was subdued now, moving just slightly at the sting of the liquid, sniffing faintly.

"Loosen your pants. Now, now, settle down," Father William crooned as his fingers slid under the waistband. "I'll take care of you." His hand reached farther down, and his other hand dropped the cloth and tugged. "Let's get you out of those."

Everything had gone dark. She could see only Father William's black cassock moving, and rising from it, the smell of something left too long in a warm, airless room, something off. The boy was crying, and Father William stretched his neck, his face lifted to the ceiling, eyes closed, skin glistening. "Let my weakness be penetrated with your strength this very day," he grunted.

Rose Marie scrambled to her feet and fled the confessional.

"Child, where are you going?" Father William's voice trailed after her. "Make an act of contrition. *I absolve you of your sins in the name of the Father, and of the Son—*"

Dear God.

She slept terribly that night, her dreams strung with rope and electrical cords, jammed with yelling, thumping, sobs, and the gurgles of strangulation.

In the room she was sharing with Sister Simon for the summer, she rose in the darkness to scribble a prayer that was running around in her mind, then dressed as soon as Sister Simon flailed awake in her bed by the window.

At Matins she couldn't sit still in the pew, and at breakfast she was able to eat only a bite of toast. No one spoke, and though she had the feeling the sisters were stealing glances at her, she wasn't able to catch any of them at it.

For the past month—ever since she had been visited by Papa, or Papa's spirit, or Papa had sent her a healing dream, whatever it was— she had been calm. Not only was she loved, but with the shadow sister and priest gone, she felt a degree of control over her life. And if she knew some things the sisters hadn't told her about, like animal spirits, seeing backwards, and dreams . . . well, she wasn't worried. She had learned from Mother Grace that revealed truths that surpass reason were mysteries to be accepted on faith. Over the years, she had accepted them all.

But now Mother Grace had spoiled everything. She was sending her away for doing nothing wrong! The small amount of control she had felt once the shadow people left was nothing but an illusion, a lie. Anything could befall her. At any time. No matter what she did.

As soon as breakfast was finished, Mother Grace steered her to the office to give her money she had "secured from the sisters' personal fund," and more warnings about buses and strangers, but Rose Marie was only half listening.

"Write to that priest on Papa's Reserve, please, Mother Grace," she interjected. "He has to tell Papa not to come here and visit. He can visit me in Black Apple instead."

From the frown on Mother Grace's face, Rose Marie knew she wasn't about to tell the priest to deliver her message to Papa, at least the part about coming to Black Apple. Oh, Mother Grace had never liked Papa, had always tried to keep him from her. Anger bubbled through her, and she turned away. If only she knew the name of the Reserve and the priest, she could write him herself. But Mother Grace wasn't about to tell her.

"Rose Marie?"

"What?" she snapped, feeling the power of her anger surge and then drain away. She was helpless again, had always been, would always be helpless at St. Mark's.

"Don't worry, Father Patrick will take care of you."

That's what I'm afraid of, she thought.

Upstairs, she packed her spare school dress, a worn sweater, a slip, three pairs of underwear, a bundle of cotton pads, one pair of stockings, two nightdresses, and a pair of shoes, then rummaged through the desk for paper and books. At twenty-five minutes to ten, she folded Sister Bernadette's raincoat under her arm, picked up her borrowed suitcase, and was about to lug it downstairs, when Sister Cilla stepped into her room.

"I need to say something to you about men," Sister blurted, her face flushing.

Rose Marie was caught off guard. "Oh."

"Once you're in Black Apple, you might meet a man who is interested in you, or who pretends to be. He might be a handsome, charming young man you think is sincere, but more than likely he only wants"—Sister Cilla cleared her throat—"to take advantage." She turned even brighter. "Most men are like that. Not all, but most. Do you know what I mean, Rose Marie?"

She could only stare.

"Listen, you can't trust any man who wants to court you. Don't let him get too familiar. By that I mean . . . well, don't let him interfere with you. Dear, oh law." She paused. "No kissing. No hands under clothing. You don't want to be ruined, and you certainly don't want a baby."

"Oh my, no!" She felt the suitcase slide from her grip and topple over on the floor. She hardly noticed Sister Cilla duck out the room. Instead, she tried to recall the prayer she had scribbled sometime between last night and this morning. *Hail, Holy Mother of Heaven and Earth.*

Then she picked up the suitcase and started down the stairs.

Waiting for her at the bottom was Sister Lucy, supported by Sister Cilla, her cheeks still pink.

"Why, Sister Lucy," she said, scarcely believing the old woman was standing before her in the main entrance, so feeble had she become in the past year. "Sister Lucy, you look pretty good," she said loud enough for Sister to hear.

"Our dear daughter," the old woman cooed, touching Rose Marie's face.

"Sister Lucy wanted to come," Sister Cilla explained. "Dear, oh law, I couldn't say no." Sister Cilla turned to the sound of Mother Grace making her way down the hall. "I couldn't say no to her, Mother Grace."

Slow and heavy footfalls on the stairs, lighter ones close behind. "Sister Margaret. Sister Joan."

Sister Simon came up quickly behind Mother Grace, and Sister Bernadette scampered from the kitchen, wiping her hands on her apron.

"Rose Marie, you must keep in touch," Mother Grace said. "Write to us once a week, at least. There are stamped envelopes in the side pocket of your suitcase."

"Yes," all the sisters chorused.

Sister Bernadette helped her into a black raincoat, and Sister Simon motioned to the gumboots by the door. Just as Mother Grace had predicted, both coat and boots were too large; she was lost in them.

It was Sister Bernadette who moved first, rushing up and throwing her short arms around her. Rose Marie felt the cool cotton of Sister's summer habit on her chin and smelled bleach and onions. Then all the sisters gathered round, pressing hard bones and jiggling flesh, their damp cheeks and warm hands against her. She had never experienced such a display of affection in all her years at St. Mark's. She couldn't stop her chest from heaving, a wail trickling from her lips.

One moment, it seemed the universe was ordained and orderly.

Then, it shattered.

* * *

In the car, Sister Cilla's white knuckles locked on the steering wheel as she accelerated down the gravel road from the school. Behind them, a plume of dust billowed. *Smoke*, Rose Marie thought. Her past burning away.

At the highway, Sister Cilla turned right in front of a transport truck and slowed to a snail's pace. Down the hill they rolled, the truck braking behind them, its air horn blasting.

"We're here," Sister Cilla announced a few minutes later as the car lurched to a stop outside a dingy gas station and adjoining café slumped against the highway. Far behind them, St. Mark's stood, a thumbprint on the vast horizon.

Once Sister Cilla had helped Sister Lucy out of the car, she turned to Rose Marie. "I have something for you." Her hands fumbled at the nape of her long neck. From under her collar, she pulled a silver chain with a small silver cross. "My brother gave this to me when I took my vows. I want you to have it, Rose Marie. For luck. Here, let me fasten it for you."

The bus pulled in then, and as Rose Marie climbed up the Greyhound steps behind an elderly Indian couple, she turned to wave good-bye to the sisters. They had grabbed hold of each other a few feet from the bus doors, and Sister Cilla seemed to wrap Sister Lucy like a wire around a windblown bale of hay. At the end of her sharp nose, a drop formed, then another, each spilling onto Sister Lucy's wimple.

Mutt and Jeff, she thought. She had seen the cartoon in the newspapers she used to wash windows and bundle up potato peels, and it had always made her chuckle. But not today. Today the contradiction of short and tall, thin and plump, young and old wasn't funny. Sisters Cilla and Lucy were staying, while she was being shipped away. Lifting her hand for one last wave, she caught something from the corner of her eye. There, under the awning of the café, someone was watching the sisters. Still as a fence post, the narrow shape stood in the shadows, only the hands moving, working something. A straw hat, she guessed.

"C'mon," the bus driver called, and she climbed the remaining steps. He pulled a lever and the doors wheezed shut behind her. Immediately she was assaulted by the smell of orange peel, cigarettes, and that unnameable acrid odour she had sometimes detected on Mother Grace's breath in the morning.

Three rows behind the driver was an empty seat, and she remembered Mother Grace's words about sitting near the front. As she neared the seat, the woman by the window plunked her purse down. Just as she started to say, "Excuse me, but is this seat free?" the woman glared at her and jerked her frizzy blond head to the back of the bus.

Rose Marie gazed down the aisle. A long bench seat made up the last row, just like on the school buses, and, on each side of the seat, a man leaned against the window, sleeping. The elderly couple who had just boarded the bus was sitting in the row just in front. Across from them were two young men. In front of the men, Rose Marie spotted another empty seat.

"Sit down," the bus driver yelled, and feeling the burn of the frizzy blond woman's eyes on her, feeling other eyes staring through Sister Bernadette's baggy black raincoat, she rustled to the back of the Greyhound. As she drew closer, she saw that everyone sitting there was dark-skinned. Indians, like her.

Taking a seat, she sensed one head still turned towards her. It wasn't the frizzy-haired woman, as she expected, but a man on the end seat of a middle row, a white man with a stubbled chin and red hair as dull as a dead fox caught in one of Papa's traps. He grinned at her with crooked teeth. She turned to the window and took a deep breath.

A lifetime before, a bus had jolted her from the narrow road that joined Mama, Auntie Constance, and Aunt Angelique's Reserve to the highway, and deposited her, stunned and queasy, at St. Mark's Residential School for Girls. How afraid she had been, a small child without a Christian bone in her body. Uncivilized.

Now, grown up, *chosen*, and practically a postulant, she felt stunned and queasy all over again as she travelled back to where she had come from, and then beyond. "For three months," Mother Grace had said. She tried to summon anger about Mother Grace's cowardice in not telling her of the possibility of being sent away, in not wanting Papa to visit her in Black Apple, and, no doubt, in demanding that Sister Cilla give her the *no men* lecture. After all, Mother Grace had been going to tell her something yesterday in her office, so why not get Sister Cilla to do it for her? Though, she had to admit, she would much rather have Sister Cilla deliver the horribly embarrassing warning than Mother Grace.

But she had no energy for anger. She was scared, and if she could just be back at St. Mark's, she would forgive Mother Grace anything.

"Hi there, little lady," a male voice greeted her from behind, and she turned in her seat.

Did she know that man? Handsome. Perhaps one of Forest Fox Crown's several relatives? She lowered her eyes, but a dart of flame made her look back up. Oh, he was like Papa, with a spirit too big for his body. Maybe twenty-two years old, maybe twenty-four, though she couldn't be sure because she had seen young men only when the farmers brought their sons to St. Mark's to deliver supplies or on the rare occasions older brothers came on visiting day. She clutched the raincoat tightly around her.

Fire Indian's hair was in neither a short residential school cut nor long like Papa's. In between. He wore a faded cowboy shirt with what was probably a ketchup stain over where his heart would be. A bolo tie made of a beaded circle with an *X* and a strip of rawhide hung around his neck. He winked, and she felt heat spread through her cheeks. She remembered to breathe—a quick inhalation, then a hiccup. Oh! She turned her eyes to the seat in front. "Put your hand in the fire, and you'll get burned," Sister Joan had warned the students many times.

The handsome man laughed, and it was like a summer blaze. Her skin was dry as late summer bark, would surely catch fire.

That Dead Fox Man was watching her again, and with him in front and Fire Indian behind, she didn't know where to turn her attention.

She closed her eyes. *Hail Mary, full of grace, the Lord is with thee. Blessed are—*

"Come sit with me," the man behind her said. "My friend will trade places with you—won'tcha, Eugene?"

Smoothing her white cotton head scarf with both palms, she bowed her head. *Blessed art thou amongst women.*

"Eugene, trade places with her. C'mon, beautiful, won'tcha—"

Maopiit! The sharp sound cut away the man's words. It had come from the seat across the aisle. The old woman had spoken Blackfoot. She must have scolded Fire Indian in Blackfoot, and suddenly he was quiet.

She had forgotten it, the language of Mama and Papa, Whitewater and Tallow. Her own once-upon-a-time, long-ago words. *The Lord, the Lord is*—she started, but the neat order of the rosary began to collapse. She turned to the window to cross herself without anyone seeing. *Hail Jesus. Hail Mary. Fruit of thy womb.* She couldn't think straight. Something about *salvation.* Closing her eyes, she listened to her breath, smelled the sour bus air flowing through her. *God, please keep me safe.* She touched Sister Cilla's cross at her throat.

The road uncoiled beside ravines and coulees; deer leapt to reveal blue and green and blue. It had been so long since she had fallen under the spell of the land, and now the wheels spinning along the white line slowly unravelled her memories—including a vague recollection of a small house in the midst of trees that trembled and danced. *A-kiitoy-iistsi*—was that the right name?

On and on they drove. Hills turned to mountains with stony fingers the bus slid through. A cluster of mountain sheep watched with shale eyes. On and on. A coyote at the side of the road disappeared in deep grass.

"Two Raven Pass," the driver called.

She might have dozed off. She might have daydreamed or been lost in thought, she wasn't sure. The bus stopped and people got off, people got on—the chorus of a hymn sung too slowly for too long.

She almost forgot Fire Indian behind her and Dead Fox Man several rows in front. After a few hours, she almost forgot St. Mark's.

At first she hardly noticed the broken mountain, nearly let it slide away like loose rock. Then she looked right at it, and the breath froze in her lungs. *The Mountain That Moved.* She knew the story, how its spine had cracked over the mine drilled deep into its belly, how it fell on houses, crushing the spirits of people eating, napping, playing, and working, grinding their lives to dust. It was what she had seen every day of her young life at home, its damaged form glinting from the creek, taking over the sky.

Fewer passengers now. They stirred, glancing at watches, pulling satchels off the overhead rack, stuffing blankets into bags. She sat forward in her seat, nervous. The bus slowed and turned off the highway, weaving along a gravel road. Shacks of tarpaper and peeling paint were crammed together on a narrow street. BLACK APPLE, a filthy roadside sign spelt out in misshapen letters. Dumbly she watched a large woman with a small boy stumble from a store not five feet from the bus, a bag of potatoes in her hand.

A siren shrieked, and the boy cried something that sounded like "Shift change, Mummy" as the woman pulled him through a puddle and down a side street. The bus passed a dilapidated building, the words DOMINION HOTEL barely discernible on the blackened wood. Leaning against the building was a clump of men, one yelling something about a "son of a bitch." Everything, everyone, looked dirty. Oh dear, she did not want to be here.

As the bus pulled up to the depot, she forced herself to remember Mother Grace's instructions. She waited for the bus driver to bellow *"Blaaack Aaapple"* before she rose, then pushed down the aisle ahead of the Fire Indian and his friend Eugene, but well behind the Dead Fox Man with his matted hair and dirty eyes. She stepped carefully down the steps, her heart banging against her ribs, past the driver, who did not take her elbow in his palm as he had with the frizzy-haired woman in front of her.

With the other passengers, she bunched around the side of the bus and waited until the driver strode through the crowd and unlocked a door near the back wheel. She retrieved her suitcase, then turned to follow the others through the door into the depot. She looked around for Father Patrick, but there was no man with a white stripe at his throat. Pushing her suitcase against her ankles, she sat on a wooden bench.

At the sound of feet shuffling nearby, she looked up to see Dead Fox Man in his dirty coat, a leer staining his face.

"Come on, honey," he drawled.

She was sure he wouldn't be the one assigned to pick her up, so she stared down at the small, diamond-shaped tiles on the floor, each one set in a perimeter of grime. She began to count them. *Two, three, four . . .*

"I got a hotel room," he whispered in her ear. "I got lotsa money." *Eight, nine, ten . . .*

Suddenly her upper arm was squeezed. Dead Fox Man yanked her to her feet.

"No!" she cried, looking around. People stared, but no one seemed ready to help. She shook her arm, frantically trying to break free of his grip. Dead Fox Man tugged her, and she stumbled towards him.

From the corner of her eye, she saw Fire Indian, Eugene close behind.

"Get away from my sister!" he shouted.

"She's not your sister," Dead Fox Man bawled. "She's with me."

Fire Indian raised a clenched fist, and Dead Fox Man let her go. "Goddamned Indians!" he spat, turning to the door.

Behind them, the clerk at the counter yelled, "No fighting in here! Go on, yous. Get out of here." He waved his hand at Fire Indian and Eugene. At her too. He was shooing them away.

She lowered her head and sat back down. It was Tuesday, she remembered, the day for contemplating sorrowful mysteries. *Mary, help me to be humble and obedient to God's will.* She felt sorrowful enough.

Where was Father Patrick? She glanced around the depot again. The crowd had thinned. Just that morning, Mother Grace had instructed her to get her suitcase and wait until she was approached by "a respectable priest, an attractive elderly man," but no one fit that description.

"Where you going? Can we walk you somewhere?" Fire Indian asked, coming over.

She shook her head. Mother Grace had warned her about strangers.

"You sure?" His eyes were no longer angry or teasing, but a flicker of orange danced through them.

"C'mon, Frank," Eugene said.

"You got someone coming for you?"

She nodded.

"Okay. Maybe I'll see you around, eh?"

For a moment, a sparrow's cry seemed to flit in her throat, but she willed it silent, pressed her lips together so the word *wait* wouldn't fly out. She was tired, so tired of waiting, her whole life spent working and waiting for her *destiny* to unfold. What she felt was *anxiety*, a new word of Sister Cilla's. "Are you feeling anxious, Rose Marie?" Sister had asked before she boarded the bus. "I suffer from anxiety from time to time myself."

One, she counted to herself, looking again at the floor tiles. *Two, three, four.* For some reason, she was cold. She pulled the raincoat tightly around herself and kept counting. When she looked back up, she was the only passenger left in the depot. And the clerk behind the big desk had his eyes trained on her.

"You can't hang around here all day," he announced. "No loitering allowed." His finger pointed to a sign just above him with that very message printed in large red type. "It says 'No Loitering Allowed,' " he repeated slowly, his finger following each syllable.

"I can read," she said. "Besides, I'm not loitering." Lifting her suitcase, she went over to his desk. "I'm waiting for Father Patrick of Our Lady of Sorrows Church. I'm training to be a holy sister." She lifted her chin slightly, as she had seen Mother Grace do on numerous occasions, particularly when challenged by Sister Joan. Or Papa.

"Gosh. You just missed his funeral!" The clerk stared at her, his scorn gone. "It was this afternoon. Father Seamus—the priest from Coal River—said the Mass."

"Funeral?" She was so shocked she could barely push the word out.

He eyed her curiously. "You didn't know he died?"

"Father Patrick?" Her heart hammered in her chest.

"Well, yeah," the clerk said, glancing at the white cotton covering her hair. "Stroke or something like that. He was here for just under a year, but everyone liked him. Except for a few of the muckamucks. You know, the high-and-mighties." He snorted.

"What will I do now?" Her *assignment*, as Mother Grace had called it, was to assist Father Patrick. "The bus," she cried. "Can I go back?"

"Long gone," the clerk told her. "Won't return till the day after tomorrow."

"Please," she begged, her voice withering to a whisper, "can you at least direct me to the church?"

34

The Orphans' Prayer

S HE STOPPED ON the muddy street and set her suitcase down. She had packed too many books, and her arm felt as if it were being wrenched from its socket.

Picking up the suitcase with her left hand this time, she trudged on. Fortunately she was wearing boots—the gumboots Sister Simon wore in the garden—"galoshes," Sister Joan called them. They were at least two sizes too big and slid back and forth as she walked, chafing her calves.

That must be the church at the end of the street, the steep roof and cross. She thought of the prayer she had started to write at Sister Simon's desk just before sunrise that very morning. She had called it the Orphans' Prayer, an appeal for all children whose relations were scattered or dead, who had no one close by to protect them. *Hail, Holy Mother of Heaven and Earth, Mother of Christ, Mother of all we who are motherless. Be our most gracious advocate and help us to accept our losses and submit to God's will.*

That's where she got stumped. The prayer was incomplete. It needed one or two more lines, but she couldn't think of what else to say to the Virgin that was suitably reverent yet expressed a child's plight. Or even that of a young woman. Possibly a young man who was beaten and then made to do things by a priest when he was just a little boy, who was so miserable when he grew up that he hanged himself.

She stopped to put down her suitcase and switch hands again. She wanted to fit in phrases like *advise God to keep us safe from those who would do us harm*, and *give us love in our lives, real true love from people who are with us, and a real true home to live in, a family, even*, but she wondered if that made her sound ungrateful. She had no right to feel sorry for herself. After all, she had Mother Grace and the nuns had taken her in. And if they didn't love her, some were fond of her. Sisters Joan and Margaret were used to having her around, at least. And Jesus Christ had revealed the sins of the past to her, a sign to the religious of St. Mark's that they might go forward, redeemed by God's forgiveness, into the future. Even Father William.

It was also a sign that she was meant to live among women of God and learn to be a holy sister, that she might one day return to St. Mark's and sleep in the small bedroom on the second floor that she had slept in each summer since her seventh birthday, though since Sister Simon's arrival, she had slept on a cot. The same room that Sister Mary of Bethany, God rest her soul, had once occupied. That's what Mother Grace had told her.

Though she had been beaten, locked up, and made fun of at school, she had not been hurt in that other way, like the big-eyed boy who became a young man who went against God's law and killed himself. She was lucky, even if she didn't feel it. She should be grateful. *Mother of Heaven and Earth.*

No one was inside the church, though the scent of incense hung heavy in the air, and vases of flowers were stuffed around the altar. Bowing, she backed out and dragged her suitcase down the stairs. Too exhausted to carry it, she pulled it along the boardwalk to the back of the church, where she found a small, flat-roofed building with faded gingham curtains hanging in the window. The rectory. Such a grand name for this stooped shack. Taking a breath, she knocked on the door.

It creaked open on a short, round woman about the same age as Mother Grace, with an apron slung over ample breasts. "Yes, dearie?"

"I'm Rose Marie Whitewater."

"Yes, dearie?" the woman repeated.

A stickiness in her throat. "I'm from St. Mark's." It caught her words like flypaper. "I've been sent here. To work." She wanted to say, *For Father Patrick*, but it wouldn't come out.

"Why, bless me, yes!"

"I'm sorry about Father Patrick, his unfortunate . . . his death. I just found out."

"Goodness gracious Sunlight soap, we forgot all about you, didn't we?" The woman's voice had a pleasing lilt, though it was different from Mother Grace's accent. With plump arms, she pressed Rose Marie against her, the smell of pastry lifting from her grey hair. "You come right in."

"Father Seamus," she called, turning her head, "it's the girl who was going to work for Father Patrick." She turned back to face her. "We've heard about you, we have. I'm Mrs. Rees, Father Patrick's—God rest his soul—housekeeper."

Father Seamus took a half step forward and glared down at her.

Still dazed by the long bus ride, by Dead Fox Man, Fire Indian, Father Patrick's death, all the terrible events of the past day and a half, and now by Mrs. Rees's effusive hug, she stared back at him, a tall, imposing man with a black beard.

"You're the residential school girl who had this—what is it your Father William calls it?" His nostrils flared. "A Visitation? I read an article about you in the *Register*—"

"Well, love," Mrs. Rees cut in, steering her to the table, "I'll get you something to eat." She tugged at the collar of Sister Bernadette's voluminous coat. "Let me hang that up for you."

Father Seamus retreated down the hall. Mrs. Rees filled the kettle, opened cupboards and cookie tins, buttered bread, and made tea, chattering all the while.

"Father Patrick's death was unexpected. In his sleep, love. Very peaceful. And such a good man, he was, working wonders in the parish." She brought Rose Marie a cup of tea, a meat pie, a biscuit, butter, raspberry jam, and two fancy squares, then sat across from her with her own cup of tea, hurriedly praying before taking a sip. Rose Marie, feeling dazed, followed suit.

"Left over from the funeral," she said. "Everyone brought something—buns, cakes, roasts—such a fuss." Glancing down the hall where Father Seamus had retreated, she lowered her voice. "Father Patrick started social evenings, bingos and monthly dinners for the down-and-out. When there was talk of a strike at the mines in spring, he was all set to offer suppers every Friday for the families. He was very popular. Father Seamus and some of the others weren't happy with, you know, the unions, dear. Say the miners are all atheist communists, don't they? Blame the Bohunks mostly, but that's not really right. It's all the miners. Tired of the long shifts, I expect. Dangerous work." She sighed, shaking her head. "At least Mr. Rees is out of the mine now."

Rose Marie, her mouth full, nodded. She had no idea what Mrs. Rees was talking about—she couldn't concentrate—but she appreciated the newsy prattle she wasn't really expected to reply to.

Hearing Father Seamus approach, Mrs. Rees popped up from her chair. "Father Seamus, a nice cup of tea?"

"No thanks, Mrs. Rees. I must be off. I can drive the girl to the Tortorelli house, if she'll hurry."

"Mrs. Tortorelli," Mrs. Rees said, leaning towards her, "agreed to board the parish worker—that's you, dear—for the three months you'll be helping out at the church."

"Mrs. Tortorelli is a devout Catholic widow," Father Seamus stated, glancing over her head and not at her face. "She runs a boardinghouse with her brother-in-law. Her late husband was most generous to the church. He was with the Knights of Columbus right up until his death."

He frowned. "Mrs. Rees, she'll have to hurry if she wants a lift. It's starting to get dark, and I have to drive back to Coal River."

"I'll get your coat, dear." Mrs. Rees scurried off, and Rose Marie carried her dishes to the sink.

"I'll just wash up and be on my way too, Father," Mrs. Rees said. "Unless there's something else you'd like me to do before I leave?"

"No. Just keep things up until I get back on Friday."

Father Seamus pulled his car in front of a grand-looking two-storey house with bay windows on both levels, and pointed. "The Tortorelli house."

Rose Marie peered through the windshield. The building, in contrast to its short, shabby neighbours, looked large and commanding, with what appeared in the gathering dusk to be a new coat of paint: gleaming white with green trim around the windows and at the eaves. Noticing that Father Seamus wasn't getting out of the car to help with her suitcase, she slid off her seat, opened the back door, grabbed the suitcase, and yanked. It toppled out, landing in a puddle and splashing her already muddy stockings. What a sight she must look.

"Thank you, Father Sea—" she began, pushing the door shut, but the car was already rolling away.

As soon as she knocked on the heavy green door, she heard high heels clicking over the floor and the door was pulled open. There stood a small, thin woman with hair gathered in a neat, grey bun. She wore a crisp white apron, but everything else she had on was black: her dress, shawl, stockings, and shiny leather shoes. A frown seemed to be etched permanently into her forehead.

"I'm Rose Marie Whitewater," she said, but the woman didn't respond. That stickiness in her throat again. "Mrs. Tortorelli?"

The woman nodded, her chin raised in Mother Grace's gesture of superiority.

"I've been told you have a room—"

"No," the woman replied. "I'm full." She pushed the door shut.

She didn't know what to do. Mrs. Rees had been about to leave the rectory when she and Father Seamus left. She'd be on her way home by now, wherever that was. Shifting from foot to foot, Rose Marie considered the possibility that Mrs. Tortorelli didn't realize she was the parish worker sent to serve the local church. Maybe she thought that young woman wouldn't be coming now that Father Patrick was dead. Maybe she had rented the room to someone else.

Rose Marie's hand trembled as she knocked a second time. "If at first you don't succeed," Sister Joan had impressed on all the girls, "try, try, try again."

This time when Mrs. Tortorelli opened the door, she was clearly annoyed. "I told you, I have no rooms left," she spat. "If you want a cheap room, try the old Mooney place."

"Where?" she managed. "Where is the old Mooney place?"

"Farther down the street. The big pink one. The only other two-storey. I run a respectable place here," she added, slamming the door. "No Indians allowed," came a muffled voice from behind the freshly painted wood.

As Rose Marie struggled down the street with her suitcase, she thought maybe she wouldn't ask Mother Mary to *give us love in our lives, real, true love and a real, true home.* That was presumptuous—a word that Mother Grace used from time to time when she thought a student or even a sister was asking for "undeserved privileges." Perhaps she would simply ask "to belong" somewhere in some sort of family or community, even if it was just a bunch of nuns. But that too suddenly seemed like an enormous request, and maybe, for her, an impossible goal. Would she ever feel like she truly belonged?

The sun was nothing but a sooty red streak skidding behind the mountains, and as she plodded towards the old Mooney house, shadows crept under its eaves, alongside the upstairs windows, and beneath the lurching porch. Once the house had been impressive, she could see, at least as grand and even bigger than the Tortorelli house, which had somehow escaped the black dust that appeared to coat every other building in the town. But now the house was neglected, the fence leaning precariously into the street, the wood rotting. The gate was completely gone and the yard overgrown with weeds. She dragged her suitcase up the steps to the front porch.

She knocked but hadn't even dropped her fist when the door swung open and she was greeted by a bright yellow light and the intermingling odours of tobacco and cooked cabbage. Then a man stepped into view. She started. Fire Indian! His laugh flickered over her skin.

"Well, well, you bin following me, haven't you?"

"No."

Frank turned his head to the interior of the house and called, "Hey, Eugene, remember that pretty little lady from the bus? She's here to take me out on a date."

"I'm here about a room," she mumbled.

"Well, come on in."

She didn't go. *Presumptuous.*

"Mrs. Mooney," Frank yelled up the stairs, "a young lady is here about a room. At least that's what she says." He turned to wink at her, then called up the stairs again. "Actually I think it's me she's after. Hey, Mrs. Mooney!" His grin again, his flashing white teeth.

"Just a minute," a voice yelled from the second floor.

"You okay?" He stepped towards her, suddenly serious, his flaring fingers touching her arm, making her skin tingle. "That bastard in the bus depot didn't—"

"No." She stepped back.

"Okay, but you let me know if he gives you any trouble."

A heavy woman trudged down the stairs, and Frank stepped out of her way. Her abnormally bright hair was gathered on top of her head in a bun that was as unruly as Mrs. Tortorelli's had been neat. Rose Marie had never seen dyed hair before, but she suspected that this hair, the colour of the oxblood shoe polish Father David had sometimes smeared in broad streaks over his brown shoes, was just that.

"Whaddaya want?"

"I'm looking for a room."

"Well, well, ain't that convenient? One just came up."

Thank you, Holy Virgin.

"Bed, dresser, closet, share the bathroom down the hall with two others: Cyril, a miner, and Ruby, who works at the hotel. Downstairs men have their own bathroom. Eighty bucks a month includes breakfast and supper. You pack yer own lunch. Pay in advance. You got a job?"

"Yes, at Our Lady of Sorrows."

Mrs. Mooney's eyes travelled over her head covering. "I see." Turning to look at Eugene, who was slinking down the stairs with a box under his arm, she bellowed, "Everyone's supposed to give a month's notice, right, Eugene?" She turned back. "So, you want it, honey?"

"Oh, yes."

"You're a lucky bugger, Eugene." Mrs. Mooney turned back to him. "If this little cookie hadn't arrived, you'd be eighty bucks in the hole." The woman grinned down at her. "He's going back to the Reserve to get married, the stupid son of a bitch."

Surprisingly, Eugene grinned too.

Rose Marie shut her mouth. "You look like you're catching flies," Sister Margaret had accused her more than once. Oh, but she couldn't help it; she wasn't used to such language. Not from grown-ups.

"That's eighty bucks, honey."

The grand total of her cash was exactly eighty dollars! Her room and board were supposed to be provided free of charge—Mother Grace had promised. If she handed the money over to Mrs. Mooney, she would have nothing left for a bus ticket home or anything else she needed. She dug into the secret pocket Sister Bernadette had sewn in the side seam of her school dress—her fingers scrabbling at the wad of bills. Reluctantly, she handed it over.

"Sure that's eighty?"

"Yes, Sis—ma'am." She had almost said "Sister." So much, dear Mother of God, so very much to get used to.

Mrs. Mooney shoved the bills down the front of her dress. "I'll get the room ready. An hour should be fine, since it's gettin' dark. I guess you can come in the kitchen and wait, or else go an' get yerself something to eat at the bus depot Chinese café. Suit yourself." She jabbed a chipped red fingernail at Rose Marie's suitcase. "You can leave your stuff here if you like."

"Yes, thank you. I'll go for a walk," she muttered, sliding her case across the doorstep. She had to get out of here, yet she was frightened of the town. She felt the same way she had when she left St. Mark's that morning: she hadn't wanted to go but she really hadn't wanted to stay either.

Twilight leached colour from the wilting tomato, potato, cabbage, and beet plants that clung to the cooling earth in the front gardens of the houses. She'd be quiet, and maybe no one would see her wandering under the sickly elms stuck haphazardly along the street. She slipped through the weedy playing field of a school, rubber boots sliding against her raw calves. Turning a corner, she sidestepped deftly into a garden as a man wove through the evening towards her. Farther along, she heard voices and glanced up, looking to the other side of the street.

The door of the Dominion Hotel swung open, and two men staggered out in a burst of music. *"Your cheatin' heart..."* twanged before the door banged shut. She froze. Dead Fox Man leaned against the side of the hotel, fumbling inside his dirty coat. He pulled out a paper bag, brought it to his lips, threw his head back, and swallowed.

He hadn't seen her. She backed away from the streetlight and crouched in the weeds of a vacant lot. Motionless, she watched the other man stagger awkwardly towards Dead Fox Man, mumbling something and grabbing for the bag.

Dead Fox Man shoved him away, but the man reached again, this time yanking the bag and its bottle from Dead Fox's mouth, spilling liquid down his chin. Pulling the bottle back, Dead Fox Man swung his other arm up from his waist in a quick arc and socked the man soundly in the jaw. The man spun, hit the side of the hotel, bounced off, and fell backwards. His head smacked the curb, bone striking stone. Rose Marie sank to her knees in the wet grass.

Dead Fox Man yelled something at the man twitching at his feet, then kicked him. He looked up and down the road. Oh, right at her! She didn't move a hair. Dead Fox Man slipped around the corner and was gone.

She ran in the other direction. She didn't care where she was going as long as it was away, far away from Dead Fox Man. Finally, dizzy and gasping, she staggered against a tree. Just down the street she spotted the cross on the peaked roof of Our Lady of Sorrows.

She darted up the church steps and pulled at the door. Locked. What church was ever locked? Down the steps. She crept along the boardwalk and peered through the window of the rectory. Dark.

She stole through the grimy streets. In lit kitchens, people drank tea and read the newspaper. A man and woman walked arm in arm down an alley, and a few minutes later, two stray dogs came yipping out of the schoolyard. Trembling, she stayed in the shadows and crept through the town, searching for the old Mooney house. Finally she spotted its high roof against the dark sky. *Hail, Holy Mother of Heaven and Earth.*

A fight, she told herself. She had witnessed a fight, just a fistfight, and most likely, part of life in this town, this Sodom and Gomorrah. She recalled the indignant expression on Father William's face as he gave a sermon about "centres of sin, profane in the eyes of the Lord." But she could no longer think about Father William without feeling a wave of nausea.

She'd be quiet and good, biding her time in this horrible town until she could return to St. Mark's. There, she'd avoid Father William as much as possible before going to the Mother House. And here, she would avoid Dead Fox Man, who had just knocked a man senseless, who might have seen her in the grass, watching. Who might have killed the man. *Please, Mother Mary, advise God to keep me safe from those who would harm me.* Her skirt and stockings were soaked, her entire body trembling.

"You okay?" Mrs. Mooney asked, glancing at her dress and stockings.

"I tripped."

Shrugging, Mrs. Mooney handed her a receipt penned in a surprisingly prim hand.

A big coal miner by the name of Cyril Brown carried her suitcase up to her room, showed her the bathroom, and pointed out his room across from hers, Ruby's room, and, at the end of the hall, Mrs. Mooney's suite.

She nodded numbly, her thoughts flitting from the Dominion Hotel to dead Father Patrick, to this boardinghouse full of men where she wasn't even supposed to be staying, and back to Dead Fox Man, his bottle and thudding fist. She caught little of what Cyril was saying, but she nodded when he looked at her with his pale eyes. *Mother of Christ, Mother of all we who are motherless.*

Her room was about twice the size of the summer bedroom she shared with Sister Simon, and though it stank of tobacco, she could see that Mrs. Mooney had given it a cursory dusting and put clean sheets on the bed.

She opened her suitcase and laid the Bible on her pillow. As she was pulling off her wet stockings, Mrs. Mooney stuck her bright head in the door. "I got some disinfectant, rags, and a mop downstairs if you want to do a proper clean tomorrow. You can use the wringer washer in the basement whenever you want."

"Yes. Thanks." *Help us to accept our losses and submit to God's will.* She really couldn't ask the Virgin for anything more, she reasoned as she yanked her dress over her head, throwing it on a wooden chair in the corner. The next day she would scrub away Eugene and all the others who had slept in the room before her. Then she would clean the bathroom down the hall. Standing at its entrance with Cyril, she had smelt urine. She would scrub the floor and toilet with bleach and scour the tub. After that, she would have a bath and soak all traces of this dirty town from her skin.

She locked the door and kissed the small cross Sister Cilla had given her, her eyes smarting. She was lost and lonely. As she put her head beside the Bible on her pillow, she whispered, "Taki, please, I need you," into the darkness.

But, of course, Anataki wasn't there.

35

Earthly Pleasures

A FEW HOURS LATER, Rose Marie clawed her way through a thick blanket of sleep and sat up in her bed. Mother Grace reached out a hand that almost touched her shoulder before it turned to paper.

"Mother Grace, where did you go?" she cried, reaching into the night. She sank back in bed.

Men fought in a dark street. Dead Fox Man saw her crouched in the grass and came after her, a rope in his hands. She fled down an alley, but slipped in a pool of mud that sucked her down. Dead Fox Man was coming for her, and she was stuck! She opened her eyes. She didn't know where she was.

A thin, haunting voice beckoned her through the floorboards, and she was drawn down to the open door of a cabin with a crackling fire and the aroma of deer stew—a home, though not the one she had once shared with Mama, Papa, and Kiaa-yo—but still, home. Her home, in the dream.

"Come in," a voice whispered to her from inside the cabin.

She opened her eyes. It was night.

"Come in." The voice called her back to the dream, a man she couldn't see clearly, though the hearth fire played over his skin. Maybe

Papa. Maybe even Fire Indian. *"Okii."* He beckoned and she started to go to him.

"Rose Marie!" Mother Grace called sharply. As she turned to her, the cabin fell into the earth.

"Rose Marie!"

Her eyes flew open. Someone was banging at the door of a strange room, not hers, not the cramped one she shared with Sister Simon that had a crucifix, palm crosses, and a picture of the Virgin Mary being told of her destiny by the Holy Spirit.

"You missed breakfast. It's nine now, and I thought I better wake you up," Mrs. Mooney called. "Hey, you in there?"

"Yes. I'm coming, Mrs. Mooney. Thanks for waking me," she added, remembering her manners.

When she went downstairs for cleaning supplies, Mrs. Mooney handed her a plate with two slices of toast. "Still some coffee on. Want some?"

"Oh. Well, thanks." She had never had coffee before. Mother Grace wouldn't allow it, warning it would stunt her growth. She was four foot ten and a half inches, the shortest senior in the school, for crying out loud.

The coffee tasted bitter. Mrs. Mooney handed her a bowl of sugar, and she dropped in a teaspoonful, enjoying the faint whisper. "Milk?" her landlady offered.

After cleaning her room and the bathroom, she had a quick bath and hurried down the stairs to head over to the rectory. The front door opened, and in walked Frank.

"There she is, Miss Rose Marie."

She nodded, her palm, gripping the banister, suddenly damp.

"No one came to get you from the bus depot yesterday, eh?"

"It was supposed to be Father Patrick. He died."

"Dwayne was saying something about that the other night. So you ended up here."

"Well, I think I was supposed to stay at the Tortorelli house. But when she saw me—"

"No, she don't like Indians." He imitated Mrs. Tortorelli's raised chin and haughty expression. "No Indians allowed-ah," he pronounced with an Italian accent, and they both laughed.

Then, suddenly nervous, she dodged by him and was out the door before she realized she should have grabbed her sweater.

Mrs. Rees opened the rectory door. "No need to knock, dearie. Come right in. I was about to get myself a bit of bread and butter. I'll make some for you too. You'll put the kettle on, won't you?" She waved an arm towards the stove. "A spot of raspberry jam, now? I made it myself."

Rose Marie waited for the kettle to boil, made the tea, and carried it to the table. She sat down while Mrs. Rees chattered on so quickly she barely had time to absorb the words.

"Not a bad town, is it, now? Not at all. Just stay away from the Dominion Hotel after dark, dear. Always walk on the other side of the street on your way home. And if you have any troubles, tell me, won't you? Me old lad will set them straight, he will." She lowered her voice. "It's the single men and the drink. And just last night Billy Nimsic found dead outside the Dominion." She shook her head, her face slumping like warm candlewax. "I wasn't going to say anything to you, but I can't help myself. I saw the blood on the sidewalk not four hours ago when Mr. Rees walked me to work."

Hot tea sloshed over the brim of Rose Marie's cup.

"Oh dear. Put that down. That's right. Now take a deep breath."

She did. Then she raised her cup again and gulped at the scalding liquid, allowing the burn to drag her attention from the bloodstained sidewalk and the sound of breaking bone.

"Billy wasn't known as a fighting man, but he was a terrible drinker since his Gladys died." Mrs. Rees crossed herself, tears springing to her eyes. "He must have fallen." She pulled the napkin from her lap and dabbed her cheeks. "Entirely too much death lately. A body can't take it."

She nodded numbly while Mrs. Rees kept chattering, her plump hands landing like chickadees on a wrist or shoulder, eyes darting from serious to sad, then crinkling in a smile. Rose Marie wasn't used to having someone confide in her, not since Taki died, but she liked it, the way Mrs. Rees's voice took over the space between them, allowing her mind to rest against the soft pillow of words.

"You never mind what Father Seamus said yesterday," Mrs. Rees consoled as they did the dishes. "He's like that. I've got plenty for you to do here, and I can use the company. That school's not expecting you back for three months, are they? You can still fulfil your duties. Can you sew, dear? The needle's getting a mite hard to hold in me old fingers, and there are all those choir gowns and robes to mend."

"Yes, I can sew," she answered, surprised by her confidence. "I can hand-stitch and use a machine, both treadle and electric."

Mrs. Rees beamed.

That evening at the old Mooney place, Rose Marie sat down timidly in the dining room with the others, most of them men. There were so many men in Black Apple, walking down the street in ones and twos, going in and out of stores, knots of them lingering outside the Dominion Hotel as she hurried by, the Mooney house filled with them. And here she was, eating with a tableful of men for the first time in her entire life.

"This here's Reggie," Cyril said. "A miner like Frank and me. And this here's Dwayne"—he jerked his thumb at a dark-haired man shaking out a napkin on his other side—"just made foreman."

"How do you do."

They nodded. Two other men came to the table, and everyone started eating—boiled potatoes, green beans from a can, meat loaf, white bread, and gravy. Heavens, not even the pretext of a prayer from any of them. She closed her eyes to silently thank the Lord while the rest dug right in.

"Heard about Billy Nimsic, I suppose?" Ruby enquired, and the others nodded, looking at her expectantly. "Jesus Christ Al-bloody-mighty," she cursed, and Rose Marie almost choked on a bean. "Back of his head split right open, the poor bugger."

"You saw him?" Mrs. Mooney asked.

"Sure did. Fell right outside the gents' door. Drunk as a bloody skunk."

"A generous guy, Billy Nimsic," Mrs. Mooney offered, "but sure as hell not one for business. Nope, it's Dickie Gerard who knows how to run that hotel. Needed Billy to be his partner on account of all that money he inherited from his old man."

"A miserable old miser, his father," one of the miners said. "Billy wasn't like him one bit."

Rose Marie sat on the edge of her chair. She wanted to cross herself, to fold her hands and say the Orphans' Prayer, but she didn't dare. On and on they went, with so many stories and so much swearing she thought her head would explode. She cut her meat loaf in small pieces and slipped them in her mouth. Once she glanced up to find Frank's eyes on her. Heat spread across her neck, and she looked away. Cyril smiled. *Holy Mother, keep me from those who would harm me.* After supper, she rose to clear the table with Ruby and Mrs. Mooney.

"You don't have to do nothing," Mrs. Mooney told her. "You paid your room and board."

"I want to help." She sounded as if she were begging—a child, not a young woman of nineteen on her way to becoming a Sister of Brotherly Love. "Please, Mrs. Mooney, I'm used to chores." Her room was the only other escape from the too-much unscheduled time, the too-many strangers, Frank, Cyril—all the men—and without work to do, the evening would be long and anxious.

"Okay, then," Mrs. Mooney agreed, and Ruby turned to grin at her, showing the spaces between her big tobacco-stained teeth. Rose Marie followed them into the kitchen.

"By the way," Mrs. Mooney said gruffly, pointing at a woman who was pushing her way through the back door, "that there's Mrs. Derkatch."

The frizzy-haired lady who had not wanted to sit next to her on the bus!

"She helps with the clean-up week nights."

Mrs. Derkatch nodded, took off her coat, and hung it on the hook behind the door, then started to scrape off dinner plates. As Ruby and Mrs. Mooney continued to talk about Billy Nimsic and the hotel, Mrs. Derkatch kept her back to them as if she were above such concerns, but Rose Marie could tell she was listening.

Rose Marie didn't want to hear any more on the subject. She bit her bottom lip, remembering how, last night, Dead Fox Man had looked right at her. She was across the street, kneeling on the ground, and it had been dark, so he might not have noticed her. He might have seen her silhouette only, or maybe just a clump of shadows. And he had not come after her, had simply slipped around the corner and vanished.

Maybe if she told anyone, he *would* come after her, like he had when she first arrived in Black Apple. Oh, but Billy Nimsic had fallen and hit his head. Dead Fox Man—whatever his name was—hadn't killed him, the fall had, the pavement: a simple accident. And it wasn't against any Commandment to avoid telling about an accident. It suddenly occurred to her that it could be against the law. Oh dear, she didn't need any trouble in this town, this awful town.

As soon as Mrs. Derkatch had scraped the dishes and stacked them on the counter, Rose Marie put them in the sink, added the cutlery, and turned on the water full blast to mask Ruby and Mrs. Mooney's conversation. Submerging her hands in hot, soapy water, she started washing.

"Aren't you afraid of cutting yerself?" barked Mrs. Mooney. "There are knives in there and real sharp."

She shook her head. There was a way to reach into water, she had learned at St. Mark's, to touch without injuring. "I always do dishes this way." That was the approach she needed in this town. She set the clean plates and bowls in the dish rack, and without looking at her, Mrs. Derkatch snatched them up and started drying. She wondered if Frizzy remembered her from the bus. The old bat acted like she wasn't worth even acknowledging. Fine. She gave her one of Sister Joan's withering looks, but Mrs. Derkatch refused to notice.

As soon as she had finished the dishes and wiped the sink and counter, she left the kitchen and slipped silently down the hall. Just outside Frank's door, she stopped. Music pulsed into the hallway, a song about a man killing another man because he wanted to see him die, and though the words were disturbing, she couldn't help but sway her head to the beat.

She was familiar with radios and the strange feelings they seemed to stir. In her second or third year at St. Mark's, the sisters had bustled importantly up to the priests' suite one evening to listen to people from across the sea declare the end of the war. She had imagined them sitting around the radio, an ornate wooden chest with a panel of thick upholstery that the sound sputtered from. It was an occasion they had talked about for months, Sister Cilla sometimes imitating the British *awk-cent* in the dorm, making everyone laugh.

When she was an intermediate, she was given the summer chore of dusting the priests' living quarters every Saturday while they were taking confession. Afraid of being discovered, she never dared turn on the radio until her second summer at the job, and once she figured out how to work the contraption, she learned the importance of pork-belly, wheat, and barley prices, information she passed on to Sister Bernadette, who then knew when to pester local farmers for donations.

Just last winter after Christmas holidays, a senior named Reba had smuggled one of the new portable radios into the dormitory. For two weeks, until they were caught and the radio was confiscated, a group of seniors had snuck into the bathroom after lights-out, giggling and dancing to tunes with names like "Earth Angel," "Tutti Frutti," and "Blueberry Hill." Probably to earn her silence, the girls had insisted she join them, and though she was older—the most senior senior, the only girl in grade twelve and supposedly "responsible"—she had allowed them to persuade her. Imitating their wiggles, shakes, and prances, Rose Marie had felt the sensation of coins jingling up her spine, something she hadn't experienced since Taki died. She had even heard herself giggle. She joined the girls for a few more nights, but she never felt the same thrill or laughed as much as on the first night. Yet for days after Sister Margaret had carted the radio away, visions of adolescent girls with jittering-fruit breasts and backs with sprouting wings danced through her mind as she was drifting off to sleep.

Clearly Frank had a radio in his room, and she was sure she had heard music coming from both Ruby's and Cyril's rooms upstairs. Yet she wouldn't allow herself to hope for a radio of her own. Soon she would be taking a vow of poverty. Material goods, Mother Grace had told her, would do nothing but impede her spiritual journey. Earthly pleasures must be forsaken. But just that morning, Mrs. Mooney had told her that whenever she wanted, she could listen to the parlour radio, even larger and grander than the one in the priests' suite. And maybe she would do just that.

She went over to it and spun the biggest wooden knob. The sudden popping of fire eating through a forest made her quickly turn it the other way. Nothing worked the way it was supposed to, and she was afraid to try the other knobs in case someone heard and came running. Smoothing her head covering, she walked towards the stairs. As she passed by the open front door, she glimpsed Cyril sitting on the porch steps, smoking. He turned and motioned her.

"Take a load off your feet," he called, indicating the step in front of him. "C'mon. I won't bite."

She paused. She really wasn't ready to go up to her room that still stank of cigarettes, and since she'd cleaned it that morning, probably disinfectant as well. She didn't want to be alone. Besides, Cyril was safe enough, a big man with eyes of water, not sparks and flames. She slipped out the door to the porch.

"Can I offer you a smoke?" Cyril stood and stiffly held out his pack to her, but she shook her head and perched on the step in front of him. "How are you taking to the place?" he asked.

Her mind raced over the crush of the men at supper, Billy Nimsic's death, Ruby's swearing, and Mrs. Mooney's dyed hair, leaving her dumbfounded. "Nice, uh, very nice," she stuttered. "Mrs. Mooney, that is."

Cyril laughed. "Some would say *real* nice, if you know what I mean, not that I blame her. She's had a hard life." He cleared his throat, and she stared blankly up at him.

"She's not really Mrs. Mooney, you know." He sat back down, his foot grazing her knee. She drew back, and Cyril didn't try to move nearer. "Her name's Delores. She just added on 'Mooney' after old Tom-cat Mooney died, leaving her this house in his will. Tom Mooney knew Delores—well, real well. Why, my mother told me he brought her from the valley when she was but fourteen years old, an orphan girl."

"Like me," Rose Marie murmured. "Well, half an orphan."

Cyril nodded, acknowledging her, but discreetly, not looking directly at her. "Maybe Tom-cat really did care for her in his own way. They say he promised to marry her, but he was already married, of course. Started her up in business, if you get my drift. A right bastard, but a rich one. And they say she was head over heels in love with him." He stopped to glance at her, an apology on his face. "I guess I'm being an old woman. Talking too much, ain't I, little girl?" He ran a broad hand through his pale hair.

"Rose Marie."

"Sorry. Rose Marie."

He went on, telling her about the town. At least he didn't bring up Billy Nimsic. Besides, his banter tempered her silence, making her feel less awkward. She was starting to discover that she liked being informed. At St. Mark's, Mother Grace told her about a tenth of what went on, and the girls in the dorm kept things from her too. She was nineteen years old, for crying out loud, and it was time she learned about life outside St. Mark's. Learning was probably what the Mother House expected her to do for three months, though she couldn't imagine they wanted her to experience everything she had in just two days in Black Apple. She had even tried coffee, and she liked it, at least with sugar and a bit of tinned milk.

"Time to turn in," Cyril said, and he waited for her to rise from the step. "Real nice talking to you, Rose Marie," he added as he held the door open. "Maybe see you tomorrow evening."

Once she was in her bedroom, she remembered to write to Mother Grace. She pulled a pad of foolscap from her suitcase. But she was restless, her situation in Black Apple was difficult to explain, and she couldn't think of what to put on the page other than the obvious.

> Dear Mother Grace,
> I arrived at Black Apple safe and sound. I am boarding at a house in town run by a widow. Unfortunately, Father Patrick has died.

No, that was too abrupt. *I am truly sorry to be the bearer of such sad news,* she added. She was about to ask if she could return to the school, when she remembered Mother Grace telling her that the Mother Superior of the order had made it "very clear" that she would have to serve her time in a parish before being admitted to the Mother House, that no special accommodation would be made. Heavens, they might send her someplace even worse than Black Apple—a town where every house had a "no Indians allowed" policy, and there was not one friendly face.

> Father Patrick's housekeeper is very nice, and I have met Father Seamus, the priest of Coal River who is filling in for the time being. Now I'll say my prayers and go to bed. I will write you a letter once I've settled in.

She got up, tucked the note in one of the stamped envelopes Mother Grace had supplied her with, and stuffed it in her raincoat pocket to mail the next day. Idly, she flipped open the Bible: *And after all thy abominations and fornications, thou hast not remembered the days of thy youth, when thou wast naked, and full of confusion, trodden under foot in thy own blood.* Oh my. She slammed the book shut.

As soon as she heard Cyril leave the bathroom, she went in. Her face in the mirror looked drawn, her eyes, staring back at herself, startled. She was frightened, yes, of course, but something else. She examined her expression. Alert. Well, she had to be alert here; danger was everywhere. Not that she was a stranger to it. If she thought about it, she had to admit that there had been all sorts of danger at St. Mark's, but like most of the other girls, she had finally grown adept at avoiding furious nuns and mean girls. She had even, more or less, become used to the shadow sister. But Black Apple was different. Here she didn't know what the dangers were or where they might come from.

She pushed onto her tiptoes and leaned closer to the mirror, examining her eyes. Yes, alert and even bright. Though the town scared her, she had met all kinds of people, and some were even nice. She had more room to manoeuvre than she'd ever had at St. Mark's, and maybe a bit of freedom to act and not just react. Maybe. She recalled the sound of bone hitting concrete and shivered. Maybe not.

After washing and brushing her teeth, she went back to her room and undressed. She was nervous, scared stiff, in fact, but the flutter in her breast felt something like excitement. She knelt by the bed and said five full decades of the rosary and then two run-throughs of the Orphans' Prayer. An hour had gone by before she had settled down enough to sleep.

36

The Letter

MRS. REES LED Rose Marie to the back of the rectory. Standing at the door of a large office with a picture of a sun-stroked Jesus hanging over the desk, she said, "This is Father Seamus's office when he's in Black Apple." She shook her head. "He wants me to wash his office floor and dust the shelves twice a week, but he cancelled the monthly Friday-night dinners for the needy because he says I don't have time for them. Peculiar, he is." She took Rose Marie's hand. "Follow me," she instructed, leading her past a spartan bedroom to the small room at the end of the hall.

"This is Father Patrick's office. Or was. I'll get you to clean it, dear. I just can't." She sighed heavily, and Rose Marie, afraid Mrs. Rees was about to weep, hurried over to the desk.

The shelves overtop were crammed with books. *Das Kapital*, she read, *The Communist Manifesto*, *The Ninety-five Theses*, *Psychology and Religion*, *NAACP and Labor*, *The Man Who Never Died*, *Heart of Darkness*, *The Origin of Species*. Heavens, she hadn't heard of one of them! Looking to the next shelf, she was comforted to see what looked like a row of Bibles, though their various names and sizes confused her: Wycliffe's Bible, the King James Version, Tanakh, the Quaker Bible, the

Geneva Bible, Webster's Revision, Concord Literal Version, Douay-Rheims Bible, Confraternity Edition.

"I'll fetch the cleaning supplies," Mrs. Rees murmured, bustling away.

As soon as she was out the door, Rose Marie picked up a photograph of a young nun from the desk, noticing how the frame was worn from handling, the glass spotted with fingerprints. Studying the sculpted ridge of cheek, the uplifted eyes, the inspired expression of a refined young woman ready to go forward and do God's work, she wondered if it was a picture of Mother Katharine Drexel, who had "worked with the less fortunate races of America"—Mother Grace had impressed upon her the previous year after Mother Katharine's death. Her gaze fell to the delicate hands pressed together, the shaped nails, and when she looked back to the eyes, she suddenly knew, despite the black-and-white of the photograph, that they were blue.

"Lovely, isn't she?" Mrs. Rees said, coming up behind her, almost causing her to jump out of her skin. "Father Patrick was always looking at that photo, he was."

"It's Mother Grace."

"They correspond, you know. Corresponded. A letter from her always put him in a good mood, and he'd read it over a few times before writing her back. Had me mail the reply at the post office, and sure enough, when I returned, he'd be burning her letter in the stove. Once I said to him, 'Father Patrick, is there something there you don't want me to see?' That tickled him. 'There's nothing in our letters you'd find anything but ordinary, Mrs. Rees, but I'm not so sure about *some*.'"

Rose Marie wondered who the *some* were, and after Mrs. Rees left, it came to her that one of them could be Father Seamus. It was normal for priests and nuns to send letters, she knew, at least concerning church business. But only when necessary. Father Seamus, she was certain, would object to anything more.

"Sacrilegious," old Father David and Father William used to warn students, "not to give a man of God the utmost respect." But she wasn't listening to Father William anymore. She wasn't so sure about Father David either.

As she dusted, washed, and polished, the room grew warmer and a soft chuckle rolled through the air. She liked Father Patrick's office; it was comfortable, and she took special care of the old leather chair he had sat in, rubbing in oil with her fingertips. When she picked up the cleaning supplies to go, she took a last look at Mother Grace—Sister Grace, then. *Good night, dearest,* she heard a man's voice murmur.

"You have written, haven't you?" Mrs. Rees asked Rose Marie during the afternoon snack she called "tea." "That school of yours? Mother Grace?"

"Yes, I dropped Mother Grace a line, but I was too tired to write much." *Anxiety.* "I don't know what to say. Mother Grace will worry if she knows I'm boarding in a house full of men."

Mrs. Rees looked troubled. "Rose Marie, there's something I need to tell you about that landlady of yours."

"I know about Mrs. Mooney's past, if that's what you mean."

"You do? Who told you, dear?"

"Cyril."

"Cyril Brown, my, my. Mr. Rees and some of his mates call him 'Tiny,' they do. Such a big man but gentle as a lamb. He'd make some girl a lovely husband."

There was no reason for her to feel embarrassed, but she did.

Her first Sunday at Black Apple, Rose Marie slept until noon. With the exception of two, possibly three times over the years when she had been ill, that had never happened before. Thankfully, she hadn't dreamt the whole night through. She had simply fallen into a deep, black pit, and then climbed out of it, stiff and groggy, at midday. She had missed Mass.

Almost a week had gone by, and she was still confused by the behaviour of the people of Black Apple: the friendliness of Frank, Cyril, Mrs. Mooney, Ruby, and Mrs. Rees, but the suspicion of Father Seamus, the coldness of Mrs. Derkatch and some of the ladies' auxiliary members too, not to mention the catcalls from men outside the Dominion Hotel as she walked past, always on the far side of the street.

The day Billy Nimsic's funeral was held at Our Lady of Sorrows, she stayed late to help Mrs. Rees and some of the church ladies wash dishes in the church hall, fold the tables and chairs, and put them away. Then she and Mrs. Rees took the good china back to the rectory to place carefully in the sideboard. It was past seven when she left, and the sun was sliding down the western sky.

Near the Dominion, as she was about to cross to the far side of the street, she noticed two women outside the gents' door. Both had long dark hair, and one was Indian, she could see, one probably Italian or part Indian—"half-breed," the miners called it—and they were both in tight dresses, their legs exposed to the cool evening. Despite her darkened eyes and bright lipstick, one of the women looked familiar.

Rose Marie slowed to study her, the shrunken yellow sweater buttoned over a stained blue dress, the broad shoulders, a prominent chin dropping as she slumped against the side of the hotel.

"Bertha," she called before she could stop herself. "Bertha Bright—"

Bertha gazed sleepily over at her, looked away, then jerked her head back, eyes narrowing.

Immediately, Rose Marie regretted calling out to her. From her very first week at St. Mark's, when Taki stole the name "Anne" from Bertha's little cousin, all their dealings had been unpleasant. Bertha had stopped physically picking on her after Sister Margaret beat them both, but once Ruth died, she started name-calling and pointing. Then,

years later, when Anataki got so sick, Bertha came down sick too. Rose
Marie had heard her boast to the other senior girls that she almost
died. But she *hadn't* died. Bertha got better, and Taki died instead. It
had taken that terrible equation of loss to neutralize their quarrel. Until
right then, when Rose Marie had so stupidly called attention to herself.

"Well, well," Bertha jeered. "If it isn't a midget in a school dress. Are
those the only clothes you got, Rose Marie Whitewater, who thinks
she's the goddamned Virgin Mary?"

It wasn't that Rose Marie couldn't think of anything to hiss back at
Bertha. She didn't have all the words for what Bertha was doing in front
of the Dominion, but she had an idea. *Hey, Miss Black Apple, what ditch
did you wander out of?* she was about to yell, when, from the corner of
her eye, she spotted a man approaching Bertha. Dead Fox Man. Head
down, she darted across the street and didn't stop to look back until
she was safely tucked in the shadow under the awning at McBride's.

Dead Fox Man's hand reached from his dirty coat and gripped
Bertha's wrist, wrenching her from her slouch against the building.
Teetering towards him on high heels, she protested, but weakly. As
he clenched an arm around her shoulders, she struggled, but half-
heartedly. He steered her towards the side door of the hotel.

Rose Marie fled to the old Mooney house, but once she arrived at
the leaning fence, she turned and walked around the block. Breathing
deeply, she surveyed the other houses, some jumbled into one another,
with old fridges and car parts rusting on leaning porches, others well
groomed with harvested front-yard gardens. She was taking a walk,
partly to calm down and partly to familiarize herself with the neigh-
bourhood as best she could in the waning light. And partly because
no one was supervising her. No one was there to tell her she couldn't.
Again, a faint flutter of excitement in her chest.

Back at the house, she went into the dining room to find the table
crowded with boarders talking over each other as they slurped coffee and shoved green Jell-O in their mouths. Mrs. Mooney slapped
a plate in front of her—a dried pork chop and a heap of crusted

potatoes—and Rose Marie ate silently, rising to help in the kitchen once she was done.

Later, on the porch, Cyril pointed out a group of stars called Orion's Belt, and she told him about the Wolf Trail, where the spirits of the dead wandered. Mama. *Anataki.*

The next afternoon, on her way home from Our Lady of Sorrows, she kept her eyes lowered as she crossed the street, walking quickly away from the Dominion even though it was only five o'clock and neither Bertha nor her companion was leaning against the building.

"Hey, little lady," a voice called from the other side of the street. "Wait up. I'll walk you home."

She looked up. Frank was running over to her, and for some reason she stood there, waiting for him.

"Explosion at the mine," he said, moving so close she could feel the heat seeping from his body right through her school dress. "I think Jake Catelli got his eardrums blown out. They closed down operations for the day."

"Oh dear."

He reached for her hand, but she pulled it away. "Just tryin' to be friendly. How was work today?"

She told him about Mrs. Rees, the ladies' auxiliary meeting, and Father Seamus, "who isn't exactly welcoming."

"He's another one don't like Indians. *Meesy.*"

She raised her eyebrows.

"That's an important Blackfoot word for people like that priest," he said, grinning. "You forgot your language while you were at that school."

"It's okay. I'm going back in a couple of months. I don't need it."

He opened the front door of the house, and at the bottom of the stairs, he leaned towards her. Before she could push past him and run up to her room, he pressed his nose to her forehead. "You never know, you just might."

Since arriving in Black Apple, she was acting the way Sister Cilla sometimes did: blushing and flustered. For no reason at all!

In her room, she thought about Frank, how he changed around people. Mornings when Reggie or Dwayne, and especially Cyril, were at the table, he was jagged edges. But the times when the other miners were on nights and went straight to bed instead of eating breakfast, Frank seemed serene, his colours falling around him like rain. "How are you, Rose Marie Whitewater?" he would ask her gently.

And Cyril. Easy to talk to, like an older brother or a young uncle. When she was finished with the after-supper cleanup, she chatted with him on the porch about this and that: the mine and the church, people they each encountered, and local gossip. Once she thought she saw Frank peering at them from the parlour window.

So much had happened, was happening around her, all the people, every kind—rough, kind, dead, sad, mean, snobby, and dangerous— Mrs. Mooney, Frank, Cyril, Father Patrick, Bertha Bright Eye, Father Seamus, Mrs. Derkatch, and Dead Fox Man. Whom should she include in a letter to Mother Grace? What should she leave out?

And what could she say about herself? So much had happened to her in such a short period of time she didn't know if she was coming or going, as Mrs. Rees put it.

First came Papa's healing dream, which had left her with a sense of calm. For the month or so before Mother Grace had sprung the *assignment* on her, she had felt loved and something else: that the world was larger and more wondrous than she'd ever imagined, and that she even had a place within it. Then she came to Black Apple with its dirt, lack of routine, and strange characters. How could she cope, let alone fit in?

Lead us not into temptation, she prayed at night. *Deliver us from evil*. She had the uncomfortable feeling that St. Mark's was receding, shrinking to a dot on the road map that was thumbtacked to the wall at the bus depot, and that the person she had been at St. Mark's was altering bit by bit, altered by this town.

* * *

The next day, when Mrs. Rees came back from the post office, her bag full of church letters and bulletins, her face was chalky, her step unsteady. Remembering Sister Lucy's decline, Rose Marie hurried to her, helping her out of her coat and into a chair. Then she put on the kettle.

"Are you all right?"

The colour started to seep back into Mrs. Rees's face after she'd had a cup of tea and a chocolate biscuit. She reached into the shopping bag at her feet and pulled out the clump of mail she'd taken from the church mailbox. Sifting through it, she withdrew a letter and handed it to Rose Marie, who recognized the flowing script.

"From Mother Grace. Oh, it's to Father Patrick." She examined the postmark. "It was mailed the day after I left. Our letters must have crossed."

"I didn't know what to do with it," Mrs. Rees said, sniffling. "You take it, dearie. You can always send it back."

That evening at supper, Rose Marie hardly noticed the squeal of sauerkraut, a food she had never before eaten, or the burn of mustard on her tongue. All she could think of was Mother Grace's letter.

"You're miles away, little girl," Cyril commented.

"Rose Marie," she automatically corrected him.

Later, in the kitchen, she was as dismissive of Mrs. Derkatch as the woman was of her, snatching each dish from Frizzy's hand as soon as she had scraped it clean. She didn't hear a word of Ruby and Mrs. Mooney's conversation, nor did she say anything herself.

When Cyril tried to draw her to the porch for their usual chat, she told him, "Can't tonight," and climbed the stairs two at a time, going straight to her room. Sitting on her chair, feet propped on the bed, she tore open the letter from Mother Grace to Father Patrick and read:

Dear Patrick,

I know that Rose Marie will be with you now, safe in your care, and I thank God for that.

Nevertheless, I need your help. I just received a letter from Father John the Baptist from the Reserve on which Rose Marie's father lived after the death of his wife, his original Reserve. It is the second letter I received from Father John. The first, which informed me of Mr. Whitewater's tuberculosis, arrived over a month ago. I have long suspected he had the illness, though over the years, it never seemed to progress.

Father John noted that Mr. Whitewater still appeared vigorous, but since he went on and on about the "heathen practices" Mr. White-water was engaged in and his "substantial following," I surmised that his concern had more to do with getting Mr. Whitewater from the Reserve and to the hospital than with any imminent danger to his life. That, Pat dear, was my mistake.

At the time, I was busy seeking an indulgence for Rose Marie, one that would allow her to go straight to the Mother House. With all the writing back and forth, I'm afraid I did not give the news the attention that, in hindsight, I see it deserved.

The day before Rose Marie was to board the bus for Black Apple, I got word that Michel Whitewater had died on the Reserve without ever setting foot in any hospital. Rose Marie was in no condition to hear that, as she had just learned she had to leave St. Mark's.

Patrick, could you possibly break the news to her in a gentle way? As I said, she knows nothing of her father's illness, so his death will come as a shock.

Rose Marie stopped reading. Papa. She stood, but suddenly dizzy, she fell back on the bed. He had died the night he came to her, she had no doubt. When he told her he loved her.

Mother Grace—whom she had trusted above all others, whom she relied on, would give her any news of Papa—had told her nothing. She had as good as lied!

Grief hit her in the stomach and seeped, hot, through her eyes. She threw the letter on the floor and stumbled across the room to the window. Peering out, she watched the sun setting behind the mountains, garish as an open wound.

Dear, dear Papa, *Blessed Wolf*. Since Mama's death, Mother Grace had kept her from him. She had denied her wish to go up north to live with him and Kiaa-yo, Papa's relations, hers too, where she should be, where she belonged. And even if Mother Grace *had* told her of Papa's illness before she left for Black Apple, she would never have allowed her to visit him. The witch, the *bitch* would have been afraid that if she left to see Papa, she would not return to St. Mark's; she would not become a holy sister. And maybe she wouldn't have. Maybe she wouldn't now!

She snatched the letter from the floor, tore it up, and threw the pieces in the air. She hated Mother Grace and all the nuns at St. Mark's, including Sister Cilla, and especially Sisters Joan and Margaret. She hated Brother Abe the disabled, and she despised Father William, the dirty kill-man!

She used the sleeve of her dress, her horrible school uniform, to wipe her nose and eyes. She would never ever write to Mother Grace again.

All night long, she prayed for Papa's soul.

37

Confession

ROSE MARIE KNEW she could not miss another Sunday Mass, and if she was going to Mass, Father Seamus insisted that his parishioners must first go to confession or be unfit for Holy Communion. "He's a mite rigid," Mrs. Rees said.

Even though Rose Marie was weighed down by grief—yes, with confusion and anger thrown in—and even though she desperately wanted to unload her burden, she didn't know what to confess to Father Seamus. Everything in her heart, mind, and soul was stuck together in an ugly black lump.

The anguish she had felt when she read of Papa's death persisted. She scarcely knew what she was doing as she moved from pew to pew in Our Lady of Sorrows, haphazardly wiping at the wooden seats.

Behind the thick blanket of fog in her head, a storm was building. She was afraid it would rip through and overwhelm her. Images of confronting Mother Grace darted through her mind. She yanked the old woman's beloved wooden cross—the one Father Patrick had made—off her office wall and threw it in her face. Then she stood at the top of the staircase on the third floor, just behind Sister Margaret as she started to descend, Sister Joan a few steps below. She shoved Sister Margaret with all her might, and the fat tub plummeted headlong into

Sister Joan. Both of them crashed to the landing, their heads striking it with the same sound Billy Nimsic's skull had made on the sidewalk outside the Dominion.

She burned with hatred.

And hatred was against one of the greatest Commandments of all, she knew. After *loving the Lord*, it was imperative that Christians *love thy neighbour as thyself.* How was she to tell Father Seamus that she hated Mother Grace, she despised Father William, and she disliked even him, her confessor? She would have to admit that she was ablaze with anger and vengeance.

As she swept the church aisles, she thought of her upcoming confession. Where to begin? Aside from breaking any of the Ten Commandments, a sin was *an offence against reason, truth, and conscience.* Yes, *wilful thought, word, deed, or omission against God's law.* But her brain was a smouldering black lump, and she didn't know where to start.

Finally, instead of trying to figure out which of her thoughts and actions were actual sins to confess, she decided to organize everything into a kind of parade to march before Father Seamus.

She had felt a twinge of conscience just before she read the letter Mother Grace had written to Father Patrick. As she unfolded the crisp pages, she had suddenly worried that Mother Grace would somehow know what she was doing. But since she wasn't contrite about that offence, she would stick it on the end of her confession.

She felt a glimmer of heat dance over her skin whenever she was near Frank, but that was like the rash Susanna Big Snake got from eating strawberries, a reaction but hardly a sin. Or, again, was she simply not contrite? And how about the conversations she had with Cyril? "Harmless enough, dear," according to Mrs. Rees, but would Father Seamus agree? That would go at the end of her confession as well.

There was just so much to confess!

*   *   *

Friday afternoon, after Father Seamus had arrived from Coal River to hear confessions in Black Apple, she waited in a pew close to the crucifix, praying for strength. In the past two days, she had grown calmer, and she had decided to start by confessing the most troubling issue of all: Billy Nimsic's fight or accident or murder—whatever it was— which pooled in her brain and sometimes seeped like sewage into her dreams. She had to confess so it would drain away. Then she could proceed with the rest of her confession—her grief and terrible anger.

She entered the confessional.

"Father, I witnessed an act of violence outside the Dominion Hotel," she said after the initial welcome and response, her voice trembling. As soon as the words were out of her mouth, she recognized that not trying to help Billy Nimsic was sinful. *Love thy neighbour.* But she had run in the opposite direction; she had not thought of him, gone to him, assisted him in any way. "Father, I did nothing—"

"Nothing?" Father Seamus's voice throbbed through the screen. "Don't excuse yourself. You did nothing? Why then were you anywhere close to the Dominion Hotel?"

"I was walking. I had just arrived in Black Apple, and—"

"And the first thing you did was head to the Dominion Hotel. That is no place for a *respectable* young woman," Father Seamus told her sternly. "You must stay away from drink. You must stay away from men. You must not court temptation of any sort. Do you hear me?" The priest's voice was loud, louder than it should be to remain unheard by the other penitents, and while she felt chastened, she also felt a spasm of humiliation, yes, and anger. Again, anger.

"Forgive me, Father, for my anger," she began, but Father Seamus, now talking about "dens of iniquity," didn't seem to hear.

"What is it about *your kind*," he demanded, "that you knowingly entice men from the path of righteousness?" His voice rose and fell in waves, just as Father William's did when he was in the throes of a sermon. *"If the serpent, the Devil, bites someone secretly, he infects that person with the venom of sin."*

"Father?" she tried, but he talked over her, demanding she make an act of contrition. She had gotten to *"I firmly resolve, with the help of Thy grace, to sin no more and to avoid the near occasions of sin . . ."* when he was giving her penance and sending her from the confessional.

He hadn't allowed her to make a complete confession. He hadn't even listened, the stupid, stupid man. They were all against her, the religious. Every last one.

38

Mass

ON SUNDAY MORNING, Rose Marie left the old Mooney place
at ten so she would have plenty of time for prayer before eleven
o'clock Mass. She was still shaken by her incomplete confession and
by Father Seamus's harsh judgement, so she wanted to arrive at Our
Lady of Sorrows early in order to set things right with God.

First, she would contemplate the mysteries of the most holy rosary
of the blessed Virgin Mary. Not only was the church named after her,
but Mother Mary was a parent, and with Papa's death, Rose Marie
was short of parents. She would beg for forgiveness of all her offences
against God, intentional or not. Then she would give St. Francis's
prayer of Spiritual Communion, and, as well as more forgiveness, she
would ask for guidance, then meditate about her vocation. What was
she even doing in this town?

She walked down the centre aisle of the empty church, smelling
the oil soap that she and Mrs. Rees always used. Even the Lord Jesus
Christ, hanging from the cross, gleamed. After confession on Friday,
angry and restless, she had waited for Father Seamus to leave, then
retrieved the ladder kept under the basement stairs, propped it against
the wall, climbed it, and dusted and washed the Saviour head to toe.

The task had calmed her. Up on the ladder she had felt close to both God and Papa. And far away from Father Seamus.

Now she desperately needed to be close to God again. She stopped at the third aisle from the front, genuflected, and took a seat in the centre of the pew. Hands folded, eyes closed, she knelt on the prayer bench and fell into the words and motions she had memorized, repeated, read, and prayed forever, it seemed. She didn't need a prayer book; she had twelve years at St. Mark's and thousands of Matins, Vespers, novenas, devotions, litanies, petitions, invocations, acts, meditations, and intercessions planted in her brain, their rhythms pumping through her heart, surging at wrist, throat, thigh, and temple. The emotions they served and expressed—longing, hope, love, fear, despair, and grace—formed a spiritual entrance that she slipped effortlessly through.

Praying at length, and in such depth, at Our Lady of Sorrows was easier than she expected, like breathing, an involuntary act as much as a duty. Biblical phrases and prayer fragments entwined with her own words, dancing through her in a language of supplication and repentance. She prayed as the religious of St. Mark's did when they were at their most humble, most sincere, and most inspired. She prayed like a saint.

After entering the spiritual realm, and reaching out to Father, Son, and Holy Ghost, the Madonna, and all the angels, Mama, Anataki, and Papa, she vaguely heard, at the edge of her consciousness, oxfords plodding, high heels snapping, and steel-heeled leather soles clicking. There were huffs, exclamations, throat clearings, and coughs, but Rose Marie, still in a state of holy meditation, was only vaguely aware of the sounds.

Finally, she opened her eyes. People were seated all around her in the church, but none in her pew. No one was directly in front of her, and no one directly behind. She saw gentlemen in dark coats, ladies in elaborate hats, and well-dressed children in shiny shoes, slicked hair, curls, and bows, but none sat close. An empty space encircled her.

As she peered around, faces looked back, some with raised eyebrows, scowls, or flared nostrils; others turned elaborately away. Mrs.
Tortorelli, wearing a veiled wide-brimmed black hat with black roses,
each one almost as big as her head, glared at Rose Marie from the front
row, and the small, grey man beside her frowned. As if Rose Marie
were contaminated. Or trespassing. Or both. It came to her that she
was being shunned.

From the back of the church came a troop of white-gowned altar
boys flanking Father Seamus, who swung a thurible, the incense rising
in suffocating gusts. She spotted Mrs. Rees walking softly down on
the right-side aisle, leading a man with wavy white hair. Mr. Rees, she
assumed—oh, but struggling, his face pale. He had been doing *poorly*,
Mrs. Rees had told her at the beginning of the week. "Emphysema,
he has, but that's just a fancy word for black lung, from working in
the coal mine."

Mr. and Mrs. Rees sat near the front of the right-side section, not
in the centre section as she had. Rose Marie looked over to the left-
side section. As on the right, the front rows seemed to be inhabited
by miners, their wives and families. The men wore white shirts, most
with suits, many of them shabby, and the women had scarves or small,
plain hats on their heads.

Behind the couples and families on both side sections were single
men and a few women, mostly older—bachelors, widows, and wid-
owers, probably. She noticed a family: a man—white—most likely a
rancher, judging from his plaid shirt and overalls, with an Indian wife.
Between them sat a string of four shiny-faced kids, *half-breeds*. There
were two other, similar families, and in the rows behind them was a
sprinkling of ragged, unshaven men, and one crazy-looking woman
with wild grey hair who wore men's clothing. In the two rows behind
them—oh, Indians. She understood. The church was another version
of the Greyhound bus. And Indians belonged at the back.

She wasn't sure what to do. Should she get up and hurry over to
the back of a side section? But Father Seamus was approaching the

altar; it was too late. Then she saw Bertha Bright Eye slumped in the back row on the right. She wore a dingy cotton dress; her eyes were lowered and her face distorted somehow. As Bertha raised her heavy chin, turning slightly to the dishevelled man beside her, Rose Marie saw that her jaw was swollen on one side, her eye black, her puffy bottom lip split. *Dear God.*

Bertha, glancing past the man, saw Rose Marie and turned abruptly away.

Heavens, she was staring at Bertha, but she couldn't stop.

Having regained her composure, Bertha looked back up and fixed her with an expression of pure hatred. Hatred again. Then she set her swollen jaw and turned to the altar.

Rose Marie looked to the front. As Father Seamus welcomed the congregation, it seemed that he too glowered at her.

"And also to you," she started to say, but as she raised her voice with the others, Mrs. Tortorelli turned, her immense hat slipping to one side, her eyes on Rose Marie, dark slivers. She shrank down in her seat, for once glad to be small, but in the centre of the empty pews, she was both isolated and conspicuous.

Once Mass ended, she couldn't get out of her seat fast enough. She fled to the aisle, but had to bunch behind others, everyone staring at her, she was sure. From the corner of her eye, she spotted Mrs. Rees waving, and she gave as much of a smile as she could manage. She was desperate to leave.

She ran all the way back to the Mooney house. Breathless, she hurried through the front door and climbed the stairs two at a time. Closing her bedroom door, she flung herself on the bed, allowing the tears she had been holding back to slip down her face. *Holy Mother of Heaven and Earth.*

Someone knocked. "Rose Marie?" It was Frank's voice. "You in there?"

For a fraction of a second she thought of opening the door and sinking into Frank's arms. She wondered if she had dreamt a similar scene, because she could see herself—taller, with larger breasts and wider eyes, almost beautiful. Frank too looked different, like a movie star on one of the posters outside the Lux Theatre downtown.

Then the fantasy vanished, leaving only anger. "Go away!" she yelled.

This time she had betrayed herself.

39

Coal Dust

THE COAL DUST in Black Apple was devious as sin itself. Rose Marie found that it soiled everything in Our Lady of Sorrows: the baptismal font, the stained glass windows, the Bible—Word of the Lord, God Almighty—Father Seamus's just-washed hands, his voice, his words at baptisms, weddings, and Sunday Mass. Outside, it dirtied the clean laundry hung on wash lines, the fresh paint on Mrs. Tortorelli's "respectable" boardinghouse, the coats of stray dogs, and the leers of men loitering outside the Dominion Hotel.

The necks of milk bottles left outside the rectory were always gritty. She imagined that the cheeks of children would feel mealy under the touch of their mothers and fathers at bedtime. The weekly *Black Apple Bulletin* had to be shaken out before being taken indoors, and the potatoes unearthed from the small corner garden at the rectory tasted of coal—that recipe of rotted plants, decomposed animals, pressure, and time. The town spent, breathed, ate, and drank coal.

Miners dug up a lost world from the belly of the mountain, heaped it in coal cars that jittered up the tipple, where it was sized, then dumped into railcars and carried away to factories in Calgary, Montreal, and Vancouver. From there, it was shipped across the wide sea to sprawling, spewing factories full of people working like machines, synchronized to sirens like the one at the mine. Men shovelled coal into belching furnaces that spewed its remains, black and sooty, into the air. It seemed to Rose Marie that the extinct past was burning its way into the future.

Each day she walked to Our Lady of Sorrows Church. Every day but Sunday, when she attended Mass—sitting with Mr. and Mrs. Rees in the second row on the right-side section—she helped Mrs. Rees clean the rectory, bake, wash, starch and iron robes and ceremonial cloths, scrub the church pews, shine the Communion tabernacle and monstrance. Once a week, Mrs. Rees sent her to pick up groceries and supplies at McBride's and Wong's; once a month, it was necessary to wash our Saviour on the cross and clean the statue of the sorrowing Virgin with her breaking Sacred Heart.

After work, if she felt like it, she would explore a part of town she wasn't familiar with. Sometimes she looked over in the direction of the Mountain That Moves and thought of her old life with Mama and Papa in their little cabin in the woods. Then came Kiaa-yo, and then came the Indian agent and Father Alphonses. It was as if her whole life had collapsed then, just the way the mountain had.

A month earlier, she had believed that God had planned things this way, that her time at the school was a blessing in disguise, leading her to greater things for His Glory. Now she wasn't so sure. She walked, she watched, and she prayed, sometimes to the Virgin, sometimes to the Holy Trinity, and every now and then to Mama and Papa. *Help me find my place, to belong somewhere.*

Soon she was taking longer walks around the town, going straight home only when she worked late, it was rainy, or she was tired. Then she tidied her room and washed her hands and face before supper. Saturdays, she always removed her white head covering and scrubbed it in the sink, trying to return it to its original white. But coal dust penetrated the cotton, and no matter how hard she scrubbed, knuckle against knuckle, no matter how much bleach and soap she added to the water or how many times she rinsed, she could not get it white.

Her vigorous scouring not only formed blisters on her fingers but also frayed the cloth, making it look ratty. By the middle of her fourth week in Black Apple, she threw her head covering away. Mrs. Rees gave her a flowered scarf to tie under her chin for Mass.

And there was still no word from Mother Grace.

On the first day of her second month in Black Apple, Rose Marie finished dusting the altar and icons in the church, then went to the rectory. As she opened the door, she could hear Father Seamus's raised voice.

"I never asked for that girl to come here. We don't have the resources to support her in this parish."

She froze.

"Father Patrick agreed to take her on," came Mrs. Rees's reply. "She's a very special girl, Father, and she comes from a respectable school."

They were at the back of the rectory, probably in Father Seamus's study.

"It's a *residential* school," Father Seamus's voice boomed. "It's a school built to provide religious and vocational training for Indian youth at the expense of the government of Canada and with the labour of the Church. A lot of good those schools do, if you look around this town. The situation is even worse in Coal River. Drunks and criminals, nearly every last one of them. At church infrequently, yet at Christmas and Easter they expect to be given Communion when they haven't even been reconciled with God at confession."

"I've got to know her, and she's a lovely young woman. Hardworking and devout."

"I have to provide spiritual leadership to this town as well as Coal River, Mrs. Rees. That is my responsibility. The church is here to support the *real* Catholics of the parish. It is the pillars of our community who supply the daily bread for the others. Let us not, in any well-meaning but misdirected way, forget that."

"Father Seamus, you've seen the article about her in the church paper. The Lord has touched her."

"According to the priest and Mother General of her *residential* school, who, if they're like the others, are always looking for handouts. No doubt her so-called *Visitation* has been exaggerated—"

"Father Seamus!"

"Never mind, Mrs. Rees, I imagine we're stuck with her now. You might as well send the month's room and board over to that, that Mrs.—whatever she calls herself these days."

"But she paid last month's rent from her own pocket, Father, money the sisters at the school gave her. She hasn't a cent left. Can we not pay back—"

"No, Mrs. Rees, we will not take the hard-earned money from our parishioners so an Indian can be given free room and board at the house of a harlot. The parish will pay her board for this month only. Please tell her that."

Rose Marie slipped out the door, easing it shut, and ran back to the church.

She began dusting the icons again. Everything she had cleaned just a few minutes earlier had already managed to attract a fine layer of coal dust.

40

The Reply

ROSE MARIE CONFIDED to Mrs. Rees that her papa had died. They were having tea in the rectory, and this time Mrs. Rees's voice was so kind, her expression so sympathetic when she asked why Rose Marie was glum, that she simply collapsed at the kitchen table, all her grief and bitterness hissing out of her like air from a balloon.

"Mother Grace should have told me he was sick," she found herself repeating. "There's no excuse for not telling me!"

Mrs. Rees didn't ask how she'd learned of Papa's death. Instead she reached over, put her plump arms around Rose Marie's shoulders, and hugged.

"She must have had her reasons, love." Then she told her to write to Mother Grace again. "She's mourning a death as well, isn't she?"

Yes, Father Patrick. But Rose Marie was not ready to write to Mother Grace. Maybe she never would be.

Six weeks she'd been in Black Apple, a month and a half of getting to know the town and its people, at least some of them. Chatting with Cyril on the porch after supper cleanup when he wasn't on evening shift had become a ritual, and sometimes when Frank was on days, he met her across from the Dominion Hotel and walked her home. If he reached out to touch her hand or arm with his fire fingers, she shook him off. She looked for him, but she dreaded seeing him. She wanted to be near him, but she was relieved when he wasn't waiting for her. He made her uncomfortable. He enticed her.

Surprisingly, she liked Ruby and Mrs. Mooney and looked forward to helping them clean up after supper. It was like summer kitchen duty with Sisters Bernadette and Cilla, but even more relaxed, certainly less censored.

She was angry, nostalgic, uneasy, confused, and lonely all at once in this town. She was also intrigued. There was a raw energy to life beyond the orderly world of the Sisters of Brotherly Love.

One evening, just after Mrs. Derkatch, her head held high, had slammed the back door on her way out, Mrs. Mooney remarked, "Maybe I should tell the 'high-and-mighty kitchen help' we don't require her precious services as long as we got you helping us, Rose Marie."

They all laughed at that.

"But don't forget I'll be gone in another month and a half," she reminded them.

Often in Black Apple, she fell into memories of her *before* life in the bush. The crackling summer fires outside and the warm comfort of the wood stove on a winter's day inside snuck up on her without warming. The smell of fresh bread wafting from the bakery at Wong's made her think of Mama's bannock, and the meat on display behind the glass counter at McBride's prompted an image of Papa bowing under a heavy bundle of venison. When she looked up to the tree-draped mountains, she could see the narrow deer trails they had walked and hear the laughter in her parents' voices as they joked. She was pretty sure that Frank danced to the radio in his room, but the scene that came to mind when she slipped past his door was Papa's compact body taking on the movements of a wolf, the heartbeat of a drum.

Yet outside her circle of acquaintances, unfamiliar people and situations confronted her daily, and what was required of her never seemed clear. She needed a friend to talk to, someone who understood her and could help her make sense of everything that had happened since she left St. Mark's. Although she couldn't turn to Mother Grace anymore, she had Mrs. Rees, Ruby, Mrs. Mooney, Cyril, and even Frank to talk to.

But she wanted Anataki.

Autumn took hold of the town. The shaking trees put on gold costumes and danced until exhausted, then dropped their leaves on the ground. Sunset came sooner, and the evening air was nippy. She wore Sister Bernadette's raincoat and Sister Simon's boots when she left the house each morning.

One evening when she was sitting on the porch with Cyril, he got up to "see a man about a dog," leaving his cigarette burning in the ashtray. Curious, she picked it up and brought it to her lips. The end was damp, so she held the tip and closed her mouth over her fingers, inhaling deeply. She did that twice more before setting it back in the ashtray.

Her throat raw and her stomach churning, she felt her head lift from her shoulders like an airborne leaf. Her thoughts teetered back to her work at the rectory that morning: washing Father Seamus's cassock collar, alb, and amice for Sunday's Mass, his bedsheets, towels, and underdrawers, then ironing them all in the afternoon. It had been a busy day, and yet insignificant. Seconds, minutes, and hours were dripping from her and falling into a shapeless lump. She wanted more than just the freedom to walk around the town after work. People still told her what to do, making her feel like she was living their lives, not her own. It had always been that way, she saw now. She was sick of having nothing that was hers and hers alone.

Standing up and leaning against a post, she watched the dirt and gravel street, the houses and front-yard gardens ooze at her feet. Only the mountains, black against the violet sky, were solid, a reminder of the landscape she knew as a child. She wanted something that was just out of reach, but she didn't know what it was. The only thing she knew for certain was that before another day passed, she must sit down and write to Mother Grace again. She could not put it off any longer.

> *Dear Mother Grace,*
>
> *Presently I am assisting Mrs. Rees in the upkeep of Our Lady of Sorrows Church, the church hall, and the rectory. She is a kind and pious woman who guides me through my chores. Overall, I am doing fine in Black Apple, but things are not as expected.*
>
> *Mrs. Mooney requires eighty dollars a month room and board. I had to make the first month's payment myself with the money you gave me, every last cent. Mrs. Rees persuaded Father Seamus to make this month's payment, but I'm sure he won't make next month's. Could you please write to Father Seamus concerning this matter?*

Once that was done, she had the urge to ask Mother Grace if she was grieving Father Patrick's death. She wanted to write, *It doesn't feel so good to be told out of the blue that someone you love has died, does it, Mother Grace?* But Mother Grace didn't know she had read her letter to Father Patrick, and she wasn't ready to admit to it.

Setting down her pen, she thought about a phrase Cyril had used a few nights back. He had been warning her of a man named Rolfe Mooney, "Old Tom-cat's son, a meaner SOB than even Tom was." As he described Rolfe—his red hair and dirt-coloured trench coat—she recognized him as Dead Fox Man.

"I know who you mean!"

"Stay away from him," Cyril warned, just as Frank had when she first arrived in town. Then Cyril told her how he, Frank, and Dwayne had thrown Rolfe out of the Dominion Hotel last Friday because Rolfe had beat up a whore, excuse his language.

"Oh" was all she had been able to say.

She knew what the word *whore* meant. Mother Grace had used it once when she was referring to Mary Magdalene. "Some say Magdalene was a"—and she had cleared her throat—"a whore. A woman who sells herself to men for money." Her voice had been stiff. "Don't you believe it, Rose Marie. The Bible says no such thing."

"I put Rolfe in a headlock," Cyril had told her, chuckling. "I says to him, 'We're not going to let you back in the Dominion. Now put that in your pipe and smoke it!'"

That was the phrase she yearned to use in her letter. *You wish you had seen Father Patrick before he kicked the bucket, don't you, Mother Grace? Well, that's how I feel too. You kept me from Papa, from my brother and all the relatives on Papa's Reserve. That was your plan. You even kept news of Papa's illness from me, and for all of that, I'm really mad at you. Maybe I'll never even speak to you again. So, put that in your pipe and smoke it!*

As she picked up her pen, it occurred to her that though she was still angry, she didn't hate Mother Grace as she had thought, as she had hoped. But she did want to get back at her.

She hated Father William, though. The kill-man. She wondered if he had hurt other boys; he could have poisoned, shot, stabbed, or hung them. Just as surely as he had hanged that little boy with the big eyes, the kid who grew up to become a haunted young man. She would avoid Father William when she returned to St. Mark's. *If* she returned. The thought darted through her mind, then crawled into a corner to sleep.

Please remind Father William that I keep his wise words in mind: "Idle hands are the Devil's workshop."

She moved her pen down the paper, about to write *Yours in Christ,* but she was not yet ready to be reunited with Mother Grace, even in spirit. And she would not ask Mother Grace to keep her in her prayers either. What good did prayers do?

Truly,
Rose Marie

41

When Skies Are Grey

MOTHER GRACE FOUND it hard to continue with her daily routine. Such a large, empty world it seemed without Patrick, and suddenly she was lost within it, left alone with no one to tell of her developing or diminishing philosophies, small blasphemies, and secret hopes. No one cared what she thought. *Désolée.* Even her favourite student, her protégée, Rose Marie Whitewater, who had delivered the wrenching news to her, was diminished to the size of a fly in her thoughts.

She should go to confession. *Non*, she didn't want to. She always found the process embarrassing. Despite decades of earnest attempts, she had never been able to forget that on the other side of the screen was a priest, one she knew, and now it was undoubtedly Father William. Over the years, she had considered him young, inexperienced, and flawed, though currently, the man was almost a friend. Not like Father Patrick, though. *Mon Dieu*, she couldn't put the two names in the same sentence. Father Patrick was her true confessor, her confidant, her love.

Dead.

How his letters had felt in her hand as she plucked them from the mail—packets of ink and ideas—substantive, challenging, yet always confirming. Even in old age, a thrill had run through her breast as she opened them, often late at night while the sisters slept. Patrick's humour—clever, sharp, and sometimes derisive, often delightfully mischievous—unfailingly caused her to laugh out loud in the hushed school. His love too; she had felt it in the texture of the paper—old and strong as a tree, as complexly grained.

In the past, when busy or ill, he had gone as many as two weeks without corresponding. When running his mission in the Badlands to the east, it had occasionally been as long as a month. She had worried only on occasion, and only slightly. If anything happened to Patrick, she would know deep within her soul. Should he be in danger or pass on, the very configuration of the world would alter, and she would most definitely feel it.

So she had thought.

Rose Marie's note informing her so bluntly of Patrick's death had hit like a sledgehammer, and she still hadn't recovered. Would she ever? She looked out the window at the sun, yellow as urine seeping into the white sheet of winter. She glanced at her hands, her once handsome nails, bitten. She couldn't remember doing it.

Despite knowing she had things to accomplish, she couldn't focus. At the very least, she should write to Rose Marie, but damn it, she couldn't summon the motivation. She wasn't sure she was even capable of scribbling more than a sentence or two.

Hélas, her last letter had been to Father Patrick, asking him to inform Rose Marie of her father's death, she suddenly realized. And what had happened to that letter? If the housekeeper had simply returned it in the mail, she should have received it by now. Perhaps the housekeeper had read it herself and then told Rose Marie the news. Or perhaps it was sitting on a dusty shelf, unopened. Had she been too familiar with Patrick in the letter, should the interim priest read it? She was unsure. Then again, it was quite possible that Rose Marie had read the letter and was heartbroken. Or furious. She couldn't deny that she had felt some guilt over the years for allowing Mr. Whitewater only limited access to his daughter.

She reached across her desk to have a look through the pile of newspapers Father Alphonses had brought her: both regional and national papers at least a week old, but sent to him by the bishop because of their coverage of the new Indian Act. Father Alphonses had driven them out to St. Mark's for her to read. "I appreciate this," she had muttered, knowing that normally she would have.

She ached from neck to wrist and had to position each newspaper in front of her on the desk in order to read it. From what she could gather, this new Indian Act conceded that residential schools had been unsuccessful in their attempts to assimilate the Indian race. *Oui*, she had known; they'd all known, but exposed in black and white for all to see, the word *failure* chilled her to the bone.

She scribbled a note, cancelling her meeting with Sister Cilla. She had hoped to solidify her strategy for the future of St. Mark's, encouraging Priscilla to rededicate herself for the greater cause. *You are the one on whom my hopes for the future of St. Mark's rest*, she had planned to remind her.

She'd meet with Sister Cilla tomorrow, or possibly the day after. When she had the strength for it.

She rose from her desk. Two in the afternoon and she was already weary, unable to spend another minute stuck to her office chair. She shook three aspirins into her mouth and, grasping one of her canes, headed towards the long and difficult staircase. On the way, she stuffed her note in Sister Cilla's mailbox.

With every step, she heard the creak of death. So much death over the years. Not surprisingly, she was learning of the passing of colleagues often these days, strong young women with whom she had attended the Mother House and sisters she had met during her years on the prairies. Then her oldest brother, Martin, gone just this past month with a heart attack. Her second-eldest brother, Stéphane, fourteen years before, and all those tubercular Indians she had worked with in hospitals. *Vieilli*, the young feverish students! So many of them. So young. Her father had died haying when she was thirty, and five years later, dear Maman had gone in her sleep. It was as if all the deaths she had ever known culminated in Patrick's passing, as if she were experiencing every last one of them again. Patrick, *cher* Patrick, *God bless your beautiful self.*

Each step caused her skirts to rub together. Widow's weeds. Of course, they were the same black and white as always, the cumbersome signification of her vows of poverty, chastity, and obedience. Perhaps too much obedience, she was beginning to think. Obedience led to compliance, which over the years had hardened to indifference—and indifference, she suspected, was the demise of the soul.

At this precise moment she felt completely indifferent to St. Mark's and its operation, the sisters, the students, and her own role. Her heart was nothing more than a dry husk. *Une veuve.* Yet she could tell no one of the depth of her grief. She took to her bed, something she had never done in all her years of serving at St. Mark's, no matter how weakened by cold, flu, or rheumatism.

Three days later, she rose from bed in the afternoon, walked to her narrow window, peered out, and from the second storey, observed that pig farmer Olaf approach Sisters Bernadette and Cilla on the front grounds, a large package—no doubt of pork kidneys or liver, wrapped like some sort of sacred offering—in his hands. From her second-storey window, she heard Sister Bernadette's giggle as she took the package. Even with her rheumy eyes, she was able to spot the flush in Sister Cilla's cheek.

For a full week, she could not muster the resources necessary to descend the stairs to her office. Except for treks to the bathroom or to her window to look out at the waning autumn sun, she remained in bed, dozing through day and night and praying for the soul of Father Patrick, her dear husband. *Mon Dieu.*

Sister Bernadette delivered a bowl of watery chicken soup and a note from Father William, but reading first of Patrick's death, and then about the new Indian Act, had damaged her eyes. Now they burned and watered whenever she tried to look at anything for longer than a few seconds.

"I'm surely going blind," she complained to Sister Bernadette, who was about to open her mouth. "Take the note back to Father William, and whatever it is you have to say, I don't care."

"It's about Sister—"

"Shush! I don't want to hear it."

She got out of bed on Sunday to listen to Father William's sermon, but watching him gesticulate in the pulpit started her eyes watering again, and she returned to her room. Sister Simon brought her dinner, which she tried valiantly to eat.

During the first week of October, she finally got up, dressed, and made her way down the hall to the priests' suite. *Onward, Christian soldiers.* With her cane, she knocked firmly on Father William's door.

"Why, Mother Grace," he greeted her, scratching his beard. "You must be feeling better. I'm, of course, very glad to see—"

"I've come for that portable radio that was confiscated from the senior girl. I'm not sure how it ended up in your suite."

"Um, actually, I want you to look at what I think you'll find an inspiring article for the *Catholic News*. I'd be interested in what you—"

"I've come for the radio."

"Of course. I'll get it. No, I can't expect you to—um, I'll carry it to your office."

"I need it now, William."

"Of course, Mother Grace. Right away."

*   *   *

Late that night, when the students were fast asleep in the third-floor dormitory, the sisters in their rooms, and Father William and Brother Abe in their suite, Mother Grace entered her office and with one creaking arm swept the newspapers from the top of her desk. Leaning forward, she switched on the radio and sat down. *Vieilli,* the "Hog Report" at this hour? She turned the dial, and music filled the absence.

You are my sunshine.

42

Bobcat with a Rabbit

TOWARDS THE END of her second month in Black Apple, Rose Marie was constantly worried. She didn't know if Mother Grace had sent Father Seamus or Mrs. Mooney a cheque for her room and board. Or if she was going to. She didn't want to ask either of them, afraid she'd be lectured, or maybe even turned out of the old Mooney place. What would she do then?

As she was clearing the dining room table after supper one night, she turned to see Frank behind her, blocking her exit to the kitchen. His reckless grin knocked her heart out of its rhythm, but then his expression turned sombre.

"I was wondering," he began, and, thankfully, he dropped his eyes to his coal-stained hands. "Would you like to come for a walk with me?" He had never asked her so formally, so seriously before.

She could smell him—not a strong scent—but a mingling of fresh earth, coal, and autumn. Shaking her head, she took a step backward, right into the dining room table. She tried to appear unperturbed; peering around at the gravy-spotted tablecloth she had flung over a chair, but when she looked back at Frank, her composure crumbled. An "undesirable," Mother Grace would label him—"unworthy," and, yes, she could see that he was. He never went to church, and he always seemed to be trying to lead her astray. She needed to get away from him, to flee to the kitchen and join the women before she did something she regretted. But with the table at her back, Frank in front, she was stuck.

"Well?"

She looked into his dark, handsome face. *Go away*, she told him inside her head. Then, also inside her head, she was running out the door, and he was chasing her, catching her hand in his.

His eyes danced, and her heart joined in. She put two fingers against her lips to push back the *yes* that wanted to pop out. "No, Frank," she whispered instead.

"I don't know why you're scared of me," he said, shaking his head. "Shouldn't be, but you are. Not yet, then, but soon you'll come with me." He started to turn away, but then stopped, willing her to look back at him.

She would not. She turned to grab the tablecloth to throw in the wash.

He moved closer. Dry hurt. A spark of mischief.

"I could show you some sights, little lady," he said, his tone altered, his breath hot against her temple. He was going to tease her; she could tell by the gunfire of his laugh. "Maybe we could go for a dip in the river together. Would you like that?" He inched closer, enjoying her embarrassment as she pressed up against the table. She had refused him, and now he was playing with her—a bobcat with a rabbit.

"Maybe you got a bathing suit you could put on, one with a little skirt?"

As he chuckled, Cyril came up behind him and cleared his throat. Frank turned and slapped the big man on the biceps. "Hi there. Best damn miner coal ever seen, Cyril," he said, looking back to her. "Except for me."

With Cyril close by, Frank was more animated, his voice playing the air like a fiddle. "Cyril is big and slow. He's a white guy—I'm an Indian, right? Like you, Rose Marie."

She looked up at both men, wondering how to get by them to the kitchen. She shifted from foot to foot, and there was an awkward silence before Frank continued, his voice bitter.

"Cyril's a regular miner, but I'm a bucker, a goddamned bucker."

Cyril stepped towards her, hitting Mrs. Mooney's tea trolley with his shin and making the cups and saucers clatter. "A bucker's a guy they call in when the coal gets jammed in the chute," he explained in the smooth radio-announcer voice he used on the porch when she was upset about Father Seamus. "The bucker has to kick the coal down and get out of the way before it lands on top of him. Frank's the best bucker there ever was."

"Yeah," Frank scoffed. "So good that they keep me doing the most dangerous job in the mine year after year. They used to get the young guys, you know, sixteen, eighteen, then move them out after a few months or as soon as they got injured. Hell, they like me so much, they just keep me at it, kicking at coal, slamming up against the wall or diving into the next room as soon as it comes hurtling down. They liked Eugene too, till he took the hint and left. Kind of gives us Indians a thrill, dodging death like that." He stared at her so hard she had to look away.

Her face burned, but she hadn't done anything wrong. She wasn't betraying anyone, not Frank, whom she hardly knew and who was trouble with a capital *T*. Not the sisters either. They were the ones who had sent her here. Not even Mama and Papa, who were dead. If anyone had betrayed anyone else, they had betrayed *her* by letting Father Alphonses and the Indian agent take her from the life she should have had at home with them in the bush, an Indian life. But that wasn't right either.

She was trapped between the dining room table and these two men, trapped in this house, this town, trapped into returning to St. Mark's in less than five weeks. She drew a deep breath. She had to deny Frank . . . yes, his *presumption*.

Her voice wavering, she managed to say, "I can't go for a walk with you. I'm supposed to become a nun, and nuns don't go for walks alone with men. Especially at night."

She would have turned to Cyril and told him, "I don't need you to fight my battles for me either. I'm nineteen years old," but the dining room was starting to list, she was dizzy, and she had to put a hand behind her back to support herself against the table.

"Maybe it's time I stopped doing what everyone else tells me I should be doing," Frank said softly. "Maybe we both should be makin' up our own minds, eh, Rose Marie?"

Sucking in breath, she pressed forward, and the two men parted to let her pass.

After finishing washing up, she made her way down the hall, past Frank's closed door to the stairs. Cyril stepped from the porch, took her elbow, and led her outside. He sat down on the top step as usual, but she didn't take her spot on the step below. The movement was too much for her; she was afraid she'd topple. Putting a hand against the post for support, she remained standing. Even though she had refused cigarettes until he had stopped offering them, tonight Cyril took his pack from the step, pulled a cigarette forward, and, reaching up, offered it to her.

She took it. "I never saw any of the nuns smoke," she said, hunching closer as he struck a match with his thumbnail for her. "Sometimes I thought I smelled tobacco on Sister Bernadette, though it could just have been burnt food." She took a shallow puff.

Cyril laughed, a happy laugh, and she talked, letting her words spill out, releasing the tightness in her chest. She told him about her parents, who had smoked a bone pipe with guests or in ceremony, sometimes cigarettes they rolled from *kinickinick*. "If they were outdoors, they used new bark instead of papers. But that was a long time ago." She took another puff. "I think it's the mountains that make me think of them so much."

"Yeah, the mountains grow on you," Cyril said, and Papa flashed through her mind, colours spilling from his skin like there was too much of him for his body to contain. Like Frank.

"Frank is always asking me to go for a walk with him," she blurted.

"I know. He's a good guy. Don't understand about your, you know, that church thing—"

"Holy vocation."

Cyril smiled. "Yeah, that. Don't worry. I'll have a talk with him. Tell him to lay off."

"No, I don't need anyone looking after me." Maybe God was trying to guide her through Cyril Brown, she thought. But she wasn't sure she wanted Him to.

"I feel like I'm just, I don't know, waiting. At St. Mark's, I always knew exactly what I had to do, where I was going, and how I would end up. Now my life feels sort of . . . uncertain." *Dust*, she thought, *blowing in the western wind.*

"Waiting? Yeah, I kind of feel like that too. What are you waiting for?"

"I guess for 'that church thing,' my holy vocation. My *destiny*." She heard the cynicism in her voice. "I don't know, exactly."

He chuckled. "Probably neither of us should be spending our lives just waiting." He took another drink of beer.

"You know, I've never tasted beer before. Only Communion wine."

"Here, take a swig," he offered, holding the bottle out to her.

"Sure." That feeling: like she wanted everything she was not supposed to have. "Hey, bubbles. I guess it's better than Communion wine." She handed the bottle back. "It's nice having you to talk to you, Cyril."

"I like talking to you too," he told her, his voice suddenly gruff.

She went up the stairs ahead of Cyril and into her room.

"Oh," she gasped, staring at a girl, young—thirteen, maybe fourteen—wearing a St. Mark's uniform, for crying out loud! Perched on the chair, the girl didn't turn her head to Rose Marie but gazed out the window, her thick black hair glowing as if struck by a shaft of sunlight.

"Taki!" she cried, running over and sliding on her knees before her so she could look up into her friend's face. "Oh my God, it's you! How I miss you."

"I'm with you lots of times, Rosie," she said, looking right at her. "You're my sister."

"Yes, I am." Laughter tickled over her ribs. "I'm so glad to see you, Taki. My life's all mixed up."

Taki smiled. "You're my sister, and I love you. Sisters are important. Brothers too. Don't feel alone, Rosie. You're not alone."

For a second, she didn't feel it.

Then she made the mistake of reaching for Taki's hands. But they were in the past and beyond the Wolf Trail, folded in memory and buried in a place she didn't know.

"Don't go, Taki," she said, though she knew it was too late.

43

Intentions

MOTHER GRACE RESUMED the execution of her duties at St. Mark's. Hour by hour, day by day, she existed, as efficient as she had ever been, as practical, as reserved, and even more commanding. Not as watchful, perhaps. Certainly not as caring. Yet, not one of the sisters could honestly complain about her performance. Not one of them could have put a finger on exactly what had changed.

It was just after breakfast on St. Jude's feast day, the twenty-eighth of October, and she was gazing out her office window at the school grounds, the rolling prairie, and, in the distance, the vague blue outline of the mountains. On nearby farms, the harvest had been completed a month and a half before, but there had been no precipitation since, and the farmers were already grumbling that they needed a dump of snow to provide moisture for planting the following spring. The weather had turned cold overnight, and now a few flakes were fluttering to the ground. Not too much snow, Mother Grace was thinking. Not yet.

Sister Cilla rushed through the door.

Startled, Mother Grace tried to rise to her feet, wincing at the dry rasp of her skirts. Her entire body felt the same as her habit. Widow's weeds, every bit of her, inside and out. As she fell back in her chair, she caught the expression on Sister Cilla's face.

"*Vieilli*, what is it?"

"Mother Grace," Sister Cilla cried. "Oh dear, oh law, I don't know how to say this!"

"Sit down. What on earth is the matter?"

Sister Cilla hunched forward in the chair, dissolving into sobs. Having no handkerchief to mop her eyes, she lifted her skirt and buried her face.

"What *is* it, Sister?"

Louder sobs broke out from behind the folds of Sister Cilla's skirt.

"Is it Sister Joan? Did she say something cruel? Or Sister Margaret?"

"No, no." Sister Cilla briefly moved her skirt from her mouth. "It's me, my position—" But she was sobbing and speaking at the same time, once more burying her face in her skirt, and her words were unintelligible.

Reaching across her desk, Mother Grace touched Sister Cilla's wrist. "Now, now, Sister, there's no problem we can't solve with the grace of God." The word *God* tasted foreign in her mouth.

Sister Cilla howled louder.

She tried to tug Sister Cilla's hand free of her face. But Cilla, as always, was strong as an ox, while Mother Grace's own strength was minimal, her arm aching with the effort.

"*Maudit*," she murmured, pressing her lips together. She really had no time for histrionics, and she pushed herself from her chair, grasping her cane. With all that had taken place recently, she had little patience left, and there was no point in pretending she did. She made her way to the door and was about to walk out of her office, when Sister Cilla wailed, "Please, Mother Grace. I can't bear you turning your back on me!"

Mother Grace turned her head. "Well, Sister, what is it?"

"Dear, oh law. At least say you'll give Olaf and me your blessing?"

"What?" She wheeled around to face Sister Cilla. "What did you say?" She stumbled backwards, and the doorknob planted itself firmly between her buttocks. "*Merde!*" she cried, unable to keep the curse to herself. For a moment, the overhead light seemed to swing in wild yellow circles. She was falling.

"Mother Grace!" Sister Cilla flew to her. She caught her up and eased her to the floor. "Should I get someone? I'll phone the doctor at Hilltop." She sprang to her feet. "I'm sorry! I'm so—"

"Help me up, Priscilla," she snapped. "And take me to my bed this instant!"

Sister Cilla took her up the stairs, half carrying her to her room, and blabbering apologies every brutal step of the way.

"Have you spoken of this, of your *intentions*, to anyone else?" Mother Grace demanded once she was propped up on her bed. Every bone in her widow's body, she could swear, had fractured.

"No, Mother Grace, I haven't. But I think Sister Bernadette suspects."

"You will say nothing of this to anyone until I give you permission, Sister Cilla. Now, brandy," she ordered. "Get me the bottle in my bottom desk drawer. Bring my cane too. And hurry. I have a few questions for you, mademoiselle."

"Aren't you being a little rash in making this decision, Sister Cilla?" she asked a few minutes later, a tumbler of brandy in her hand. "Surely you don't think you're the only sister who has ever been in love?"

Sister Cilla looked down at her, astonished. "Dear, oh law, I never ... Well, I guess not, Mother Grace."

"And Sister Bernadette was certainly remiss if she ever left you alone with that man."

"Dear, it's not Sister Bernadette's fault."

"I really have to wonder if the younger generation has any concept of sacrifice, any idea of what service to the Lord means, any desire to labour for the greater good!" Looking up at Cilla, she saw her face crumple. "*Mon Dieu*, sit down before you fall down, Priscilla."

"I tried, Mother Grace," Sister Cilla wailed, collapsing on the end of Mother Grace's bed. "Time and again, I really did." She snatched up her skirt and wiped her nose. "For eight years, Olaf has been asking me to marry him. I thought he was joking at first—we like to share a laugh—and I shrugged it off. Later I knew he was serious, but I turned him down. I prayed. I put myself at God's mercy."

Sister Cilla's face was blotchy, her eyes were a little wild, but Mother Grace noticed that her voice had steadied.

She took another good long swallow of brandy, fully aware that Cilla could probably use a drink herself. *Tant pis,* she was too annoyed to offer her one.

"This time when Olaf proposed, I knew that I wanted what he wanted: a family. I knew my heart wasn't in my work here anymore. And most of all, Mother Grace, I knew that I love him."

"Love?" Mother Grace uttered the word like the punch line of a bad joke. Her intention was to imply that in light of the divine, romantic love was ridiculous, a parody of God's love. That was how she *should* feel. In fact, before Patrick's death, it was how she believed she *did* feel. "Love," she said again, more softly. "Well, Sister Cilla, I'll summon you tomorrow when I have more to say on this matter. *Va t'en.*" Since it was St. Jude's Day and since he was the patron saint of desperate causes, she'd say a prayer or two about keeping Sister Cilla at St. Mark's.

The following day, Mother Grace awoke in a grim mood. Despite her prayers to St. Jude, she had the feeling Sister Cilla would not remain a Sister of Brotherly Love and, when the time came, take the reins from her and run the school. She had seen the set of Cilla's jaw and heard a winsome note in her voice when she said Olaf's name. *Oui,* and her departure would irrevocably alter the future of St. Mark's as she had imagined it, as she had hoped and prayed it would be.

Her misfortunes had started with Rose Marie's departure, she realized. Then came the terrible news of Patrick's death. After that, the order to close some residential schools—not St. Mark's, at least. Now Sister Cilla was running off with a man like, like *une catin.* What was God doing?

Mon Dieu, but she was old and useless. The knowledge carved its way through her with a twisted blade as she dressed and struggled downstairs to her office. *How could you, Jesus?* she muttered, staring up at Patrick's cross. *How could you take so much from me?*

Yet she still had the girl. She must not forget that. What was that precious little saying Sister Bernadette chirped from time to time? *God doesn't close a door without opening a window.*

Dear Rose Marie, she would write. *By the time you get this, it will be a month before your return to St. Mark's, the order's requirements fulfilled. After a recuperation period, you will travel by train to the Mother House. Your destiny awaits you, child! After two years, God willing, you will return here as an ordained Sister of Brotherly Love. It is all unfolding, Rose Marie, just as God intended.* She'd write those exact words without mentioning that Sister Cilla would not be her chaperone to the Mother House, that it would have to be Sister Simon instead, and possibly Sister Bernadette too.

Was there something else she had to attend to concerning Rose Marie? She had the feeling there was, but she couldn't focus, and truth be known, she didn't care enough to try.

With Rose Marie gone to the Mother House, what would be in store for *her*? Well, she considered, taking the nail file from her top drawer, she could begin to chronicle Rose Marie's childhood and the details of the Visitation, her first miracle. *Oui*, Rose Marie was her window. The loss of Cilla was simply the price she had to pay for indulging in self-pity after Patrick's death. She had ignored the needs of others when they had most required her. She sank to the floor beside her chair and knelt on her stiff knees.

Lord. But as she closed her eyes, it wasn't the cross Patrick had made her that burned into her brain; it was the crucifix hanging over her bed upstairs. Bronze—the face, cut by shadows, dark and craggy. An Indian face. *Forgive us, Père, we know not what we do.* Tears trickled down her old cheeks.

44

Undeserved Extravagances

ANOTHER DAY GONE," Rose Marie muttered to herself as she slipped into bed each night. Another night closer to her return to St. Mark's. Yet each dawn made her feel farther from the school and the sisters, especially from Mother Grace, who still had not written. Didn't the old bat care about her anymore?

Her room and board was due in two days, Mrs. Mooney told her at breakfast. "Better write to that school of yours again, cookie. Father Seamus won't pay it. He's tighter than a nun's cunt."

Ruby and the men roared at that, and Rose Marie felt her face flush. She had no idea what *cunt* meant. Knowing Mrs. Mooney, it was something vulgar.

The coming month would be her last in Black Apple. She wasn't sad, glad, excited, or despondent. Just confused. *Mother of all we who are motherless, I want to belong somewhere; I want a home,* she found herself praying into her milky coffee. Then, to be respectful, she added, *Help me to accept my losses and submit to God's will.* Whatever "God's will" was. She didn't even know her own.

As she walked through the town from the rectory that evening, she wondered if Mother Grace had mailed the cheque yet, or at least contacted Father Seamus about covering her room and board.

Mother Grace was well known for her convincing letters, her words carefully chosen, her script so perfectly formed it legitimized any request she made. Usually. But there was no *usually* about anything in Black Apple.

As she looked at the mountains illuminated by the setting sun, euphoria rose in her. She recalled Mama's laundry bushes and Papa's trap shack; the fishers, badgers, bears, deer, and coyotes in her country; how her family had lived among them, and she hadn't known how happy she was until the men came and took her away. She imagined her childhood home hollowed out and leaning precariously under a buildup of snow, the front porch sagging to the ground—and her joy drained away.

She needed someone.

For seven years at St. Mark's, she had enjoyed Anataki's friendship. How Taki's jokes and giggles had warmed the miserable dormitory. How her death, like Mama's and now Papa's, made the world a colder, emptier place. For the five years following Taki's death, she had little more than lukewarm friendships with the other girls her age and not much more than the acceptance of the sisters. Well, Sisters Cilla and Bernadette liked her; she was pretty sure of that. And Mother Grace had considered her special. Actually, Mother Grace liked her a lot, she had to admit.

During catechism, Mother Grace's bluebottle eyes had sparkled when she answered questions correctly or asked her own. Yet Mother Grace had not told her about Papa's death. She had not sent her room and board or settled with Father Seamus either. She had abandoned her. Just like everyone else.

Since being taken to St. Mark's, she had travelled a long way in both distance and experience, finally becoming an almost-nun. But here in Black Apple, she was an Indian first of all, it seemed: someone to use and beat up, according to Rolfe Mooney. Disreputable, according to Mrs. Tortorelli. A drunk and a criminal, as far as Father Seamus was concerned.

To Cyril she was his "little girl" friend, but to Frank, she was a woman. A shiver ran through her.

Still and always, she was daughter of Michel and Ernestine and sister of Joseph. Yes, and friend-sister to Anataki, who had come back to her. *Sisters are important, Rosie,* Taki had said. *Brothers too.*

That night, she dreamt of her brother.

She was floating in a vast lake. Raising her head, she looked around, but there was nothing but water. Then a face surfaced a few feet away. "Kiaa-yo!" she called, then "Joseph!" But the water moved swiftly; the lake became a river and carried her away. Soon he was just a speck bobbing in the distance.

Was Joseph a God-fearing boy? she wondered when she awoke in her dark bedroom. He was her brother, but she knew almost nothing about him. Her own blood. Perhaps he was a wild young man, maybe even more than Frank. Or he could be traditional, like Papa. The thought warmed her. Maybe, like Papa, he danced and healed and hunted.

The following day was hectic. Though Father Seamus had cancelled many of Father Patrick's community events, he was permitting a luncheon after the special service celebrating All Saints' Day. Rose Marie made sandwiches, cut the squares Mrs. Rees had baked that morning, rushed around filling plates and pouring tea, and then did the dishes so that Mrs. Rees, who had been run off her feet, could have "a cuppa and a sit-down."

By the time she left the rectory at ten to six, fatigue stuck to her like a coat of grime. She arrived at the old Mooney place in time to wave off Mrs. Mooney's insistence that she eat.

"I'm stuffed full of sandwiches," she said.

With Ruby working a double shift at the Dominion, and Mrs. Mooney hurrying off to the curling briar, she decided to indulge herself, to take a bath in the deep tub with the chipped enamel lip. She loved baths, she had discovered. Saturday-night assembly-line showers had been the only form of full-body bathing available at St. Mark's, and in her first few years at the school, when Sister Margaret was in charge of the dorm, the girls had to shower in their underwear. Sister Cilla, when she took over, had found that notion silly and told them to disrobe so they could wash behind the oilcloth curtains, "as God intended."

During her first week at the boardinghouse, Mrs. Mooney had told her that she was welcome to two full baths a week, and short, shallow ones "when necessary." The men of the boardinghouse were permitted just one bath per week. "They got showers at the mine. Just make sure you don't tie up the bathroom for long."

Three weeks after Rose Marie's arrival, Mrs. Mooney stopped depositing the standard Ivory in the upstairs bathroom and indulged Rose Marie, Ruby, and herself by purchasing sculpted oval cakes dyed pink, green, or mauve in "American Beauty Rose," "Spring Blossom," and "Lilac Splendour" scents. Each cake of soap had a woman's silhouetted head stamped in the centre, and its flowery smell drifted invitingly down the hall. At least, Rose Marie thought it inviting. Cyril complained that the soap made him smell like a cheap whore, excuse his language.

That evening presented the perfect opportunity for a long soak. And who would know if she spent an hour locked in the bathroom? Ruby and Mrs. Mooney were out, Cyril and Frank were having a nightcap in Cyril's room, and the downstairs miners were gone, either working or washing coal dust down their throats at the Dominion Hotel. If they needed to, Cyril and Frank could use the downstairs bathroom, for heaven's sake.

She ran her bath, then sank into it, inch by luscious inch, allowing the water to rinse worry and sandwich spread away. She shampooed her hair with Halo, piled it on her head, then stood in the bath to survey her coiffure in the steamy cabinet mirror. *Glamorous.* She liked the exotic sound of that word. And the fact that it had never ever been used at St. Mark's. *Lavish.* Lying back in the tub, she rinsed her hair, imagining drifting in a tropical sea. She had seen pictures of Hawaii and the Caribbean in the *National Geographic* at Wong's. "Honeymooners' Paradise," the article was captioned.

The day before, as they had their tea, Mrs. Rees had told her a story that she couldn't stop thinking about.

"Forty-four years ago today, I came here," she said, her eyes peering through her past. "My two older brothers, Evan and Daffyd, sent for me. Said they had a husband picked out and mailed me a ticket on a steamship."

Mrs. Rees had come to Black Apple from somewhere else and things had worked out for her. "He was a dour one, this Gilbert they had picked. Worked in the same coal room in the mine as Daffyd, and always grumbling about stiff joints and all the miners who'd died."

Nibbling a scone, she wondered if Gilbert was the ailing Mr. Rees, the "old darlin'" Mrs. Rees often took a saucer of sweets to from the rectory kitchen, the husband who insisted on walking her at least halfway to work each morning despite his emphysema, the kind man she sat beside at Mass.

"I was coming out of McBride's after picking up a nice roast for dinner—Dafydd had invited Gilbert again—and I was already carrying a twenty-pound bag of potatoes from Wong's. Right then a nice-looking young man walked past, saw me, and stopped."

He was a few inches taller than Mrs. Rees—Miss Brocket, then—with brown wavy hair.

" 'Please, my dear,' he said, 'let me help you.' He walked me home, carrying both bags. We were approaching my brothers' shack when he spied Evan sitting on the front step smoking, and it turned out they knew each other from the mine."

" 'Hello there, Brocket,' he called, not knowing Evan's my brother. 'I see you're green with envy, but you're not getting near this lovely lady, because I'm going to make her my wife.' "

" 'Well then, mate,' says Evan, 'I'd better invite you in for supper if we're going to be family.' Two months later, when Gilbert told me we better talk seriously about getting married, I was already engaged to Theo."

Mrs. Rees had laughed then, giggled like the girls in the dormitory sometimes did, like she and Anataki had. "Gilbert's an old man now, sour as a pickle but healthy as a horse! Never married, did he."

She imagined the young Miss Brocket and Theo in each other's arms, his hands—callused from work, a little coal-stained around the nails where a brush wouldn't reach—pulling her close, a tang of sweat pressing against the scent of shaving lather.

Rose Marie slid her hand to the straw and silk between her legs. Her thighs tingled.

When she climbed out of the bath, she opened the cupboard and pulled out one of the thick lavender towels Mrs. Mooney had told her and Ruby they could use. "Just for us girls," she had said. "The men can use those old ones. As if they'd know the difference."

She dried her face and neck, skimming quickly over her nipples and belly, ignoring the wet between her thighs, then scoured her legs until tiny rolls of dry skin peeled away. Clean. She pulled her St. Mark's cotton nightdress over her head, wrapped her hair in the towel, and tied the dressing gown Mrs. Mooney had lent her. It was miles too big, but she remembered Sister Margaret always warning, "Don't look a gift horse in the mouth."

She opened the door and started down the hall. Walking on air. That's what Mrs. Rees had said. "Going down the aisle on my wedding day, I was walking on air." Rose Marie felt that way too.

She turned the corner and ran smack into Frank.

"Oh!"

He leaned into her, and she smelled alcohol on his breath; then his fresh earth scent engulfed her. He drew her close, his nose pressing her forehead.

"Oh," she said again, her hand on his chest pushing him back.

"Rose Marie," he whispered. *"Niita-wah-kah-taan."* He reached for her again, and this time she fell into him, let his mouth find hers. She understood.

"Come," he whispered, pulling her to his side. His arm around her, they started towards the stairs.

"No," she said, shocked by her response to his warmth and scent. "No," as he pulled her closer.

She heard Cyril's door swing open.

"Frank," Cyril said firmly, "you leave her alone. I told you. She's a church girl, for Christ's sake!"

Frank lunged at Cyril, pushing him against the wall, lightning crackling around him. "And I told *you*, stop interfering with her and me!" He punched Cyril in the jaw.

Cyril's head hit the wall. For a fraction of a second, he looked dazed. Then he charged, his weight catapulting Frank towards the staircase. Frank flew down a few stairs, but one sinewy arm caught the banister, and he flung himself upright. He rushed back up at Cyril.

"Stop!" she screamed, jumping between the two men. She pushed one hand against Cyril's chest, the other against Frank's. "That's quite enough. You're acting like children!" She recognized Mother Grace's authority in her voice, Sister Joan's words.

"What the fuck's going on up there?" a man yelled from below. Reggie, coming through the front door. "Frank, is that you? For Christ's sake, quit it, or I'm calling the fuckin' cops!"

Cyril pushed in front of her and glowered at Frank.

Frank looked from Cyril down the stairs to Reggie, who glared up at him. Shoulders rounded, he shook his head. "I wouldn't hurt her," he said to Cyril. "Jesus, you know damn well I wouldn't do nothing to hurt her."

For a few moments, it was so quiet that Rose Marie could hear each one of them breathing.

Then Cyril said, "Get the hell out of here."

Frank slunk down the stairs and slammed through the door.

"Are you all right?" Cyril asked, turning to her.

"Yes." But she was gasping and hiccuping at the same time. She couldn't catch her breath.

"Frank likes you, but don't understand about that thing you said—"

"My holy vocation."

She should turn away and walk across the hall to her room. Oh, but she couldn't trust her legs, was afraid that if she tried to move, she'd topple right down the stairs. Father William's warnings rang in her ears, words she had never fully understood—*shame, weakness, sin*—notions that until that very minute hadn't meant a thing to her. She couldn't stop trembling.

"Hey." Cyril's big hand rubbed her back. "You look scared. But it's all right now. Frank won't bother you no more. He knows he has to deal with me. Look, would you like a drink to get rid of them hiccups? Come on," he urged. "It's all right."

The bed was dimpled where Cyril or Frank had been sitting, and a chair was shoved close. A troop of dust bunnies under the bed shivered in the breeze that cut between the propped-open window and the door.

"Sit down," he said gently, indicating the chair. He shut the door. "Just one drink. Good stuff. Single malt. Frank and me was just celebrating the pay hike." He handed her a cloudy tumbler.

She took it, tippling the glass to her lips. The stuff smelled like the furniture polish remover she and Mrs. Rees used to scrub waxy buildup from the church floors, topped off with a dash of coyote piss, but she took a sip anyway, feeling it scorch her tongue. Closing her eyes, she gulped. The liquid burned all the way down to her stomach, and just as she was beginning to wonder why anyone would voluntarily drink such a concoction, a warm glow radiated through her.

"I think it's working." She held out her glass, and Cyril sloshed more of the amber fluid inside. She took a gulp. *"I am weak, but thou art strong. Jesus keep me from all wrong,"* she sang, rocking on the chair.

"I'll get you some music." Cyril rose from his bed and turned on his radio. " 'Fascination.' I like that song. I heard it on the radio in the parlour."

"Madam?" he said, holding his hand out to her. "May I have the honour of dancing with you?"

"Why not?" She teetered to her feet. "You know, one year, probably my fourth or fifth at St. Mark's, Sister Cilla taught us the waltz. 'One, two, three, one, two, three,' Sister called out as she swung around the floor, her skirts swooping like crazy. She's not the most graceful person in the world, and real tall. Not as tall as you, though."

Cyril placed his big hand on her shoulder and smiled down at her. "A dancing nun? You don't say."

"Sister had the girls pair off by size, and each couple stumbled around the gym, saying 'one, two, three, one, two, three.' Yeah, like that. My friend, Anne, was sick, and no one else was close to my size, so Sister Cilla grabbed me and whirled me around until I thought I'd puke."

Cyril chuckled. "I can't dance worth a damn," he said, "and I wouldn't try if I didn't have half a bottle of scotch in my gut." He drew her close until her nose was just below his armpit. She could smell American Beauty Rose soap and the damp cotton of his shirt. *One, two, three, one, two, three.*

The song ended.

Cyril kissed her forehead.

A voice glided from the radio. "And this one goes out to all you miners and your wives. Requested by Madge, it's Tennessee Ernie Ford with 'Sixteen Tons.'"

"Da-duh-duh-duh-duh-de-duh-duh," she and Cyril chimed to the music.

With a plush lavender towel wrapped around her Halo-shampooed hair, a man's big arms around her, "Sixteen Tons" playing on the radio, and single-malt scotch blazing in her belly, she felt pure pleasure. The music guided her feet, and Cyril's arm tightened at her waist. Her head fell back into music that lifted her through the humming air.

Then the lavender towel toppled from her head. She reached to pick it up and stumbled, landing on Cyril's bed. She laughed. A turtle on its back. She couldn't seem to find her feet. When she closed her eyes, Cyril was laughing right beside her.

Maybe God blinked. Maybe He chose that particular moment to test her. Or maybe Satan found the cracked-open window that poured tinny music and gleeful laughter into the night and projected his dark form through it.

That had to be it, because Cyril felt safe to her: his American Beauty Rose smell and his big cool hands. He had saved her from the temptation of Frank, and he felt safe to her as he whispered, "Sweet little Rose Marie, just as sweet as she can be," as his mouth opened on hers.

He kissed her, long and slow, his fingers sliding over the cotton blouse Ruby had given her and she had taken in. When he cupped her breasts, she turned her chin to protest, but his mouth held hers and then a tingle skittered up her neck, down her ribs.

She closed her eyes and kissed him back. As his hands reached under her skirt, she quivered and the thought of trying to control her dizzy body flitted through her mind. She should turn from Cyril, prop herself up, crawl over the rippling mattress, and stand up, if she could manage it. She should go to her room, and she would, but Cyril's unhurried kiss and touch told her she had all the time in the world.

Her entire body felt like a string of Christmas lights that had just been plugged in and she felt good, fully, dizzily alive. Besides, Cyril felt safe to her. Even as he pulled off her stockings.

45

Stud

NIGHT, THIRSTY, DRANK up the dregs of the day.

Rose Marie slept poorly, her dreams pulling her in and out of sensations and sleep, from drifting to struggle to paralysis, then back again in a nauseating vortex.

She was in a river being carried by a strong current; she was drowning. Mother Grace threw her a rope, but it unravelled as soon as it hit the water. Mrs. Rees said, "Get out here, love, where it's safe." Rose Marie staggered up the bank, and there was Cyril, reaching. He pulled her to shallow water, but let go, and suddenly her school dress was heavy, weighing her down. She fell back in the water. She was being swept away. Up on the riverbank, Papa danced in his medicine shirt. Or was it Frank?

She woke up shivering.

She was standing at the top of the stairs at the old Mooney place. Cyril kissed her forehead. Frank flew forward, socking him in the face. Cyril pushed Frank down the stairs. She ran to the rectory, but Father Seamus blocked the door and wouldn't let her enter.

In the morning, she was groggy and disoriented, not knowing if it was Sunday, and she had to get ready for church, or a workday. Her dreams had left her so exhausted she could hardly climb out of bed. Why all these dreams? Why now?

It was turning cold. Rose Marie had to pull on both pairs of woollen stockings under her long skirt and wear a sweater under her coat to walk to Our Lady of Sorrows. The pools of water in the road were frozen, and when she stepped on them, the sound ricocheted off the mountains, breaking open the day.

In twenty days, she would return to St. Mark's. In the meantime, she must steer clear of Cyril and Frank, she decided. No more talks on the porch. No more walks home from the Dominion. She would take a longer route to the old Mooney place, avoiding not only Frank but also Bertha Bright Eye slouching by the gents' with her stains and bruises.

"Not even three weeks, is it?" Mrs. Rees exclaimed in the rectory. "I'll be lost without you."

Rose Marie smiled. "You did just fine without me before."

"It wasn't the same, dear."

A soft arm encircled her shoulders.

"I'm sure going to miss you, Mrs. Rees," she cried.

"Lost without you." Mrs. Rees sniffled. "I'll make us a cuppa."

Minutes later, pouring tea, Mrs. Rees ventured, "Cyril Brown's a good chap."

"What?" Rose Marie stiffened. How could Mrs. Rees know about Cyril and her? She hadn't even confessed it. Oh, she just couldn't face Father Seamus talking all over her in the confessional, shaming and condemning her. She touched Sister Cilla's cross at her neck. "No kissing," Sister had warned. "No hands under clothing. You don't want to be ruined."

Was she ruined?

"It's just that Cyril fancies you. That's what they're all saying," Mrs. Rees said. "You could do worse, you know."

*   *   *

Late in the afternoon, the temperature dropped further, and the sky turned the colour of the bottled ink she had written her school notes in. It was almost dark when they sat down to eat supper, and she could feel Cyril's pale eyes on her. Frank's dark eyes were watching her too.

She studied the bowl of stew in front of her. As soon as she was finished eating, she went straight to the kitchen. Let Ruby or Mrs. Mooney clear the table for a change.

After washing the dishes, she crept down the hall as quietly as possible, past Frank's room, past the parlour with the radio, stopping just before reaching the door to the porch. Thankfully, the night was too chilly to sit outside, but she stood on her tiptoes, peering through the window to make sure Cyril wasn't waiting for her. Then she raced up the stairs to her room.

She knew that Mother Grace had, on occasion, said St. Francis's Spiritual Communion prayer when she wasn't feeling well or, more likely, couldn't force herself to confess to Father William. Just like Rose Marie, now, couldn't face Father Seamus.

I believe that You, O Jesus, are in the most holy Sacrament. I love You and desire You. Come into my heart. And please forgive me, Jesus, for my terrible sin of the flesh. Dear God.

More water in her dream that night.

Her long-ago creek had swollen. It swirled around her feet, grew higher, pulling at her thighs. "Help!" she screamed to the people onshore—pale figures she couldn't identify—as she was swept up in the cold rush. She didn't know where the river was taking her, and she couldn't break from the current.

At Our Lady of Sorrows Church, she cleaned and served at the Peacock and Santorini baptisms, and a few days later at the Catholic Women's League tea. One afternoon after polishing the monstrance, she climbed the ladder to wash Jesus on the cross. Kissing His feet, she asked Him to forgive her, to guide her, to show her a sign. *Dear Lord, I don't know what to do.* At the end of each day, she walked through Black Apple, avoiding going home until the last possible minute.

Cold air blew in from the mountains, freezing grass, trees, and her brain. Although she chatted to Mrs. Rees when they were together, afterwards she couldn't recall what they had said. Cyril's name came up from time to time. She changed the subject.

It was the same situation with Mrs. Mooney and Ruby. They said things, she said things, then she wondered what they had talked about. At least Mrs. Derkatch wasn't at the house anymore. Mrs. Mooney really had told her she wouldn't need her help while Rose Marie was there. "Good riddance to bad rubbish," Ruby snickered when Mrs. Mooney told them.

Leaving the kitchen, Rose Marie went straight upstairs.

"There's snow in the air tonight," Cyril said, stepping out of the shadows and scaring her half to death.

"Heavens!"

"It'll be real cold for you to go to work in the morning, Rose Marie."

She shifted from foot to foot as he looked down at her. This man had been her friend.

"You'll need a winter coat."

She opened her mouth, but she didn't know what to say to him anymore.

"Why don't you meet me at McBride's after work tomorrow and—"

Deftly, she slipped by him and rushed into her room.

Again after supper, Cyril waited for her. "I'm not going to touch you or nothing like that." He moved closer. "I'm worried about you, is all. That coat of yours ain't gonna keep you warm walking to the church and back. Don't even fit you right."

"I'm fine," she muttered, scurrying away.

"Rose Marie, I want to talk to you," he called after her.

Safely in her room, she locked the door.

Mother Mary, keep me safe from those who would do me harm. Whoever they are. Wherever.

The following night, Cyril was parked right outside the kitchen when she came through the door. He grabbed her elbow and tried to turn her, to make her look him full in the face.

She lowered her eyes.

"It's all right, little girl. I just want to say something."

She tried to squeeze by him.

"Please, Rose Marie."

She had nowhere to go except back where she'd come from. She spun around and pushed through the kitchen door.

"Jesus Christ!" Ruby looked up from the kitchen table, where she sat smoking with Mrs. Mooney. "What the hell happened to you?"

"Sit down," Mrs. Mooney ordered. "Here." She handed her a cigarette. "You look like you need one."

Rose Marie brought the cigarette to her mouth, and Mrs. Mooney lit it. She drew the smoke deep into her lungs, then exhaled, floating away on its grey back. She wanted to float right into another house, another town, another life.

"I know just what the doctor ordered," Mrs. Mooney told her.

"What?"

"Ya need to learn how to play Stud."

"Stud?"

Ruby and Mrs. Mooney laughed raucously.

"Poker," Ruby said.

"Oh." She remembered learning in catechism that gambling for fun, like bingo, wasn't intrinsically evil. "I guess so."

"We bet with matchsticks. That way you can't lose nothing."

"Thank God."

*   *   *

The next day, Cyril started the afternoon shift, and Frank was back on days. As Rose Marie sat across from him at supper—hash, mashed potatoes, and peas—she could feel him watching her. She glanced up and saw a question in his eyes. Like the question in Cyril's eyes. She ate a few bites, then picked up her plate and slipped into the kitchen.

As she scrubbed the frying pan, she heard chairs scrape and Dwayne ask Frank if he wanted to go for a beer at the Dominion with him and Reg.

"No," Frank answered. "Think I'll turn in early."

Ruby and Mrs. Mooney brought dirty plates and leftover food into the kitchen and the cleanup ritual began.

After they finished, Rose Marie put her hand on the kitchen door, but thought better of swinging it open. Instead, she crouched down and peered underneath. Frank's feet. Sure enough, he was waiting for her.

"I thought you left," Mrs. Mooney said as she came back to the sink.

"I don't want to see Frank," she whispered.

"Wouldn't mind a game of Stud," Mrs. Mooney said. "You, Ruby?"

"You betcha. Rose Marie?"

"Sure."

Rose Marie stayed in the kitchen that night, the next night, and the night after that. Mrs. Mooney and Ruby taught her about flushes, full houses, bluffing, shuffling, and wild cards. From time to time, one of them would reach into her pile of matches, light a cigarette, blow out the match, and drop it back in the pile. At ten minutes to nine, when Ruby pulled away from the table, put on her coat, and headed out the back door to the cab that took her to work, most of the matchsticks were blackened, and the kitchen air was blue with smoke.

As they played cards, the women gossiped. Wong's was running bets out the back door, Ruby said. Everyone knew that Mr. Tortorelli had died of "the clap," and Mrs. Derkatch's son had fathered half the babies born in the last year, according to Mrs. Mooney. "That's from Dr. Radford, straight from the horse's ass."

At first Rose Marie was shocked by the stories, then intrigued, and finally amused. "Heard anything new?" she would ask as she counted her matches at the start of each evening's game. No one's secrets were safe. Stories blossomed like cigarette smoke from the women's lips.

From time to time she heard Frank come from his room and stand outside the kitchen door, waiting, but he never came in.

Rolfe Mooney's name came up more than once.

"A chip off the old block," said Ruby.

"Dying's too good for him." Mrs. Mooney nodded.

"I know something about him," Rose Marie ventured, and both women turned to her. "I saw him punch a man my first night in Black Apple. I think it was Billy Nimsic. I think he killed—"

"Quiet!" hissed Mrs. Mooney. "Don't say nothing you can't prove. You don't want that bastard on your back."

"Can't say I'm surprised," Ruby murmured as she shuffled the deck.

The next evening, as Frank paced outside the kitchen door and Mrs. Mooney dealt cards, she turned to Rose Marie. "Cookie, you can't hide from them two men forever. You can cut the tension round here with a knife."

"That's a fact," Ruby said, grinding her butt in the ashtray. "It ain't no better at the hotel neither. Soon as Cyril got off shift last night, he went straight to the Dominion and straight at Frank. Dickie Gerard says to me, 'What happened? I thought those two was buddies.' I says, 'A girl happened.'" She grinned, showing her big teeth.

Rose Marie lit herself a cigarette and inhaled deeply. She knew that both Ruby and Mrs. Mooney expected her to do something. It seemed Mrs. Rees did too. But she didn't know what to do and the words to ask them were lost in the snowstorm in her head. It had been building since the night she took the bath, since Frank and Cyril's fight. Since Cyril had *interfered* with her. Since she had let him.

Look to the future, she told herself, but she couldn't see a damn thing but cigarette smoke.

Over lunch, she complained to Mrs. Rees that she still hadn't heard from Mother Grace. Mrs. Mooney hadn't received the rent yet, and no bus ticket had arrived in the mail.

"I'm sure something will come soon," Mrs. Rees consoled, spooning bread pudding into a dish for her. "Don't you worry. If you don't hear from Mother Grace soon, just let me know. I can't do anything about your room and board, but I can speak to Father Seamus about getting you a bus ticket." Mrs. Rees set the bowl in front of her then stroked her hair. "Cheap as a ha'penny, he is, but I think I can get him to agree."

"Thanks, Mrs. Rees."

"You could always stay in Black Apple." Mrs. Rees's eyes were bright as she sat down across from her. "I could speak to Mattie McBride and see if she'd hire you as salesclerk at her store. Betty Watson is leaving at the end of the month to get married to Mario Olivera, who won't give her a moment's peace. Mattie will need someone. You could stay, dear, if you wanted. And if you wouldn't mind, you could still come here once a week to help with the sewing."

"Of course I would, Mrs. Rees. If I stayed, that is. I'm grateful, I really am, but living in Black Apple wouldn't be the right thing. I mean, I'm supposed to become a nun." Her tone, she couldn't help but notice, was plaintive.

"It's wonderful work, dear, being a nun. God's work, and He has given you a special gift. Doesn't mean you're meant to be a nun, though. Are you sure, Rose Marie, about your vocation?"

"I used to think so. Everyone at St. Mark's did."

"Have you considered marriage? Has it ever been something you wanted?"

She shrugged. "Not really." A cabin with a blazing fire leapt into her mind. "Well, not much." She shut her mouth before tears spilled into her words. For no reason.

"No shortage of men who fancy you. Like I said, you could do worse than Cyril Brown."

"What about Frank?" she ventured. "Frank Bouchie?"

"Worse."

"Why?" A flare of anger. "Is it because he's Ind—"

"Yes, dear. People wouldn't treat you so well. At least, if you stayed in town. You wouldn't want to go live on the Reserve, would you?"

She hadn't thought of that, but now her dream of the little house came back to her, a man's voice calling out to her. "Maybe," she answered. "I hadn't really thought—"

"You need to think, dear. Do you want to become a nun, or would you rather be a shopgirl, or a wife?"

Rose Marie pressed her fingers against the bridge of her nose the way Mother Grace always did. *Mon Dieu.*

"I don't want to upset you." Mrs. Rees's soft hand rested on her arm. "But would they send your children away to St. Mark's or St. Gerard's if you married Frank?"

"Oh, I never thought of that."

"You have to consider everything, don't you?"

"Maybe there would be a day school by then. Maybe they wouldn't take the kids so far away or for so long." Rose Marie touched the dark spot over her left eye, a reminder of the beating Sister Joan had administered her first year at St. Mark's, before Mother Grace had taken her under her wing. She thought of the big-eyed boy who'd hanged himself, and then of Anataki's body turning from feverish hot to stone cold as she lay beside her in the dormitory.

No.

Then she remembered a smiling Taki, sitting on the chair in Rose Marie's bedroom in the old Mooney house and gazing out the window. Now she wondered what Taki had seen. The sinking sun, the dirty street, or maybe the same blizzard that raged in her own head? She could just make out a shape floundering in the wind. Maybe Taki had seen it more clearly. Maybe she knew what it was.

The next day and the day after, as she walked to work, cleaned the church, played Stud in the kitchen, and knelt by her bed at night, she could feel the vibration of heavy wings against her chest. Something was coming towards her, its movements growing more certain as it got closer.

46

Departure

MOTHER GRACE wouldn't let Sister Cilla leave the way errant sisters usually did, she decided, as she sat in the dining room, the school's accounts spread before her. She was totalling expenditures and projecting costs as she did at the end of every month. As if she cared whether or not minimal needs were met and the school's budget was balanced. As if nothing had changed.

She recalled one dull morning at the Mother House, more than fifty years before, when, eating her porridge at the table the postulants shared in the basement, it occurred to her that someone was missing. The chair of Claire Dubois—a scattered but cheerful girl who usually sat beside her chattering about anything that came into her disorganized head—was empty. She hadn't seen her at Matins either.

"I wonder where Claire is," she had commented.

Sister Sebastian, at the head of the table, cleared her throat and, raising a finger to her lips, gave her an admonishing glare. Obediently, Grace finished her breakfast without saying another word.

Later, as she washed her hands in the bathroom sink, the plump young woman who had been seated across from her at breakfast approached her. Judy or Julie, if she remembered correctly, first bent down to look under the cubicle doors, making sure they were alone.

"Claire's gone," she whispered, straightening. "Her door closed late last night, and then I heard her on the stairs. This morning her room was empty. I looked in her bureau and—"

Someone came through the bathroom door then, and Julie or Judy stopped midsentence, dried her hands, and promptly left. As if it were a crime to so much as acknowledge that other life that was no longer involved with theirs. Their holy vocation. As if leaving it was something shameful.

Madeleine Bournais left in her second year at the House, and another young woman disappeared a month later. All slipped away in the night without so much as a good-bye, and she never found out what had happened to any of them. They had disappeared, leaving small holes in the daily routine at the Mother House. Tracks in the snow.

She wouldn't have Sister Cilla sneak out in the dark and climb into a waiting pickup, driving through the night to some cramped house on a pig farm, miles away. She and the sisters would acknowledge Cilla's years at St. Mark's, her speed, strength, and genuine concern. She would tell Cilla that she could not disappear into the country air never to be seen again, or to be glimpsed only by accident, slipping in or out of the post office at Hilltop.

She couldn't bear that.

At breakfast, she waited until the sisters were all seated. Leaning forward on both canes, she pulled herself up. "I have something important to tell you," she announced.

"Sister Cilla," Sister Lucy blurted, her head bobbing. "Where's Sister Cilla?"

Mother Grace stared down at the old woman. Sister Lucy knew something was afoot. Half blind, deaf, and forgetful as she was, she still had that inexplicable perception about people, though now it was buried under ancient memories and jumbled thoughts, a golden thread in a mound of mattress stuffing.

"What I need to tell you is that Sister Cilla has a few words for all of us," she announced, her voice fraying. She had wanted to make this announcement in a perfunctory manner, just to get the damn thing over with, but it was all she could do to control the pitch of her voice. She turned to the dining room entrance. "Sister Cilla," she called. "Sister, come in here."

There Cilla was in a faded blue dress that sagged in the bosom and barely covered her knees. Mother Grace had no idea where the thing had come from.

Cilla stepped awkwardly forward on white nursing shoes that seemed to squeeze her feet into hooves, shortening her steps. Her hair, surprisingly long, was gathered in a knot at the back of her neck, and as she hobbled to the table of stupefied sisters, a flush spread over her face and down her neck. Reaching their table, she raised her hands to her cheeks and, blinking rapidly, tried to speak. All that came out was a sob. She swallowed, hands fluttering at her chest, her eyes spilling.

Well, someone had to take control of the situation. "Sister Priscilla is leaving us," Mother Grace declared. "She will be staying at the house of a Hilltop parishioner until Saturday at three thirty p.m., when she will marry Olaf Johanson. Father Alphonses has agreed to conduct the ceremony."

The sisters gasped in unison. Clearly, they hadn't seen this coming. Except Sister Bernadette. A small smile danced over her lips, but she quickly covered her mouth and forced herself to frown.

"Any of you who wish to, may attend," Mother Grace finished, her words running out of sound. She sat down.

Except for the sniffles coming from Sister Cilla, the room was silent.

Regaining her composure, Mother Grace looked around. From the sisters' expressions, she could tell that no one had any desire to witness the ceremony, save Sister Bernadette, who was again trying to stop her lips from curling at the edges. *Oui*, Sister Bernadette had suspected a romance. And she had tried to tell her. Never mind, the two of them would go together to the ceremony.

Late the previous night, she had decided to do this one thing, difficult though it would be. For the sake of Sister Cilla, who, as soon as she walked out the door, would no longer be *Sister* Cilla, she would put her disappointment aside and, *oui*, her pride. She rose stiffly to escort Cilla to the front door. As they walked from the dining room, she heard Sister Margaret declare, "Well, if that don't beat all!"

"If you ask me," Sister Joan began, but Mother Grace stopped listening. Instead she raised an arm and pressed it against the small of Sister Cilla's back. She had expected it to need the support she had to offer, but Sister Cilla's spine was straight and strong. As she glanced up at the younger woman, she noticed a gleam of resolution behind her tears. Sister Cilla was sad and perhaps embarrassed, but she was not tentative. She would not be returning to St. Mark's.

There it was: a paper bag waiting at the front mat, a winter coat in a ball beside it. Sister Cilla strode forward and put on the coat in one swift motion. Before Mother Grace could blink, she had opened the front door.

Peering out, Mother Grace saw Olaf's truck, a skiff of snow blowing over its hood. Just as they must have planned. Olaf, his hair watered down and his battered hat conspicuous by its absence, sat upright at the steering wheel, an equally long-boned but greying woman in the seat beside him. He grinned eagerly at Sister Cilla and started to get out of the truck, but she waved him back.

Abruptly, Cilla turned and kissed Mother Grace on the cheek.

Mon Dieu, she hadn't been actually kissed for—well, she didn't know how long—and it flustered her. She wasn't sure what she said, but whatever it was, it made Sister Cilla smile. As dear Priscilla ducked through the door, she looked genuinely happy.

As she herself couldn't be. Not even hope could grow in barren ground.

Dreadfully weak, she wasn't sure how she'd make it down the hall to her office. Foolishly, she had left her second cane in the dining hall. But she'd get there. Just as she always did.

Minutes later, slumping in her desk chair, drained, Mother Grace realized she hadn't sent Rose Marie her last month's board and a bus ticket. *Vieilli*, she should have mailed them over a week ago. What was wrong with her?

No point fretting about it. Rose Marie's landlady, no doubt a good Christian soul, would exercise patience. And soon Rose Marie would again be at her side, for at least a month while arrangements were made for her trip to the Mother House. She did miss the girl, she realized. She was capable of feeling something other than grief, after all.

Once Rose Marie's two years were up, God willing, she would return to her, to all of them at St. Mark's. By then, Mother Grace would surely have recovered from Patrick's death and be able to experience hope once again. Perhaps through Rose Marie, her protégée.

She wrote a cheque, enough for both the board and the return bus ticket, then scratched a quick note. She'd give the letter to Father Alphonses when he arrived that afternoon rather than wait for the local delivery. *Mon Dieu*, she should have been more diligent, but circumstances had conspired against her. She crossed herself. These days, it seemed, she was never vigilant enough. "Forgive me, Lord," she muttered, rubbing her watery eyes.

There was a knock on the door. "Father Alphonses," she said, rising, "I've a letter for you to mail."

47

Possibilities

R OSE MARIE SAT on the edge of her bed, writing on the pad of foolscap she had brought from St. Mark's. Her hand no longer seemed to be connected to her body; she couldn't control it, and her words sprawled clumsily across the page, a mess! She scrunched up the paper, flung it across the room, and started again on a new sheet.

Dear Mother Grace . . .

A knock on the door. She dropped her pen, leaving a smear of ink down the page.

Heavens, it was Cyril.

"Rose Marie," he said, looking her straight in the eye, "I need to talk to you, and you have to listen."

"I can't. I'm busy. And exhausted." Suddenly she was, slumping against the door frame, hardly able to hold herself upright.

"Come outside with me." He took her hand, and she let him lead her down the stairs. Throwing his huge jacket over her shoulders, he guided her out the front door.

There it was, the porch where, starting back in mid-August, they had met in the evening. Through September and October, when Cyril wasn't on shift, they had talked—often laughing, sometimes smoking, occasionally sharing a beer—while the sun slid down the sky. Tonight was dark and chilly, the moon a lopsided grin among hundreds of blinking eyes. Rose Marie shivered, watching her breath bloom a white bouquet.

"I'm sorry for what I did. I didn't plan to . . ." Cyril muttered. "You know."

Her face grew warm in the porch light, but Cyril's eyes held hers and she couldn't look away. She couldn't run either, though she wanted to. And she didn't want to.

"You might not believe me, Rose Marie, but it's true. I didn't think about you that way, but since that night, you've been on my mind every minute."

She tried to breathe normally.

"I think we're good together, the way I can talk to you, and you to me." He reached for her, and she found herself pushing her arms around his thick waist. Pressed against the bulk of his muscle and flesh, she felt protected from the shadows and whispers of the town. She would never end up like Bertha Bright Eye.

"Look." He cleared his throat. "It's time I settled down. If you'll have me." He nuzzled her hair.

"What? What do you mean?"

"Marriage."

She hadn't expected this! Pulling back, she gazed up at him. He smiled and pulled her close again, his lips slow and cool on her forehead.

Glancing at the dark street, she allowed her mind to wander downtown. She saw herself standing at the cash register behind the counter at McBride's, a confident young woman in a white blouse—brand-new, not a hand-me-down—and a pretty red skirt.

She would get a job at McBride's, and the women who came in would nod at her in a friendly, familiar way. Maybe not Mrs. Tortorelli and a few of the others, but many of them would. "How are you doing, Rose Marie?" some would ask. "Have you and that man of yours set a date?" Just as she had heard them ask Betty Watson.

"A little house," he whispered. "I got some savings."

She would become Mrs. Cyril Brown, married to a big, strong white man. His name just as much as his physical presence would keep Rolfe Mooney, and everyone like him, at bay. She'd have her own little house, and she'd get to know other miners' wives—Mrs. Rees would have to help with that—and once or twice a week, she'd drop by the rectory to sew while Mrs. Rees gave her tea and lemon loaf, all the while chattering. *"Have you got your living room furniture yet, Rose Marie? I saw a nice sofa in the Eaton's catalogue."* It was possible, and she could feel the words start to take shape in her mouth. *Yes, Cyril. I'll have you*, but she bit her lip to stop them.

"You know how I feel about you."

A line from the Orphans' Prayer slipped through her mind: *Give me love in my life, real, true love and a real, true home.*

"How do you feel about me?" she asked him. She needed him to tell her in his best radio announcer's voice, to convince her that they could make a home together and have a good life, a *meaningful* life. And love.

He cleared his throat. "Well," he started, but stopped. "I think you know," he finally said, nervously stroking her hair.

But she didn't. She wanted more, a complete declaration. She needed it.

They stood on the porch watching the stars. Finally, she pulled away from Cyril.

"You'll think about it, won't you?" he asked, and she said, "Yes, I will."

Together they walked up the stairs and went to their separate rooms.

Rose Marie couldn't get to sleep. Once she was able to get Cyril off her mind, it went immediately to Mother Grace. Who had brought her up since she was seven years old, for crying out loud. But who had kept her from Papa, had not even told her when he was sick, who had made it impossible for her to see him before he died. Whom she wanted to hate but couldn't seem to.

Why hadn't Mother Grace sent her room and board or bus ticket? What could be wrong? Finally she drifted to sleep.

The current was strong, but swimming hard for the shore, she was making progress.

She woke up and felt Cyril's body, strong and protective against hers. And then he was on top of her, crushing her beneath him. She screamed.

She had screamed, the sound ripping through her belly. Too late.

Alone in her room, she was shivering cold, her blankets thrown off. "Hey, little girl," Cyril had said as she pulled up her underwear, about to leave his room that night. "You don't have to go, do you?"

"I'm not a little girl."

"No, you're not."

She waded into her creek. Looking at the shore, she saw a man dancing. It looked like Papa, and she called out to him. As he turned towards her, she realized it was a younger man, but the sun flared over his shoulder, and his face was blotted by shadow. Frank?

When her alarm rang, her brain was muddled, and she thrashed at the clock, knocking it to the floor. Her dreams exhausted her, and she was too tired to get out of bed. By the time she made her way downstairs for breakfast, everyone had gone. The only thing on the table was a plate with a congealed egg, a greasy clump of bacon, and cold toast.

Frank came out of his room and watched her eat. As she got up from the table, he said, "I'll walk you to that church."

"No, you don't have to."

At the door, he handed her a toque. "Wear this. Don't want to freeze your ears."

"Won't you be late for work?" she asked once they were outside.

"I don't care," he said, trudging stiffly beside her through the snow. "I'm sick of bucking. Yesterday, I told my foreman to make me a regular miner or I'm quitting."

"Aren't you worried about losing your job?"

"I ain't worried. Besides, I got something to say to you, Sinopaki."

She stopped. He knew her home name! Someone from the Reserve must have told him, but he hadn't gone back there since she'd arrived. From time to time, friends and relatives passed through, and maybe someone had told him, someone who knew Aunt Angelique, her mother's sister. Whom she never saw anymore and had all but forgotten. She had forgotten so much. She smiled up at Frank, her old name—her real name—a small treasure between them. Maybe it was time to start remembering.

There is so much I have to tell you, Mother Grace, she would write that evening. *I hardly know where to begin.*

"You belong with me," he said, taking her hand in his fire fingers. "I know who you are and where you come from."

I have worked hard at Our Lady of Sorrows. I have prayed, asking the Lord for guidance and the Virgin Mother for intercession. I wanted to be pious and faithful. I have tried.

"We can have a good life together," he said.

"What kind of life?" She needed him to explain, to convince her.

"A good life," he repeated. "Maybe in the old way." He glanced over her shoulder at the cars buzzing by them on the road.

"What do you mean, exactly?" She willed him to look at her, but he just shrugged and started to walk, letting her hand drop.

"Maybe live in the bush like your parents," he said after a few minutes, as if he were considering the idea for the first time. "We could look for their old house. Or I could build us a place if I can find land no one owns."

"Is there enough game to live on?" She thought of Papa with his gun, traps, snowshoes, and Mama's snares. Her parents had been known as skillful hunters, but there were days when winter had dragged its frozen carcass into spring, and the family had nothing left to eat but a few licks of powdery dried meat and shrivelled berries. Now, with the white men hunting too, there might not be enough to go around.

She ached for the old life as she remembered it—sun, creek, bush, mountain, and sky with Mama and Papa and their snug bed of hides, with Kiaa-yo too—but she wasn't sure it was possible anymore. She needed to know. She needed someone who knew.

"The Reserve, then." Frank sounded uncertain. Then his gunfire laugh. "We could even stay in Black Apple. Union says they're going to get us accident insurance. If the mine won't get me out of bucking, we could live on that while you push me around in my wheelchair." He grinned, but she didn't grin back.

She went to work, and all day long, she blinked a blizzard from her eyes.

She had planned to finish her letter to Mother Grace that night, but she couldn't. The storm in her head pushed against her skull, and even her eyes throbbed. She put down her pen and crawled into bed. She didn't even pray.

She was watching the dancer onshore, trying to see his face, when the water began to rise around her. He kept dancing, unbuttoning his white shirt as his thighs drummed, his feet rose and fell. Sliding off the shirt, he unzipped his woollen pants. The water pulled at her knees, splashing up her legs. Floundering, she cried out as it sucked her in.

The dancer wore nothing but a breechcloth. He stopped dancing and looked over. Finally, he saw her. He dove into the water.

She woke up. The blizzard was gone. She stared into the deep night. She knew what she would write to Mother Grace:

I have watched a shape moving towards me. As it gets closer, I can see it more clearly. You would call it my destiny perhaps, Mother Grace. It's possibility, I think. Possibilities. There are as many as there are feathers on a bird, and it has not been easy choosing among them, believe me. Believe in me, Mother Grace.

But the dream was pulling her back.

Lifting his face from the river, Joseph snapped his head back, flinging water from his long hair. "Come home, Sinopaki," he said, reaching for her arm. "Where you belong."

Laughing, she shook off her brother's hand. She didn't need his help. She was quite capable of swimming on her own if she knew where to go, if she really tried. Her arms pulling, legs kicking, she slid through the water like a fish.

She awoke before dawn and finished the letter to Mother Grace.

Love, she wrote at the bottom, then stared at the word, amazed.

Rose Marie.

48

Her Own

MOTHER GRACE COULD not sleep. Lying in bed, she felt the pages of the letter she had just received from Rose Marie in her fingers. Dry as shed skin.

That afternoon in her office, she had bent over until she thought her back would break. It took every ounce of her strength to wrench open the bottom drawer of her file cabinet. Pressing one hand against its frame to steady herself, she had reached in and stuffed the letter at the back, her fingers running over the dusty photographs of those two wretched religious she had hidden there twelve years before.

Sister Mary and Father Damien had haunted her for the seven years until Rose Marie's Visitation had answered her questions and sent them back to the past.

Now, in her dark bedroom, the words of Rose Marie's letter knocked through her mind. *I hope you can forgive me, Mother Grace. I hope I can forgive you.*

She closed her eyes and willed her thoughts away from the weight of those words. *Dieu Tout-Puissant, ayez pitié de moi.*

Outside, the wind wailed, a thin, haunting sound. *Come, wind*, she found herself thinking. *Carry me away.*

And there it was at her window. As she lay still, she heard it rattle the small panes. The rattling grew louder, more insistent. The storm was picking up. So many storms over the years. *I've had enough.*

Crash! Glass shattered and cold air blasted through the tiny bedroom. Despite the bone-chilling gust, she didn't have the strength to rise and hobble downstairs. She curled herself into as tight a ball as her stiff bones would allow, just as if she were a child.

The wind whirled through the room, trying to find her. Then it was on her bed, swooping at the covers clutched in her fists. It took her temples in its icy fingers and lifted her bed cap. *Mon Dieu!* She felt a frosty breath in her ear, surprisingly gentle. A breeze slid through her mind, blowing her thoughts clean.

The sky was black as ink. *Oui,* black as all the words and numbers she had ever written in letters and ledgers, all the quotations, pleas, revenues, and expenses—the amounts—what she amounted to. But they were fading. Their black-and-white certainty was being swept away.

Up, she rose. She flew. *Immortel!* She was sailing through night to daybreak, flying through the sky from St. Mark's to somewhere else. Morning sun spilled over the horizon and blanched her old bones. Far below, diamonds glittered in new snow.

The land was different, no longer an expanse of prairie, but well treed. Briefly, she wondered if she had returned to her childhood home, and suddenly she yearned to see her big brothers throwing snowballs, yelling and cantering through the drifts on their strong young legs, the little ones squealing with delight.

Instead, she found herself above a road. A mountain loomed ahead, a skirt of trees falling from its stone waist. This was not Tête Rouge. *Non,* not her family farm.

As she drifted gently down, she could hear boots crunching snow, and in the distance she made out a man walking towards her. She half expected it to be Brother Abraham, but no, she didn't know this man.

He carried a suitcase. Trailing behind him was someone else, a youth, it appeared, one hand gripping the handles of a paper bag; their breath broken pillows in the air, white down spilling, and they kept their eyes lowered. There was a solemnity about their procession, as if a serious business was to be carried out. Possibly they were travelling to a funeral, or maybe one of them would be leaving, perhaps the youth.

Still in single file, first one, then the other turned down a wider street, the hills of snow on each side soiled by exhaust fumes. From an alley, a third figure emerged, falling in line behind the youth. All three trudged towards a dingy building with a Greyhound bus parked outside. The youth wore a hat, scarf, new overcoat, and boots, and though overwhelmed by clothing, the young limbs moved easily through winter. As young limbs do.

Mother Grace turned her attention to the man at the end of the procession. He looked Indian, with shaggy hair.

Was this a dream? Yet she was not asleep, she could swear.

She felt an urge to get closer to this odd little parade making its way to the bus.

And then she was right behind the first man, could reach out and touch his broad wool back if she wanted. She could hear his steady breathing as he took the suitcase to the side of the bus and set it in the baggage compartment. A big man, he turned to the youth, drawing close. "Keep in touch," he said, his voice low. "Let me know you're safe. You know I'll be waiting for you." His eyes were such a pale grey, they looked almost clear.

The young face lifted to his words.

It couldn't be.

They embraced. The man closed his eyes. He kissed the strand of dark hair spilling over the youth's forehead, while the Indian man shuffled uncomfortably behind. "Remember I'll be here, waiting."

As they broke apart, the Indian man moved to the youth. "If you don't find him," he said, stepping in front of the bigger man, "you know where you belong, Sinopaki." He pulled off the youth's hat and laughed.

C'est vrai!

Long, gleaming black hair tumbled around Rose Marie's face. She was a woman, not a youth, not even a girl, her face fuller and softer than it had been when she left St. Mark's three months before. She embraced this man too.

"Thank you," she said, turning to include them both, "for everything."

"Keep in touch," the big man repeated.

"Make sure you do," agreed the Indian.

"I will."

She took the bag and climbed the bus steps. The men shuffled closer, following her with their eyes until she had moved past the bus driver and disappeared behind steel and glass.

The men remained standing outside, but Mother Grace had left them, was somehow with Rose Marie, watching them through the window. She sat down in the same bus seat and felt a young heart beat in her breast, driving out her old aches and pains.

The motor coughed and turned over; the bus doors wheezed shut. Pressing her forehead against the cold glass, Rose Marie waved at the two men.

Frank, both hands in his pockets, had moved back from the bus and was peering into the sun. Cyril found her in her seat, and stepping forward, he touched the window near her mouth. She could almost feel his fingers through the glass.

As the bus backed up, she swelled with anticipation and waved excitedly at Cyril and the glow of Frank, who was moving forward and squinting now, trying to see her inside. She kept waving as the bus started down the road. She waved until it turned the corner and they vanished behind Wong's General Store.

The bus picked up speed as it headed for the highway. Then, suddenly, it started to slide, brakes squealing, passengers sprawling across the seats. As it screeched to a stop, she was thrown against the window.

Rolfe Mooney rose up on the other side of the glass, his face not two feet from hers. Fear flooded Rose Marie, and a small sound of alarm escaped her lips. Mother Grace's heart seized.

Scowling, Rolfe staggered backwards.

"Drunk as a skunk," someone had said somewhere about someone, and she heard the bus driver open the door and yell, "Get the hell off the road!"

The bus started up again, and she rubbed her hands together, jittery with anticipation and fear. She was journeying north to find little Kiaa-yo, big Kiaa-yo now—Joseph, her brother—and her aunt, her uncle, her cousins, all the relatives she hadn't yet met.

Ahead, the road unwound like a ball of wool. The sky was a brilliant blue, the snow a slurry of constellations. *Mon Dieu, mon Dieu,* such beauty in the world. Why had she so seldom seen it?

Reaching into the large McBride's shopping bag, Rose Marie pushed aside the carton of cigarettes Mrs. Mooney had given her and pulled out the lunch Mrs. Rees had made. As she peered inside at the sandwiches, butter tarts, an apple, two thick slices of lemon loaf, and an orange, she thought of the new dressing gown Ruby had sewn her, now tucked inside her suitcase. She felt humbled; she felt rich. At the front of her skirt, in the secret pocket Sister Bernadette had added three months before, was a crisp fifty-dollar bill from Cyril and two twenties from Frank.

She had gained a little weight while in Black Apple, and the waistband was snug; she'd have to move the button once she arrived on Papa's Reserve. She would be in a new place, a young woman making decisions for herself. She had already made one.

Even if she couldn't find Joseph or Aunt Katie right away—if the information about the Reserve that Frank had found from Forest Fox Crown was wrong, or if they were away somewhere, or their house was hard to get to—she'd be fine, she told herself. After all, she knew about people like Rolfe Mooney, Mrs. Tortorelli, and Father Seamus. If she could steer clear of troublemakers and instead find relatives and friends, she'd be fine. And if worse came to worst, she'd go to the priest on the Reserve or to the band office.

But she expected to find her relations.

And beyond that, she was out of expectations. They hadn't done her any good in the past. Recently she had discovered choices, something she had never had before, and she wanted to make her own, not be caught up by the ambitions others cast out like nets, catching her up and dragging her behind them.

The sky pressed against the bus windows, singing with snow. Ahead, the road kept tugging them on. From the corner of her eye, she spotted a silver wolf slipping into the woods, its luminous coat and star eyes glowing. There, piercing the air, a raven flew ahead of the bus, its wings flapping like Sister Cilla's habit used to when she ran.

She was the air in the bus, the wind chirping at the window, that raven, ragged in the wind but flying strong.

She was Sinopaki at the beginning of her life. She was Mother Grace at the end.

She had never been so free.

Afterword

I N 2 0 1 5, T H E Truth and Reconciliation Commission of Canada re-
leased a report based on extensive evidence of the egregious treatment
of children at the residential schools, with the goal of educating all Canadians
about this dark era in Canadian history.

In *Black Apple*, I visit the residential school environment not because I
want to—it's a disturbing setting—but because with my characters and their
time frame it couldn't be avoided. Nor should the reality of residential schools
in North America, their political aims, often horrendous conditions, and dire
consequences be forgotten. Those survivors who reveal their experiences,
whether openly or confidentially, do so at great personal cost in order to
break the conspiracy of silence around Canada's residential schools, a reality
that continues to affect generation after generation.

At the same time, *Black Apple* is a work of fiction. I wanted to explore the
psychology of those who worked at the schools, often well-meaning indi-
viduals whose sense of religious, cultural, and/or racial superiority allowed
them to think of their service as a personal sacrifice for the greater good,
one for which they were neither adequately compensated by the government
nor admired by their charges, the result sometimes being acts of cruelty and
depravity of which their younger selves would never have believed their
older selves capable.

A few former residential students do speak of kind and loving people who made their experience more bearable. Rare as they were, those people had a sense of truth and conscience not tied to a particular institutional policy but rather to true wisdom and an attitude of respect.

In *Black Apple*, I wanted to show the many sides of human behaviour, to find, through fictional re-creation, a greater truth about who all of us are as a people.

Acknowledgements

IN THE WRITING, editing, and publishing of this book, I owe so much to so many.

First of all, my sincerest thanks to those who shared their experiences with me. I am truly grateful.

Thanks as well to Canada Council for their assistance in the writing of this book.

I'd also like to thank several writer friends for their considered advice: Kimmy Beach, Leslie Greentree, Carolynn Hoy, Joann McCaig, Blaine Newton, Susan Ouriou, Roberta Rees, Jill Robinson, Cathy Simmons, and Barb Scott. I am indebted to Ruby Eagle Child for help with the Blackfoot language, to Judy Dussault for information about life within a religious order, and to the people at Sage Hill Writing Experience. I very much appreciate the insight, patience, and advice of my editor, Phyllis Bruce, as well as her team at Simon & Schuster Canada, and the support of Martha Webb, my agent.

Love and thanks to my partner, Kamal Serhal, to my four amazing children who always stand behind me, their partners, and my two wonderful grandchildren.

My research took me to many beautiful places in British Columbia and Saskatchewan, but most of my time was spent in southern Alberta. I also searched through some websites and many history books. Books that were particularly valuable include *Shingwauk's Vision: A History of Native Residential Schools* by J. R. Miller; *Residential Schools, The Stolen Years,* edited by Linda Jaine; *Resistance and Renewal: Surviving the Indian Residential School* by Celia Haig-Brown; and *Indian School Days* by Basil H. Johnston.